SONG of VALEROS

By E.A. STEWART

ACCIDENTAL HERETICS SERIES
Book 1: *Bone-mend and Salt*
Book 2: *Trebuchets in the Garden*
Book 3: *Crux Lunata*
Book 4: *Song of Valerós*
The Mad Woman of La Catalane: A Novella
The Blue Door… and More Accidental Heretics Tales

LEGENDS OF VALERÓS SERIES
Wheel and Serpent: 1
Traitor: 2
Hero: 3

RAIN CITY INCIDENTS SERIES
(as Annie Pearson)
The Grrrl of Limberlost
Artemis in the Desert
Nine Volt Heart
The Pirate King

SONG of VALEROS

ACCIDENTAL HERETICS: BOOK 4

E.A. STEWART

Jūgum Press

For Jacyn, who always wants a story to read.

Contents

"On This Expedition of Peace"

The History:
In 1212, the Tunisian-born caliph of Córdoba tried to rally the local emirs to resist the invasion of Al-Andalus by the united Christian army. But the generations-old clans, both Moors and Mozarabs, resented the Almohad caliphate that had installed itself after a coup by overly righteous Berber mercenaries. To build an army, the caliph was forced to hire mercenaries from northern Africa and Europe.

Andalusia and the Occitan

Pedro d'Aragón had planned and provisioned an expedition into Andalusia for five years. Alfonso of Castile still struggled to get his cousins in León and Navarre to join in the effort to "reclaim" territory from the Muslim caliphate. In Europe, the archbishops offered remission of sins for any who joined this expedition of peace and faith. The pope suspended all fighting against the so-called Albigensian heresy. Rumors in the troubadours' world claimed that the heretics had invited the caliph to invade Christendom. No tales anywhere could be trusted. What's at stake? The future of Europe.

The Accidental Heretics Story So Far:

Isabella of Valerós, after surviving murderous attacks, now journeys with Chrétien and Durán to warn Pedro of a plot by the traitorous Crux Lunata. Sebastián is with Pedro's force, leading Valerós mercenaries in Iberia. Tomás, believing Isabella dead, is spying in Al-Andalus for Pedro, but finds his work hampered by his son Yusuf and by a passel of Mozarab cousins with conflicting desires and demands. What's crucial for a safe future for the bonfraires?

> A general's pet djinni.
> A Celtic soldier-troubadour.
> A resurrected noble woman.
> A monk, accidentally turned renegade.
> A young Catalan soldier, battle-ready but lonely.
> A Moorish mercenary, spying.
> A heretic eager to get home.

Characters

In These Chronicles
Chrétien, Tomás's foster-brother
Durán, Sebastian's half-brother; seigneur of Montcava estates
Felip de Xirgú, a donzel of Girona
Isabella of Valerós; called "Vidal" on the road
Sebastián, Isabella's son; heir to Valerós and Montcava
Tomás de Morella y Cyprus, Isabella's husband
Yusuf, Tomás's son, born in Cairo

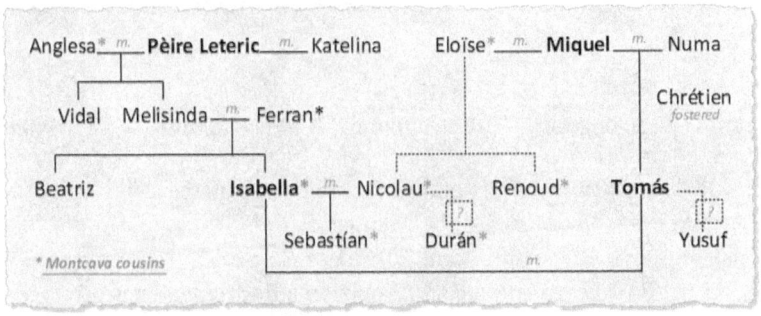

Houses of Valerós, Cyprus, and Morella
Anselm, the chaplain; a former crusader
Dolç of St-Féliu, a kinswoman of Pedro d'Aragón
Fortuno, a child from Morella
Guillem, marshal of the Valerós knights; a Sicilian Norman
Jacques and Thierry, Montcava mercenaries
Miquel de Morella y Cyprus (deceased)
Numa, Miquel's wife; a Kurdish noblewoman
Pèire Leteric, an old crusader, seigneur of Valerós (deceased)

Houses of Beaurain, Montcava, and Xirgú

Colomb, a half-brother to Hugues de Beaurain
Esak, a Churchman traveling with Arnau Amalric
Hugues, Marques de Beaurain; a crusader (deceased)
Matheus de Xirgú, Felip's brother
Nicolau, Isabella's Montcava husband (deceased)
Renoud, Nicolau's younger brother (deceased)

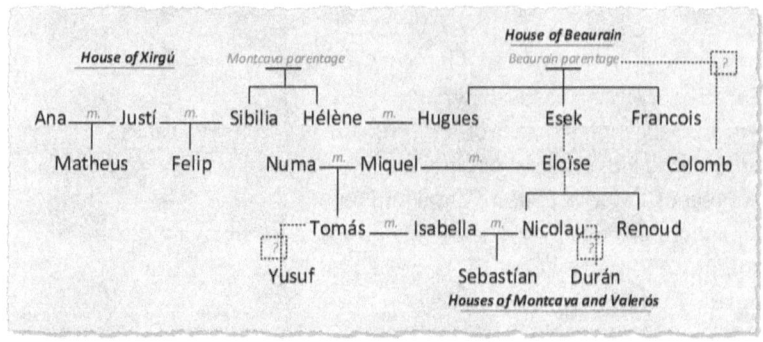

In Al-Andalus

Al-Hasan *Abu Jossep* ibn Muhammad ibn Ishaq al-Shahid, a taifa general
    on the frontier
Al-Makkzan, Tomás's great-grandfather; a Berber mercenary
Jafar ibn Jafar, a poet and scribe from Jaén
Qasim al-Jalal, "the magnificent," Tomás's servant
Rashid al-Rashid ibn Abd al-Aziz, a vizier; a Rodriguez cousin
Ríma, wife of Abu Jossep; a Rodriguez cousin
Rodriguez, a Mozarab clan; inheritors of the old Visigoth kings
Tuma ibn Mikhail ibn al-Makkzan, Tomás in Al-Andalus
Zaheid al-Quti, "the Goth," guard to Ríma; a Rodriguez cousin

Among the Courts, Crusaders, and People of the Towns

Baudoïs de Montpelhièr, a seigneur at Lérida
Doménec, Pedro's personal clerk
Don Carlos, an emissary of the king of Castile
Petronilla, a cousin of Pedro d'Aragón; Don Carlos' wife
Serena Péletier, a neighbor to the Xirgú domus in Girona
Taresa, a laundry girl

Historic Figures
In the Languedoc and Aragón
Arnau Amalric, a Church prelate, now archbishop of Narbonne

María de Montpelhièr, Pedro's wife

Pedro II, King of Aragón and Count of Barcelona

Ramón-roger, Count of Foix

Raymond, Count of Toulouse

Simon de Montfort, leader of the French invaders; viscount of Carcassonne

In Iberia
Afonso II, king of Portugal

Alfonso VIII, king of Castile, leading the united Reconquista army

Alfonso IX, king of León and Galicia

Diego Lopez II de Haro, a nobleman in Castile

Roderick, Visigoth king in Iberia ("last king of the Goths")

Rodrigo Jiménez de Rada, archbishop of Toledo

Sancho IV, king of Navarre

Elsewhere in Christendom
Innocent III, papal head of the Holy Roman Church

Philippe II, King of France; called *Philippe Augustus*

In Al-Andalus and Dar Al-Islam
Muhammad *Al-Nasir*, the fourth caliph of the Almohads from Tunis; called *Mirammolin* in Christendom

Rodrigo Díaz de Vivar, "El Cid," a Castilian nobleman and warrior who seized Valencia from the Moors (deceased)

Salah ad-Din Yusuf ibn Ayyub, first Ayyubid Sultan of Egypt and Syria; called *Saladin* in Christendom (deceased)

SONG of VALEROS

PART ONE
On Summer's Eve, 1212

TO ARNAU, MY BELOVED BROTHER IN CHRIST,

Please, dear brother, be assured. I took your caution to heart. After prayer and searching my soul, I affirmed my deep Spirit-blessed belief that God has granted me the gift of these visions. After two years of prayer and fasting under your guidance, I have found both redemption and great joy. I thank God, but I also thank you, who led me to the path of righteousness for His Name's Sake.

Last feast day, St-Jordí in his golden helm came to me again with a message in the half-built church in Girona. His face shone with God's light. All around him were torn rainbows and a haze of glory. As he always does, he spoke sweetly, beseeching me to pour the libation of God's holy justice from that Cup we call the Grail. Each time he appears, St-Jordí demands that I lead my Crux Lunata brethren to fight evil. Whenever St-Jordí departs from me, the air remains filled with incense. That odor provokes sweet sadness for the great efforts our Saints undertake to help with our salvation. After each blessed vision, I suffer, half-blind for a day, yet I come with great speed to join you, to march under the banner of heaven in Castile and Andalusia, to defeat the Saracen infidelity to God.

We shall help Alfonso of Castile stop the caliphate in Iberia. But more important, we must tread silently but boldly to tear down that unnatural man, Pedro d'Aragón. If you and I stop this viper, we are one step closer to eradicating the foul dualist heresy that grips Christendom.

1

A brother-in-arms was attacked in Girona. I must stop here with him, praying that God grant that noble knight strength, for the sake of our holy enterprise. I know not what more we will be called upon to endure in our work to carry the Cross to the Saracens—while carrying the Cup and the Sword to destroy a wicked king. But St-Jordí promises that victory shall be ours. The Sword of the Cid has passed from the saints to the Crux Lunata, those soldier-priests who fight both Saracens and heresy. The Cup has strayed from our grasp, but we shall soon seize it again.

God promises to deliver us from living under iniquity, if we promise to do His work in this quest.

I send this hasty message with Crux Lunata couriers. We shall meet soon on the road to vanquish the caliph. Over this journey, may all blessings from heaven fall on your head and your heart.

— *Esak de Beaurain*
Your brother in the Lord, from Girona,
in the Thirteenth Year of Our Blessed Pontificate

1

Hesitation

*Tomás in Baeza,
on the Al-Andalus frontier
early June*

THE FORMERLY HANDSOME TUMA IBN MIKHAIL—the name Tomás
of Morella was called while spying in Al-Andalus for the king of
Aragón—disarmed his foe and pinned him in the dust under a lemon
tree in the courtyard.

"I do not admit defeat." His cousin Rashid grinned, his teeth
flashing white in the dusky twilight. The scent of lemons overwhelmed
the senses after a day baking in the heat of June.

"You have no weapon." Tomás tightened his grip. "I have conquered the caliph's best vizier."

"Ah, but you dropped your sword too." Rashid, slick with sweat
from sparring, wiggled but couldn't break free from Tomás's superior hold.

"Yet you can't escape my grasp, Rashid al-Aziz. You advise the
caliph. What can a vizier do when he's defeated in such a way?"

"Shall I call Abu Jossep's army to crush you?" Rashid laughed
at that idea. The taifa general they both worked for no longer cared
to fight. That was what Tomás had come to Al-Andalus to achieve—
and the opposite of what Rashid must achieve for the caliph.

"The same way the sultan Salah al-Din crushed the infidels at
the Horns of Hattin?"

"The way my cook crushes a weevil." Even with the strong odor
of sunbaked lemons in the courtyard, Rashid smelled like a clean,
honest fighter, a balm for a mercenary like Tomás.

"O great vizier, you seek to wound me with words when you cannot win a fair fight."

"More like a slave mashes a gnat. To my knowledge, you never fight fair, Tuma."

"Fine. Stop talking." One hand slid from Rashid's sweat-slick shoulder as Tomás prepared to release him. "We're late for dinner. But fetch your sword. I'll show you moves when there are too many attackers."

"I practiced that defense when I was twelve years old."

"*Ai*, but this is a method of attack, not a defense. It uses a series of movements known only to me and my brother."

"Does sharing this secret mean I'm your brother?" Rashid's cheek twitched, betraying that the question meant more to him than a simple tease.

"It means that I can trust you to fight by my side. First, one brother makes the sign to start." Tomás shared the odd wave his foster brother Chrétien had invented when they trained together in Cairo. "Then you step this way to disarm your attacker."

Rashid imitated the movement perfectly on his first attempt. Tomás's cousin in Al-Andalus was a talented fighter.

"In the next move, I step to protect you. To do this, I must—"

A cry rang out from the rooftop of Rashid's house.

"*Desperta, Ferro!*"

Before Tomás's servant Qasim could shriek a second time, Tomás scrambled up the trellised bougainvillea, sword in one hand. Atop the wall, he pulled the swaddling from his sword blade and then leaped in among black-clad men attacking people on the rooftop. They glanced up from a victim, two with dripping daggers in their hands, so surprised at Tomás's arrival that one was looking at the burst of blood from where his hand had been before the other two could act. Tomás left that man to bleed while slashing at the closest assassin, who thrust his dagger in defense, but then clutched his middle and collapsed.

Rashid appeared at the rooftop doorway, hacking at the third assassin who advanced on Tomás. The black-clad figure fell onto Tomás, who let the dying man down onto the roof and stepped away.

"They killed Vizier Marzuq!" Yusuf shouted.

Yusuf and Qasim, backed into a corner by the far wall, both brandished daggers. Qasim kept pushing Yusuf behind him. Ibn Jafar the poet, who was Marzuq's scribe, hid behind both of them.

Four bodies lay strewn across the rooftop, as if it were a battlefield, one being the vizier Marzuq al-Jayyani, who had appeared in Baeza the month before to help Rashid convince the general, Abu Jossep, to send his army to the Caliph. The gaping slice in Marzuq's throat meant he was now beyond any help.

Tomás instead whispered to Yusuf, who was his son—though to keep him safe, Tomás had decided no one here should know that secret, even Qasim. "Are you hurt?"

"My pride suffered. Qasim saw the threat before I did." Yusuf glanced at the bodies, betraying no revulsion. Then he faced Tomás, all the strife now gone that had separated them ever since Tomás's wife Isabella died. "Thank you for your service, Ibn Mikhail."

Tomás pointed to Qasim al-Jalal, his priceless servant hired from the docks of Valencia. "We must honor you, Qasim the Magnificent. You are the best of men."

The lad puffed up, proud for having called out the words Tomás taught him, words Qasim didn't understand. *Desperta, Ferro!*

Rashid inspected the bodies of the attackers. "Cork sandals. Black shifts and *sarawil* trousers. Black turbans. What were they shouting?"

"'Faith. Truth.' And…" Yusuf glanced over at Ibn Jafar, the still-cowering poet. "An imprecation to keep a soul from heaven."

"Marzuq's guards are dead at the foot of the stairs. Their throats cut." Rashid pulled the veil from one of the murderers and commanded Tomás's attention. "Are these the famous Nizari assassins?"

Tomás pulled back the veil from another and used it to wipe his sword. "Those assassins were wiped out years ago by the Ayyubid caliph in Cairo. These are Berber youths, barely old enough to be mercenaries."

The poet spoke, addressing Tomás, his voice quavering. "You fight like the Nizari swordsmen, Ibn Mikhail. I saw them once in secret fight dens in Cairo."

Tomás carefully deflected that notion. "Any remaining disciples of the originals now live far north, high up in the stronghold of the Old Man of the Mountain."

The poet nodded, seeming to agree. "Three of their black-robed assassins could not appear here on the frontier."

"Poor Marzuq!" Rashid pulled a cloth over the dead vizier's face.

Tomás ignored the poet. "Ah, cousin. Marzuq wanted to climb the caliph's lofty towers by standing on your balls. No one will weep in mourning unless you pay good silver for their tears."

"I'll still have to explain my failure to Abu Jossep. I didn't protect a man who lived as a guest in the city I am protecting."

"But we kept the general's djinni safe." Tomás claimed heroism, though what he'd really done was protect his son, the way a father should. Abu Jossep also claimed Yusuf as a "son," having acquired him from the people who rescued the boy from a shipwreck and then spread rumors that Yusuf was a djinni. In truth, Yusuf was only smart, learned, extraordinarily aware, and stubborn.

At Rashid's shouted command, soldiers appeared and removed the mangled vizier and the assassins. Then servants washed away pools of blood and sprinkled sand on the tiles.

Tomás caught Qasim by the shoulder when Abu Jossep's guards came to escort Yusuf home.

"You saved his life," Tomás whispered in his servant's ear. "I owe you everything."

Qasim cast a doubting glance that he must have learned from Yusuf. "The assassins came for the vizier. We were never in danger."

"Yes. Unfortunate for Marzuq."

Qasim shook his head, denying that. "No, they came for Rashid. And perhaps for you. But they found only Marzuq because you were late for supper."

The lad slipped away to follow Yusuf, his nighttime chore.

Tomás's nerves thrummed. Too much blood in his heart.

That abused organ had pumped oceans of blood when Qasim screamed, "*Desperta, Ferro!*" His heart burst his ribs at the sound of the words he'd told the boys to shout if they needed him. The Valerós battle cry. Surely no one in this goat town recognized Catalan-bastardized Latin.

The scent of lemons in the courtyard again tickled Tomás's nose. No more odor of massacre. By rush light Tomás checked his stinging, bruised flesh for cuts. He'd likely strained sinew and muscle

6

scaling that wall, and he'd feel it in the morning. His old masters in Cairo would take the iron rod to his hide for even a single cut from hired bandits who proved to be only lads dressed in someone's idea of assassins.

Boys no older than Yusuf and Qasim.

What enemy hired young untrained mercenaries? Or smuggled those Berber boys through the city gates?

The answer had to be that his moon-touched cousin Ríma, who days before had begged Tomás to dispose of her former husband Marzuq. Perhaps she'd been helped by that poet, the untouched man in the rooftop melee. Tomás's breathing turned ragged again, disturbed by the memory of Yusuf brandishing the long dagger his stepbrother Sebastián had given him. Yet how good it felt, seeing Yusuf defend himself.

And how good to fight with Rashid at his side like a true brother. Unfortunately, they'd unknowingly battled desperate Berber boys.

•

"Our action seemed valiant. Fighting beside each other."

Rashid stood close by Tomás at the city gate, staring up at the three bodies hung in gibbets, stripped naked and exposed to the morning sun. He'd just finished shouting Abu Jossep's message to the city: *Evildoers and traitors are always found. Judgment is swift.*

"Until their veils were lifted to reveal mere boys."

"I prayed at dawn," Rashid said, "for the strength of mind to focus my disgust on the man who hired them. I feel no remorse for our actions. They were young, but they were hired to kill."

"We didn't know they were boys when we interrupted their butchery." Tomás shifted Rashid's attention away from the spiritual. "Our cousin Ríma wanted Marzuq dead. She asked me to kill him."

Zaheid stepped beside them, a rough giant among local men. Yet another Rodriguez cousin, he'd been sent by the clan to serve as Ríma's guard. The Rodriguez clan was a collection of ambitious, double-dealing, and secretive cousins and aunts and uncles. While Rashid was sent in service to the caliph, Zaheid was Tomás's secret contact for sending messages home to Pedro d'Aragón.

"Makes you think." Zaheid's words slurred behind his Morella accent, the accent of his childhood village. The village that Tomás's father Miquel had escaped as a youth. The dirt-poor village that called Tomás their don, their landlord, though no rents were ever paid. Where he'd never visited. "About the price of allegiance. Poor sods."

"Do you suppose these boys' families were paid well?" Rashid shifted his gaze from the gibbets to the crowd below the gate, looking to see who else might be studying the outcome from the previous night's attack. "What price led them to gamble all?"

"They were too young to know how to gamble," Tomás said.

"What's your price, Tuma?" Zaheid prodded Tomás with an elbow, likely meant for his ribs, but bumping his shoulder.

"I'm a mercenary. I accept the best rate offered."

Rashid waved his hand to scatter a clutch of boys preparing to throw rocks at the gibbets. His eyes turned luminescent in the sunlight. "I give all freely to my family and my brothers-at-arms. I believe you do the same, Tuma. Brothers first, always."

"Yes." Tomás breathed the word as a sigh of longing, thinking of his own brother and his true bonfraires before thinking about how his cousin Rashid came to be his newfound brother.

But then Rashid made a thoughtless move, touched his mouth, tipping his head the way a girl does to attract attention. Their friendship had drifted too far; Tomás needed to guard each moment, to direct Rashid's beliefs and hopes elsewhere. "Family, yes. Except we need to worry about our cousin Ríma."

"The servants say our cousin Ríma is willful." Rashid shooed away another passel of town boys. "It's our aunts' fault. It's an enormous evil for a young girl to be told she's greater than she is."

"Is that how Ríma was raised?"

"My aunts and her mother dressed Ríma better than her cousins and sisters, always saying that God knew she was a princess, that if the old kings had fought harder, she'd be a queen here. It's not good. It makes a woman…" Rashid considered his words. "Too proud. Too independent. We serve the clan, and we serve our caliph. But to teach a girl she's better than others, it does no one any good."

"But didn't we learn that way, too?" Tomás considered how Pèire Leteric had let Isabella run free as steward at Valerós. She, too, had a strong will, but not like moon-touched Ríma. "My father insisted that I was born to be better than any other knight. Your uncles sent you to the caliph because…why?"

"Because I was born to be the best of my clan. We're men," Rashid said. "We have to fight for it, but we can be everything our fathers and uncles told us. However, a woman such as Ríma?"

"She was beaten by her husband and needed her cousin to take her away, to find another husband." Zaheid asserted his role.

Tomás said, "Now she makes herself a tyrant in Abu Jossep's private life."

"Indeed." Rashid nodded, though surely he had no idea how well acquainted Tomás had become with Ríma. "Abu Jossep never restrains her. Ríma is still the willful child my aunts raised her to be. Like how Abu Jossep lets that djinni run amok."

"We live in strange times." Zaheid gazed upwards, hands behind his back.

"And yet, Ríma will do as she was raised," Rashid said. "We were all paddled by the same strict aunties and righteous uncles."

"Truly." Zaheid glanced at Rashid, who was a fellow clansman but of an unusually high station. "But weren't we raised to believe that if you do good to people, you'll enslave their hearts?"

The big man always managed to appear as innocent as an enthusiastic puppy, looking merely curious. Yet he'd just repeated the code phrase that connected Tomás and Zaheid as Pedro's agents. Their cousin didn't answer as Tomás had:

I'm as famous as fire on a mountain.

"I'm not sure that's true." Rashid pondered the idea, his face grave. "Abu Jossep treats the men in his army well, takes care of their families. But they're deserting like traitorous fleas."

"Are they deserting the general? Or the caliph?" Tomás took a chance, challenging Rashid with such a question. He couldn't confess his private joy at the growing desertions.

Zaheid said, "My mistress Ríma says we were all betrayed when those Berber caliphs first stole our land. I believe her heart is with the deserters. Like all the Rodriquez women, she longs to see the clan's ancient lands restored."

"Our cousin Ríma," Rashid spoke slowly, his jaw jutting, as if he bit and chewed each word, "should take care that her tongue doesn't cut her neck. She must honor Abu Jossep for saving her from her bad husband. She must keep our aunties' wild ideas to herself. Can you advise her?"

Zaheid laughed, which is a meager way of describing how he roared, his beard and belly shaking. He wiped at his face, as if brushing away tears. "Write your advice in a letter, and I will deliver it. Me, I need to keep my post. My children in Jaén prefer to eat and sleep under a roof."

"If Rodriguez men were ever kings," Rashid grew more heated, "it's five hundred years ago. Yet our aunts still raised us to resent land stolen and power lost. Though our clan has grown as rich as any in Al-Andalus."

"At least we have each other. We must protect our cousins and brothers." Zaheid faced Rashid. He stood more than a head taller than either Rashid or Tomás, but the three of them were several shades darker than Ríma after a season in the sun. The branch who'd married into the clan in Morella came from a late wave of invaders. Al-Makkzan, their mutual great-grandfather, was a Berber-dark mercenary from Tunis who married a Mozarab woman with a legacy her family traced back through the infamous Cid to the Visigoths. The Rodriguez clan accepted the infusion, but only Rashid had risen in rank under the new caliphate.

"Those poor dead bastards in the iron basket up there probably said the same thing." Rashid brushed away flies, renegades that had dropped from the bodies hanging above. "I'll find a way to speak to Ríma. But I have business in the camps."

Tomás followed Zaheid, waving farewell to his cousin the vizier. They'd spend the day in the camps too. To Rashid's knowledge, Tomás offered informal training for farmer-solders, teaching simple hand-to-hand techniques.

Not rumor mongering.

∎

For much of the afternoon, Tomás followed Zaheid, meeting his acquaintances in the camps, tossing dice with local men while spreading rumors by asking innocent questions. *Is it true the caliph pays mercenaries but expects men from here to pay their own way? If the caliph requisitions all the burros, how will the wives of fighting men manage the harvest or the fall plowing?*

Then the summer day turned to night without a difference in the heat. Tomás waited outside the city gate for Zaheid to meet him, then caught sight of his giant cousin before Zaheid saw him. Zaheid was in deep conversation with a man, a Mozarab with odd-shaped ears and a broken nose. The Mozarab wandered off, getting lost amid the vendors selling *mutawwama* and sheep's cheese-and-bread.

When Zaheid greeted him, Tomás didn't ask whether that man with the odd ears was one of Pedro's couriers. Better not to know. Instead, Tomás picked up what they'd been discussing earlier in the day. "What a mess I have. I came here to help Pedro in Al-Andalus. But now I need to rescue a significant portion of my clan. What to do next?"

Zaheid said, "It's simple, Ibn Mikhail. If God gave you family, then you must put family first. For the rest, just do the best you can. The only danger…"

"Yes?"

"Is that the moon fell on our cousin Ríma. We know what to do with Rashid al-Aziz, because he longs to be the caliph's right hand."

And he's in love with me. Tomás considered this problem often, seeking a way to avoid heartbreak. Then Tomás knelt at prayers beside Zaheid, who held his big body as still as a stone, composed and upright in the cool and quiet of the hall. As soon as they exited through the hall's carved door, retrieving their shoes, Zaheid became animated once more.

"Come, my friend. I hope you preserved your appetite."

He hurried Tomás along so there wasn't time to admonish Qasim, who rushed to his job as Yusuf's nighttime bodyguard. As large as Zaheid was, he moved quickly when he had a goal. And Zaheid talked as rapidly as he walked, tossing words back to Tomás. "My friend Umar is growing wealthy cooking for men like me, the ones who miss their homes. He's my dear friend now…"

They dodged a cart hauling one last load of wood to a rich man's kitchen. The drover took a stick to his burro, nearly knocking Tomás a good one on the head. Tomás ducked and moved to the center of the alley, trying to stay close to Zaheid, who never paused for breath.

"It's only by chance that I found Umar. A friend at the custard stand in the central market—you know that stand? Sweetest date creams this side of the frontier—mentioned that his cousin Umar served men like me. He took me around one night. Like a taste of Paradise."

In the village outside the city walls, Zaheid strode through a trio of small dogs that a young boy was herding back into his house. One miniscule beast tripped up Tomás, forcing him to scramble to avoid stepping on either animal or child and then to catch up with Zaheid, who came to a sudden stop before a whitewashed house at the edge of the village. Zaheid straightened his tunic, tucked his hair back under his modest turban, and kicked his sandals together to remove the dust. Before he knocked, he studied Tomás.

"Am I presentable?" Tomás asked.

"Best that can be expected." Zaheid nodded, as if he were a sartorial judge.

"Your camel shall spit gold before I'd ever seek to shame you." Tomás repeated what his father always said to tease his mother.

Zaheid's shoulders lifted in surprise. "Have you seen a camel? Is it a real beast?"

"Of course. I've ridden camels."

"It's just a large dog, no? These poets and singers, they are fabulists, don't you think? If they were regular men, we'd call them liars."

"It's bigger than a horse. I'll tell you over dinner."

Zaheid nodded, accepting the delay. He knocked on the door, and then whispered, "You are about to enter Paradise."

The massive cypress-wood door opened on silent, well-oiled hinges into a foyer, where the arches revealed an open-air courtyard with a fountain and two tall date palms amid a riot of flowering bushes. From the behind the door, a pretty girl-child peeked to see who entered. As tall as Tomás, but far slimmer, the child bowed and murmured a welcome. It required a second look before Tomás saw it was a young man dressed in simple, flowing silks.

"Is Umar at home tonight?" Zaheid asked.

The boy said, "You have come to dine, master?"

"You know me well, boy," Zaheid said. "This is Umar's night for saffron stew, isn't it?"

Zaheid kicked off his sandals. Tomás pried off his own boots, and then crossed the foyer to wash in a basin of rosewater. The boy stood ready with linen toweling, the way a rich man's servant cares for guests. Tomás handed back the towel, smiling at the lad.

Who stared at Tomás's scarred face. The boy's lips twitched as he repressed a shudder. Tomás again offered his best smile, wishing to reassure the frightened boy, who led them to a curtained alcove off the courtyard.

"It is indeed the night for saffron, kind master. Umar is absent tonight, but cautioned that we care for you as he would."

The too-pretty boy left them to settle on cushions, returning with two silver basins. He tied back the striped awning that hung over the alcove's archway, murmuring that they must wish to catch the breeze while enjoying themselves. Then he poured water from a tall ewer and knelt to wash their feet, sprinkling herbs to scent the water.

"You come here for two things," Zaheid said. "To be treated like a king, and to eat food like only a mother or wife can prepare for you. Now, as for saffron, my oldest boy said he'd beg on the street if that's what it took to procure saffron for his mother's magic." He settled more comfortably into the cushions. "But that's why I'm laboring here in the wilderness, so my lads don't have to beg in the streets."

Across the courtyard, another pair of visitors entered an alcove, and then two young beauties, similar to the one washing Zaheid's feet, slipped inside and let the striped awning fall closed.

"Umar makes all his money off men like me," Zaheid said. "If you're homesick, Umar has what you need. Food like your wife makes—at least, if you live in Jaén—and comforts that make you long for home and hearth."

That sweet young thing stared up at Tomás while washing his feet, smiling, washing further up Tomás's calf. Tomás shook his head. The fountain in the courtyard burbled noisily, so no words could be heard from other curtained alcoves. That boy padded in and out on bare feet, first carrying away the wash basins and then returning with a platter of bread and fruit. The yeasty smell of the bread answered the question about what other perfume Tomás had smelled when they first entered the courtyard. It was the homely scent of freshly baked bread.

"We have limes for you, master," the boy said, "and the first of this year's fresh figs. Shall I bring—"

"What I always want!" Zaheid clapped his hands in appreciation, then rubbed them together before seizing a piece of warm bread and slathering it with honey and butter. "If Umar isn't here, then that rascal in the kitchen hasn't prepared anything new tonight."

The lad left to fetch food.

"This is the night every week when there's saffron in the stew," Zaheid said. "This is always where you'll find me for supper. It's usually lamb in the spring. Now that summer's here, it's roasted goat, though I'm only partial to goat when it's prepared exactly as my wife does."

"I agree." Tomás caught a bite of bread before the honey could drip. Across the way, a third lad slipped into the curtained alcove. "To prepare goat properly, you must have a big pit. It's never done right in the city."

Their stew arrived, generous portions dished into large crockery bowls. The boy also set before them a platter heaped with filled bread rolls.

"Ah! You win my heart once again!" Zaheid bit into a roll. Motioning that it was too hot, he paused a moment, unable to talk, and then took a second bite. "Come, cousin, try this. It's pigeon. The best use of those bastard birds."

Tomás took a bite, then tried to interpret what he tasted. Coriander. Cinnamon.

"Your women don't take this good care of you in your country, eh, cousin? It's not possible." Zaheid paused between bites to praise the food again. "My wife, it takes her all day to prepare this dish. She stews the birds with onions and spices, then fries the little beasts in oil before she rolls them in thin dough and bakes them in the oven. Only she in all of Al-Andalus can roll the dough thinner than Umar's cook can achieve."

The spices burst in Tomás's mouth with each bite.

14

Zaheid stopped midbite. "But then that's the sadness which strikes me when I come here for Umar's food. My wife is far away in Jaén, making my sons happy. I'm here alone among strangers, just for the sake of silver." He finished the bite, savoring it with his eyes closed, a tear trickling down his massive cheeks. Zaheid opened his eyes. "But I've got you for company, cousin. What's to mourn when I can share bounty like this with another man who's as much a stranger here as I am?"

They ate in companionable silence while that lad passed in and out of their alcove bearing dishes heaped with fried eggplant, greens, and fruits. At last, the boy left them alone with a plate of membrillo slices and cheese with sugared almonds.

"What do you think, cousin?" Zaheid picked his teeth with a silver toothpick from one of the plates. "Life is good."

Three boys slipped out of the alcove across the way, now shirtless. They held the awning aside for another two boys who waited in the courtyard, bearing silver basins and herbs for washing.

"The djinni says that your mistress Ríma is dangerous."

Zaheid chuckled, a sound that bubbled up from deep inside. "I wouldn't trust Ríma as far as I could toss her. A spindly sprite like her, I could toss plenty far."

"Is she responsible for Marzuq's death last night? Yusuf thinks she killed Abu Jossep's first wife."

Zaheid held slices of membrillo and cheese delicately, using only his thumb and index finger. "Marzuq? That's likely. He was a right bastard of a husband. The general's wife? Why go to the trouble for a poor woman already dying of a wasting disease?"

Tomás took one sugared almond, staring at it rather than nibbling.

"Our cousin Ríma does what she wants," Zaheid said. "But you've come this far in life, you know to be careful of a wild and jealous woman." He took a bite, savoring the sweet membrillo. "Especially one with griffons and otters playing upstairs in the broken minaret of her mind."

Tomás sat back on the cushion and asked what he'd wanted to know all day.

"Who's the fourth dead man hanging in the gibbet at the gate? One of your men?"

Zaheid sobered, but shook his head. "Don't know the poor bastard. Perhaps one of Alfonso's agents. They've been active here."

"Offering the clans their old lands if they support the Christian forces?" Tomás asked. In the camps, where he stirred trouble, he never repeated the rumor, but rather always asked it as a question: Is it true that the king of Castile promised to restore ancient Visigoth land to the clans? "Who is taking Alfonso's offer?"

"All of them will, if it becomes certain the caliph will lose. Otherwise, no one. Most clans believe they are better off allied with the Moors. Those kings in Castile never amount to much. Our Rodriquez cousins aren't looking to join the Roman Church, only to snatch back their Visigoth legacy."

"My message to send—"

Zaheid brushed his big lips, requesting silence.

The boy appeared by their table again. Another basin of water, more toweling. Another too-young, ill-taught seductive glance at Tomás, who once more shook his head.

When the boy was treading back across the courtyard, Zaheid whispered, "What?"

"The caliph has only thirty thousand men. And locals are indeed deserting. They don't care to fight."

Zaheid sighed, shifting on the cushions. "And you should know what I learned today. The infidel army is low on supplies. Pedro's army and the *franj* knights have to go home in the next fortnight. Or starve."

Tomás closed his eyes. Failure to help Pedro in any significant way sat heavy in his belly. Pedro had spent years planning, and now Tomás had only a fortnight left to do anything useful.

"Let's go, friend!"

Zaheid heaved to his feet with the grace of a much smaller man. "My mistress Ríma will be distressed if I'm not dozing at her doorway soon, guarding against whatever trouble she goes looking for in the night."

Tomás followed, that serving boy again close behind him.

"I don't know how Umar does it," Zaheid exclaimed again in the foyer. "He must rely on an ancient inheritance to offer us these delights at so little cost."

Tomás reached for the purse tied at his waist, but Zaheid waived aside his offer to pay for their feast.

"Just leave an extra dirham for the servants." Zaheid again stood by Tomás, washing in rosewater, fanned by the willowy serving boys. "Umar can't possibly afford more than the food and roof over these servants' heads."

"*Ai*, Zaheid!" Tomás embraced him at the gate, where they parted ways. "You wonderful man! I love you like my own brother."

"Didn't I tell you?" His friend chuckled. "Umar's food and comforts are glorious. Don't ever say I did you no favors. I've shown you Paradise. Right here in the middle of hell on earth."

Behind Zaheid, the spooky scribe Jafar ibn Jafar emerged from one of the curtained alcoves. The scribe, or poet or whatever he called himself, straightened his *jubba*, speaking to someone who remained in the alcove. Tomás looked back at the array of alcoves around the courtyard, judging how close the caliph's man had been while he and Zaheid had dined.

Ibn Jafar trod through the courtyard, absorbed in thought, as if indifferent to his surroundings. He traipsed past Zaheid and Tomás without acknowledging that he knew them or that Tomás had saved his life the night before.

Unless Tomás and Rashid broke up a different plot, perhaps one Ibn Jafar knew.

．

Long, long past midnight, Tomás sat on a narrow bench in the alcove where he slept. He removed his boots.

"Hail the king who was, and the king who is to come."

Ríma settled at his feet, the scent of lavender wafting up from her hair. The tall sorceress who claimed to be the secret queen of Visigoths rested her head in his lap, one hand on his sword's leather-and-wood scabbard.

"The Rodriguez clan honors you, Ibn Mikhail. You are our protection and our hope. Our fathers' grandfathers and our children's grandchildren sing your glory."

"My father would find no glory in fighting other men's children."
He moved her exploring hand. "I do not agree with what you choose
to do for revenge on Marzuq."

"Defense. Not revenge." She raked her nails down the length of
the scabbard. "The caliph sent those assassins for Rashid. And you
used the sword of our last mighty king to protect your clan."

"How do you know? About those assassins and Rashid?" He
didn't expect an honest answer. Ríma moved in the general's court
like a spirit, listening and meddling.

"When you feed hungry boys, they talk to you." She traced the
scar on his face, which she knew by now he hated. "The same way
you enslaved your Qasim's heart. Well-fed and over-promised."

"Do not send boys disguised as men again." He didn't mask his
disgust. "It's devil's work. It's beneath the scheming of a queen. If
that's what you long to be, behave with honor."

"I'm the only person you can trust in this lonely place." Ríma's
deep voice trumpeted. She was taller than Tomás. Her long hair fell
free over his hand, unencumbered by a veil, and she glowed moon-
white in the dim light of his alcove. "It's a blessing from heaven that
I'm here to offer you comfort. You've been more lost than the moon
in winter."

"God knows I've never endured a strange land on my own."
Tomás resisted the impulse to laugh. The scant breeze prickled his
skin. Night offered no relief from early summer heat.

"You must repay heaven's blessings. Restore the rightful king
in Iberia."

He hadn't seen her in the light since his first day in Baeza, but
he had an impression that her eyes never fully opened, as if she saw
the world in a dream.

"I'm a gambling man, and heaven owes me a substantial debt."
Sweating in the heat, Tomás tried to ease away from her, but Ríma
clung close. "And our cousin Rashid is also my friend. He's like a
brother. Abu Jossep showers me with kindness."

"If Rashid knew what you are, he'd kill you." She traced the scar
on his lips again. "Abu Jossep kills traitors. No one here is your true
friend. Except me."

"Stop that." He removed her hand.

"You and I have much work to do." She wiggled her hand free and grasped his wrist. "It's time to destroy the caliph and the general. I need you to act."

"I work for Pedro."

"You can't love the king of Aragón more than me." Her low voice rang with steely intentions. "I alone am faithful."

"Don't whisper monkey piss. Pedro is a brother to me."

"You just called Rashid your brother. What if Rashid learns about Pedro? Or that Yusuf is your son?" She stretched. "My courier leaves today. What secrets do you want to send to Pedro?"

Tomás pondered his secrets. A taifa general's wife arranged the murder of the caliph's vizier. His son Yusuf had stolen the attentions of that general. A righteous vizier longed for Tomás's loyalty. And his fanatical cousin Ríma, who either was or wasn't Pedro's agent, embodied danger. "Tell him Abu Jossep's army will soon join the caliph."

"That's not how we restore the ancient throne of Roderick."

"Stop!" he cried. "The devil's adulterous sister would tell you to leave a man to his own business."

Ríma rose up, holding out her long hair like two wings of an angel. Or demon. "*Ai*, Abu Yusuf ibn Mikhail ibn Rodrigo al-Cid. God will deliver justice. You and I shall rise up as the incarnation of the Divine, you on the left hand as consort, I on the right."

"Surely every goat in town dies before that happens."

"Do not mock, Tomás. Swear that you will be true."

He laid a finger on her lips, trying once more to quiet her mad notions. Bad enough that she asked to touch his sword every time she appeared. He carried a sword from his father Miquel that Ríma believed came from their Rodriguez ancestor El Cid, the famous warrior from a hundred years ago. She also believed that his sword had magical powers to restore the inheritors of the old Visigoth kings to power in Iberia.

As with most things, Tomás believed as his father did. In the case of this sword, he believed it was forged thirty years ago in Damascus, where Miquel had stolen it.

"What do you want me to be true to?"

"To me, Ibn Mikhail. Your consort."

"Vich d'ase." He hissed a reference to donkey anatomy. "I gave an oath to my father, my brother, my wife. And to Pedro. No more in this life."

"You and I owe heaven the promise of true hearts."

"I'm not your consort." Hell is right here on earth. He was lonely when he dreamed of Isabella, lonelier still when Ríma came near him, reeking of lavender and madness. "The Visigoths died five hundred years ago."

"Can't you see the curve of Fate under heaven? I will be queen and you my consort, ruling together from Roderick's throne."

He couldn't help laughing aloud. "When the caliph is defeated, the Christian kings will carve up Al-Andalus like a roasted lamb pulled from the fire pit. They'll reward their knights. That will not be you or me, sweetheart. Unless you have a connection with one of the military orders. Knights Templar, perhaps? Order of Calatrava?"

"I know all your secrets," she whispered, nuzzling against him, the scent of lavender making his eyes water. "Do as I require. Or Abu Jossep will hear the truth about your magical child."

Tomás seized her wrist. *"Jhezu del Tron,* do not threaten me."

Ríma laughed, such that all of Baeza must hear her. "They quarrel in Christendom over whether their Jesus was Man or God, and whether Woman was created by Good or Evil. Jesus in heaven doesn't matter to a man like you."

"'Their Jesus'?" Tomás asked, wondering how Pedro had enlisted such a woman to serve as his agent. "Are you not Christian?"

"I meant Jesus as some describe him. Don't quibble like a false scholar. The power of God is the force of life. That is what I serve, neither king nor priest."

"I serve Pedro. You, it seems, serve lunacy and heresy."

"All evil comes from men denying their divine nature." She raked a nail down his arm. "Like you, refusing God's call to serve our family and our kingdom."

"No, all evil is just one man or woman choosing to do ill rather than good."

"I understand your weakness, Ibn Mikhail. You cannot let go of that ghost you are in love with. Please know, I do not need a consort. I can command without you."

"How will you do that? You're a woman who was forced to run to Abu Jossep for protection. You depend entirely on your husband and your clan."

"I have allies provided by heaven."

"The chickens you cut up in the orchard? You may call those allies, because I won't help you."

"Then I pray your bones turn to air. I deal harshly with foes."

He left her in the alcove and jumped down the stairwell noisily, skipping steps. In the courtyard, he glanced up to judge how near dawn might be, when the baths opened. He refused to ponder whether that moonstruck sorceress intended to send an assassin after him.

The cloying scent of lavender lingered.

When the doors to the baths opened, Tomás slipped inside alone, soaking away that odor. He rubbed the square bonfraires' brand on the back of his wrist, thinking how pleasant it would be if he were with Sebastián now, breathing only the yeasty and fetid odor of ten thousand men on campaign. Living in the controlled order of a well-armed camp, not this man-trap of a city. Lucky Sebastián, on the road, playing honest solder.

.

Jafar ibn Jafar the poet finished his letter to the caliph, then toyed with preparing another pen.

In early spring, Ibn Jafar had delighted the caliph with a collection of odes that explicated the struggle between Dark and Light. Half of Al-Andalus could recite the briny dialog between the Angel and the Djinni. And his family made it through the last winter on gold earned from love odes composed for the caliph's first wife. A true poet, Ibn Jafar now knew, should never sample the delights of love. Desires of the flesh led him to this frontier town, scribing for a vulgar vizier in order to earn sufficient silver to feed five children, two wives, and the minimum number of servants those women declared necessary for a life worth living.

And for all Ibn Jafar knew, his labors might be feeding strangers in Jaén in his absence. Did other men sit at his table and sleep in his wives' beds? Ibn Jafar wrapped his second-hand linen *jubba* tightly, the one Marzuq discarded because of spice-and-grease stains the laundry women couldn't remove, even though Marzuq berated and beat them. Ibn Jafar's wives had warned him. They claimed all men beat their wives, but not with the vigor of the vizier Marzuq.

Ibn Jafar began another letter.

．

ALL BLESSINGS UPON YOU, MY DEAREST WIVES.

With all thanks due to Allah, I survived a shocking night. I held the two of you in my heart through the horror I endured. The moment before tragedy unfolded, I sat on a rooftop in Baeza overwhelmed by the odor of sun-ripe lemons from the courtyard, reminding me of how you both scrub your hands with lemons to purge evil. Little did I know the kind of purification I was to witness.

Since the caliph sent me to serve the inelegant vizier Marzuq al-Jayyani, I have endured his sulks and complaints about this backward town. Indeed, the ceaseless war drums and the stink of goat pervade all. Angry about supper being late, Marzuq moaned, "Why are we here? Only to suffer?"

I repeated the text of the caliph's letter to the general. "We are here to help Rashid al-Aziz guide the great general Abu Jossep, guardian of the Al-Andalus frontier. To bring his army to the caliph's battle to protect Dar al-Islam against invading infidels."

You two guessed the truth when the caliph sent me here. Marzuq was asked to subvert Rashid al-Aziz, because of his ties to the Rodriquez clan. I understand that the future of Dar al-Islam is at stake, and so I do what I can to help the caliph, for there lies our future and the future of our children.

Marzuq and I were on the rooftop with that odd creature Abu Jossep keeps. This lad appeared several fortnights ago, touted as a djinni, the lone survivor of a shipwreck and a marvelous scholar of wit and learning. Abu Jossep adopted him, so the oddity is called Yusuf ibn Hasan.

I see last night's tragedy unfold whenever I close my eyes. The overly righteous Marzuq sat like a toad in a green silk *jubba*. The shell of his cranium, not at all well hid under a green woolen skullcap, with the convex swelling above his ears indicated a strongly destructive nature. The swelling at the lower back of his skull indicated great carnality. At a glance, one could see a man given to possessive rage, unable to resist calls of the flesh.

While we waited on the roof for supper, Marzuq invited me to debate that upstart youth Abu Jossep calls his djinni. Other guests were late. Stars poked pricks of light through the fabric of dusk. Marzuq interrupted Yusuf-the-child-scholar in the midst of his argument. "But is that truly what it says in the Quran?"

The lad Yusuf, his face devoid of emotion, scrutinized the vizier, but did not state the obvious, that we weren't discussing the Quran. Instead, the lad was explicating one of my odes with noble scholarly deference to me. The boy said only, "It shall all be as it pleases Allah."

At the sound of servants on the stairs, Yusuf's servant roused from where he lay on a crumpled *jubba* in the shadows. As the door to the roof opened, he began screeching in the tongue of ifrits, nothing I've ever heard in Arabic, even amid the mangled dialect that farmers speak in these hills.

A servant passed me, dropping a napkin in my lap, with large childish words scrawled across it in charcoal.

"You have nothing to fear."

At that same moment, Rashid al-Aziz's wild cousin stood on the rooftop's half wall, sword in hand. He landed beside me with a leap. The servants stepped away from Marzuq, who choked in dismay. But no, the portly vizier bled from a slash at his neck. As the ferric smell of blood filled my nose, I nearly said it aloud, that this wasn't the plan.

In a few horrific heartbeats, one servant lay bleeding on the rooftop. Rashid emerged from the stairs, and soon all three assassins lay dead on the rooftop.

Rashid's cousin jutted his mangled face up close to mine, his breath hot, flecks of sweat splashing onto my face and hands. Who came to my defense? Rashid, the vizier who was supposed to be dead at that moment. "Leave him alone. He's only a poet."

When that wild warrior cousin stood so close to me, I saw that he'd been a handsome man once upon a time, even more handsome than his cousin Rashid. He'd once been the kind of man that women risk the world to sleep with. You know the type from the caliph's court. I shall write an ode, wondering what it costs a man to lose God's gift of beauty.

I also noticed a slight gesture from that scholar the general calls his jinni. The boy touched that warrior's hand, bloody as it was, the way a boy reaches out to an older brother. Or a father. No, they must be brothers. Whatever this man had been in the past, no woman would sleep with a man so hideously scarred for fear of conceiving a mangled child. But the boy's rude slave caught me watching. I felt marked for seeing what I shouldn't.

As you may imagine, I remain so unnerved that I must quarrel with my pen frequently while I write to you by rush light. My letter to the caliph already done, I was about to sleep. But can you guess who appeared in my room? That woman you two called a sorceress when she lived in Jaén, Ríma of the Rodriquez clan. She's now the general's wife, yet her presence in my room shows how she remains untamed. I'm reminded of what you both often claimed, that the Rodriquez clan cannot attend to its own problems. They all endanger the caliph's work to preserve peace in this land, where we seek to serve God with word and deed.

I wish I had you here to share your wisdom, to tell me the meaning of what Ríma said to me. "The room is now cleared and the chair made ready for a new king. Does your caliph know?" I said no and pretended to fear her. All I can do is to help the caliph tear all power away from the Rodriquez clan.

Though you need not worry for me. Every rumor says that the Christian army of vermin shall soon give up and return to their warrens. And then I shall return to the joy and serenity of our own home.

— *Ibn Jafar, The Poet*
From Baeza, Jaén
serving at the command of the Caliph of Córdoba,
at the last full moon before the solstice

2

Provisions

Sebastián at Calatrava,
on the Castilian frontier
June 1

"IF YOU DEPART NOW, CARRION will take your soul," Sebastián of Valerós shouted. "You stain your father's honor."

He spat into the dust, emphasizing his disgust, expecting he spat blood, since the shouting ripped at his throat. Sweat poured into his eyes, and the sun burned through his skull. Here in their stinking camp outside Calatrava, the Castilian general Diego Lopez de Haro stood behind Sebastián, mute and never moving. It came down to Sebastián to stop the deserters from his camp since Diego had not been able to act since the travesty at Malagón. Tens of thousands of ultramontanos had already departed from Castile's army camps. Sebastián shouted again, desperate to protect his own forces from mass desertion, smothering the heart-pounding fear that he might have to report failure to Pedro d'Aragón.

"Did your grandfathers abandon Jerusalem because it was too hot? Is that why Saracens now eat and drive their goats where our Savior walked?"

Sebastián bellowed until he was hoarse, then paused to let men holler their protests:

"The pope demanded only forty days of crusade!"

"Pas cinquanta jorns pudent!"

"Not fifty stinking days."

"We paid for our sins. Who will pay for our horses?"

"The kings let the Saracens escape at night."

"The lords gave Calatrava to their favorites."

These men screeched the same grievances as the herd of ultra-montanos who had decamped earlier that morning. One-third of the united army packed and headed back over the mountains to Anjou, the Aquitaine, Cahors, and the Pays de France.

The continual unhappiness of the ultramontanos had changed to mutiny when, after several days' siege at Calatrava, the kings' counselors entered Calatrava to negotiate a surrender. To prevent another massacre like Malagón, the Castilian captains let the caliph's garrison ride away under the night's full moon with whatever possessions they could carry. In the morning, the captains gave the empty city to the Order of the Knights of Calatrava, the same holy order that lost the citadel to the Moors a decade earlier.

First the ultramontanos rioted. Then, their sins forgiven for having rendered forty days on crusade (and disregarding new sins committed in passage), the Frankish ultramontanos packed their tents, sand and fleas and all, and returned north.

Which confirmed Sebastián's belief that they were a foul, worthless drag on the united armies.

"Complaining is what soldiers do best."

Father Anselm surveyed the remaining angry horde from where he stood with Sebastián atop the now Christian-held walls of Calatrava. Anselm was the one man in camp with a place in Sebastián's heart, since they'd endured the siege of Minerve two years before. A true crusader, a loyal advisor, Father Anselm shared wisdom, having spent decades in the Holy Land with Pèire Leteric, Sebastián's great-grandfather.

The remaining ultramontanos under Diego's and Sebastián's command still bawled complaints, milling beneath the city walls. When it was quiet enough for his words to be heard, Sebastián shouted again, in every dialect he knew.

"The next step you take shows the world how you care for your father's honor." In Catalan, Aragón, Narbonne, and Toulousain dialects, Sebastián added, "And for paratge. For your home and families. For the brother right beside you, who you must protect."

A voice lost in the ranks cried out in French. *"Can't eat your paratge. Can't reclaim the dead pledge I made in order to get enough gold to come here."*

Dead pledge. *Mort gage.*

It set Sebastián to wondering how much the usurers were earning from these ultramontanos. One set of sinners was growing wealthy off another set seeking redemption on crusade.

By midday, when Sebastián finished shouting, Valerós lost only a dozen ultramontanos, all men of the most troublesome nature. Valerós retained the motley bands of Narbonnese knights, Catalan bordoniers, and Mozarab archers that Pedro had assigned to Sebastián's camp. The only men Sebastián could truly count on were the dozen Valerós knights that Pedro had hired to train his Aragón knights. Now, Pedro seemed to believe that Valerós could manage any fighters disdained by generals from Castile and Aragón.

Sebastián watched as the departing ultramontanos migrated across the plain to travel under a banner of the Knights of the Lunate Cross, who were most dissatisfied about yesterday's conquest being handed over to the Order of the Knights of Calatrava. But what else could they have expected? The allotment of battle spoils belonged to Alfonso of Castile, not bishops from Rome and the Toulousain.

When Sebastián glanced back, Diego had disappeared, like the half-ghost he had become, ever seeking solitude.

Then a messenger from newly arrived knights demanded the presence of the Master of Valerós. Pedro and his personal guard knights had ridden out ahead of the main army and caught up with Diego's band at the vanguard. The king wanted a report.

■

"Master of Valerós? What say you?"

Pedro d'Aragón stood taller than most in any gathering, but coated in La Mancha dust, he appeared no different from others who rode hard that day. Sebastián also noticed that, instead of gazing up, he could now look the king in the eye because he'd grown so much since Twelfth Night. He strove to appear as relaxed and respectful as Father Anselm did beside him.

The king tugged off his dusty gambeson and signaled for Sebastián to help with his chainmail. Behind them, camp stewards erected a hasty pavilion and unfolded camp chairs. Then the stewards left Pedro and Sebastián with Father Anselm and the king's clerk, Doménec.

"I'm sorry, Monsenyor, that I couldn't keep more men here. However, it's the worst of the worst who departed. Untrained grumblers."

"Saves us the trouble of feeding them." Pedro's eyes glimmered more than Sebastián remembered, perhaps because the king had tied his hair back for travel. "The archbishops heard me insist on our need for money, not more men than we can feed."

Father Anselm nodded. "Our best hope comes from the years you spent provisioning, Monsenyor."

Sebastián stood even more stiffly, aware that he'd just shouted and worried for a whole morning over the wrong problem. The real problem was what his grandfather Pèire claimed when he scratched the outlines of a battle in the dirt: *"Horses move on grass and water, soldiers need beans and mutton."*

"I will admit," Pedro spoke coolly, "your speech stirred my bones, Valerós. All the captains are repeating your glorious words." He was dusty from the road, streaked with sweat, and removing unadorned armor that wasn't his own. "Diego Lopez did well, letting you speak. A youth shamed grown men, reminding them what our forefathers endured outside Jerusalem."

"Though their fathers and grandfathers also left the Outremer because of the heat," Father Anselm said. The priest slumped on a camp stool, weary from ceaseless sun, saddle sores, and bad food. "That and suppurating wounds."

Pedro studied Anselm but spoke to Sebastián. "However, I don't believe the famous general Diego Lopez gave the Master of Valerós those words to speak."

"It's as Diego taught me." Sebastián didn't venture near the precincts of disloyalty. He owed the silent, battled-shocked Diego Lopez respect. "For generations here, one side captures a citadel and flies its flag. Then its neighbor takes it back the next summer. The ultramontanos mistake slaughter for valor."

"Very pretty," Pedro said. "I must add to my testament that you are to speak at my funerary memorial. Did you learn that silver tongue from Pèire Leteric or your stepfather Tomás?" He grinned,

28

but then pointed a finger at Sebastián. "Why hasn't Diego Lopez answered my messengers' request for a meeting? Why does Sebastián of Valerós command these men instead of Diego Lopez?"

Was this an opportunity to complain to the king? Guillem, the Valerós marshal, had been sent back to protect Castel-de-Valerós from heretic hunters. Father Anselm, ill, used all his strength to console diarrheic foot soldiers. Tomás lived, or perhaps died, in Andalusia. And Diego, the Castilian guardian of Sebastián's future wife (whom he'd never met), walked the earth like a living ghost, leaving Sebastián to figure out how to command two thousand men withering under the La Mancha sun. He'd never been so lonely.

Pedro tipped his head, waiting for an answer.

"God spoke to Senhór Diego amid the travesty at Malagón." Sebastián weighed every word. "He's been silent since witnessing an apparition of the peace-loving St-Martín, who—"

"*Jhezu del tron!*" Besides calling on Jesus in heaven, Pedro tapped the camp table where his clerk Doménec worked. "We need a priest here. One who speaks the Castellano tongue."

Father Anselm stirred. "I tried, but I can't break Diego free from his Malagón nightmares."

"*Ai*, gentle soul," Pedro said. Yet everyone (except perhaps Doménec) knew that Anselm had served as a far-less-than-gentle warrior for thirty years before turning priest. "We need someone from Alfonso's camp who shares his tongue. Doménec, why do you hesitate? Fetch the best man among the priests from Castile. They should be arriving here by now."

When Doménec left, Pedro settled back, as easy in a camp chair as any man could be. "I needed Diego to help me convince Alfonso to continue on. But no luck for me today." Then he bolted upright in his chair. "You are ill, good Father."

Anselm shrugged. "It will pass."

"Yes, if you rest," Pedro said. "I want you in the rear, with the bishops' men."

"I'd prefer…" Anselm's voice wavered.

Pedro grasped Anselm's wrist, encompassing the square brand burned there. Sebastián also bore that mark, indicating that they were bonfraires, inheritors of Pèire Leteric's confraternity of knights.

"For my benefit, I'd like at least one man among the bishops' soldiers to know what it is to be in battle. Go now, I beg you, *mon amic.*"

Anselm rose to do as Pedro bid. Sebastián felt the baked La Mancha dirt shift beneath his feet. Anselm gone from his side, his last ally, his last friend.

"I'm forced to ask more of you, Valerós." Pedro pointed for him to sit. Sebastián complied, though uncomfortable at the motion. "The bishops' ultramontanos ate their way through our provisions before deserting. Alfonso's resolve is wavering. I have to know that at least part of my force is reliable. Is that you?"

"*Òc,* Monsenyor. You can ask anything. We will be prepared."

"*Ai,* bonfraire. Perhaps that's all I needed to hear. Tell me what you learned from life with Castile's captains."

"That the word 'honor' sounds almost the same in their tongue as when the roughest Catalan shepherd speaks it. Yet it tears at their hearts and bowels to speak the word, instead of giving them wings."

That made Pedro laugh. "Not useful information for strategy, Valerós. What do Diego's captains think of us?"

"That we're all mere ultramontanos, not to be trusted. That we are fools held enthralled to the pope, crusading for gold, and we'll all go home with no thought to next summer's strategy. That none of our knights can sit a horse well enough to swoop in fast on a raid and then be gone."

"That's the worst?"

"They think we'll all turn for home before the new moon. Because only fools would stay here longer. That we'll starve."

"What do you think, Sebastián?" The king's use of his common name caught him by surprise.

"I've been hungrier than this. The horses seem fine. Since my sins are all forgiven, I'm free to do whatever I want."

Pedro's lip twitched in amusement, then he continued to be disconcerting. "I'm sorry Tomás isn't here with us."

"*Òc,* Monsenyor. He likes grousing in the dust. He's missing all our festivities. Have you heard from him?"

"Not for the last fortnight. Now, let me again ask more from you. We have a contingent of Almogavars who want to fight Saracens, but Castile's generals don't want them. You know who they are?"

"Farmers and shepherds from the frontier mountains. Raiders."
More riffraff for Sebastián to control.

"Òc. It's said they're good fighters, but Alfonso doesn't want to
promise to share any more booty. He's still making promises to his
cousins from Navarre."

There was no possible way to say no. "Fine, Monsenyor. Send
their captains to me."

"And one more thing I must ask. Can you keep your men moving forward until the Feast of St-Peter and St-Paul? At the new moon?
And help them keep the faith if we have to turn our heads to home
without battling the caliph?"

"I believe so. I succeeded today."

"Can I tell Alfonso to look at Valerós if he wants to see men more
committed than his own? He's wavering."

Don't make promises you can't keep. Pèire said it often.

"I can try."

"Do you recognize our greatest enemy in this battle?"

Sebastián hesitated, wanting to be right. "I've spent too much
time thinking it's thieving ultramontanos, Monsenyor."

"It's the sun and moon. Time running out faster than our food."

"I'm not sure how to battle that enemy, Monsenyor."

"If you figure it out, you'll be a great general. Perhaps your
Almogavars know how to squeeze milk from stones, make bread
from all this dust. It's said they know how to live off the land."

"I shall ask their captains, Monsenyor."

"It was a jest, bonfraire. For right now, what do you need that I
can lend you?" Pedro stood, which seemed to indicate that their meeting had ended.

"Our men need rest." Sebastián stood too, noting again that he
was as tall as the king. "And laundry women to comb out the lice."

"The supply train arrives tonight, at the latest," Pedro said. "The
whole army will rest here for a few days. But I asked what do you
need? You, the Master of Valerós."

Sebastián, after three months on the road, did not request what
he wanted most, which was Tomás at his side, or at least another sane
man to talk to. He asked what his grandfather Pèire Leteric would.
"A bath. A clean shirt, if one can be found anywhere."

"God provided a river over there. And I must have a spare shirt." Pedro pulled at the ties of his own linen undershirt. "But are your desires truly so small?"

"The rest are impossible, Monsenyor." Sebastián twitched inside his own itchy, sweat-damp shirt. "I wish God might send a plague on the fleas and mosquitoes. That the blessed angels might heal my men of their farts and moaning. I want wide open fields of grassland for the horses. And clouds over the midday sun. Rain."

"The shirt, Valerós. I can only offer the shirt."

Sebastián carried away the shirt, thinking it was too nice a shirt for him, more like what his brother Durán wore in the city.

Sebastián headed off to tell his men that the king of Aragón admired their skill and fortitude, and that the king begged them to travel with him into the heart of Andalusia. Sebastián had committed to following what proved to be a random trail in the wilderness, believing that the results would help his brothers and family live in peace.

Yet here he was, eating dirt like a wild dog on the frontier, to protect his brothers. Even his stepbrother Yusuf must be living a better life, lost in his studies and dreams in Barcelona.

Before speaking to his men, Sebastián put on the soft white linen shirt from Pedro, as proof that the king of Aragón admired Valerós. But the shirt made him imagine the life Durán must lead now.

Lots to eat, prepared by Tomás's mother at the family domus.

Real baths.

Carousing in the city with Chrétien.

Only Chrétien would put up with the life Sebastián led. Surely Durán would never choose an armed camp in the wilderness.

3

Obligation

Durán in La Mancha, beyond Zaragoza
May 16, at the full moon

FOR OUR GRACIOUS LORD AND PATRON, Ramón-roger, Count of Foix, we dispatch this testimony of our progress.

Our band of one hundred and twenty southern knights and mercenaries traveled safely from our parting in Narbonne into Aragón, and on our way to the plains of Castile and then to the frontier, where we hope to join Pedro d'Aragón in the expedition to bring the Cross to the land of the Moors, resisting the nefarious plans of the Caliph of Córdoba to invade Christendom.

The men from Foix and Toulouse are in good health and make speedy progress in our effort to join the king of Aragón. However, our band endured a division after an accident befell Matheus de Xirgú in Girona. He was badly injured, such that his mercenaries are led by Felip de Xirgú, who is the scribe of this missive.

You shall find of interest that the band of knights traveling with Matheus departed from our company, those knights who call themselves the Order of the Knights of the Lunate Cross, whom you know as Crux Lunata. Remaining with us are the mercenaries riding under the banner of Maria de Montpelhièr and her captain, Colomb de Beaurain. I am advised by Durán, our master, to say to you: "We do as our lord bids to make friends of our enemies and brothers of those who would destroy us."

We hope you are finding peace at home, with our pope calling for a pause in the struggle against heretics this fighting season. Like all Christian knights on this expedition, we are grateful to be able to fight the Saracens. I am again advised by Durán, our master, to say to you: "We are united as brothers to serve the peace that Pedro d'Aragón seeks in Christendom."

Felip de Xirgú, May 1212
Written for Seigneur Durán of Montcava,
Master of knights from Foix, Montcava, and Montpelhièr
for this expedition of peace and mercy

.

Durán outside Zaragoza
late May

"I stand for Valerós!"

Once again, Durán watched his *bon amic* Chrétien hold a swathed sword over his head and shout before stripping to fight, his long, bare torso glistening with sweat in the midday sun, his blond hair bound up in a battle-ready knot.

As part of the training ritual at each midday break in their journey, Durán shouted, "Montcava and Foix yield to Valerós!" And then he stared at the ground, not to be distracted while Chrétien was half naked. No one in this army needed to catch the Master of Montcava staring at that manifestation of glory, a gift from the Good God of light and love.

At each midday break, the band of knights and mercenaries on their way to join Pedro d'Aragón practiced close-hand battle, until each group's champion called for one last fight. Privately, Durán despaired at the futility of man-on-man brutality, but the Montcava and Foix men shouted their support for Chrétien. The captains had agreed weeks earlier that Montcava, Foix, and Xirgú knights and mercenaries rode as one united force.

"Xirgú yields to Valerós!" Felip shouted. The big shy monk Felip was now the Master of Xirgú since his brother Matheus lay dying in Girona. The Xirgú knights and mercenaries always yielded to Valerós. Any of them who'd ever fought Chrétien at midday practice didn't want to repeat the experience.

"*Vivètz Valerós!*"

Vidal of Valerós and the Montcava mercenaries cheered. They were all loyal bonfraires who kept a secret, that Vidal was Tomás's widow, Isabella.

That left one captain to fight Chrétien: Colomb. Half-brother of the famous crusader Hugues de Beaurain, he'd been paid by Maria de Montpelhièr to lead her mercenaries into Andalusia. But Maria also wanted her husband Pedro dead so her son Jaime could be king of Aragón. Durán and his friends worried that her gold had also bought Colomb's services as assassin. But on this journey, what Colomb wanted most, it seemed, was to harangue each of them.

At every *migdiada,* Colomb stripped to do battle with Chrétien, who was half his age. He was a broader, more muscled man than the sinew-thin Chrétien and was remarkably strong, the streaks of white in his hair the sole sign that he was ten years older than his body revealed. Durán, the second-generation bastard of another Beaurain younger brother, saw himself in his great-uncle Colomb as if gazing in a warped mirror.

Colomb stepped into the center of the ring and faced Chrétien while raising his wrapped blade to urge his men to cheer. After the fighters' first two steps, nothing that happened looked like the simple fight steps Durán had learned from Chrétien. Instead, Colomb and Chrétien provided master lessons in brutal fighting, which Durán privately considered a worthless waste of human time and energy. For Durán, Chrétien's daily fight mostly meant Durán had to be careful of that man's bruises while trying to find a comfortable way to sleep at night.

Colomb and Chrétien had fought so often that the two fighters were familiar with the other's habits. Each stepped back as rapidly as the other stepped forward. Each man used his shield as another weapon, holding a smaller shield than used for fighting from horse-back. Colomb held a slightly wider, heavier blade.

Since both men fought with swaddled blades, no one should mistake this as a life-and-death trial. Colomb's first moves attempted to cut to Chrétien's feet and shins, which Chrétien parried with the flat of his blade, falling back with an enormous grin on this face and then stepping forward quickly to strike for Colomb's middle, except instead of making the brutal *swack* of a "cut" with his wrapped blade, he merely swiped across his foe's belly. Colomb's reaction was a thrust intended for Chrétien's face while kicking Chrétien's middle.

Watching, Durán grabbed his own middle, as if feeling the pain himself. But Chrétien stood his ground, not even swaying with the kick, and lifted his sword to strike from high guard. Colomb deflected Chrétien's blade with the hilt of his sword. Chrétien stepped back, and when Colomb next thrust for his middle, Chrétien trapped the blade with his hilt. With a sweeping kick, Chrétien knocked Colomb's sword from his hand and sent it spinning so that four men had to jump out of the way. Chrétien was again victor.

Colomb bent to retrieve his blade in the dust and then sauntered back to grasp Chrétien's elbow, pulled him close, and spoke in his ear.

Stepping back as if repelled, Chrétien paled under his sunburn, lines of white-hot anger around his nose and mouth. He stalked away. Colomb, laughing in spite of his defeat, swaggered back to his side of camp. Chrétien shoved his way through the ring of men and returned to join Durán and Isabella in the Montcava camp, where he poured water from a leather bucket over his head.

"What did Colomb say to you?" Durán had endured a series of mocking encounters with his great-uncle since Toulouse, like a thistle jammed in his soul.

"He said that we're both orphan bastards," Chrétien bared his teeth, scowling.

"Me too," Durán said.

"Then he added, 'But your dead brother and father will never greet mine in heaven.'"

Chrétien unbound his hair and shook it free. It flew in a whirl before cascading in long white locks down his beautiful, wet shoulder blades to that narrow indentation at his waist.

"*Jhezu del tron!*" Isabella glanced across the clearing in the camp to where Colomb was donning his shirt and jerkin, and apparently telling jokes, since his companions clutched each other, laughing.

"But you don't believe in heaven." Durán puzzled over Chrétien's anger. "Or so you always say."

"He insulted Tomás and Miquel."

Durán said, "You insult my father whenever you speak of him."

"Sadly," Chrétien laid a wet hand on Durán's shoulder, "your father had no honor. I clutch my brother's and my father's honor as what remains of them here on earth."

36

"Does Colomb know…?" Isabella didn't finish the question. She exchanged a glance with Chrétien. Durán saw that his two friends still teetered on the edge of an abyss of grief. Tomás was dead, which Chrétien had learned in a letter from Pedro just before they found Isabella in Girona two weeks ago. Chrétien chose not to tell her that Tomás had survived the massacre months before, arguing that she didn't need to experience the loss again, like Chrétien had.

"That Hugues and Miquel were *bon amics*?" Still wet, Chrétien tugged on his linen shirt and leather jerkin, finally covering his distracting, beautiful bare ribs. "If there is a heaven, Hugues de Beaurain is arguing with God to make sure Miquel gets in."

"Does he know about you and Tomás and Hugues in Béziers?" Durán asked.

"Who know what Colomb knows? Go ask him." Chrétien grasped Durán's shoulders and shook him. It passed for a farewell embrace. "I'm riding for Lérida now. Jacques has already packed our horses."

"I want to come with you." Isabella kept arguing this. In Barcelona they'd heard that Pedro d'Aragón tarried in Lérida on his way to Andalusia. They'd undertaken this journey to warn Pedro about the Crux Lunata conspiracies against him, so the detour was necessary.

"It's only a week's detour," Chrétien said, "and you're needed here. Keep Durán from leading the army into heresy."

Chrétien could ride faster and with greater safety than anyone else, so Durán couldn't resent Chrétien's mission. But he did resent the coming days of loneliness. Durán threw his arms up in a southerner's gesture of anguish and shambled off to rouse the Montcava mercenaries to mount up and resume their ride into Iberia to join Pedro's army.

A week without Chrétien? Durán hadn't gone two days without him since they came home after the siege of Minerve ended. The painful thump in his heart warned that bad things were about to happen and he'd have to face it alone. With Colomb breathing down his neck.

.

Felip on the Aragón frontier
early June

The local farmers had allowed them to pasture horses for the afternoon, so the men, the horses, and the donkeys got their rest at *migdiada*, but Felip had learned that Durán and the captains seldom slept at the midday break.

"Come, Felip. We need to purchase provisions in town."

When Durán spoke, Felip stopped staring at his tin cup of lentils and onions and rose to follow him. Felip kept a promise to himself, to endure whatever his fellow travelers did. This was just another day with no chance of a midday sleep, though it was already late in the afternoon to call this part of the day *migdiada*.

Durán led the way up the narrow, deserted path to the huddle of tile-roofed houses at the edge of the hillock. Halfway up, they met a fellow carrying a lamb on his way down. He was dressed in the summer linen and sandals of a herder, though the flocks should all be in the higher hills now.

"*Hola, señor!*" Durán greeted the man in that odd Castellano tongue people spoke here. He asked who might sell provisions.

The fellow pointed to a dirt path that led up a steep rocky rise. "At *migdiada*, our elder rests in his casa. Behind the church."

"Gracias." Durán resumed the steep hike.

Felip said, "We should have asked to buy his lamb."

"It was sick," Durán said. "Its thin bleating broke my heart."

That comment seemed typical of Durán, which Felip found reassuring, since Durán was always kind, even when Felip offered ideas that proved to be ignorant or foolish.

"I hope silver will tempt the village elder," Felip said. They'd paid good silver to rest along a stream where their horses could forage in grasslands the sheep had abandoned for the summer.

"Don't let your hopes run wild," Durán said. "It might require an apparition of angels, like everyone we meet talks about."

In the village, the outlying casas were rock-heaps, seemingly abandoned while the sheep were in the higher altitudes. A dozen stone-and-plaster huts crowded around the church, which was merely a slightly larger stone shell with a cross raised on its roof beam. In front of the church, a small girl in a dusty linen shift sat on the steps crying, wailing a broken-hearted loss like only a child can do. When Felip and Durán appeared, she shuddered. Covering her face with her hands, the weeping child ran up a narrow alley between the church and the casas, shrieking.

"My chickens! My dear hearts!"

From the same alley she ran up, more children and dogs descended, all small and too young to follow the shepherds up into the mountains. Their noisy begging broke the *migdiada* silence, the same noise that greeted the travelers whenever another army had already ridden through their village and offered the children bribes. They demanded more of the visitors

"Sesame! Silver! Sugar!"

Durán distributed a half dozen pennies among the urchins and again asked about the elder's casa, trying the same butchered Castellano dialect he spoke with the man on the path.

"Is this the right way?" he asked.

"*Si*," one of the infants shouted. "With the other crusaders." The boy said *crozadas*, which must mean…

Behind the church, Colomb and a half dozen of his men paraded down the pathway, each clutching five or six glossy-black chickens with shocking red combs and ghost-white faces, all still cackling in a ruckus over their capture.

The crying girl's beloved chickens, Felip guessed.

Durán stepped close to Colomb, acting the same way Colomb did whenever he scolded Felip.

"Foraging provisions for our men, Senhór Colomb? How cunning. Did you pay?" Durán remained adamant about the camp rule: silver was to be paid to the locals for all food. No theft. And no demands to surrender food for the sake of a holy war.

Chickens squawked. Colomb bared his teeth. Felip stepped back, startled.

Durán signaled for Colomb's men to leave. "Join the others, and seize what's left of midday rest."

The six mercenaries looked to Colomb for confirmation, which Felip felt must aggravate Durán to the bone. Before Colomb could answer, Durán said, "I'm the master of the united army. Your captain always agrees with my command."

Complaining chickens and slouching men followed the trail out of the village till all that could be heard of them was the calls of discombobulated black-feathered fowl, leaving Durán and Colomb, with Felip as the sole audience.

"Do I owe the village people silver for chickens?" Durán stepped closer to Colomb. Durán was three fingers' breadth taller, but Felip had never before seen Durán draw up to look like a masterful fighter. "Or do I replace the silver you laid out to provision our men?"

Colomb folded his arms, forcing space between them. He spit just to the side of Durán's dust-encrusted boot.

"Are you a Beaurain?" He sneered, a look that Felip found too familiar, having been scolded so often in that same way. "Does your blood run thick with valor and paratge? Or are you a lapdog for Valerós? Those wrong-headed children who betray the Church by protecting heretics?"

Durán spit in the other direction, mirroring his uncle. "Paratge is what you promise your kin and your domus. I owe my life to my brother Sebastián, the master of Valerós. But I owe nothing to my wicked Beaurain grandfather. It's always a Beaurain who betrays me and my brother."

"Here's a church. Let's step inside while I denounce your heresy."

"Which of your brothers taught you about honor? My grandfather?" Durán said. "Hugues de Beaurain would never betray his own kin."

Colomb balled his fists. "I should beat you for saying my brother's name." A rictus of anger froze his taunting grin in place. "What right do you have, heretic, to call on Hugues' honor?"

"The weeks I spent with him in Béziers. Hugues was the best of teachers."

"May God condemn you for telling lies. You never knew my brother. And the archbishop of Narbonne surely is right, that you do not know the true God."

The heat between the two men could ignite a wild fire in the matorral. Standing nose to nose with his fierce uncle, Durán spoke quietly. "I lived through hell with your brother Hugues. Hate me if you will, but do not call me a liar."

Cloudless sky above. Doves cooing in a hidden dovecote. Felip caught a shadow flittering in Colomb's eyes. Durán must have seen it too, because he pressed on.

"Perhaps your other brother never shared his many evils. How he forced himself on my grandmother. Beaurain bastards like you and me can preach paratge only as a caution."

Colomb's watery eyes flicked to the left, then up toward heaven. His lips parted, but it took two heartbeats before he spoke.

"You perverse heretic whelp."

Anger wafted from Colomb like a heat-haze on the plains. Durán stepped back, treading on Felip's boot. Yet Durán spoke with admirable calm.

"Ancient Beaurain sins are not relevant to our duty here, uncle. María pledged her army to the Count of Foix, who made me master. We abide by what our benefactors agreed." Durán pointed to the village elder's casa. "This army pays for provisions. We share among the entire army. That is the way of honor, which is a duty for a Beaurain. Now, do we owe silver to this village? Or do I owe you for your good work to provision the army?"

Colomb still breathed heavily. Felip smelled his anger, as if it poisoned the knight's sweat. "We paid for the chickens. You owe nothing from your purse."

"*Bon.* Then we're done here." Durán stepped back again, missing Felip's boot this time, though Felip stumbled getting out of his way. They walked away from Colomb, back around the church.

"What do you want from the House of Beaurain?" Colomb called, waiting until Felip and Durán had walked far enough away that he had to shout. "What do you beg your heretic God to grant you, Master of Montcava?"

Durán faced his uncle again. "I want what Hugues wanted. For paratge to always defeat evil ambition." He widened his stance, hands on his hips, mirroring Colomb again. "And there is no House of Beaurain. Hugues gave everything to Jean-Luc de Chartrain, as recompense for Beaurain perfidy."

Colomb, jingling that string of coins he carried, stood in challenge, the same way he did at every midday fight. But Durán jogged down the pathway to return to camp. He seemed happy, given that he'd just endured another harangue from his uncle.

"What I want most," Felip hurried alongside Durán, "is for God to strike Colomb mute. And then strike him with a plague of midges and mosquitoes." Durán didn't reply, but Felip persisted. "Colomb makes it so personal, the way he torments us. What did he mean about the archbishop of Narbonne?"

"Arnau Amalric wants to burn me as a heretic. It's why I'm obliged to be here on this expedition, to prove to the archbishop that I'm not worth burning."

As if that was a sufficient explanation, Durán fell silent. But Felip asked the question that had bothered him since he first met Durán.

"Do you p–people pray? P–Please don't be offended. I'm only curious. I've never known a Good Christian."

"Of course, you know us," Durán said. "As is true for every don, dòmna, and donzel in the south, most of your servants and half your aunties and cousins are Good Christians."

"No, I—"

"Òc. I assure you."

"What do you pray for? If you believe in two Gods, how do you choose which one to pray to?"

"Peace," Durán said. "Doesn't matter whether it's the God of darkness or light. We pray for peace."

"Yet here you are, a Good Christian leading an army."

"I'm not a very good Good Christian. And leading an army is just one day's drudgery done over again the next new day. To keep Arnau Amalric from burning me as a heretic and seizing my family's domus and villages."

"If I ever knew any G–Good C–Christian, I never knew anyone who might be burned as a heretic."

"You know Isabella. She had to be pulled from the pyre at Minerve after the tinder had already been lit."

They reached the edge of camp. Durán waved to Isabella where she tended her horse. "I have to tell her what we learned."

"About chickens?"

"No, that Colomb doesn't know about Hugues de Beaurain and Tomás and Chrétien in Béziers."

"What happened in Béziers? Besides the Franks' conquest?"

"Colomb's brother, who was my grandfather, kept us in prison for a month." Durán lifted his arms in that southern gesture of despair. "The French conquest? Béziers reeked of scorched stones and charred timbers. I kept thinking we smelled the burned people. And I smell it again each time Colomb taunts me."

.

Durán beyond Zaragoza
early June

"Can't even pee in peace."

That was Durán's first thought when he rose each morning, or when it was time to saddle up and ride after *migdiata*.

It wasn't worth beseeching any God to answer a prayer, just a persistent longing while waiting for Chrétien to return. Without Chrétien, Durán naturally wanted to be alone, but there wasn't a single action or moment when he was left in solitude. He endured a prodigious burden of work, while the other captains and knights rode in front of their men without a care. He had to account for the food stores daily, which he'd grown used to, serving as the Montcava seigneur, except now the stores moved over the landscape on mules. Unlike home, he couldn't trust that men guarding the stores weren't removing shares through business ventures with the locals.

Thanks to Chrétien, Durán knew how to use his knuckles and fingers to add and subtract, so that he could judge whether the numbers changed when his victualer brought tallies to him. However, he had to trust at least a few of the men. He'd chosen Thierry, the Norman captain from his own mercenaries, and Bernart Bovon, the captain of the Foix men. Not as tall as Durán, Bernart was sturdy and handsome, with broad shoulders and muscled thighs. Though it was probably foolish to trust the man who had misdirected Durán to a brothel in Narbonne when all Durán wanted was a haircut.

Otherwise, the business of leadership proved to be lonely. And frightening. Chrétien might laugh at that fear, but Durán was responsible for keeping one hundred and twenty men and their horses and mules alive and functioning over hundreds of leagues across Aragón and into Castile and Andalusia.

And one thing continued to be as sure as sunrise. Colomb appeared at every turn, censorious, haughty, hand on his sword hilt. At any glance from Colomb, Durán raised his shoulders, stood straight in resistance, not pondering what a vain, ignorant twig he'd been back in his life in Toulouse.

Durán and his brother Sebastián both shared Beaurain blood, as did Colomb. Beaurain blood is warrior blood, Sebastián said. Except the Beaurain grandfather that Sebastián and Durán shared was a mendacious priest, not a famous crusader hero. And Durán didn't feel the fire Chrétien said burned in the belly of warriors. Growing up in Toulouse, Durán chose to shelter with Good Christians in Toulouse, the kindly people who had rescued his starving mother when his Beaurain sire discarded her.

What Durán felt in his belly: two kinds of hunger. The first and most important was to figure out each day how to feed the men and beasts for which he was responsible.

His deeper and more enduring hunger was for Chrétien. He wanted his *bon amic* near again. After two years together, a fortnight's loss reawakened the beast of loneliness that had stalked him up until Chrétien came to Toulouse. Durán found small comfort from envisioning Chrétien away on his noble mission to warn Pedro of the Crux Lunata conspiracy.

The promise of the next painful fight with Colomb did not shake the aching of loneliness and loss. As if Chrétien had taken a limb or an organ with him. A piece of Durán's heart.

Time to go be beaten and bruised for that day's *migdiada* break.

·

"Pedro's head!"

Thierry inspected the piece of silver where it lay in the dust, then called the results of the coin toss.

Durán obviously despaired.

Isabella reached out to stop him. "You don't have to do this. I can fight my own battles."

He shook his head. "I have to assert that I'm master."

Each day, at the end of the sparring during the *migdiada* break, Colomb de Beaurain won the final toss of a brass or silver coin and

44

got to choose his fight partner. Every single day, every midday break. Different coin each day, same result.

"Vidal of Valerós." Colomb pointed to Vidal the scribe, picking the same fight partner each day.

Once again Durán removed his jerkin and repeated what he said each day.

"My scribe doesn't fight."

Durán recited the same message each day, that his scribe didn't fight yesterday or the day before and wouldn't fight tomorrow.

"Master Vidal has never trained. I will fight in his stead."

Sotto voce, Durán said to Isabella, "I wish Chrétien would catch up. We don't know how to gamble." Then he picked up his quarterstaff and stood in the ring opposite his great-uncle Colomb. The same height. The same build. At least thirty years separating them. One a scarred warrior, the other a peaceful Good Christian sworn to hurt no living thing, but who'd already lost his chance at a better incarnation in the next life.

Colomb unbuckled the two swords he always wore, one short, one longer, and he too stripped to just a linen shirt.

At every *migdiada,* Durán asserted that he was the leader of this army and took a beating while his men cheered, as if Durán had a chance to win. On good days, Durán fought Colomb to a draw. At the end of each fight, Colomb clutched Durán's forearm in the traditional way of southern knights—supposedly to show brotherhood—and drew Durán close to whisper a taunt in his ear. This day's taunt:

"You have an obligation to God and the House of Beaurain."

"My obligation," Durán said, "is to uphold the honor of my brother Sebastián and our domus."

"A true Beaurain knows the true God and knows how to care for his men. It's born in the blood."

"I'm a true bastard that the Beaurains abandoned in the street," Durán said. "My obligation is to paratge and true brotherhood. Your protégé Matheus has no idea of honor and betrayed his own brothers."

"Noble words from a Valerós lapdog."

Colomb bent to pick up the coin from that day's toss. He'd invented a new tradition, and each day he drilled a hole in the tossed coin and added it to the jangling bunch of coins that he wore on a tether at his waist.

Coin in hand, Colomb spit in the dust and turned his back, holding up two fingers in insult. Which was when Durán saw it for the first time: The Crux Lunata tattoo on Colomb's forearm.

Shaking off bruising pain, Durán returned to his friends.

"Colomb has a crescent cross on his arm."

Isabella nodded, instantly understanding what this meant, that Colomb was more than a Beaurain mentor to his nephew Matheus. He was an active member of the plot to destroy Pedro d'Aragón. Meanwhile, Felip chattered about which of the two fighters was most battered that day.

"Please, I can count my own bruises." Durán bit back saying more, irritated by Felip's naiveté, then felt bad when Felip ducked down in that wretched posture of meekness that made Durán want to elbow him in the ribs. "Please notice instead how much better I'm getting with the quarterstaff, training under one of the great fight masters in Christendom."

"Who also trained my brother Matheus, the traitor."

After Felip slouched off and Isabella departed to tend to the horses, Durán scratched at his beard—he hated the damn ragged bush—and went to beg the kitchen sergeants for extra water, so he could wash off that day's chicken-hearted fear and failure. Then he tramped over to the side of camp where he'd pitched a lean-to shelter for shade. Durán held a hand up to the sun, judging how much time he had to rest. Four fingers until the sun angled to the place on the horizon when the whole stinking army would remount and ride.

Durán lay in the shelter of the lean-to, which didn't offer enough shade to keep the sun from baking his legs. He fumbled in his jerkin for a hank of linen and draped it across his face to keep off the flying critters that buzzed even in the heat of the day. And he thought about praying.

He didn't believe in supplication. That's one of the benefits he found when he began to commune with the Good Christians. If you weren't begging God for favors, then you didn't have to argue with yourself all the time about why God didn't grant your plea.

Pray for peace.

He intended to keep his resolution never to raise steel in battle. And just accept bruises on every part of his body. Like the old days from before he met Chrétien, scrambling to stay alive on the streets of Toulouse, before anyone ever hailed him as seigneur.

What Durán sought now was to govern his wishes and longing. He wished for Chrétien to return, wanting the company, not the protection. To talk over problems.

Beaurain or Valerós lapdog?

Neither. Merely Durán from the marketplace united with an orphan jongleur from the Outremer crusader camp. Neither of them had a father who'd acknowledged them, though he and Chrétien shared a set of obligations to their brothers.

Of anyone on this adventure, Durán had the purest reasons for joining the invasion of Andalusia. He wanted to save Valerós and Montcava, to deny efforts of the archbishop of Narbonne and the Church to seize those villages. To avoid being judged a heretic and therefore endangering those villages, Durán chose to do what no truly Good Christian would, to take up arms and lead an army.

Baking in that infernal plain didn't feel like a noble endeavor. Instead, Durán imagined how it felt when the other half of his soul lay alongside him. Not even needing to touch. Merely breathing the same air. The sound of Chrétien's voice. No, not singing. The way that words came from deep inside Chrétien's chest, reverberated in the ground, crossed over and rose up inside Durán's own core. What he'd whisper in caustic poetry. What it would feel like if Chrétien were here now, lying beside Durán through *migdiada* rest. What he'd given Durán permission to say the first time they lay beside each other. The first time Durán felt the peace for which he'd prayed.

Eu vos amor.

What did he want? To finish this obligation to the family that had discovered him only a blue moon ago. To be done running fool's errands for counts and kings. To be home again.

No, he just wanted Chrétien to finish his current errand and join them on the trail, so that Durán could lie in his friend's arms and find comfort for just one moment. What kept Chrétien away? What could possibly demand that Chrétien be anywhere but here?

4

Discovery

Dolç in Lérida, Castell del Rei
early June

DOLÇ CAME WITH TREPIDATION TO the common room of Petronilla's house, even though the servant who summoned her insisted that a guest had asked for Dolç by name.

Petronilla, a closer cousin to Pedro than Dolç, liked playing queen-of-the-house now that her husband Don Carlos and most of the other men were gone to fight in Andalusia. Whenever a guest arrived, Petronilla became overly busy, claiming her role as hostess and introducing that knight who was her constant companion now that Carlos was gone. Carlos was an important man, an emissary to Aragón for the king of Castile. Dolç didn't understand why Petronilla chose to spend so much time with a lesser knight when she had a grand husband.

"Baudoïs de Montpelhièr is here with us. We are sheltering safely here in the royal city while our husbands and champions are away. Those of us who have husbands." However coolly she spoke at that moment, Petronilla was not oblivious to the insult. She'd urged Dolç to leave Barcelona and join her for protection in Lérida, and then never lost a chance to needle Dolç for having a betraying, banished husband.

That ponderous knight Baudoïs, large enough that one might have sympathy for his horse, moved elegantly in chambers and in the dining hall. He seemed healthy enough to be on crusade, but begged off in spite of Don Carlos's urging, and he was explaining to the new, unseen visitor why he'd stayed home.

"I won remission of my sins in Constantinople. That's enough for any man. If the Saracens come this far, of course I'll be ready to fight again."

"Never made it as far as Constantinople." The voice spoke an Occitan-Catalan patois, with an odd accent Dolç had heard from only one other man, her husband. Who was no longer her husband. "And I kept on sinning. I owe God this expedition."

"It's an honor to have one of Pedro's knights visit us." Petronilla fawned over the visitor.

"I'm only a jongleur, a singer of others' songs."

Dolç entered the common room to find a tall Celt dressed in chain-mail and a gambeson with the same insignia her husband Tomás wore. While Baudoïs maintained his perpetual knightly stance, part rigor, part menace, this knight swept a deep bow upon seeing Dolç, seemingly unencumbered by his armor or weapons.

"Ma dòmna, I am Chrétien of St-Joachim, brother to Tomás of Morella. And I am seeking Dolç of St. Félíu. Is that senhóra you?"

Petronilla answered him, as if Dolç were a child to be ignored. "St-Joachim belongs to the Count of Barcelona, who grants it to favored seigneurs."

"And not bastard Celts?" The tall, magnificent knight smiled. "My brother Tomás lost the St-Joachim estate to me at dice. I have allowed the charade that Tomás was the master there. But now, here I am, come to see how I can be of service. Dolç of St. Félíu?"

With one hand, Dolç clutched Quelo even closer under her shawl, embarrassed by her hostess's rude disapproval. The other hand she offered him in greeting.

"My cousin Dolç's friends are mine too." Again, Petronilla in-truded. And nothing in her voice rang as welcoming.

Senhór Chrétien made a courtly bow, then focused his attention on Dolç, seeming to disregard Petronilla. "I'm on my way to join Pedro, but must first ask if I can be of service in any way to my brother's wife."

"Our marriage was annulled." Dolç said it aloud (she repeated it to herself daily, so that she'd learn to believe it), but her voice was lost while Petronilla vented her persistent rage for Tomás.

"That bastard traitor!" Petronilla used ill language whenever Tomás's name was mentioned.

"I am my family's only bastard." Chrétien remained affable and lighthearted, seeming to ignore the rude outburst. "Tomás is our father's true son. And I do need to speak of Tomás's business with you, ma dòmna."

Dolç indicated the archway that lead to her chambers. "Shall we talk business in my room?"

Chrétien followed, walking backward while offering thanks to Senhóra Petronilla in the drawling accents of a backcountry Catalan sheepherder.

Inside Dolç's chamber, the girls glanced up shyly from the corner where they'd been carding wool since breakfast. Fortuno stitched away at pieces of leather to construct a vest he called a cuirass. Dolç had punched holes with an awl, so the chore took concentration, not strength, and Fortuno bit his lip, absorbed until Dolç opened the door wider for Chrétien to enter.

"We have a guest. Senhór Chrétien is Don Tomás's brother."

Fortuno looked up from where he sat, which was a long way up since yellow-haired Chrétien was unnaturally tall. Fortuno jumped up, his work clattering to the floor.

"Did you bring news from my master?"

It had proved to be a chore to teach a half-wild boy from the frontier how to honor his betters, to be silent in company. Though perhaps Dolç simply didn't understand boys.

But Chrétien stopped as if stunned.

"Whose boy are you?"

"This is Fortuno." Dolç rested her hand on the black-haired boy with the same dark-lashed beautiful eyes as Tomás and the same warm color. "He's an orphan from Morella that...Sebastián found in Barcelona. We consider him family."

Chrétien opened his mouth as if to speak, but no words came.

"He must look like my husband as a child." She'd made that mistake, thinking at first that Fortuno was Tomás's son.

"Yes, very like him." Chrétien swallowed. Finally, he spoke. "I would like to meet all of you."

She called the girls over for introductions, proud that they bowed honorably, their eyes round at meeting a knight up close, still in his traveling clothes.

"You have your tasks, children." She sent Fortuno away with the girls to attend to their chores. "Senhór Chrétien and I have business to discuss."

Dolç settled on a bench. The babe, immediately restless, made tiny sounds. She dropped the shawl over him and then ensured that he latched onto her breast properly. Over the past anxious days, she'd lost all modesty.

"Quelo came too early." She pulled the shawl more tightly over the babe. "The travel here proved too much. Or perhaps he's as eager as his father to be out in the world doing things. And therefore, I have a seven-month babe in my care."

"Neither Pedro nor Tomás wrote to me about you. Or about…" Chrétien settled back in his chair, silent while she fussed with the tiny sweet thing.

"Tomás doesn't know. The boy is called Miquel—Quelo—after your father." The babe managed to keep sucking and settled peacefully against her. "We consulted an excellent physician, Na Floreta. She advised me to keep him bundled close to my heart. It seems to be working."

"He's Quelo of Morella." Fortuno sprang up, dropping his work, excited again. "The young donzel will be my master, because I'm from Morella and—"

"Fortuno, you—" Before Dolç could say more, Senhór Chrétien had his hand up, gently interfering.

"You are from Morella, *fadrín*?" Chrétien motioned for the lad to come to him. "I'm Tomás's brother. In his absence any man under Tomás's rule must obey me."

"Òc, senhór." The boy spoke the household tongue now, heavily inflected with the accents of the Aragón frontier.

"Sit here by me, *fadrín*. A good soldier never interrupts a woman when she is speaking."

"Òc, but I want to tell you—"

"Silence, *fadrín*. The senhóra is telling us how Quelo fares."

51

Fortuno settled in beside the tall knight. Whenever the boy stirred as if he might speak again, Chrétien tapped his shoulder, obtaining the perfect obedience that Dolç never gained over the excitable boy.

"Our confessor here believes that Sancta Maria touches our lives," Dolç said. "I begged the Holy Mother to save my son, and She promised Quelo's life to me. Her voice guides me every moment of the day. But perhaps you think the idea of a guiding saint is women's foolishness."

"Never in this life, ma dòmna."

"Quelo grows stronger every day. I thank the Blessed Mother of our Lord for keeping us safe."

"It must be hard for you." Chrétien had left his levity behind in the foyer with Petronilla.

"Pedro provided me with good stewards. We have all the silver we need. And Pedro empowered the stewards and his guard to—"

"I mean for you, ma dòmna. Alone here. Without Tomás."

She bent her head. "I don't believe what Petronilla claims, that Tomás betrayed the king. Pedro sent guards the day Tomás left, which I think means that—"

"Things aren't as they seem." Senhór Chrétien finished her words for her. He seemed uncertain about what to say next. After a moment he began again. "I didn't know about you until I knocked on your villa gate in Barcelona."

"Thanks be to God!" She used a Narbonne dialect with him. "Except my cousin says—"

"The witch I met in the outer hall?"

"She means well." Dolç habitually defended Petronilla. "She invited me here after Pedro left Barcelona, because we're cousins. May I invite you to stay the night with us?"

He became serious again. "I have to say goodbye and return to my journey."

Fortuno broke the bond of silence Chrétien had laid on him. "Take me! I'm a soldier. I'm ready to help Pedro drive the Saracens back into the sea."

"Peace, *fadrin*." Chrétien had a hand on the boy's shoulder but looked to Dolç, who nodded.

"Best if you take him with you," she said. "Morella must send men to support Pedro."

Fortuno nearly wiggled out of his skin with joy.

"Go pack, *fadrin*. One satchel." Chrétien dismissed him, then turned back to Dolç. "What did Sebastián and Yusuf say about losing Tomás in Barcelona?"

"Nothing. They traveled into Iberia with Pedro, leaving the same day Tomás did. Neither gave me a chance to say goodbye."

"I've felt lost without Tomás." Chrétien paused. "Now, meeting you, I feel in the deepest caverns of my heart…"

He didn't seem able to go on. Dolç wanted to rescue him from what must be said.

"Please remember that Pedro d'Aragón had our marriage annulled. Tomás didn't want the marriage, then didn't want me to be alone when he left."

"Ma dòmna." He touched her. No one but the children and the physician had touched her since she came to Lérida. "Annulled is what the Church does. Our family will never abandon you." He shifted forward, whispering in her ear. "Pedro wrote to me that Tomás is dead. You are now in my care."

She had by then mastered hiding her tears; children shouldn't see their mother weep. They sat in silence for so long that she had to move Quelo to her other breast and the girls shuffled with unease.

When Fortuno burst once more into the room, Chrétien said, "Can you give me dinner, ma dòmna? Then I'll be on my way. Every moment I tarry, my friends are riding farther into La Mancha."

"I'd be honored to serve you, senhór. Will you sing for us? Sebastián claimed that one cannot have truly enjoyed life without hearing you sing."

·

Throughout dinner Petronilla sat close by Dolç's side. She persisted in attempts to engage Chrétien's attention, speaking Dolç's name and yet excluding her.

Petronilla's friend, the fastidious giant Baudoïs, watched Senhór Chrétien like a cat at a mouse hole, never smiling at even the broadest of Chrétien's jests, never looking away, except one moment when he caught Dolç watching the watcher.

Petronilla's voice rose, piercingly. "Naturally, I don't want to speak ill of the dead or those who aren't here. But what was our cousin Pedro thinking to put our dear Dolç in such a quandary? All these children and no one to champion her."

"*Ai*, Pedro was thinking of me." Chrétien had his hand on his heart, smiling warmly, as if Petronilla offered another jest like his. Then his smile disappeared into cold sobriety. "Because he knows I'd move mountains to come to Senhóra Dolç as fast as I could,"

Before the food was cleared away, the Celtic jongleur sang *cançós de guèrra*, dedicating two songs to Outremer crusaders now in Abraham's bosom. When Chrétien performed a long portion of the *cançós d'Arturo*, Dolç felt as if her heart might burst. He sang Guinevere in a sweet falsetto, and then made everyone in the room love Lancelot for his bravery and great beauty.

"A true knight of paratge." Chrétien paused for a long sip of wine. "Except for betraying his king."

Then he sang *cançós d'amor* written by the count of Foix, a poet in the Pyrenees foothills. He sang the one where a shepherdess humiliates the priest who had seduced her, and the one where the three mistresses capture a fickle, lying knight and cut his locks. Petronilla laughed heartily at the humiliated lover-priest. The best song, Dolç believed, was the one where the humble woodcutter proved to be a true knight of the Cross, united in the end with the love of his heart, singing his homage to the highborn dòmna who loved him.

Her oldest girl whispered in Dolç's ear with a request. Dolç said, "Fortuno, sing for us before you go, please."

The boy stood in front of Chrétien and sang, in a high, swelling voice that made everyone forget what an earnest scamp he was. The song was "*Ab nou cor*," except the boy sang of loving the dearest cow who gave the sweetest milk that made the best of cheeses. A country grandmother had made over the words of that raucous love song for a little boy to sing. The way Fortuno crooned, the song still revealed all the joy and longing for the beloved. The girls, hanging close to Dolç, listened with sad sweet smiles, then rushed to embrace Fortuno and wish him good health and success on crusade.

Fortuno came to receive a farewell kiss. Dolç said, "May God's hand guide you if your good companions ever fail you."

■

"His voice leaves a lingering afterglow." Chrétien, standing by Dolç and the children to say goodbye, watched Fortuno load his small pack onto the back of the horse. "He must sing better than the angels."

"It's one more reason why Fortuno should be with you," Dolç said. "There's a life for that boy if someone helps him find his way. And yet...

"Òc?" Chrétien turned his handsome, smiling countenance on her. He'd taken advantage of the bath she'd offered, and he'd shaved, so that a stunningly beautiful, glowing man stood before her. Dolç felt her face grow hot under his kind attention.

"Can a little boy survive in the middle of an army?"

"I did. Tomás did." He smiled again, his hand on her shoulder to reassure her. "He won't be near battle. I'll leave him with the laundry women, which is the safest place on God's creation. You know that Saladin returned the crusaders' laundry women? Didn't even hold them for ransom."

She took his hand, the way her own mother used to when she needed reassurance. "I cannot offer enough thanks that you came. That you care enough to..."

Her three girls chose that moment to clutch at her skirts, pulling at her so that she had to shift Quelo to one arm in order to comfort them with the other.

"Ma dòmna, listen." He touched each of the girls' heads, tousling their curls. "I am your brother. Do you understand? I owe you all that body and soul can do."

She nodded, not wanting him to see her fears.

"I'll be with Pedro when he returns, ma dòmna. Then you shall come home with me. My mother Numa will welcome you."

To keep that magnificent man from seeing how this overwhelmed her, Dolç called for Fortuno to come, and she made him stand still while she said a prayer to protect him. The girls hugged and cried over Fortuno, which kept her from betraying her own melancholy. A soft cry from Quelo meant that he needed her most, so she hurried the girls inside to calm them and to let Chrétien depart.

In her own private room, though, chaos broke out among the girls. Fortuno had forgotten his leather vest. She tied Quelo more closely to her with a shawl and ran down to the courtyard. Behind the woodcutter's wagon, the vest slipped from her hands. She bent to pick it up.

"Thank you, senhór knight." Petronilla's voice rang out over the cobbled yard. Peeking under the wagon, Dolç saw that the woman stood with a servant who was prepared to close the gate behind Chrétien and his friends. Petronilla stalked away, calling back, "Thank you for taking out the trash."

With that knight Baudoïs at her side, Petronilla returned inside, her nose too far in the air to see Dolç behind the wagon. The Montcava mercenary who'd arrived with Chrétien stood silently with refreshed horses. The panniers had been resupplied with food and fodder as Dolç had asked.

"Jacques." Chrétien pulled his companion aside, near the wagon. "Stay here. Guard the senhóra of St-Féliu and her children. Watch out for that giant who calls himself a knight."

The little Norman spat. "Surely you jest. This is the first war in years that might make us rich."

"I don't trust that *putana* cousin. And that knight Baudoïs has a Crux Lunata tattoo on his hairy forearm. Both my gut and the creeping at the back of my neck shout that danger lurks here. Don't leave Petronilla or that knight alone with Senhóra Dolç or her children."

"My gut says I'm not a nursemaid. I swore to Tomás that I'd stay and help you protect Montcava, but—"

"I'll give you half my booty."

"That's foolish wages for babysitting," the man Jacques said.

"The tiny ma dòmna holds Tomás's child in her arms."

"*Bon Dieu!* But Senhóra Isabella…"

"Will never be spoken of while you are here. Neither wife knows the other lives. That's Pedro's riddle to solve when he has the leisure."

Isabella. Dolç recognized the name which Tomás, that poor wretched man, cried out in his sleep. The woman that Sebastián and Yusuf called mother.

Now Chrétien had two widows to whom he must attend.

Jacques walked back with Chrétien and hoisted Fortuno atop the palfrey, admonishing him about letting the horse have her head, while Fortuno swore every horse made by God loved him. Then Jacques waved as Chrétien and Fortuno headed out to find the road to Toledo. Fortuno sang out the first line of a traveling song. Chrétien joined in the song as the gate closed behind them.

Jacques, taking up the reins of his horse, led it toward the stable, his head down as he walked.

"*Salut!*" Dolç called to him in French, since she had overhead enough to know that was his language. He didn't know her voice, wouldn't notice that she was about to break into tears. "It's Master Jacques, isn't it?"

"Oui, madame."

"Can you please chase after Fortuno to give him his cuirass? Then I will find a bed for you. Will you dine with us? What more do you need to be comfortable?"

"I'm used to a pallet with the guards, madame."

"We can do better than that. Chrétien asked you to live in the king's city for my sake. You won't be sleeping in the stable."

5
Fidelity

*Vidal on the Aragón Frontier
a hundred leagues beyond Zaragoza
mid-June*

DAY OR NIGHT: HEAT, DUST, gnats, fleas, mosquitoes, sweat. Yet here on this hot, dusty plain, Isabella found that her heart had wings. The knowledge of Sebastián—alive!—gave her energy while the long ride wore others down. No more bargains with the devil. Just take care of the horses and help her companions.

For a while, at least through this summer and fall, she had to be Vidal the scribe, wrapped up in leather traveling clothes, master of his horse, owning nothing except rediscovered friends. And hope, not just that she'd see Sebastián, but that they'd get to Pedro in time to warn him.

Isabella had so much hope that she was first in the saddle each morning, last to dismount for *migdiada* or for the night's encampment. The wind pushed her across montañas and plains, with only the empty Iberian wilderness separating her from Sebastián.

To her relief, no priest rode with them. She'd been rescued by heretics and then harassed by a renegade abbot over the months she hid in the monastery at St-Pere. In the moments of solitude she stole each day, she offered gratitude and begged for Tomás's soul, pleading that he be admitted to heaven and cradling the relics from her winter of terror, that bejeweled finger bone from a forgotten saint and the gilded icon of Sancta Maria, Queen of Heaven.

The most precious relic was Tomás's recaptured short-sword. She wore it at her side, slept with it amid the heat and dust and mosquitos. She retained the nagging concern that Crux Lunata knights pursued her for that poor dead abbot at the monastery, or for leaving Matheus at death's door in Girona. But no more nightmares, reliving the moments when false crusaders murdered Tomás.

No more torments like those she'd endured while hiding in the monastery at St-Pere. Only faded memories of lying helpless in the cave of the heretics who had rescued her.

And now she knew Sebastián and Yusuf were safe and riding with Marshall Guillem and Father Anselm and the best of Valerós knights, in the safety of Pedro's immense army. Her goal, after finding her sons, was to warn Pedro about Crux Lunata. Pedro had to return home alive and a hero in Christendom, because he was the only leader who could persuade the pope to restore peace in Toulouse. Valerós. All of the plains and hills and valleys of the south.

After Chrétien left to find Pedro and warn him of the Crux Lunata plot, Isabella had insisted that the captains gradually increase the pace of travel. Her goal was to join Pedro's army as soon as possible, where she'd find Sebastián. She had to argue the case with Durán, who didn't want them to be separated too rapidly from where Chrétien might find them.

"Chrétien riding alone can travel at twice the pace of your army, Durán. He will find us."

On the first day after she won this argument with Durán, they added two leagues to the day's travel distance; the second, adding five leagues. Spring had arrived, and the blooming countryside filled the air with the perfume of rosemary and thyme. Swallowtail butterflies hovered over star clover in bloom. By the third day, the army achieved fifteen leagues and then kept that pace each day.

When they left the cultivated regions of Aragón territory, they divided the ride into early-morning and evening bursts to avoid the blaring midday heat. No baggage train, only palfreys and mules. Instead, scouts bought supplies with the gold sewn in the captains' cloaks. Otherwise, the army scavenged rabbits and roots in the wild and pushed on toward the next provisioning station.

Isabella would happily ride this army into the ground, except she cared too much for the horses to abuse them in this heat. With the hard pace set, each man and his beasts were in constant pain from riding and sunburn. If they camped near a lake, flies swarmed in the sun and mosquitoes crawled up shirts and leggings in the night. Some men were so bitten that their swollen faces were hard to recognize. Hot as it was in the dead of night, many men built fires, because the extra heat, a smoky cough, and irritated eyes were better than being eaten alive by mosquitoes. If scavengers found no wood for smoky fires, the army rode as late into the night as the horses tolerated, rather than sit still to be consumed by insects.

But Isabella was doing what she'd once bragged about from the safety of Castel-de-Valerós, when her grandfather shook his head sadly at the idea, claiming that the time had passed for women to lead. *No more queens like Eleanor d'Aquitaine,* he'd said. Yet here was Isabella, at the forefront of one hundred and twenty knights, riding through the dry-land wilderness, crossing hundreds of leagues to join Pedro d'Aragón.

Pink and white rockrose with dusted-grey leaves crowded the road, interspersed with yellow broom. Rose garlic bloomed in the grass where the horses grazed. The air smelled of spring's new life, and her horse—not a Valerós horse, but a good one—enjoyed the ride as much as she did. Except for the prickling fear that they were still pursued by Crux Lunata knights seeking revenge for what happened at St-Pere monastery, when that greedy abbot managed to get himself killed while attempting to assassinate Isabella.

And Colomb de Beaurain, a Crux Lunata relic, riding in their midst. Watching, haranguing, waiting.

Did he believe that Felip and "Vidal" caused havoc at St-Pere? Or had Colomb guessed who she was? Exactly how much danger did they gamble with, battling Colomb every day?

.

"*Bon Dèu,* I'm hungry."

Outside the provisioning agent's casa, Isabella took the reins from Durán and Felip to hold their horses.

"Here." Durán reached into the pouch at his waist and produced a hank of linen, then unwrapping a clutch of quail's eggs. "Thierry found these while checking beyond the camp at dawn. Boiled them and sent them as a gift."

They had two eggs each, and Isabella cracked and ate both of hers while Durán still argued that his share belonged to Felip. It took Felip the usual embarrassing exchanges before he accepted the morsels. It wasn't a sacrifice. As a Good Christian, Durán endeavored not to eat meat or the product of the congress of animals, but often failed. He practiced his beliefs more diligently when Chrétien wasn't around to persuade him otherwise. Isabella repeated what Chrétien would say.

"A traveling warrior can't survive on weeds and beans."

For a fortnight, Isabella wished for Chrétien to catch up with them. He'd begged her, in his farewell, to watch out for the two untested captains, Durán and Felip. She resolved never to offer unasked advice, to let Durán and Felip learn their duties, though it often meant biting her tongue raw while they guessed what to do next.

How could two men nearly the same size could be so different? Durán had the build and strength of a streetfighter, except he'd taken a Good Christian's vow never to harm a living thing. Dark-haired Felip, who wore a monk's habit when they first met, had the broad shape and God-given power of the knightly class he was born to, but had never learned to wield even a knife until he joined this army.

"My grandfather claimed that crusaders travel on God's paths of glory," Felip said. "Perhaps angels will show us the way."

"I have doubts," Durán said. "Chrétien insists that every army travels on beans, not glory. It's just one more supply puzzle after another. I'd be lost if he hadn't taught me *mathematica*."

That day, Isabella, Felip, and Durán stood in the baked dust, begging for supplies from the keeper of one of Pedro's frontier provisioning stations. The local trail guide they'd hired, García, was nowhere to be found whenever they needed his help. Durán, the leader of the Montcava and Foix knights, dickered for supplies.

"We have nothing for you, senhór," the stationmaster said. "Pedro d'Aragón demands all be saved until after the new moon in July. He wants that men who live to come home from the war will have food and fodder."

A doughty white-haired fellow with an Aragónese accent, this stationmaster claimed to understand their distress, having crusaded in the Outremer with men from the Aquitaine. Then the ancient crusader-turned-provisioner said that a band of knights passing through the previous day took the last available supplies for the outward journey, on their way to join the unified army south of Toledo.

Durán appeared calm, given the tragedy just announced. He scratched at his beard while studying the list that identified where to purchase food and fodder, the list that the count of Foix had received from Pedro d'Aragón. "The next provisioning station is two days away."

Tucking his list inside his cuirass, Durán showed the stationmaster a bag of gold. Not so much gold as to attract bandits, but enough to entice people in small, dirt-poor villages.

"Who has stores that they'll sell me?"

The ancient soldier spread his open hands. "Pedro paid our shepherds and farmers to give up all they can spare, to the glory of God. If the Blessed Mother of Our Lord appeared with the loaves and fishes, I dare not sell it to you."

"Who came here yesterday?" Felip asked, voicing Isabella's continual dread that they'd been hunted since leaving St-Pere.

"Knights from the holy orders," the stationmaster said. "Some were Templars, who think they're holier than John the Baptist. Same as they were in the Outremer."

"*Ai, mon amic.* That's what I've heard." Durán asked more, evoking the stationmaster's tale of mistreatment in the Holy Land. He had a knack for making friends with provision-keepers. At the end of the tale, Durán asked again about the last travelers.

"The others? It was fellows what never was in the Outremer." The old man rubbed his sunburned bald spot. "The Knights of the Rosy Cross, was it?"

In spite of her resolve to be silent, Isabella blurted, "They wore red crosses? Or black?"

The ancient stationmaster squinted into the sun. "A moon cross? That might be it."

"The Knights of the Lunate Cross?" Durán asked. "Little red crescents at the end of the black crosses they wore?"

"*Si.* They told stories of apparitions. How saints are appearing on the land."

"You gave them Pedro's stores?" Durán said it softly, not wanting to show his immense frustration.

"No. Had a letter from the archbishop, they did. To take whatever stores they needed and the archbishop will pay the king. They got the last of the fodder and beans that I could allow."

After they said farewell and untethered their waiting horses, Felip complained. "Colomb says in real wars the army takes what it needs while traveling. Pedro's new ways are untested."

"Chrétien says," Durán cited his sole authority, "that Pedro planned provisions for years. He forbids his knights to steal crops or animals. We pay our way."

"Shouldn't every man on the frontier support the fight against the Saracens? I gave up all my land for this crusade." Felip folded his arms. Yet, as Isabella saw it, Felip had been swindled out of his inheritance by his brother Matheus.

She said, "Pedro has to govern here when this enterprise is done. He doesn't want starving, unhappy people after the army returns."

The stationmaster called after them just as they prepared to mount and ride. "Those rosy knights who came yesterday. They be seeking a pair of heretic monks, the dark-robed kind, who murdered a Christian abbot. Keep your eyes wide, like a fox."

Durán waved farewell. "God keep us safe from the heretics."

Isabella pressed at the dust-rag she tied over her face, half-laughing, half-horrified to have her fears confirmed.

They made some distance before Felip exclaimed, "Why do rumors accuse us of heresy? It's worse than—"

"Peace, *mon fraire*." Durán spoke just loud enough to be heard over the clopping of their horses. "No one believes you're anything but a fine seigneur from Girona."

"Except Colomb de Beaurain," Felip muttered.

"Let's think the best," Isabella said. "Colomb hasn't murdered us or turned us over to the Church courts."

"Yet," Durán and Felip said at the same time.

At camp, they were saved from having to explain the new rationing required until the next supply station. Colomb and a quartet of his men were divvying up supplies: lentils, flour, salted meat, and—*Bon Dèu*—sheep's cheese. Paniers with a dozen live chickens were loaded onto mules that also carried arms and blankets.

"We aren't robbing the countryside!"

Watching Colomb and Durán quarrel, Isabella once more saw how Durán had inherited Hugues de Beaurain's ability to assert himself. She'd met Hugues, that famous knight, and recognized the same nobility in Durán. Colomb? Every grimace, demeaning laugh, and dismissive gesture reminded her of other Beaurain men: Matheus, who she'd nearly killed in Girona; and worse, her dead husband Nicolau.

Durán whirled away from the argument, commanding the captains to prepare to ride. Colomb called after him, openly mocking in front of his mercenaries.

"A Beaurain army is well-trained and sticks together. Are you glue, *fadrin*? What did God make you? Wheat-paste or plaster?"

This continual harassment reminded her of life in Toulouse, where Nicolau and Renoud bullied her, saying evil things over and again, just to drive her mad.

She'd lived through too much since then to be silent now.

·

Isabella approached while Colomb was currying one of his horses. He took admirable care of his horses. While she watched, he dropped the jangling currycomb and embraced the horse, grabbing its ears to whisper endearments, offering up a tiny dried apple. Then he threw on a blanket and began to saddle the horse.

"Pèire Leteric taught his men to harness horses that way." She pointed to the crossed-breast double-strapping. "He brought a saddle like yours back from the Outremer."

Colomb didn't glance up. "I rode with Pèire briefly. The few months I was on crusade with my brother Hugues in the Outremer. Learned from both men." After he cinched up the strapping, he again paused to make love to his horse. "Are you Pèire Leteric's spawn? You look like him. But Pèire didn't have a string of bastards, so what are you? Maybe his brother's castoff, looking for a bigger scrap of Pèire's legacy by hanging onto your cousins?"

"Your horse has Arab blood, but I'm not asking about his mother and father. It isn't what a courtly man does in our part of the world."

She stuck out her jaw, imitating how Tomás offered challenges, but also aware, standing this close to their adversary, how Durán and

Felip and the Montcava mercenaries always surrounded her, kept her safe. And here she was alone with their enemy.

He slipped his horse another morsel of dried apple. "Pèire was a good man. We bastard sons should stick together, the way brothers do. Wish I could make your *bon amics* understand. We owe it to God to help set the world right again."

"I'm loyal to Pèire's brotherhood, the Confraria de la Crotz. Hugues de Beaurain was also." She bared her wrist, showing the square burn of the crossbow bolt, then hastily pulled down her sleeve, her wrist seeming too thin, too vulnerable to show an enemy. "Bastards or not, we uphold paratge and the honor of the south."

"Brotherhood?" Colomb scoffed, which startled his horse, so he had to pet it and say again how much he loved it. "The children of good men have gone mad, claiming land and power while protecting heretics."

"You prefer Crux Lunata." She boldly pointed to his forearm, where Durán had seen the moon-cross tattoo. "But you didn't leave with the Crux Lunata knights in Girona. Why?"

"I'm leading Maria de Montpelhièr's mercenaries. She sent me with the Count of Foix's army. The Knights of the Lunate Cross have their own captains."

"But you're a knight in that order."

"Just this year. My brother was an early initiate. I'm walking in the footsteps of a noble, devout man who convinced me that God wants us to restore order in the south."

"Why work for Maria?" Isabella asked. "The Count of Foix surely pays better."

"I owe loyalty when she calls on me."

"Loyalty? Then why not serve Pedro d'Aragón? He's working to unite our world."

"Because I'm a Beaurain." He talked his horse into taking the double-reined bit. "We owe fealty first to Philippe Auguste, not Pedro. Who works only for his own glory, not God's."

"*Ai*, Philippe? The king who let his knights invade to steal our land and booty?" Resentment burned in her soul. "Whose captains made a devil's bargain and burned heretics."

"You disagree, little man?" He clapped his hand on Isabella's shoulder with force, more than the kind of slap any man in the army gives another while talking. "The saints come to good Catholics. Can the heretics claim that? Can Pedro?"

"I don't know anyone who's met a saint, whether Catholic or Good Christian."

"I do. I've seen what a man looks like in the ecstasy of an apparition. Can you say that about your heretic friends?"

"I don't know about other people. I pray only for peace and forgiveness, not the visitation of saints."

"Truly?" He loomed over her. She stood straighter. "Looking like Pèire, you're not pretty enough to be prey for *cavallers fada* like that Celtic madman Durán sleeps with. But you're the *fada* who ran off with Matheus's baby brother."

"We merely left the monks' life behind. We didn't run away."

He laughed. His horse stepped sideways until he gathered the reins and tugged. "Neither of you has enough spunk to kill Lorenç, so I'm guessing he was attacked by heretics, who all lie about wanting peace. Back home, they're breaking the pope's call for the Peace of God and wreaking revenge on their betters. Are you in that rat's nest of heretics the Crux Lunata seek to save from damnation?"

"No. And I have not seen Crux Lunata knights save souls, Captain Colomb. But I've seen them murder innocents."

He shook his head, the way one does with a recalcitrant child. "The archbishop of Narbonne gave me only until the first new moon in the summer."

"For what?" *The same day Crux Lunata seeks to destroy Pedro.*

"To bring my heretic Beaurain nephew to serve the Church." He kissed his horse's nose. "If you once hankered for the monk's life, then you must love God in the caverns of your heart. Help bring your friends back from the dark valleys of heresy. You carry Pèire's blood. Lead Durán to the path of righteousness."

"I didn't know you too hankered after God's love." *But I now know that you do indeed spy on us for Crux Lunata.* "Are we arguing how to lead men, or about the ways of angels and saints?"

"It doesn't matter to me," Colomb spoke slowly, as if explaining to a child, "if angels and saints unite to taunt Saracen devils."

"What then? What do you care about most?"

"That southern lords stop arguing with the Church. The House of Beaurain must bow to the Church and turn over their heretics. Then we can come together as brothers and fight to keep the south for our own people."

"Simon de Montfort is hurting people, not saving souls. You are mistaken if you think he's doing God's work."

Colomb stopped stroking his horse, scowling. "You won't uphold Pèire Leteric's honor? You won't serve the one true God? Are we enemies then?"

"I don't hope for the blessing of an apparition, but I strive to serve God with every breath I take. And I know Simon is not right with God." She touched one of the highly polished brass stirrup, running a finger over the inscription. "How unusual. Where did you find these?"

"Constantinople. I fought beside my brother there." Colomb spoke like a knight talking about his greatest glory. "Where my brother taught me how to fight for God and salvation."

Isabella knew stories from Constantinople, how Hugues de Beaurain was tricked into believing Jean-Luc de Chartrain was a thief and a Cain. "A place of hard lessons."

"Indeed." He too touched the polished brass stirrup. "It's why I prize these. A reminder of what I learned there. It's what I strive to teach as a captain."

"Surely not."

"Òc." He frowned at her quibble. "The left one says, 'Praise the Mother of our Lord.' This one says, 'Glory to God.'"

"No, that's not what these Greek letters mean." She knew from ten years guided by Katelina of Naxos, who loved Pèire Leteric and tutored Isabella and her sisters. "This one says, 'Steal my wife, not my horse.'" She ran a finger again over the left stirrup's inscription. "This one curses God. With crude words I won't speak aloud."

For that moment, Colomb seemed stunned.

"Durán's farrier can hammer that out for you. Ask him when we camp tonight." She offered a soldierly farewell wave. "Meanwhile, Captain Colomb, I won't tell your secret. We both know things aren't always as they seem. You and I aren't innocents."

6

Apparitions

Felip in La Mancha, beyond Toledo
mid-June

FELIP CARRIED A SECRET IN HIS heart, a belief that God might strike him dead for pretending to be a crusader. By fire? Lightning? And inside his jerkin he secretly carried his uncle Lorenç's cup, stolen from the abbot when Felip and "Vidal" had fled the monastery.

One secret that Felip could not hide from his new friends was that he struggled as the leader of the Xirgú mercenaries. He was raised to be a priest and had taken the Xirgú mantle only because his grandmother begged him to uphold paratge and his father's honor.

That was after Isabella of Valerós had stabbed Felip's brother Matheus. Who wasn't actually his brother.

Because Felip owed a huge debt to his father's honor, and because Durán had welcomed him as a captain, Felip continued to struggle each day, trying to transform the novice priest inside him into a leader of the Xirgú men.

Yet each day on the journey, he was confronted by Colomb de Beaurain, Matheus's defender. Harangued when saddling his horse, supervising the food supply, or setting or breaking camp. Durán complained of being scolded in whispers each time he encountered his great-uncle, but Felip was outright laughed at each time he encountered Colomb.

Since that day in the village with the black-feathered chickens, Colomb seemed to avoid Durán, except during midday fighting. But Colomb continued to harass Felip without relief. Every night, Felip went to sleep with the image of Colomb, hands on his hips, mocking him. And then he got up in the morning with the dread that he'd hear it again, the clink of chainmail, words spoken through a croak of laughter.

"Xirgú bought an army, but what is the price of salvation in that heretics' nest?"

Colomb tapped a long, gnarled finger right over Felip's heart, upbraiding him in the same way that one ancient monk at St-Pere used to, asking if Felip carried the Blessed Savior where it mattered. Like asking a child if lessons have been learned. Felip knocked Colomb's hand away.

"Sleep well last night, Xirgú? Snuggling up with murderers and heretics?"

Colomb, though the same height as Felip, hunched whenever he confronted his prey, arched over like a rough-legged buzzard, sun glinting golden in his eyes, as if Felip were the hunted hare. Yet whenever Colomb tapped him, Felip respond the same way he did with that aged, nagging St-Pere monk, repeating a benediction instead of a curse.

"I'm blessed to follow the path God intended for me."

As if responding at mass, each time Colomb answered, "At the end of that path, your father turns in his grave."

Then Felip would step aside to take a wide path around Colomb de Beaurain, ignoring that the knight laughed at him. And then at night, Felip examined how much he feared Colomb, and how much he wished he could show Durán that he was worthy to lead the Xirgú men, that he appreciated what he was learning from his new friends.

■

At *migdiada*, Felip's insides clenched again when he heard the call during midday sparring.

"Pedro's head!"

The mercenary Thierry bent to look at the coin in the dust, declaring the results of the toss. Durán had offered his own coin, hoping to defeat any trickery, but the results proved to be the same as every other day.

"I can fight my own fights." Isabella clutched Durán's arm, but he shrugged out from under her grip and began to strip his shirt.

"I have to deny Colomb's challenges. The count of Foix made me master of this army."

But that day, Felip decided to pay what he owed his father's honor. He stepped in front of Durán and said the words.

"The s–s–scribe doesn't fight. The Xirgú seigneur fights in his s–stead." Felip began to peel off his cuirass. Inside, he heard Chrétien's voice and wanted to prove him wrong. *"Xirgú couldn't win a fight to save himself."*

"Jhezu del tron!" Isabella swore softly, her sleeve smothering most of the words.

"Peace, Master Vidal. Let him try," Thierry said, blessedly kind mercenary that he was.

Felip stripped his shirt, carefully swaddling the cup he secretly carried and setting it aside with his cuirass. Then he stepped into the fight circle, cradling the quarterstaff Chrétien gave him when they first met.

Colomb removed his own linen shirt, his usual grin in place. He did not appear near his true age: broad, muscled shoulders, a chest as firm as a young man's, only grey-haired.

"Xirgú fights for whose honor?" Colomb taunted. He didn't speak once the fight began, where Felip proceeded to forget every lesson Chrétien taught about the quarterstaff.

Felip escaped with only a broken nose, blood pouring over his sunburned face, Colomb grasped Felip's forearm, hauled him to his feet, whispered in his ear, and then released him so suddenly that Felip stumbled. Colomb picked up the tossed coin from the dirt and swaggered back to join his men in their own encampment, rattling the string of coins he carried at his waist.

Serving as barber-surgeon, Durán spoke consoling words, while Isabella watched, wincing the way she often did at the sign of even a trickle of blood. Durán tilted Felip's head back to staunch the bleeding. "Chrétien would say—"

Isabella interrupted. "If you can't resist a taunt, then practice more with Thierry and Durán. I don't like seeing you bleed, Senhór Felip."

"Colomb wants mutiny," Felip said. "He called me a boy lover."

"It's not the worst thing in the world." Durán cupped Felip's nose, seized it just below the bridge, and tugged the flesh back in place. When Felip shrieked, his blood splattered onto Isabella's bare hand, which she shook while skittering away, as if touched by poison.

"*Jhezu adouçar*, Felip," she scolded. "No more stunts like that."

"A stunt?" Felip gargled on his own blood and had to swallow before he could speak clearly. "I was protecting y–you."

"No, you did it because Colomb got you riled, calling names." Isabella returned to Felip's side, resting her hand on his shoulder. Felip guessed that meant she wasn't truly angry, since she seldom touched him. "Thank you, *mon amic*. I appreciate what you tried. But don't go into battle when you don't know the stakes."

Durán prodded gently at Felip's bones, checking to see whether anything else was broken.

"What are the stakes?" Felip remained bewildered. "Colomb talks about honor, while he's taunting us. I try to serve my father's honor, but both Colomb and Chrétien scorn me for it. Aren't we on this journey to serve paratge?"

"*Òc*. And why does Colomb keep telling me to behave like a Beaurain?" Durán finished washing up the last of Felip's wounds.

"He means Hugues. Of course," Isabella said. "He thinks that means serving the Church and surrendering heretics. Felip, what did Colomb say at the end of your fight?"

Felip sniffed, then gagged at the results. He swiped at his miserable nose. "One of his disgusting taunts. He's worse than Chrétien, goading me."

"What did Colomb say?" Durán asked, much more gently than Isabella had demanded.

"He said, 'Well done, Xirgú. Your men liked that. God bless you for being a man.' Yet everyone saw him humiliate me."

"All your men cheered you on," Durán said. "They clapped and shouted your name, even though you lost."

Felip jerked in surprise. Blood dripped from his nose once more. Isabella glanced away, then got busy cleaning up the campsite, preparing to ride after the midday rest.

"Colomb wants to convince us to join him," she said, "on the path of righteousness."

•

71

Three days later, Felip prepared to rest with his men at *migdiada*. He unloaded his palfrey and tugged off his chainmail tunic. Midday rest became more necessary each day, with rising heat and miserable nights after interminable days on horseback.

Isabella also cast aside her chainmail, but instead of leaving her horse to browse with the others, she called to Felip. "Let's ride up the hill to see who's behind us. Or in front."

"The Crux Lunata knights who left us in Girona are in front, wreaking havoc." Yet Felip left his pack and chainmail with his men, left his palfrey to browse with the others, and followed her.

Felip never said no to anything she asked.

Therefore, while everyone napped, Isabella galloped ahead and Felip struggled to catch up, as usual. Beyond Girona, Barcelona, and Zaragoza, into the uncultivated wilderness, they'd still heard rumors of the renegade monks of St-Pere de Selva. Therefore, Isabella continued to worry about who might be pursuing them. "Crux Lunata will take any opportunity to attack Valerós."

Hands shading her eyes, Isabella peered into the distance, a torn linen shirt tied over her head, a length left free to wrap over her nose and mouth so that she appeared more Saracen than Christian, neither a proper Roman one nor a Good heretic.

Felip rode up alongside her. "If anyone is following, it's your friend Chrétien. He'll catch up soon."

"We can hope," she murmured. "Durán worries, since it's been three weeks now."

Felip gazed north to follow what she observed, but had to squint in the too-bright midday sun that threatened to parch a man's brain. She pointed back up the trail, to a village they'd passed earlier that day. "There's the shrine to the Virgin Mary we passed. That flock of doves just rested on its roof."

"Here on the far edge of Christendom," Felip said, "each one of these ignorant shepherds speaks of Santa María ten times before any mention of our Lord and Savior."

"*Bon Dèu.* These people can't tithe enough for the Church to send a priest this far into the wilderness. They find what comfort they can."

"You repeat heresy."

"Be careful of that word. Our Savior didn't tell us to pay a priest to forgive our sins." She kept saying that, even though she was on a crusade with one hundred and twenty men who sought remission from their sins by fighting for the glory of God.

Done scanning the horizon, they rode down to let their mounts rest and to inspect the horses, where Felip listened closely to everything Isabella said, because she was always right. She checked a couple of animals for lameness, feeling up each horse's leg, fetlock, tendons, knee, and shoulder.

"*Ai*, this poor fellow. The ones with pale noses get sunburned, just like us." She rubbed her own peeling nose. "We need to find a healing woman who has a salve for sunburn. And you and Durán must tell your men to hood their horses during the day."

She needed that salve more than the horse she tended. Her face glowed with sunburn, her lips as badly chapped and peeling as her nose, her hair pure white. No man would find her beautiful. Then again, only Durán, the mercenary Thierry, and Felip knew she was a woman. Though Felip had once worshipped Vidal the scribe, now that seemed to him like an illness, a fever that should have been treated with healing herbs.

Her finger pointed, circling the valley where the hobbled horses grazed while the men slept. "García, that guide Durán hired in Zaragoza, promised to lead us to trails the main army didn't take. Yet these fields are trampled and overgrazed. Our horses need twice as much pasture as this."

Felip agreed. "Every trail that García takes us down is already pounded to dust."

"He'd better find fodder to purchase soon, if he can't produce fields for grazing. Each horse needs twenty pounds of feed a day. And the more food the horses have to carry, the slower we go."

Isabella seemed to be musing aloud, not requiring an answer. She surveyed the valley again.

"Stop!" She grabbed Felip's elbow, which startled him, since she rarely touched him. "See that lamb lost among the horses."

He squinted into the slanted afternoon sun. Thunderheads glided overhead, so shadows obscured the view, but he finally saw the small animal at the far edge of the horses. "It must be from a nearby village. Aren't all the herds up in the mountains?"

"Let's find this critter's home. Maybe we'll find a healer with the salve that horse needs."

"Without a doubt. Though we need shelter soon."

"Those clouds?" Isabella bent her head back to gaze skyward, her white neck bared in the cloud-filtered light. "Rumbling for nothing. There won't be rain. But it'll be cool enough to ride soon."

Catching the lamb was the easy part of her plan. On foot, they explored the edges of the small valley that curved among a series of limestone hills. The lamb bucked from Felip's arms, knocking against the chalice he kept bundled inside his jerkin. His secret. The tiny beast scuttled up a narrow path between two sharp outcroppings. Isabella followed quickly and wrestled the animal back into her arms.

"*Hola*, little fellow. Let's find your home."

They climbed a trail that zigzagged up one side of a steep hill. It leveled out at the top, where they found a clearing with a tumbled-down hut at the edge, moldering amid overgrown rockroses. In the center of the clearing, a circular herb garden grew, each fanned arc holding a different plant, a low stone wall marking it off from the sandy ground. Most of the garden plants had bolted and dried, spring blooms gone to seed. At the circle's center stood an iron cross, twice as tall as Felip, its crosspiece lashed in place with braided leather that was losing its grip, so the arm of the cross tilted, pointing directly at Felip. Unreasonable, twitching fear crawled up his neck.

"Black henna. Datura." Isabella inventoried the garden. "Valerian. Chicory. Spurge. If we find the gardener, we'll find good medicines."

"Witch-weeds?" Felip wrinkled his nose.

"These healing plants are gifts directly from God, without the intercession of saints or angels."

The air here was heavy. Stagnant. Unease rippled along his spine. "I don't like how this place feels."

"It's the thunderclouds. It tickles the small hairs on your arms and neck when—"

A blinding light.

An unending roar in his ears.

He tried to breathe.

Couldn't.

That's all he wanted. To breathe.

He sucked air, but his chest wouldn't move.

As if a beast squeezed his middle. No room for air to come in.

At last air. He coughed.

And then the fire and the pain came.

Roaring, bursting his head from the inside.

Felip made it to his knees, his heart pounding hard enough to break his ribs. That secret packet in his jerkin burned, as if it had been set on fire. His fingers and toes stung like a thousand bees. Smoke filled the garden, wafting over him. The dried garden weeds burned, flashing flames upward in a perfect circle inside its rock walls. The cross had fallen into the fire.

Isabella sprawled across a rock pile, farther from the fire than Felip. When she stood, she still clutched that lamb, which slumped in her arms, shaking. She seemed to be speaking, but he couldn't hear because of the booming in his ears. Lamb in her arms, Isabella stumbled over to where Felip struggled to stand.

Isabella spoke. He only knew because he saw her lips move.

"I can't hear." Felip couldn't remember why they were in a smoke-filled field.

"*Sancta María, Mare de Dèu!*" she cried, sounding like a Catalan sheepherder over the roar in his ears.

A figure appeared on the other side of the burning circle. Felip squinted again, trying to make his eyes and his body work properly. A woman in black, leaning on a walking stick. A very old woman.

"*Hola, señora!*" Isabella shouted in terrible Castellano. "Is this your lamb that we found?"

The woman stood as still as a frightened mouse hoping not to draw the cat's attack. She gaped at the strangers. Isabella called again, repeating in Catalan and other dialects.

"We saved this lamb from the valley below. Is it yours?"

Lightning flashed again, striking the next hill over. Then thunder pounded inside Felip's head. His heart leaped with fright.

The lamb bolted from Isabella's arms and ran toward the woman, skirting the smoldering circle. When it reached the woman, nuzzling her hem, she ran off. The lamb scampered behind.

Isabella, near Felip's roaring ears, shouted again. "We never got a chance to ask her for a salve."

The walk back to the horses was the most painful of his life. His fingers and toes stung, as if his gloves and boots were filled with bees. His limbs ached and wouldn't do what he ordered, as if he'd melt at each step. He kept looking over his shoulder, his frightened heartbeat warning along with the roar in his head that danger was near.

The storm blew itself further west, leaving the plain to swelter once more in the heat, unrelieved by rain. When Felip and Isabella returned to camp, the army had packed up, prepared to ride out. Isabella and Felip had missed all of the midday rest.

"All hail the fiends of hell!" Colomb called when Felip arrived. Felip made a bold move, standing in the posture Colomb usually did while chiding him, hands on his hips. "Blackened by a devil's burning fire? Or just mired in sin? Touched a bruja?" Colomb laughed. "You'll fit in well with the Moors in Andalusia."

Behind Colomb, Durán pretended to rub at his face, a silent motion meant for Felip, who stripped off his gloves and touched his face. His tingling fingers felt nothing. Then he looked at his hand, which came away with a film of charcoal. He touched his eyebrows. The edges of his beard. His tingling fingers detected that his hair was singed stiff, his face burned deeper than the sun had managed.

Across the backs of his hands, red flowers appeared in blotches, running up into his sleeves, as if his blood bloomed but couldn't break through his skin. That promised to make the coming night with mosquitoes and smoke even more unpleasant. That and the burned circle on his chest, where he had Lorenç's cup bound inside his shirt.

He'd been touched by God's purging fire. And lived.

Did coming to the presence of God change a man forever, as the old monks claimed at St-Pere? Or did it only signify that God had accepted him as an obedient servant on this crusade?

Isabella smiled at Felip in her kindest way. She spoke, but he couldn't hear over the roaring in his ears.

.

AN APPARITION OF OUR LADY AT SANTA EULALIA
Testimony of Mafalda, June 1212

A child of God, Mafalda, witnessed the apparition of the Holy Mother of our Lord at the shrine to Our Lady above the village of Santa Eulalia where she lives. Mafalda is the ancient-in-years mother-in-law of the brother of an elder in the village. All village members give good account of this woman in her simple black dress, always with her walking stick, as a kindly healer who blesses her salves and powders with prayers received from a priest who once resided in the village during a pilgrimage to Covadonga. They say only her son-in-law has ever called her bruja, and he would not testify to this under oath.

The woman Mafalda had gone to tend her garden near the old shrine on the hill. As she approached her herb garden, an image of Sancta Maria rose up before her, taller than a human can be, bathed in light, and moving as if animated by the breath of life.

The spirit called to Senora Mafalda. "I am Maria, the Mother of God!"

At that moment, a bolt of fire from heaven struck the Cross in front of that ancient shrine. Fire consumed a perfect circle around the Cross, which had fallen to the earth, the death of Our Savior defeated once more by the powers of Heaven.

Again, the figure of Sancta Maria called to Mafalda. "Behold the Lamb of God. Our Father in Heaven sent me, so that all will believe and be saved."

Sancta Maria held aloft a holy and innocent lamb, which flew as if carried by angels, settling beside Mafalda. The woman Mafalda did bow in honor and awe to the figure of Sancta Maria. When Mafalda rose, the sainted mother of Our Lord had disappeared.

People of the village returned to the shrine with Mafalda, who showed them where the spirit of Sancta Maria had appeared. As she described, a perfect circle had burned around the broken and destroyed Cross. When men dug the Cross to free it from the ground and preserve it, they found the perfect image of the Infant Jesus formed in glass, glittering as if made of gold.

The lamb that the Holy Mother released from her arms also bore a figure of the Infant Jesus burned in its wool. Senora Angelica, the wife of the chief village elder, snipped that wool from the lamb, and it is preserved in an oak box and kept in the old shrine.

The village, working together, has repaired that ancient shrine, destroyed when the Moors conquered this land twenty-five generations ago. The gold-glass image of the Infant Jesus and a new carved image of the Mother of Our Lord are preserved in the shrine, and the village comes to pray there on all holy days.

This Mafalda did witness before all elders of the village, as written and confirmed before the notary from Teruel, who journeyed to the village after hearing the story of these marvels.

PART TWO
Lo Lunfèrn dins la Tèrra

TO ARNAU
Who, like St-James, is my beloved brother in Christ,

It is a blessed time to be alive and to be here in a land where God once more allows the saints to walk among us. At each humble church where I stop to pray, people's stories are being written and turned to song, voices lifted to drown out those heretic troubadours and their obscene poetry.

Instead, we hear how Sancta Maria, the holy mother of our Savior, appears to heal and bless those who are true to the Church. Each apparition is a sign that you and I were blessed to be born when God's kingdom is to be regained everywhere. I am filled with a charge, as if on fire inside, with each visit from St-Jordí that God allows. I'm eager to do the important work we have.

Will we succeed by the Feast of All Saints this year? We hope by then to have heretics and Saracens all banished, their souls taken to God while we live to see the glory of our Lord's kingdom on earth.

Please pray for our glorious knight Matheus of Xirgú that he may rise from his grave injuries to take his place again as the Crux Lunata leader. We will join you on the road to Andalusia, where under the banner of heaven we shall deliver a mighty blow for Christendom.

We are impatient, like St-Paul, to begin God's work, to perform real acts for God, destroying heretics and declaring our Lord and Savior valiant.

— *Esak, your brother in the lord*
Ten days after Pentecost 1212,
in the Thirteenth Year of Our Blessed Pontificate

7
Betrayal

Tomás in Baeza
early June

"THE MORNING SUN SHINES ON Ibn Mikhail! And the gratitude of our caliph rains gold upon him!"

When Tomás entered the general's court the morning after the murders on the rooftop, Abu Jossep jangled a purse of coins and tossed it toward the archway. Surprised, Tomás caught the leather pouch on instinct, happy to hear the ring of silver against gold, since he'd seriously depleted his own coin, gambling in the army camps while rumor-mongering for Pedro.

"The sun rises and sets every day." Abu Jossep tapped his great misshapen nose, then thumbed his huge lips, indicating that he was about to impart wisdom. "The frontier is burning under the summer sun. Those Christian kings cannot continue to feed the seventy thousand infidels they brought to our borders."

The general was in a jolly mood, seemingly unaffected by the death of the vizier Marzuq. He motioned for Yusuf to sit at his side. Abu Jossep's awe and fascination for his djinni had transmuted to affection and respect for Yusuf's intellect and young wisdom. In their friendship, Yusuf seemed to offer filial devotion along with his scholarly divination. Abu Jossep touched the boy's head, rested a hand on his shoulder, murmured in his ear. Yusuf tipped his head with humility, then looked up at Abu Jossep, smiling warmly.

Tomás sat cross-legged beside Rashid, a surge of blood rushing to his head. A pain shot like an arrow for his heart. He quelled jealousy. He'd regained friendship with his son, but now Yusuf knew about Tomás's work in Al-Andalus, which put the lad in danger.

81

"The caliph sent messages." Abu Jossep called down blessings upon God and his leader. "He's reaped a great harvest from Ibn Mikhail's picture of how the infidel kings will array their armies."

Tomás hoped his face expressed only modesty. Not pride from having succeeded at subterfuge for Pedro d'Aragón.

Abu Jossep said, "The caliph has put three traitors to the sword, men who came to him with false stories about the infidels' battle plans. Each spy cried out to the prophet Jesus as he died. You are indeed to be rewarded, Ibn Mikhail."

Ibn Jafar the poet, who also sat by the general, seemed annoyed. "The sword only? Were the traitors' families punished?"

Tomás fingered the pouch of coins, listening to the jangle of his reward while considering the less fortunate three. They too were soldiers in the vanguard of the coming battle between enormous armies. And yet...

"The caliph is always wise in his judgment," Abu Jossep said. "Perhaps only God knows why a traitor betrays his own people."

The poet cleared his throat. "I've written to the caliph about our loss of the vizier Marzuq, assuring our caliph that you'll find the author of that villainy." His gaze settled on Tomás.

Sweat gathered in the small hairs at the back of Tomás's neck. The day was already too warm, though the sun had lifted itself only three fingers' width above the horizon.

"Please read the caliph's other message to us, my son." Abu Jossep passed a piece of parchment to his djinni, then rested his beefy paw on the boy's shoulder.

"I shall read, *Walidi*." Yusuf looked up at Abu Jossep with the same expression as when Tomás came to Cairo to fetch his estranged son. Mild. Innocent. Masked. Tomás needed a new plan, and another horse, provisions, and knowledge of a passage through the mountains to where the Aragón army camped. He needed to escape with Yusuf from this vipers' nest.

Yusuf pitched his voice like a poet reciting in the streets. In the same heartbeat, the infantry parade drums began to beat, the way they did every morning, pounding all day. "'For the most honored Al-Hasan Abu Jossep ibn Muhammad...'"

"Skip that, my lovely boy. It's pure drivel and flattery." Abu Jossep twitched a finger to indicate that Yusuf should continue.

"'On these days,'" Yusuf recited dates from the week before, "'the infidels who entered Dar al-Islam through its back gates did attack our citadel at Malagón. The number of the unholy devil's spawn was seventy thousand. The number of the defending faithful, a mere two hundred. Then did...'" Yusuf stopped.

"Go on, my dear boy." Abu Jossep cradled Yusuf's thin shoulder in his huge palm. "We never hoped to hold that remote outpost. Their captain knew to surrender." The general chuckled. "The kings of Castile and Aragón will have yet more people to feed as they advance upon Al-Andalus."

Yusuf swiped a finger at his eyes and read more. "'Then did the infidel army enter the city, crying glory to their Lord and God as they put every Man and Woman to the sword.'"

Abu Jossep sat back. "No, that's not right, lad. I know Alfonso of old, when we threw him out of Al-Arcos. He would never taint his honor by killing hostages."

Yusuf blinked twice, then resumed reading. "'Woman, child, and man, each was consigned to die in their own blood, or worse, and the animals and goods of the city were carried away. They garrisoned Malagón with only one hundred men, and then they did march—'"

"Stop!" Abu Jossep cried. "What do you say, Ibn Mikhail? Could the king who enslaved you do such evil?"

"No." Muscles in Tomás's jaw twitched. His throat was parched, Tomás imagined Pedro surveying that slaughter. Never in this life. "The infidel armies have *franj* and Angevine fighters, like that cur Richard who butchered hostages outside Jerusalem."

"But that king called for burning the infidels they call heretics." The pouches beneath Abu Jossep's eyes were black and swollen. Beyond grief, the general seemed ill. "What's his name, Ibn Mikhail? Is it Pasqual?"

Miserable, Yusuf bent over that scroll he was reading. Tomás had sweated through his linen shirt, the sour stench choking other sensations in the court. "Who do you mean, gracious lord?"

"That infidel who held you as slave. What's his name?"

"You would say Butrus. He calls himself Pedro. They say he regrets his intemperate, youthful writings. He preaches the virtue of mercy to his soldiers. And I was a mercenary, not a slave."

"These infidel kings are like bees." Abu Jossep ignored the tears running down his cheeks. "Their mouths carry sweet honey and their tails poison."

"Shall I read more?" Yusuf asked, his voice hollow.

"Yes, dear son of my heart." Abu Jossep patted Yusuf's hand, offering sad comfort.

Yusuf read rapidly. "'From Malagón, the infidel army marched to Calatrava, which guards the road to Córdoba.'"

"We couldn't defend there," Abu Jossep murmured. Rashid sat impassively, no flicker of emotion passing over the chiseled planes of his face. Ibn Jafar the poet stared ahead at a mesmerizing spot on the marble floor of the court. "We only captured it back from their Knights Templar—how many years past?"

"Seventeen years, gracious lord," Rashid said. "You took it after defeating Alfonso at Al-Arcos."

"Allah delivers all victory," Abu Jossep said. "We hope for His peace for Calatrava. Tell us what happened there, my son."

"'Outside the citadel,'" Yusuf paused to swallow, "'that army of demons shouted over the sermons of their kings and priests, denouncing them for showing mercy to Jews and Arabs. At dusk, the kings conferred with our brave captain defending Calatrava.'"

"One hundred fifty infantry and archers," Abu Jossep said. "All I could send. The frontier cannot be defended. We will have to take back those citadels next season."

Yusuf tugged at Abu Jossep's sleeve. "*Walidi,* please let me read the rest."

"Yes, lad." Abu Jossep wiped at his eyes with his sleeve, his nose fiery red, his cheeks flushed with grief.

"'During the night,'" Yusuf read, "'the people of Calatrava were allowed to depart, with all the goods they could carry. The soldiers of Aragón led our people to safety on the road to Córdoba.'"

"Praise Allah who is the author of all goodness!" Abu Jossep lifted his hands to heaven, inadvertently slapping Yusuf with his metal-studded sleeve.

"But what do we make of these kings?" Rashid said. "Slaughter one town, and then free the next?"

Even more vehemently than Rashid, Ibn Jafar pleaded, "Can these kings not rule their own people?"

"There is more in this message." Yusuf interrupted that tirade, earning a glare from Ibn Jafar. "'In the dawn when the infidel army learned they had been deprived of booty, great numbers of the *franj* rose up in anger and broke camp. Thirty thousand knights and infantry departed for their homes in the north.'"

"That's half the army!" Tomás exclaimed.

Yusuf continued to read, ignoring Tomás's outburst. "'In Córdoba, our great caliph Al-Nasir has gathered two hundred thousand men who now march to Jaén, to fight for the glory of Allah. In the face of our superior might and with the desertion of the *franj*, the infidel forces cannot advance into Al-Andalus.'"

Abu Jossep settled back, light returning to his face. "Then we don't need to send the men of Baeza off to war. We need only prepare for next year's raids to recapture the citadels."

"No, *Walidi*." Yusuf tugged at his sleeve. "At the end, the caliph asks more." He trailed a finger along the bottom of the message as he read. "'The caliph commands the great general Abu Jossep to join his army with our effort. All men are called to show their faith. We shall advance together to crush the infidels no later than the summer's first new moon.'"

The feast of St-Peter and St-Paul. The day that Pedro insisted his army needed to be on its way home—or starve. Tomás had to delay departure of the army from Baeza for only another fortnight.

"You shall join in the caliph's great victory," Ibn Jafar the poet said. "And gain the best fruits of the spoils."

"Do you truly believe that?" Abu Jossep asked.

"Yes." Ibn Jafar seemed impassioned. "The caliph arrays his forces like locusts prepared to devour the harvest."

Less passionately, Abu Jossep said, "The caliph will place all the local men in the front to receive glory. He pays his mercenaries less, shares fewer spoils. If we go to battle at all, he wants us only as locusts in the field."

The general implied that the caliph placed less-trained locals in the front line in order to slow and tire out the Christian knights, who always like to be the first to ride into battle. The caliph's mounted knights would remain safe and fresh.

Locusts in the field? The caliph planned to make the local men into martyrs.

·

Abu Jossep wiped away the last of his tears. "You are a poet, Jafar ibn Jafar. Can you write an ode for this pretty story?"

"Excellency?" The poet seemed confused.

The general chortled. "If the infidels cross the mountains, they march straight into our caliph's arms. If they stay where they are, they bake in the sun and starve."

"It is a dilemma," the poet said. "Not a story."

"There is no dilemma," Rashid said. "The caliph commands us to bring our army to Jaén."

"Shall we join the caliph merely to watch our Creator's blazing sun char these dogs?" Abu Jossep pointed a thick, gnarled finger at Rashid. "Or do you wish for a slaughter, the way these Christian dogs did to our people in Malagón?"

"I wish only that it may be as it pleases Allah." Rashid rose. "I shall prepare our men to march, as the caliph commands."

"Let us confer first with my djinni," Abu Jossep said. "In haste, regret is roused. In taking time, hope and peace awaken."

"Or perhaps in taking time we shall be judged by the caliph as traitors to Dar al-Islam," Rashid said.

Abu Jossep tapped his great, ugly nose as if thinking. "Perhaps you can join my djinni tonight to learn how the stars are arrayed, to tell us the most auspicious hour to travel."

Rashid paused, his long lashes sweeping above bone-hard cheeks. "Perhaps your djinni can join me today to learn how the best army in Dar al-Islam is arrayed."

"No," Abu Jossep said. "I need my djinni today to explain a troubling dream." Again, he rested his hand on Yusuf's head. "In all His wisdom, Allah could not have chosen better recompense for my lost son, the one born of my loins. This son is born of my heart. Wondrous are His ways."

"Indeed, and you have the most beautiful woman in Al-Andalus as your wife," Rashid said. Tomás glanced sideways, wondering what the vizier intended to evoke from the general.

Abu Jossep startled them with a bellowing bray of laughter.

"No, no. What use do I have for a wife after this?" The general thumped his wooden leg. "I took my new wife only as a duty, to keep other men from abusing her. No, Allah sent this lad to remind me what it is to both lead and be led by a son."

"*Walidi*, I'm here only as your friend," Yusuf said.

Abu Jossep beamed at his djinni. "What a glorious gift from Allah, to grant me the chore of leading a boy to his manhood! This lad is everything a father might hope for the Creator to make. Wisdom beyond his years. Bravery. You heard how he escaped pirates in Almería? And escaped the assassins on the rooftop?"

Tomás again tasted jealousy as if it were bile.

"Only the deaf could fail to hear," Rashid said.

Nodding as if complimented, Abu Jossep continued. "Blessed is the man Allah chose to beget this lad, and blessed am I to rear him in my house. Now tell me what you mean to do, Rashid al-Aziz."

"What I do every day. Prepare your army to march."

"Today you need to find the traitor who sends assassins and persuades men to desert. Feed the gibbet and keep our men in camp."

With that, Abu Jossep rose to leave, leaning on his djinni for support. He got his crutch caught up in the sheath of the dagger Yusuf hung from his belt. The dagger Tomás had given Sebastián years before, the steel too old to keep a sharp edge.

Yusuf straightened his belt and sheath. "Please tell me what troubles you, *Walidi*."

Abu Jossep rested his hand on Yusuf's head. "I so like it when you call me father."

Tomás closed his eyes to keep anyone from peering into his soul while the general hobbled from the room, that wispy poet trailing behind, leaving Tomás and Rashid alone in the council room.

Rashid muttered, "Why did the caliph not write to me? Where is a message for me?"

"Your message, cousin, was on that rooftop at twilight yesterday. Qasim says those assassins were seeking Rashid al-Aziz. You. The caliph wants you dead." He walked with Rashid from the council room into the courtyard.

"No, Tuma. Your servant repeats falsehoods."

"Qasim is never one to try milking a he-goat. You're from the Rodriquez clan. Given all the rumors about the clans' bargain with the king of Castile, you are in danger."

"No, I'm doing the work the caliph gave me, which proves my loyalty. If I persuade Abu Jossep to move his army, then I shall plead for my clan's loyalty, so that rumors don't ruin us."

Tomás touched Rashid's sleeve. "My friend, do not waste time here. Let us work together..."

Rashid stopped, his internal fire dampened. "As what?"

"As cousins. Brothers, even. If you'd been born in this city, you'd be the general, not serving as vizier."

"You and I..." Rashid gripped Tomás's forearms, as soldiers did here when greeting each other. "We would have been raised as brothers if our great-grandfathers had stayed together. Is that why you can read my heart? How shall we work as brothers?"

Tomás stared into the dark eyes of the man he'd been sent to betray. If this army never marched, it gave Pedro the best chance. And all these people could remain safe in remote, walled Baeza, which no army could ever defeat in siege. Words strangled in his throat as he sought the most truthful commitment.

"The dogs of evil have come here. We need to leave, you and me. As a brother, I beg you."

"Hail!" A soldier's voice shouted outside the courtyard. "Rashid al-Rashid ibn Abd al-Aziz is called to the field."

With that interruption, Rashid departed, casting a contemplative glance backward. In the empty courtyard, a fountain plashed. Doves cooed on rooftops. The parade drums beat in the distance. The sweat on Tomás's neck, stinking of fear, trickled down into the hollow above his heart.

Tomás had proved to be of no use to Pedro, merely adding fire to rumors in the camps, losing silver at dice while encouraging farmers-turned-infantry to follow their instincts and go home. The sole most effective thing he could do for Pedro now was to keep the general's army from joining the caliph. Past the archway, he found Qasim lingering in the foyer.

"When Yusuf reads the stars tonight, I hope the poet and the general are both confounded." Tomás noted Qasim's assent in a flicker of his eyes. "And after you get our clothes to the laundry women, let's see what's good in the market stalls."

"The laundry women already have our clothes, so we can go to the market now." Qasim slumped though, not perked up with the prospect of food. "We aren't leaving today or tomorrow, are we?"

"No."

"I'm sorry, master. I have not yet found a way to free Yusuf from the general's guard. After that attack on the roof, we are never alone."

Qasim began an inventory of what he'd collected and stored for when they would escape into the wild hills.

While Tomás walked alongside Qasim to find food in the marketplace, he made his own inventory.

Two boys to protect.

A sorceress to avoid.

A tremendous friend in his cousin Zaheid, who'd need protection from the general's search for traitors.

And Rashid, who juggled his own Greek-fire grenades about how to best act. For the caliph? For Abu Jossep? For his own clan?

From all possible choices, Tomás was most convinced that leaving Baeza and Al-Andalus was the only safe choice for Rashid. How to save his cousin without betraying him?

A street urchin tugged at Qasim, pulled him down to whisper in his ear. Startled, Qasim called out.

"My master! One hundred burros!"

•

Qasim's words sounded like a malformed curse but instead offered a warning: a significant number of men had deserted, heading for the higher hills with a herd of burros. A messenger called Tomás to join Rashid.

It proved to be only twenty-five burros once Rashid learned the details. Still, that many stolen burros warranted pursuit of the deserters. A dozen men prepared to ride out. This chore didn't require the vizier's skill, but the prospect of a hunt offered relief from the boredom of camp, even in the midday heat.

Qasim brought Tomás his horse, lightly packed and ready for a ride through the countryside. Clattering hooves and riders' shouts allowed slim chance for a private word. Tomás slipped Qasim a square dirham. "Here's silver. Tell your friends in the market that Abu Jossep wants only the burros back."

"Who takes a burro when a horse…" Qasim clamped his mouth at the dagger-sharp glance from Tomás.

The knights rode out, spears and white shields flashing in the hot dusted-lemon sunshine, trekking up the heavily beaten path into the hills. After the second olive orchard, where the trail forked into three arroyos, and then forked again, the burro trails scattered in five directions. The knights broke into trios and quartets. Rashid and Tomás set off as a duo, up the steepest path into a narrow cork- and oak-lined canyon.

"You saved my life on our way to Baeza, Tuma. Why would I choose another man for chores like this?"

"You don't need my protection here. I am only a swordsman."

"Peace, my friend. Let me pay you a compliment."

"I only meant," Tomás began again, "that these deserters would not choose to murder the caliph's vizier. It would bring all hell on their tails."

"Hell?" Rashid mused. "You perhaps spent too much time with the infidels?"

"Best word to describe it." Tomás made the most of his error, not having Qasim here to help guard his tongue.

They let the horses choose the way up the trail. The tickle of sweat under chainmail brought out memories of other long rides under too-hot sun. Tomás pulled at his gambeson and mail, hoping a stray breeze might find its way down his tunic.

They paused to let the horses rest where a stream rushed among the rocks and the limestone outcropping offered enough shade that the two knights could lean against the rocks. Tomás faced up the rocky trail while his cousin gazed behind them over the farmland and orchards that sheltered the army camp. Tomás offered Rashid a handful of dried figs and oil-cured olives from the packet Qasim had tied to his saddle.

Instead of declining the offered morsel, Rashid accepted with thanks, and then prayed over them.

Tomás felt free to eat his lunch and ignore piety.

"You have no prayers, Tuma?"

Tomás drank still-cool water from a leather flask. Qasim did an excellent job of packing it away from the sun's burning rays. "Not out here where my mother can't force it on me."

"Ah." Rashid accepted Tomás's water, though he had his own tied to his saddle. "My mother died when I was so young I don't remember her. My father was killed in a border raid. I was raised by my aunts, including Ríma's mother. They're Mozarab. They believe—"

"In the prophet Jesus?" Tomás felt compelled to help Rashid tell what seemed to be a troubling story.

"They taught me to pray to the One True God."

"My mother is from Saladin's own tribe, but she's Christian." Tomás stretched. Behind Rashid's shoulder, up the trail where the vizier couldn't see, a shepherd boy peeked over a rock, surely no older than that lad Fortuno on the streets of Barcelona. His eyes big as quail's eggs, a hank of dark hair tied up with a string like a grain shock. Tomás stretched taller, signaling with two fingers in the sign he'd seen Qasim trade with market urchins. The lad dropped behind the rock. "She taught me to pray from the cradle."

Rashid nodded at that shared confidence. "I was eleven when a distant uncle took me into the army. I didn't know how to live with fighting men."

"That's why my father sent me to Cairo." Tomás passed two more figs to Rashid, who accepted and bit into one while staring back down that trail. "Despite the many knights in our household, my mother ruled us."

"Your masters also had to teach you to pray properly? I also learned to lead men and to always…"

"Win. Be the best." Tomás said. Though his masters taught curs-
ing, the sword, and deceit, they also insisted on supremacy in every
fight. "That's what I learned in Cairo."

"It must have been a test of your soul, living as a servant in Barcelona." Rashid mistook Tomás's intent. "I cannot imagine how you
swallowed that humiliation."

Tomás twitched, then made it look like a nod while his insides
roiled. What he'd lived through. It should have been him left to the
wolves in that forest outside Narbonne. And now he told tiny lies
while his cousin offered truths he'd never shared with another man.

"To be the best, to become this," Rashid pointed to the badge on
his gambeson, a symbol of his power as vizier, "I say and do all that
a man subject to the caliph of Córdoba must do."

"You worked much harder than me," Tomás said. The lad appeared again, a rope harness in his hands, waving it over his head.
Tomás stretched once more, signaling come-hither and hoping Rashid
continued his meditation on the plateau below. "I let fate shift me
from one world to another. But people say that God has blessed you.
That you—"

Rashid slashed the air with his hand, demanding silence.

"My aunt, Rima's mother, said it was not a problem to God,
which oath I swore when I went to serve the caliph, because God
cares most how you take care of family."

"As my father taught." Tomás closed his mind to the repeated
memory of how he'd failed, first Miquel, then Isabella.

"For generations, Mozarab clans have served in the caliph's
army. But I didn't see how different one way of life was from the
other until..." Rashid let the thought die.

"Until the caliph made you a vizier?"

"Yes, then—"

A shrieking burro, running as fast as a stubborn animal can,
clattered past. It stumbled as it entered the narrow passage between
the men and their horses, its rump knocking against Rashid's horse.
Startled, the horse shook free its feedbag and screamed after the
burro and reared up. Tomás pulled Rashid out of the way, keeping
him from grabbing the horse's reins just as the animal lost its footing
and began to slide down the hill, scrambling to get purchase amid

baby gall oaks and prickly juniper struggling to grow on the steep ravine sides. Many horse-lengths below, the horse slid rather than fell, coming to rest on its side, caught against a thicket of young oaks and wild olives.

Before the horse ended its fall, Tomás began sliding down the ravine after it, breathing dust and animal fear, skidding in gravel to stop his own fall.

The horse, awake but not trying to rise, flicked foam from its nose, its eyes wide with fright. Tomás began to murmur, in Arabic for an Arabian horse, the way he'd seen Isabella comfort frightened horses, calling it his one true love in a soft voice, waiting until the animal could accept his hand, repeating words over and over until the horse heaved a sigh and tried to get up.

Above, Rashid chided Tomás's horse. "I'm tying you here for your own good."

And then he too slid down the ravine to help rescue his horse.

Tomás caught Rashid at the bottom, keeping him from falling further down the ravine, jerking both of them against the thicket of gall oaks.

"Again, Tuma?" Rashid murmured. "You once more do for me what a brother would?"

When Tomás released him, Rashid regained his footing and carefully brushed the dirt from his once immaculate white trousers and tunic.

Together, they coaxed the horse back up the ravine, traversing to find the most stable footing, taking all the time in the world.

At the top, Rashid's horse nosed Tomás's, sharing something between them. The shaken horse seemed bruised, but not lame, with scratches but no significant wounds.

"We'll have to ride back together," Tomás said as he and Rashid rubbed down the jittery horse and then made sure both horses had enough water. "We'll let yours find its way behind us."

·

While they stood by the trail, giving the horses more time to rest, Tomás offered Rashid water again.

93

"You were telling me how you must decide whether to serve our clan or the caliph."

Rashid breathed easily, as if nothing had happened. "Any man from this country, like Abu Jossep, will choose his clan first."

"But you, cousin. Which do you value first?"

Rashid's dark-eyed stare probed Tomás, who asked but dreaded whatever secret his cousin wanted to share. Rashid coughed before he spoke.

"Since the day they found my brother's battered body, every moment of life has been a hole I can never fill. Because of him, I still say the prayers I learned as a child for Jesus to save his soul. It's not wrong, but I can't speak of it to anyone."

"I too learned prayers from people who followed two different prophets. My father's household sheltered many kinds of believers."

"In this, we are again like brothers. How did you choose which path to follow?"

"I was lucky to have a father to guide me," Tomás said.

"How did he teach you to pray?" In his eagerness, Rashid spilled from the flask, his eyes begging an answer.

"My father said there's one true God. Who cannot be begged to intercede, however any man chooses to pray. Who doesn't care what we do."

Rashid jerked back as if struck, stopped by the limestone rock where he leaned. "No scholar writes that. It's the…the emptiness of a *batini*. A man who believes nothing."

"*Batini* is just a word. The events of my life bear witness to what my father taught."

"The life of a servant?"

"A mercenary. Do not pretend they are the same thing. The caliph hired thousands upon thousands of mercenaries. My life has been much more than that of a servant."

"Yet you are not a happy man, Tuma."

"You aren't seeking happiness in this life, are you, cousin?"

"Al-Andalus has never known a more pious caliph." Rashid hedged his answer, made nervous by Tomás's question. "The caliph always carries a Quran he wrote himself, along with his grave clothes. He tolerates Mozarabs in his army, but only true believers can come close to him. Any man who prays as the caliph does and then rejects it …" Rashid's voice quavered. "Apostasy means death."

"I'm honored that you trust me, like a brother, to share this." Tomás spoke softly. He did feel honored. He also wanted angels from heaven to pick him up and drop him in a far desert, where he hadn't promised Pedro to betray the man who turned out to be his friend. "But an honorable man cannot go against his clan to serve a caliph. Especially not a caliph who…"

Rashid raised his hand, eyes closed, as if he didn't want to hear what Tomás was about to say.

Tomás dropped his voice further, though no one else could hear him. "A caliph who isn't from this land, who came here from Tunis. And will return there. A foreign lord who will sacrifice local foot soldiers for the sake of his mercenaries."

Rashid shaded his eyes against the glare to peer into the valley. "The caliph fights only for Islam. Others—like our clan—fight to keep the land that is ours. Our orchards and our brass smelters. The canals our ancestors dug here. Our own windmills and cotton fields and silver mines." He paused and glanced at Tomás. "Why are you here? What's worth dying for here?"

"I fight for money," Tomás said. "And I never believe that it'll be me who dies."

The horses stirred. This time Tomás's horse, Al-Malik, showed the whites of his eyes. Noise of a rumbling pebble-fall echoed down from the upper trail. Hooves on stone.

Rashid leaped up, untethering his horse and urging it away from the trail's edge. Tomás secured the flask of water and bit into the last of the figs before mounting his horse and doing what he could to calm and steady it.

The burros were upon them by the time Tomás settled into the saddle. He held out an arm, and Rashid mounted behind him. The burro at the fore, with a pack of fodder in its panniers, was disconcerted by the many friends that insisted on following him.

"Was it fated thus?" Rashid called over Tomás's shoulder as they rode back to Baeza. His own horse trailed along behind.

"That these burros would decide to come home?"

"No." Rashid laughed joyfully, which Tomás had seldom heard. "That the God of our grandfathers would send you here. That I'd find a true friend for this first time."

Riding with his cousin, in a thoughtless moment Tomás grasped Rashid's knee. "As your friend, I tell you again, the caliph will destroy you because of your clan. Let's leave now. Find adventure elsewhere."

Rashid cupped Tomás's hand, held it on his knee. "You know I cannot. Don't ask me to desert our clan in the middle of all this turmoil. Family must come first."

·

Back in town, the burros were returned to corrals in the valley. Rashid sent messengers out to call the other knights back to camp. Just inside the city gates, the gibbet had been refreshed, a man's body hanging, his tongue black and his skin blistering in the sun. A parchment rag that said only "Traitor" hung around his neck.

Tomás, not recognizing the dead man, looked away but then spotted Zaheid in the crowd. That cousin shook his head. Neither had a word to share that night.

Rashid said, "Let the stable boys water and brush the horses. I can give you supper at my house."

He dismounted, which gave Tomás room to climb from his horse. Rashid had a hand on Tomás's shoulder, inviting him, wanting to prolong their time together.

"Thank you." Tomás couldn't shake off his cousin's touch. Inside he shrank under it. "But I must be sure Qasim attends to his chores."

·

A crescent moon hung above the city walls when Tomás left the baths and slipped into the small alcove Abu Jossep had given him as his sleeping place. Walls so close, he felt crushed within them, even with the arched window that opened above a gallery.

Tomás closed his eyes, thinking the day's efforts should reward him with sleep. Though he summoned sleep with the strongest commands and prayers, instead he drifted, feeling Baeza all around. Ensnared, like a man wrapped and unable to rise from a hammock. Civilized mutterings echoed from the dovecote, where the doves cooed complaints about an intruder waking them—one of the guards in his soft leather boots—and then fluttered back into silence. The soft thud of the guards' feet treading along the city walls. A cat slinking along the roof in hopes of a bat or mouse hiding in the tiles.

Overhead, a nightjar churred, perhaps out stealing milk from goats, its call rising and falling as it lured his ladylove.

Because Abu Jossep loved his horses, the stables were close enough that Tomás could smell, even taste, the mucked-out midden heap, sweet with the scent of grass and fodder.

The weak scent of the nearby jacaranda tree wafted in the thin breeze. You wouldn't know what that odor was if you didn't know the tree stood so close, its purple blossoms the strongest color in the city during this season.

The strongest scent of all was the summer smell of lemon trees from the courtyard, like in his mother's house-garden in Famagusta on Cyprus where he and Chrétien played as infants, brushing aside fallen leaves, heaping dirt to make tiny citadels, with sticks to serve as conquering armies, Chrétien chattering, endlessly repeating the stories they'd heard from their father and the other aging knights of the household, always making sure to repeat each story exactly as it had been told. They'd gleaned lemons after a downpour cast fruit to the ground, and brought their mother a bowlful so that she could make them a squash with cold well-water.

Tomás had never been so unsure, not knowing how to take action. Caught up in the life of a cousin who wanted to be his brother, a woman who wanted to be his consort, and a son whose friendship he'd lost and then found again.

He wasn't the honorable man he wanted to be with Rashid.

Restless, he battered his fleece-stuffed pallet into shape, his fingers stopped by something hard. Tearing at the seam, he opened the canvas pallet and found a broken knife blade. In the dim light he couldn't see colors, but felt rust on its edge and thread-and-hair wrapping its length. He left the blade at the archway, intending to drop it in the latrine come morning. There just wasn't time or need to accommodate a mad sorceress in all his other worries.

Every fiber of his being wanted to escape Baeza and find the crusader army. Yet he had little more chance of that than those deserting burros of finding a way out of this hell on earth.

The only thread he held onto was the fibers of his father's honor, though he didn't know how to twist that into a rope that would save either him or Yusuf. With no new answers or renewed hope, he drifted into the grey world that served as sleep, yearning for a dream of Isabella nearby, whispering in the night, "Only you. *Eu vos amor.*"

And once again he woke from dreaming of Isabella to find Ríma beside his bed, offering him a flagon of wine, insisting they talk. As if he lived in two worlds at the same time.

"I don't want you here," he said. "I am not your consort. Keep away from me."

"God will change your mind, perhaps in time to save your life," she said. Tomás seized her wandering hands. "Congratulate me. I convinced my husband to move his army and join the caliph."

"Why did you do that?" He whispered his despair, having failed to achieve anything for Pedro.

"For you, so you can act for the clan instead of only living for that djinni and the king you're in love with. Don't you want to thank me for this gift?"

"What gift?"

"The freedom of the road."

8

Saracens

"NO, SEÑOR. EL REY Y *Dios nos dieron este camino.*"

Isabella struggled to understand the man's backcountry Castellano. Did he say, "*God and the king gave us this road*"?

García, their unreliable trail guide, had introduced them to Asencio, an aging sheepherder who didn't even remove his battered leather hat while he refused to yield right of way on a narrow road. Tall and broad, and as grey as the burro he rode and as impassive as a kestrel on a bare oak branch, Asencio was the chief elder in this seven-hut village and the leader of the shepherds, who tramped along with their slow-moving flock.

"We cannot wait for you to pass ahead of us." Asencio's voice rumbled like a brown bear in the brush. "For a fortnight we held our flocks back to let crusaders pass."

Isabella understood most of those words. Each conversation with the locals seemed to start with *No, señor.* The guide García was never any help, except to explain that the local people worried about the coming Saracen invasion.

Felip said, "Don't these people want Christian soldiers to stand between them and the caliph's army? The sheep aren't going to protect them."

A large, mixed flock of sheep and goats blocked the narrow passage between two hills. Durán and Felip conferred, agreeing that riding overland to circumvent the flock would harm the locals' fields. They asked the shepherds to hold back their flock, so that their knights could join Pedro and Alfonso to defeat the Saracens. The shepherds stood defiant, dressed in wool breeches, hose, and tunics, spun so spider-web thin as to indecently reveal details of the herders' manhood. They cared only about moving their flock up into the mountains for summer grazing.

Asencio shook his head, as if refusing a child's request. "First we halted for a passel of strangers who insisted they were crusaders. Then for a parade of Hospitallers and Knights Templar. Our animals need good green grass from up higher into the monte to thrive."

Felip tried the argument that worked at a few villages. "For the sake of the Good Virgin Mary—"

"*Si, señor.*" Asencio's rumbled from deep inside the barrel of his chest. The shepherds nodded behind him, like a silent chorus. "We pray every day that our Savior's mother might remind King Alfonso of the concession he promised. Our Council owns the rights here, however much kings need to fight Saracens for the remission of their sins. Our sheep have the right of way on this road."

Durán offered silver, which seemed to offend the dignity of each man aligned behind Asencio.

"God gave us these sheep," Asencio intoned, "to provide for us if we take proper care of our herds. We cannot accept gold in trade for what we owe to God."

Therefore, the travelers waited, not just for the trail to be clear of sheep traveling from the matorral into the mountains for summer grazing, but for the streams to clear, so that they had clean water for riders and horses. The waiting prevented a full morning's ride, so that they camped for *migdiada* after traveling only three leagues. Rather than hand-to-hand training, the captains agreed that in this heat, fight-work was a hardship along with flies, mosquitoes, and low rations.

Leaving camp, Isabella, Felip, and Durán went to purchase sheep for a few nights' stew. The last provisioning stop had again been empty, having just been visited by a band of fifty knights under the banner of the Order of the Knights of the Lunate Cross. Durán asked two different men along the way whether anyone in the neighborhood might sell a sheep or two. No luck.

Then Asencio reappeared, riding back toward them on his burro, harness jingling, as slow as a green turtle moseying down the road.

The day's heat had progressed so that the man had sweated through his linen tunic.

"*Hola!*" Durán shouted in the rough Castellano they all practiced. "We hope you changed your mind."

Another voice called out behind them.

"*Bonjorn!*" Colomb smirked, holding up his hand to greet them, that string of coins jingling when he waved. He led three pack horses. "Pray God I'm not too late to help."

Felip had the best mastery of the local dialect, called to Asencio, "*Hola, señor*. Did you change your mind about selling mutton?"

"*Si, señor.*" Asencio offered Felip and Durán a bota of watered wine. "You are men of the world. You understand that those poor men, they only know their wool and mutton and cheese. It's not market season, so they think their animals will be worth much more when autumn comes."

Felip and Asencio agreed on the number of sheep for an amount of silver. Felip fumbled for the purse in his jerkin.

"You will meet me at the place I tell you," Asencio said. "Tonight, when the moon is four fingers above the horizon."

"We intend to be on the road and far ahead of you tonight," Durán said. "We need to take possession of the sheep now."

Asencio held out the purse he'd received from Felip, as if offering it back. "Then I'm sorry. It's tonight. The only way."

"We need meat." Colomb spoke, though no one asked his view. "We can't arrive starved and exhausted before the battle begins."

The purse disappeared inside Asencio's shirt. "Where this road turns to the south, a trail leads to the west. It's too narrow for your army to pass. A dozen horses can come, no more. Where the trail fords a river, there's a shrine. Older than our grandfathers' grandfathers. I'll meet you there."

"What fools do you take us to be?" Colomb growled.

Asencio shook his head, as mournful as the oldest monks at St-Pere reciting the last of the day's Divine Hours. "The shrine was made holy by St-Hermenegild himself, before the Saracens came to spoil this land. I swear on that saint's own bones to meet you there."

"Who in the golden heavens is Hermenegild? A pagan idol made holy?" Colomb had taken over the transaction. Felip scowled.

"He was beheaded by his own father, in the days of the old kings," Asencio said. "He so believed in the Holy Church that he chose death over dishonor to his own vows."

The business concluded, the travelers headed back to camp.

"That fornicator of sheep likely just stole your silver," Colomb said. "Let's hope we find our sheep among the relics of martyrs up that trail."

"If Señor Asencio is not there tonight, we'll find him tomorrow," Durán said. "It's not as if we can't find a herd that large."

"It's not as if you care about a sheep for anything more than a cuddle, Senhór Montcava," Colomb said. "Damn Good Christian heretic that you are, pecking away at horse feed and grass."

The grand Beaurain knight spurred his mount ahead, his pack horses in line behind him, leaving the other riders in the dust.

Isabella found it admirable when Durán clapped Felip's shoulder. "It's not the way I'd have done it, Xirgú. But you did what you could. We need provisions."

.

"The s–s–smoke keeps the m–mosquitoes away."

Isabella heard Felip's jest as a call for bravery amid the flames.

Only Colomb laughed aloud.

No one had invited Colomb on the journey to claim their purchased sheep, but there he was, bringing up the rear, leading four pack horses when the rest of them managed only one each on this narrow trail.

Along which a grass fire raced, lighting the trail better than the twilight did.

"Lightning out of a clear sky strikes and sets a fire," Durán said. "Who'd believe it?"

"Only a fool," Colomb called from the rear of their column.

"And only fools like us would be here now," Durán said.

"And yet here I am." Colomb laughed until he coughed.

Durán and Isabella rode at the front of the line, both sitting rigidly in their saddles. The rest—Thierry and four men from the Montcava mercenaries—also sat military style. For a few moments, the only sound was the peculiar hollow thumps of the horses' hooves, beating a rhythm, then shuffling when one horse danced away from the smoldering grass at the edge of the trail.

"Speaking of fools," Colomb said, "why is your scribe leading this chore, Senhór Felip? To chronicle our feats of daring and our wondrous adventures?"

"M–Master Vidal knows the horses best."

"Marvelous talents. Pen and curry comb." Colomb cleared his throat and spat, loud enough to be heard along the whole column of riders. "Who'd believe it?"

"Master Vidal is from Valerós." Isabella's voice rang out over the sound of horses and the crackling of esparto grass afire. "We never stay home when there's work to be done."

In the distance—west, since the broad glow behind the hills must be the sunset—flames rose from a new fire, as if Hell's gates had opened. The trail turned, taking them toward the new flames.

"Shall we continue, *cavallers*?" Colomb called. "Or go back?"

"Stop shouting, all of you," Durán said. "Keep your horses calm. We go on."

The men, riding in file, passed Durán's order back to the end of the line. At least those instructions quieted Colomb.

She hoped that Felip could remember everything she'd taught him about how to reassure horses, but she couldn't see through the haze to tell how well he was doing. Her eyes burned, leaving her scarcely able to see the trail in the smoke. Her horse did better than she could, of course.

A new fire flared nearby, to the east this time. A terrifying scream sent the horses stepping sideways, snorting their fear.

Pounding along the trail.

Another scream.

A burro came tearing down the trail toward them, its eyes wide and white with fear, running heedlessly through the line of horses and riders.

Durán's horse reared. Isabella reached for his reins and quieted it. The loose, crazed burro shook its head and reared near Felip's pack horse. Colomb slashed at it with his lash, so the beast ran off the trail and into the flames to the east. Rearing, it stumbled back, then found the trail again and ran down where they had just climbed.

"More space," Colomb growled. "*Dolç Jhezu*, give the horses space to move."

In a few more thudding heartbeats, the line of riders came to rest in a narrow clearing. Isabella and Durán dismounted to speak with Asencio.

"May the Blessed Holy Mother protect you!" the shepherd's voice boomed.

Several of the horses startled again at the noise. The Montcava mercenaries quieted their horses in a Norman dialect. Felip walked his horses over beside Durán, while Colomb hung close by Isabella.

"Who started the fires?" Colomb demanded.

"God Himself," Asencio said. "Or perhaps God's enemies."

Colomb snorted. Or perhaps it was one of the unhappy horses.

"*Se dice*," Asencio began with *They say*, like every rumor monger in the wilderness, "that the Saracens draw near."

"The caliph's army is gathered outside Jaén." Colomb repeated what they'd heard at every provisioning station. "Much better chance of Knights Templars appearing in this hellhole than Saracens."

Asencio shrugged, offering a sheepherder's hand-raising surrender to heaven in reply. He hadn't brought anyone to help, so the travelers struggled to bind the sheep they'd purchased and load them into wicker panniers. Then they loaded the horses. Hot, sweaty, frustrating work that none of them had been bred or trained to do.

"A drink of water before you go?"

Asencio motioned them to the hut at the edge of the clearing where a rush lamp burned. The whole band of them—parched, filthy with mutton-smelling lanolin, fire smudge, and sweat—glanced at each other, eager to finish the chore and return to camp.

"Or perhaps a sip of wine and a bite of cheese?" Asencio headed for the hut, while at his side, Durán argued that they were short two lambs. Asencio insisted that he had turned them over, but the travelers had lost them in the ruckus while loading horses.

At the entry of the filth-ridden shepherds' hut, Isabella paused, unsure whether to enter. Colomb stepped in front of her rather than lingering behind, just out of reach.

First, the hut stank of dirt and vermin. Fleas and bugs festered in the rushes on the dirt floor, perhaps left behind long ago by the ancient kings of Iberia. The lamplight attracted a mass of flying vermin and illuminated the old, cracked timber lintels of an archway that led into a hillside cave. From the painted figures scratched in the walls, this must have once been a chapel, including a cross with a hanging figure that must be Jesus. Fiery flames engulfed another figure, perhaps a cloaked woman. Perhaps fifty generations earlier. Now, unwashed shepherds used it for shelter.

While Asencio continued to argue with Durán, Isabella studied the walls. From a pile of rubble near the archway leading back into the hillside, she picked up a stone and studied it.

"*Mise en garde!* Xirgú! Montcava!"

The mercenaries yelled from outside. Horses screamed.

Metal clashed on metal.

"Saracens!" Asencio screamed, rushing out through the arch.

Colomb had both his swords in hand, offering the shorter of the two to Felip as he rushed into the clearing. Isabella followed, pulling a linen rag over her mouth and nose while drawing her dagger. Outside, the Montcava mercenaries fought with attackers who seemed more intent on getting at the horses than attacking the soldiers.

"You aren't going out there!" Felip pushed Isabella back inside, which surprised her so much that she didn't resist.

But then a firebrand hurtled past them, crashing into a pile of trash and filth that immediately ignited, searing hot. They ran together for the doorway, flames behind them. Isabella wrenched free of Felip's grasp and ran for the horses just as a figure jumped toward them. Felip swung his still-sheathed sword, its handle crunching into the dark figure, who howled and fell back.

In the clearing, Colomb fought a man he towered over, hampered by another man wrapped around his back. Isabella struggled with a trio of horses. Felip ran, again swinging his sword, still in its scabbard, aiming for the neck and shoulders of the man riding Colomb's back.

Colomb called, "Thank you, Xirgú. The horses!"

Felip grabbed at the reins of two horses, saying the things she'd taught him, reaching to reassure each frightened animal.

"*Don't be afraid, my friend, peace.*"

She let go of one fear—for the horses—hearing Felip call reassurances while he gained control of each animal.

"*Vivètz Xirgú! Vivètz Montcava!*" Colomb shouted. He waved a sword. If he wanted to kill any of them, all of them, it could have happened in this melee. At this moment, he seemed instead to cheer them on.

After eons, calm descended on the clearing. The smoky haze, though not gone, no longer blinded them. The fire still smoldered inside that vermin-infested hut, but the flames along the road and in the fields had burned out. The horses stomped, more gently now, where they'd been led to the opposite side of the clearing from the burning hut.

Durán stood above the sole body of an attacker, every other assailant having disappeared into the night, along with the fire and smoke. He held only his quarterstaff.

"Saracen infantry." Durán hovered, ghostly in the dwindling firelight. "I saw cloaks like this in the Zaragoza market. Crusader booty."

Colomb knelt at Durán's side, pulling free the attacker's cloak. He carried the striped, hooded robe to where the travelers had gathered with the horses.

"Bought at a market," Isabella and Colomb said at the same time.

Colomb shook his head, laughing again. "We were robbed by those herders. They stole back their own sheep."

"C–Christians attacking other Christians?" Felip was astounded.

"Many Christians are only as good as the others around them." Colomb spat.

"I killed one of them." Durán croaked, his smoke-infused voice barely above a whisper. "Just a poor shepherd."

Isabella went to his side, hoping to offer comfort, because she heard his pain, but not knowing what to say. What had helped her, after that hideous moment when she'd once killed a man?

"God sees what's in your heart," she said.

Durán stared, the whites of his eyes lit by the last of the fire. He tipped his head as if he didn't understand, as if she spoke in another tongue. "I killed a man," he whispered.

"*Vivètz Beaurain!*" Colomb called. "Can I tell the archbishop you aren't a heart-bleeding heretic after all?"

.

They returned to camp at dawn, having urged their tired, dispirited horses back down the trail. The men in camp were dousing fires and packing their horses, preparing to ride. The sheep were a welcome sight to travelers tired of beans and farro. Those who'd stayed at camp enjoyed both the adventure tale and the news that they'd stay in camp until after *migdiada*, so the fire-weary horses could rest.

"Fresh meat for breakfast!" Thierry announced to the captains.

Tired to the bone, Isabella watched men scurry to rebuild fires and begin butchering the mutton they'd risked their lives to fetch. After counting, they proved to be five sheep short of the original purchase number.

And García the unreliable trail guide had disappeared, along with one of Durán's pack horses.

"Thank you, Xirgú." Colomb brushed close as he passed, knocking Felip off balance. "You did well tonight. What did you learn?"

Colomb had already advanced a dozen paces, not waiting for Felip to answer his taunt.

"Xirgú!" Jaufrés, the Xirgú captain appeared, hailing Felip. "Senhór, your men sent me with a gift. They thank you for upholding their honor at arms practice and for last night's work."

Jaufrés passed over a much-used bota, three-quarters full of a sweet wine, a kind they hadn't tasted since leaving Zaragoza. A precious horde.

Felip grasped Jaufrés' forearm. "Thank you. I'll come drink it with our men right now." He paused and then called, "Captain Colomb, will you join us?"

"I prefer sleep. You and Master Durán have worn me out tonight."

"Òc, Senhór Beaurain. But we learned. Don't p–pay for provender until it's d–delivered."

Colomb paused near where Durán had folded himself up alongside one of the cook fires. "It's good that you'll never get a taste for it, senhór. Better before God than all the glory-seekers."

Durán didn't acknowledge his uncle, didn't even glance around when Isabella offered him a flask of water.

Colomb persisted, not seeming to recognize Durán's misery. "A true scion of Hugues de Beaurain knows how to care for his men. You've proved that it's born in the blood."

Hands on his hips, Colomb waited for an answer, then tossed up his hands and walked away.

Isabella pondered that rare compliment. All the Beaurain grandchildren that she must either protect or protect herself from sprang from that evil priest Esak, a different Beaurain brother.

Hugues de Beaurain had no children.

.

An Apparition of Sancta Maria at Herencia
Testimony of Asencio, Age Forty, June 1212

Asencio, the chief elder of Herencia, did testify before the scrivener and notary public, together with all elders and the village people of Herencia about the apparition of Sancta Maria, the Mother of Our Lord and Savior, which appeared to people of Herencia at midsummer during the season of the Saracen raids.

On the feast day of St-John the Baptist, while moving the flocks of Herencia into the mountains for the summer, Asencio and the other shepherds of Herencia took shelter at the shrine made holy by St-Hermenegild, which was destroyed by the Moors many generations ago. The flocks had been safely corralled for the night, with two of the elders serving as watchmen while the other exhausted shepherds lay down to rest.

Then did a Saracen army descend on the place, intending to steal the flocks to feed the gathering army of the caliph of Córdoba. They did light fires with torches to herd the animals away from their Christian shepherds.

When the watchmen wakened the shepherds, crying, "God preserve us from the Musslemen!" the others did rush out of the shrine with their staffs and spears to defend the flocks.

The numbers of the Saracens were too many, and the shepherds did fear for the loss of the flocks and their own lives. As they together cried for mercy and help from the Mother of Our Lord, then did the Archangel Michael appear, riding a black horse as tall as a house, his sword blazing with the fire of Heaven.

The Saracens did cry in fright. One despicable demon among them hurtled a torch into the shrine of St-Hermenegild, alighting the shrine inside.

Then did the figure of Sancta María, the Mother of Our Lord and Savior, appear, coming from the shrine amid all the flames. She held her cloak out, sheltering the shepherds as a Good Mother does her children, murmuring prayers to bless and keep them.

The image of Our Lady did glow, and with the Angel Michael behind her, they did shine light greater than the fires of the Saracens. Christian and Musslemen alike could not bear to look upon that light.

The attacking army of the unholy caliphate stepped back in awe and wonder. Our Lady did pray, saying the prayer taught to us by Her Loving Son. The Saracens cried out in fear and fled.

With the departure of the Saracens, the light that shined from the angel and Our Lady dimmed. When the shepherds turned to behold the saint who had saved them, her spirit had departed. The burning shrine cooled in the dawn of the next morning, and the shepherds entered, where they found the image of Our Lady now etched on the shrine's rear wall, flames burned into the wall circled her image. Our Lady can be seen to be lifting her hand in a gesture of blessing.

Then did they work together to gather their flocks, giving thanks to God that all but a dozen from the flocks had been spared from the Saracens. Alas, that dozen belonged wholly to Melendo from Herencia who had remained home, too ill, infirm, and elderly to accompany his flock into the mountains for summer grazing.

With the blessings and kindness of Sancta Maria filling their hearts, Asencio and the other shepherds did vow to rebuild the shrine, and to pledge all donations from the shrine to Melendo to compensate for loss of his flock. The man, however, did not live to accept the pledges and prayers, having succumbed within three days to his illness, his heart broken from loss of his sheep. Pledges to the shrine are instead managed by the village elders, for the Glory of God and in gratitude to the blessings of Our Lady, the Holy Mother of God.

I, Ordoño of Manzanares, scrivener and notary, was present when the witnesses testified after midsummer in June 1212, including Asencio and five elders of Herencia, being Gregorio, Larios, Pascasio, Yague, and Fagundo. At the request of the elders of Herencia, I have put this in writing on two sheets of parchment and sealed it with six strokes of ink, in witness of the truth.

9
Pedro's Head

Durán on the frontier, near Valdepeñas
mid-June

"PEDRO'S HEAD!"

Thierry called the coin toss in the day's last fight match, for the fifteenth time since they began the trek across La Mancha.

Durán dreamed of a future when they no longer lived like Israelites fleeing the pharaoh. He longed for Chrétien to return, and he wished each morning for one festering *migdiada* that didn't end with Colomb's call.

Under close inspection by the archbishop in Narbonne, Durán had been forced to swear an oath to prove he wasn't a heretic. But he'd promised only to serve God and his family with an honest heart. Since then, Durán had become Montcava's respected leader, and had accidentally become the murdering soldier he didn't want to be. Now, it was time to take yet another beating.

"Pedro's head."

"Vidal of Valerós." Colomb pointed, grinning.

Durán stirred slowly to avoid the bruise on his spine from the previous day's fight with Colomb. He closed his eyes and forced himself upright. To take and administer another beating.

Except Isabella already stood in the circle. She cradled Durán's quarterstaff.

She discarded her baldric and dagger and then stripped off the head cloth she usually wore, so her white hair glistened in the glaring *migdiada* sun. Under her leather cuirass from the Zaragoza marketplace, she wore a thin linen shirt.

111

Felip jumped up, but Durán held him back. "We have to stop interfering," he whispered.

Durán and Colomb fought with equal-sized oak staffs, about an arm's length taller than they were. Which meant that Isabella held a staff that was an arm's length longer than the one Chrétien gave her for training. Durán tried to read her face. Angry? Eager? Fearful? No, just the calm concentration with which she did all her chores.

She and Colomb circled each other, with Colomb making repeated feints, yet not stepping close enough to engage her. She made the first actual strike, which Colomb easily blocked. They launched a beginner's round of rhythmic strike-and-block moves. Then Isabella came down under Colomb's pole, pushing it aside and coming back quickly with a thrust, which Colomb just as easily blocked.

She smiled. Nodded, the way Chrétien did in training when congratulating you for learning a move. She called to him.

"*Vivètz Beaurain!*"

The two stepped up the pace of strikes and blocks. She seemed to focus on striking his shins and feet, to undercut him. Colomb never thrust for her head or face, only her midsection.

At a moment when Durán blinked, Isabella changed her stick to the other side of her body, so that she held the pole left hand forward, her dominant hand. She thrust, pushing the pole forward, hard into Colomb's check. He stepped back, then came forward to strike and block her, thrusting through her defenses to strike at her middle. Isabella stepped sideways with the force of that blow. Smiling again, she raised her pole to strike, but it was a feint, so that when Colomb moved to block, she thrust hard, mashing his hand on his stick.

Colomb dropped his staff.

He bent to fetch it and rose with that grin, that infuriating grin which made you want to smash his gullet. Then he bowed with great ceremony. "The scribbling bum-boy has some spunk."

Colomb grasped her forearm, pulling her close to whisper in her ear, the same way he always did with Durán. When Colomb picked up the coin in the dust, the way he did every day, he examined it and then tossed it to Durán, who caught it, though it had been hurled so hard that his hand stung.

Colomb strode back to his camp, where the twelve knights in his entourage glanced back over their shoulders, as if suspicious that more than their leader's quarterstaff had been knocked about.

"All honor to the House of Beaurain," Isabella called after him. Colomb raised two fingers in response.

Isabella stood stiffly, grasping her quarterstaff, watching them go. She then began a slow, very erect walk to Durán's camp.

She sat on a campstool and closed her eyes again.

"I think my rib is broken," she gasped.

·

"What did Colomb say?" Durán demanded.

Isabella still struggled to catch her breath. Durán had taken a quarterstaff in the ribs often enough to know breathing must hurt. He and Felip begged her to move inside the tent, so they could peel off her clothes and tend her wounds away from prying eyes.

"He said..." Isabella gasped with pain, paused. "'Valerós breeds heroes. But Pèire Leteric cannot protect any of you.'"

Smothering small gasps, she sat up straight so Durán and Felip could wrap her ribs. Under his hand, Durán imagined he felt the pain shooting through her torso.

"Why can't Colomb leave us be?" Felip cried. "He's as bad as my brother, one taunt after another."

"I hope not that bad," Durán said. "Maybe he's just...What's this?" He touched gently where a perfectly round bruise appeared on her ribs, larger than the other bruises from Colomb's quarterstaff.

"That icon," she muttered.

Felip picked up her cuirass. From inside, he pulled a stone disc. After staring at it, he passed it to Durán, who studied the image of a woman surrounded by flames, carved in the stone.

"Found it in that shepherd's hut, just before..." Isabella took five breaths, panting in pain "...the fire."

"I don't see how you can sit a horse." Durán returned the stone to Isabella, who slipped it back into her leather cuirass.

"There's no...choice." She paused again as a wave of pain passed through her. "I did this falling off...a horse once. It's just...a few days' discomfort."

"There's bound to be an herb-witch in the next village we pass," Felip said. "I'll fetch her."

Isabella said, "Thank you both. You remind me each day how good it is to be with friends."

Durán helped her back into her shirt. "If you accepted your friends' help, your rib wouldn't be broken right now."

"Colomb wouldn't stop until I took his challenge."

Felip scoffed. "Then he'll cease taunting us now?"

With a firm and obscene street-vendor's gesture for "no," Durán said, "Colomb will keep at it, because he's preparing to turn me over to the bishop of Narbonne as a heretic." He repeated what Colomb whispered in his ear after every sparring session.

With the least movement possible, Isabella shook her head. "No, he is persuadable. I think he's been misled."

A melodious Cyprian accent said, "Lovely family scene. Have we any wine?"

To Durán's relief, Chrétien rejoined them, leading a pair of tired horses, one ridden by a grubby little boy dressed in the Morella house-colors Tomás and Chrétien used to wear.

"*Hola, mon amic!*" Durán pretended that his heart didn't pound from seeing Chrétien's face again. "Your new boy looks just like your brother."

Isabella quivered under Durán's fingertips while he tied her shirt back in place. Durán held her shoulder still, more to keep from running to greet Chrétien than to restrain Isabella.

"*Òc,*" Chrétien said. "Fortuno is from Morella. Perhaps he's some sort of nephew. But who knows?" He ruffled the boy's hair. "The good news is, Fortuno can sing."

"I'm glad you found us," Isabella said.

Chrétien nudged the grubby child in Isabella's direction. "You like lost boys, Master Vidal. Here's one who can't ride a horse or shoot an arrow, but you're good at finishing half-made things. Just give him back at supper time, so he can sing."

Felip pouted. "You are calling me a half-made thing?"

Chrétien glanced at Felip, surprised. "I refer to my brother."

"*Ai,* you can't steal boys away from their homes," Durán said.

"Why not? It worked out well for my mother." Chrétien was laughing at him.

"You were found, not stolen." Durán persisted. "And Numa became your mother. She's not like—"

"The warrior Vidal?" Chrétien asked. "Our Vidal cared for a host of lost souls when Minerve came under siege. Anyway, I didn't steal this boy. He was found, the same way I was. And he wanted to come. Didn't you, Fortuno?"

The boy nodded vigorously, though he clutched the edge of Chrétien's gambeson like a waif from the streets.

"He does look like your brother," Isabella said.

A torrent of words flooded from the boy Fortuno, who spoke in a backcountry dialect, but in high, sweet tones. "My father fought for our domus. I alone am left to bring honor to my house. I will fight where God leads me, to defeat Saracens or heretics or bandits. My fathers' paratge will be redeemed, and all the sons of my village will never again fear the Saracen."

Chrétien's hand settled on the boy's head, silencing him. "Master Vidal, teach him to say *Vivètz Valerós* with the proper accent."

"I can't take care of a boy." Isabella winced when she spoke. "Better if he goes with Thierry and the Montcava band."

Durán interceded. "Vidal just won a fight with Colomb, but came away with bruised ribs."

"Vidal needs care?" Chrétien said. "The boy Fortuno can help."

"*Òc*," Fortuno piped. "My new master says I am to be servant here. If I am obedient, he'll teach me the sword." He stood next to Chrétien, about as tall as the sword that hung from the Celt's belt. "Then I shall be a sergeant like my father. I will fight the unholy Moors and join in the victories that God will give us."

Felip took the child's hand, leading him away. "First, let's wash you. A man who honors his father keeps himself clean. And let's help Master Vidal to rest in the comfort of his tent."

When they were gone, Durán touched Chrétien's hand, then grasped it as soldiers do when greeting each other.

"Too long, *mon amic*. Too lonely," Durán whispered.

"*Ai Deu,* how I have longed for the comfort of ordinary camp life." Chrétien tugged at Durán's beard. "Are you disguised as a wild sheep? Same ruddy fur."

"I have stories to tell, adventures that left me with an abiding fear of sheep."

"Can I shave this for you?" Chrétien stroked his cheek, as he always had done.

"I wouldn't trust another soul."

"What else do you wish for, *cor dolç*?"

"To be home. And alone." It took everything for him to stand and not lay his head on Chrétien's shoulder and weep. "A man died because of me. I killed him."

10

Bonfraires

AFTER LEAVING THE BOY FORTUNO with Thierry and the Montcava mercenaries, Felip found the Xirgú captains and gave instructions for the night. When they'd all said *bon nuoit*, Felip kindled a small smoky fire. He hadn't been able to sleep since God's lightning struck four days ago, and didn't want to spend the long waking hours battling gnats and midges.

Felip crouched near the fire, thinking about Chrétien's return. Excited to see the sword-carrying Celtic jongleur again, Durán never asked one significant question. The little boy Chrétien had brought, his face shining like a beatified saint, was as ecstatic to be among crusaders as Felip had been his first day in camp. Felip admired that Durán kept silent about his battle glories, not bragging how brave and victorious he'd been in that affair with the sheep and the fire. Durán had proved that he was a real crusader, a leader of men. Rumors were spreading through the camp like that wildfire, recounting how Durán had fought and won. Though it must be Montcava mercenaries—surely not Colomb—spreading those rumors. They'd want their seigneur to be well regarded.

Naturally, Felip pondered whether he'd acquitted himself as well as Durán had when they fought their attackers. He'd felt fear for only a single heartbeat before acting. Would his father have praised that effort? He still had much more to prove as the Xirgú leader if this crusade was going to expiate all his sins. Though, of course, as Chrétien always said, this isn't a crusade. They were on an expedition of faith and peace.

117

When Felip poked his mosquito-fighting campfire, that cup hidden inside his jerkin abraded his burned chest again. Those burns from the lightning adventure were slow to heal, and the red dots on his arms had bloomed into fern-like flowers since that day. Whenever he rested, his fingers and toes tingled again. He kept hearing thunder, but the skies had been cloudless since that iron cross burned.

Distracted by his ailments, Felip didn't hear the jongleur shuffle up to the smoky fire. He was followed by Isabella and Durán (now clean shaven). The two men squatted on their haunches beside Felip, while Isabella sat gingerly on the ground, favoring her injured rib.

"Xirgú, *bon nuoit*." Chrétien thrust a crossbow bolt into the fire. "You've had some adventures since we last met."

"We all have." Felip couldn't claim anything compared to what Durán had endured while Chrétien was absent.

"We need to ask you a question," Isabella said.

"Are you with us, *mon amic*?" Chrétien seemed somber. No easy jokester, no false fool.

"I'm riding to join Pedro, like you are," Felip said. "For my father, for paratge."

"Will you swear allegiance to your brothers in arms in the way your father did?" she asked.

"I'm sworn to Pedro as a seigneur."

"Can you swear more than what a southern seigneur swears to a king?" Chrétien asked. "Can you swear to God in Heaven to support and trust us as brothers, through everything? If we offer you the same oath?"

"That's an enormous request." His heart lurched, the way it did when lightning struck.

"We want to trust you, and we want you to trust us," Chrétien said. "Like brothers do."

Felip looked to Durán for explanation, because Chrétien remained a puzzle most of the time.

Durán said, "Chrétien, Isabella, her son, Pedro *El Rey*, they are part of a crusader brotherhood. The bonfraires. La Confraria de la Crotz began in the Outremer two generations ago."

"We each swore an oath that…" Chrétien paused, gazing off into the night. "That to break would be to surrender my immortal soul. Can you swear that oath? Durán promises that he can."

Felip glanced at Durán, having learned on this expedition that Good Christians didn't swear oaths. Durán seemed as solemn as his friends were.

Isabella said, "Can we trust you with our lives?"

"*Ai…*" Felip's heart beat only twice in the time it took to understand at last why Isabella greeted these men in Girona with such joy, why her heart opened to them in a way she never allowed him. "*Òc.* But why do I need to swear?"

"Because we require more than an ordinary promise," Chrétien said. "You need to commit your father's own honor."

"Paratge," Felip said. "As a man, I already—"

"More than that," Chrétien said. "More than most men could ever promise each other."

Struck by Chrétien's solemnity, Felip nodded. "What do I do?"

"I'll say this one brief prayer," Chrétien said. "The rest of our rites are for pageantry, not promises."

He softly chanted a prayer in clear, simple Latin that Felip understood easily.

"Now you must swear using these words," Chrétien said. "Put your hands on this cross." He held out his sword, placing both of Felip's hands on its crosspiece. "*Sodalitas, fidelitas, virtus.* Upon my honor I swear absolute loyalty to my brothers when called to arms."

Felip repeated the words, while Durán stared into the fire.

Chrétien chanted more words for Felip to repeat. "I swear on the name of Our Savior and on St-Jordí to stand by my lord and king. I swear to stand ever ready to serve as a defender of the poor and of all who love God."

At the exact moment Felip repeated the last words, Isabella grasped his forearm. In a swift move, Chrétien snatched that iron bolt from the fire and touched its tip to Felip's wrist.

"*Jhezu y María! Mercé Dèu!*"

Felip shouted more from surprise than pain.

"No use telling the whole cat-sucking camp," Chrétien said. "Learn to keep our secrets."

"And you, Durán?" Isabella said. "Are you one of us?"

The Master of Montcava still stared into the fire. "Òc. You have my heart, my life, my honor. I'll defend my brothers and the poor. And I love God as best I can." He stretched out his arm, laying his hand loosely on the crosspiece of the sword. Chrétien touched the bolt to Durán's wrist. This time, Felip smelled the burned flesh, just a whiff, as if an essence of spirit floated around them and then was gone on the night air.

Far away, across the clearing in the Montcava camp, Fortuno called Chrétien's name, begging him to come sing. Chrétien rose, took his sword from Durán, and sauntered away with Isabella following. In a moment, a song drifted in the still air. An ancient *cançós de guèrra,* the kind that only old men sing.

.

Durán remained behind, lounging beside Felip while the smoky fire settled to embers. That crossbow bolt lay in the dust by Durán's foot.

"They are all good men, the Confraria." Durán passed over a leather bota of unwatered wine. "You didn't make a mistake. Chrétien says the only work is to keep promises. And to come when a brother calls."

"Brothers." Staring into the fire, Felip saw in the embers the face of the man he'd always believed was his brother, nearly killed by a friend Felip believed was a man. Until she jumped out that window.

"I like the confraternity part. With our brothers," Durán said. "With these friends, I built a life I never could have dreamed of when I shivered with my mother in our hut. I'm safer and happier. But then that's what sent me out here with the army, the enormous fear that I'd lose all of it. And bring harm to my new family." Then Durán asked, straight on, "What are you most afraid of, bonfraire?"

Felip couldn't answer for a moment. With years of being tortured by his brother Matheus, he'd never considered admitting his real fears to anyone.

"That G–God will strike me dead, I suppose. For my sins."

"God has had a few chances already, hasn't He? The lightning? That fire in the mountain pass?"

"We are lucky."

"Or perhaps your sins aren't so grievous." Durán took back that bota of wine. "I also fear I will fail as the Montcava leader, and not just because I don't want to kill people in this war. But because I fail at my duty to keep others safe."

"Can I ask you?" There wasn't one other person in the camp Felip trusted to speak with like this.

"I'll try to answer." Durán passed the bota back to Felip.

"When Isabella was at the m–m–monastery, in disguise…" Felip took a breath, wishing to ask his question without stuttering.

"Who knows how that woman thinks?" Durán murmured. "She must surprise even herself."

"I was in love with her."

Durán glanced at Felip, smiling. "I'm sure it's her kindness. That's how she won my heart."

"B–but I thought she was a m–man."

"Nature does help her pull a blindfold over people's eyes. She looks like a broomstick when she isn't dressed as a man."

"But I never thought that b–before. I d–d–dreamed of Serena from next door, and servant girls. Then…"

"Ah, I see." Durán, still stretched out, propped on his elbow, smiling. "Felip, you dear boy, do you think I'm beautiful?"

"D–don't call me a boy."

"Forgive me. I meant it as an endearment, *mon fraire.* But tell me, how did you see me when we first met?"

"I saw a soldier. Tall, strong." Felip found this embarrassing. When Isabella introduced her two friends, she explained that Durán was Felip's third cousin on the Montcava side. Then Chrétien had tapped Durán on the chin, saying he was also a piss-poor heretic. Felip hadn't met a heretic before. That whole meeting was confusion. "You and your friend captured Isabella's attention. I was jealous."

"And Chrétien? What did you think when you first saw him?"

"That he's not from these parts. Maybe a northerner?"

"You don't see a man who's far more beautiful than a poet could write in a song?"

"No. He's arrogant. And c–cynical. He teases t–too much."

Durán stretched out again, folding his hands behind his head. "You aren't going to fall in love with a man, if that's what you're worried about. The beast in you knew Isabella was a woman. Even if your eyes lied to you."

A spark popped. Felip dropped another two sticks on the fire, each no thicker than a thumb, for that's all they'd scavenged here. He took up that crossbow bolt, idly drawing in the dust.

"Durán, please tell me who you all are. The secrets here are thick as dust."

"First, as Isabella described, you and I are third-degree cousins. Through your mother and my father. The Church never lets relatives marry who are that close."

"Excuse me?"

"I mean if you were...never mind." Durán shook his head. "Chrétien's father—that is, his adopted father Miquel—founded the Confraria with Pèire Leteric, who is Isabella's grandfather."

Felip roused, hearing a name he knew. "My father traveled with Pèire Leteric when he went on crusade to Jerusalem."

"Then perhaps the circle turns, and you are now where you were always intended to be."

"How can Isabella be part of a soldiers' fraternity?" Felip used that crossbow bolt to poke the fire, moving unburned portions of the smoldering sticks onto the embers.

"In the siege of Minerve two years ago, she was a hero, for how she helped people there."

"Dressed as a man?"

"Not then, no. But at times, in certain places, Isabella travels dressed as a man. For safety."

"Her husband didn't object?"

"Her first husband Nicolau was..." Durán sat up, folding his long limbs to sit cross-legged. "Nicolau was my father. Who sowed bastards in others' fields."

"In my father's house." Felip felt relief wash over him, at last able to speak of those revelations in Girona. "That means that Isabella's son is Matheus's half-brother."

"Unless Matheus's father is Renoud, Nicolau's brother. Then Sebastián is only his cousin."

"You and her son are half-brothers?"

"Òc, though we don't look much alike. Sebastián takes after his mother. And I, unfortunately, resemble my father."

Felip bashed at a half-burned stick, shattering it so it fell in the embers. "Matheus isn't my brother."

"Seems like I'm stuck with him." Durán shrugged. "But now you're with the bonfraires, so you have brothers in many places. Like Sebastián."

"How can she have a son old enough to ride to war?"

"Sebastián is fourteen. She—"

"She was t–twelve." Felip performed simple *mathematica*. "How could she mourn a man who—"

"Different husband. Nicolau died at Constantinople." Durán's mouth twitched, visible even in the smoky darkness. "She married Chrétien's foster brother, Tomás. That's who she mourns."

"She told me about that bandit attack. How could anyone live through such carnage?"

"When we catch up with Pedro's army, Sebastián can tell us how he and Tomás survived."

"Her husband survived?" Once again Felip heard her voice, from when she was Vidal the scribe, explaining grief: "*I lost my entire family to Simon de Montfort's francimand crusaders.*"

A hand gripped Felip's shoulder, sending pain shooting up into his head. Chrétien's long fingers held him in place. "You will not tell her that Tomás survived that bandit attack."

"You have to tell her the t–truth." Felip gasped in pain. "It hurt her soul to lose him."

"Tell her what?" Durán whispered. "That Tomás is dead again?"

The brand burned at Felip's wrist. "I can't keep secrets from her."

"You must." Chrétien grabbed Felip, rubbing the raw, scorched place. "*Sodalitas, fidelitas, virtus.* I command you to keep the secret, as your brother in arms."

"No matter." Isabella appeared by the fire, looking like a ghost. "Your Fortuno told me. Tomás was alive, but now he's dead again. That little boy can't talk about Tomás without crying, because his new son will grow up without a father." She slumped down by the fire, toying with that crossbow bolt. "You should have told me."

"Forgive me, Vidal." Chrétien sat beside Durán and wrapped his arms around his long, folded legs. "Pedro forced Tomás to marry, to protect lands from Simon de Montfort. I was silent because I didn't want to burden you with more cares."

She stared across the fire at Chrétien. Felip guessed they might quarrel, but instead, Isabella laughed. She seized that crossbow bolt and began to poke at the fire while reciting words like a litany.

"I endured years of torment living with those bastard Beaurain brothers in Toulouse. I rode across all of the Toulousain when Renoud stole my son. I lived in a city starved under siege, and barely escaped the heretics' pyre."

The bolt scattered coals, its tip now red again. She spoke the next verse of her litany.

"I used my dagger to stop my husband from murdering my son."

Poke and sparks. Another verse in the litany in her raw voice.

"I saw my family killed, and came away more than half-dead, living in a cave, where Matheus massacred my friends."

She bashed mightily at the coals so that sparks flew.

"Why, Chrétien, why on God's good earth would I be upset that Tomás had another wife and a child?"

The three men sat in silence, while Felip calculated how badly he had misunderstood both "Vidal the scribe" and the woman Isabella of Valerós.

"I'm all done with weeping," Isabella said at last. "But it's so sad that yet another mother has to protect a fatherless child."

"I made sure she's cared for," Chrétien said. "I left Jacques with her at the king's palace in Lérida. So Dolç and her children are safe in their beds. We can trust Jacques to be sure of that."

11

Risk

Dolç in Lérida
mid-June

THE PLAN BEGAN WITH A ridiculous question Jacques asked, that little mercenary who Chrétien left as her guard. Dolç was so alone, there wasn't anyone to whom she might tell the story. It had taken them a fortnight to get used to each other. They spoke in Jacques's native tongue, since few here seemed to understand French. Then, one day Jacques asked that strange question.

"Did you know the Cid was Don Tomás's great-great-grand-father, the hero who captured Valencia a hundred years ago?"

"He never spoke of it." Dolç answered cautiously. Tomás had never told her one thing about his world. What little she knew, she'd learned from Sebastián and Yusuf.

"You know that boy, Raoul, the servant in Petronilla's house, the one who's been following me everywhere? The lad has tricked himself into thinking I might get him out of service and into some lord's army." Jacques could turn any story into a many-stanza epic. Once he started, his tales would rival *La Chanson de Roland*. "He begged a lesson in swords in exchange for big secrets he knew, though I didn't believe he had any secrets to make his own granny's heart beat fast. But it seems our Petronilla entertained certain monk-knights on their way to Toledo. And Raoul served them. This was while you were laid up with your *bébé* Quelo."

"What's the secret?" Dolç served him the meal she'd prepared over the fire in her room, though the extra heat made the closed room too warm for midsummer. She'd been bribing Jacques to keep her company most afternoons by feeding him, since it was bone-crunchingly lonely in Lérida.

"Those knights said prayers and shared wine and bread, and then sang a ditty, laughing hard and then singing it again." Jacques repeated the song.

> 'When the Grail and the Cid's sword are enchained,
> One man dies so the best can reign.
> Iberia passes to the Cid's anointed son.
> What was divided becomes one.'

Dolç frowned. "I've heard it before, so it isn't a secret."

"It's not the song that's the secret," Jacques said. "Petronilla, your cousin who brought you here, told her monk-guests that a son of the Cid lives in her house."

Still fatigued from childbed and nursing the girls from one bout of stomach troubles to another, Dolç wished her head would clear. The kitten the girls had adopted from the stable leapt from a chair to the table top. She scooped it up and put it on the floor. It rubbed against her ankle.

"Don't you see?" Jacques said. "It's why Chrétien worried. That tall witch-woman wants your Quelo because Tomás's great-grand-father was that hero, the Cid."

"Whatever for?" Fear jolted behind her breast, like the day Don Tomás departed, but worse now that the child was bound to her, his heart beating beside hers.

"To hear Raoul tell it, the monk-knights want Quelo for some kind of magic."

They sat in silence, though Dolç's room was never truly silent. The fire crackled. The little girls moaned about their bellies. Quelo snuffled in his sleep. The kitten mewled. Jacques idly tapped his knife on the table top. When she spoke, it was like breaking the tension atop the water in a too-full cup.

"Where is the safest place, Jacques?"

"Not here, ma dòmna." He'd lived in the south long enough that he peppered his French with local words. She'd simmered chicken pieces and dressed them in a sauce of ground almonds, fennel, and her own spice mix, scavenged from the household kitchen. Cinnamon, cloves, and ginger. Plus the saffron she'd brought from her kitchen in Barcelona.

"Is my cousin's dinner table safe?" It was past time to admit her suspicions about why her girls had been throwing up for two days. She had taken to preparing all their food here in her room.

"I think not, ma dòmna." Jacques licked his fingers, clearly savoring the food. It gave her pleasure that he enjoyed what she served him; Don Tomás never did.

"Is my bed safe?" She'd found a wax doll wrapped in red thread in the rushes under her bed and went as far as the main kitchens to throw the whole mess into the fire.

"No, ma dòmna. Though I do my best."

"If I'm not safe within these stone walls, then am I not safer in my own home?"

"That's a long journey, ma dòmna. Hard for your little girls."

"These are hard times, Jacques. They need to grow up strong."

"Are you asking me to be more than a guard? To prepare for a journey?" He broke off a piece of the bread-bowl that served as his trencher, scattering crumbs as he bit into it.

"Can you do what you believe Senhór Chrétien would do, please? I have silver."

"I shall scout for wagons or find—"

"No wagons. Only horses or burros."

"Can your girls ride that well?"

"They can learn. Wagons might make us easy targets."

"Chrétien will have a pike up my rear end if I fail." Jacques wiped his fingers on his jerkin. "If your cousin Pedro doesn't get his hands on me first."

"They aren't here to help. Let's not worry about them. Can you take me home?"

Jacques worked his lower lip, chewing thoughtfully. "I'd best do what Chrétien would. We'll keep our souls stitched inside our skins better at his house."

Quelo cried softly, waking from sleep. Feeling her milk let down at the first note of his cry, Dolç shifted him closer where he lay bound under her robe. He latched on hard, but she only sighed, because she liked to feel him growing strong. He suckled while she considered how naïve she'd been about the people she chose to trust, like the cousin who had begged Dolç to leave Barcelona.

Quelo's hunger cry didn't disturb the girls, who scarcely stirred where they slept, still ill from the last meal they'd eaten at Petronilla's table.

"The sparrows sing beautifully. God has made a beautiful day." Jacques spoke softly in French. "I'd best get busy with my chores."

The kitten rubbed at Dolç's ankle again. "I suppose we can't take much. That makes it simpler."

∎

Dolç along the River Segre
June 24

At a tavern outside the Lérida city walls, Jacques had encountered old friends on their way home from the expedition into Andalusia.

"They didn't make any money on that jaunt," Jacques told Dolç. "And God maybe forgave their sins for a bungled crusade, but they can't eat forgiveness. I hired them cheap."

"The battle is over?" Dolç asked, excited. "Then Chrétien and Sebastián will be home soon."

"No, ma dòmna, not over. Many French lords abandoned the cause as futile. We have hired six men for the same silver I thought might buy only three. It's only bandits we need to worry about on the road, not the men going home from Iberia. Those wild Pyrenees mountain men are fierce, they say."

They departed the next day, since Dolç had prepared as soon as the decision was made, gathering blankets, food, mint, and medicine for the still-ill girls, and shifts and stockings. Ten horses and their riders left Lérida when the guard changed at dawn, having paid safe-passage money to servants inside and guards at the gates.

"Bribes is what we call them in my tongue," Jacques said. Their travel companions laughed, all of them speaking French, usually too fast for Dolç to keep up. Three of the men nestled bundled children as they rode, trading off every league or so with the other men. At Jacques's insistence, Dolç rode with him all of the first day, Quelo swaddled within her light cloak.

"It's not like you're one straw heavier than your oldest girl," Jacques said when Dolç suggested that she could ride on her own.

None of the girls had gotten comfortable, nor had Dolç, by the time their little band reached the forest on the southern side of the Pyrenees where the pine and juniper trees, sunbaked in the July heat, released pitchy perfume. She hoped that perfume masked the scent of the travelers from any who might follow.

Jacques had told the bribed servants and guards, confidentially, that they were headed home to Barcelona, but after departing the city, Jacques's mercenaries and their charges instead followed a narrower trail up through the Serra del Montsec, where they found sufficient water and forage for the horses. While making their way, Dolç baked bread in the campfire at night, and Jacques and his friends traded tiny amounts of silver with shepherds for meat—usually chamois, but sometimes roe deer—and learned which trails to follow to find passages in the next valley and which trails were least plagued by bandits.

During the day, Dolç racked her memory to teach the girls what she'd learned during her childhood in the mountains. How to avoid unsafe rock piles where vipers lurk. How to spy rabbits and chamois and pine martens without disturbing them. How to know the names of birds and flowers.

Peregrine.

Booted eagle.

Capercaillies.

Gentian.

Buttercup.

Crucifer.

12

The Serpent

ISABELLA, OUT IN THE WILDERNESS, far from the mountains she loved, lay among one hundred twenty men, gazing at the stars. Untold numbers crossed midheaven, illuminating the fishbone skeletons of trees that murmured with each other in the faint breeze. With summer here, the night sky seemed friendly, unlike last winter when the stars scattered like ice shards and the wind-torn branches of Aleppo pines grabbed at her. When the world wanted her dead.

Perhaps Isabella of Valerós had not yet been resurrected. Perhaps that old Isabella still lay crushed and broken where Matheus of Xirgú and his Crux Lunata knights had massacred her family.

Except they had lived. But then Tomás died again. Her thoughts trailed off into the night when she whispered prayers begging for mercy for Tomás's soul. With so much talk about Tomás around the last night's campfire, she now heard only Tomás's voice.

"I believe as my father did. That God doesn't care about us."

She shook off that ghostly whisper and said aloud what she'd said to Tomás long ago, "We believe as we're taught, for the good of the domus as well as for our own souls."

At the next day's *migdiada*, the travelers' midday break, Isabella accepted a scoop of potage, cold from the cook's baggage, and ate quickly. Durán cautiously checked the potage Chrétien handed him, habitually making sure it contained no meat.

"*Cor dolç*, at least trust me," Chrétien said. "I love you more than the world itself. I'm not going to sneak sins on you. But give up that heretical nonsense, not eating meat. A man your size needs succor."

"I trust you," Durán said. "It's just habit."

While they enjoyed bickering, Isabella left the camp to take care of her personal needs. Usually Thierry slipped away with her and stood guard, but she'd delayed today, and he was already asleep, like most of the dusty, exhausted travelers. She traipsed a narrow path upstream into a small side canyon. When the path turned into a deer trail, she hopped limestone boulders, stopping where a creek emptied into the canyon, where the mist of the waterfall encouraged royal ferns in the outcroppings.

Sebastián and Yusuf lived.

Her sons still walked God's earth, breathing the same air she did. And Chrétien swore they'd find the two boys with Pedro.

After satisfying her personal needs, taking care to avoid loose stones and other vermin-friendly places, she pulled off her linen tunic—still painful from the fight with Colomb—and carefully set aside her relics from within the wrapping that bound her chest: that silver-crusted saint's finger and the painted icon that she'd taken from Rubea's cave; the ancient stone icon she'd picked up from the shrine-turned-shepherds' shelter before the bandit attack. Then she wetted her shirt in the stream to rid it of many days' dust and spread it to dry in the sun.

Isabella drenched her head cloth, wrapped it around the stone icon from the shepherds' shelter, and held it to her ribs. The wet cloth and stone, which seemed to be always cold, eased the pain as she lay in dappled shade on a flat boulder, listening to the water rush over stones. A dark warbler, the kind with the cocked tail, hung on a branch near the stream, trilling its melody. The crickets persisted with their own raucous song.

That core satisfaction warmed her bones. Her sons lived! She prayed for patience (as usual) for how slowly she was forced to ride while dragging one hundred twenty men across this wasteland. She included another prayer of gratitude for her close companions. Felip had proved to be a kind, thoughtful man in spite of the family he'd been born into, though he still worried about living up to his father's glory. She offered gratitude for Chrétien's return, for Durán's sake most of all.

Peace. This must be better than purgatory, waiting for fire to anneal all sins. Waiting to start the next part, where she'd find Sebastián and Yusuf and then choose action for Valerós, not just running to save Pedro as the sole option for the salvation of their domus and villages. They'd run home to Valerós together.

To make sure the new mills worked properly.

To repair the orchards.

To help people who'd fled Simon de Montfort's persecution.

She'd call on Pedro for the protection he promised, so people at Valerós could tend their orchards and protect their sheep from wolves instead of defending against heretic-hunting invaders.

The clouds parted and the sun glared down again. Isabella wrapped her head cloth, which was still wet enough to be cool and refreshing. She nabbed her half-dry shirt and struggled into it, following the ritual postures she'd invented to avoid jostling that injured rib. As the shirt rucked over her head, blinding her, a sound echoed in the narrow canyon.

A snap. A crunch.

Not a deer or small mammal. Not otters climbing the bank.

The sound that only a human makes.

"Thierry?" She called one name.

Only water gurgled and glugged in the hot silence. The crickets ceased their sawing.

She gathered up her relics, tucked them inside her shirt, and scrambled down from the boulder and retraced her steps along the deer trail, listening, glancing back. After a hundred paces she stopped and listened again. Her heart beat just a jot harder than the hum of heat and trickle of water

"Felip?" she again called, convinced she was followed.

Another hundred steps and the real path appeared again, but it wound uphill toward the top of the canyon. Certain that she'd taken a path that followed along the bottom of the canyon, she again hopped boulders.

A crack in the brush behind her confirmed that she was followed. Someone who refused to answer her call. She glanced back repeatedly for a sign of who it was, now feeling hunted. Her side ached from boulder hopping and hard breathing. Used to a horse, and not boulder climbing, her thighs strained when she chose larger, widely space boulders alongside the creek. One more large stone, and the true path appeared. She leaped to a last low, flat rock, and teetered, stopping.

A grey viper lay where she wanted to leap next, its zigzag pattern unmistakable. It lifted its head when she landed on the nearby stone, so close that the horn on its nose and the yellow tip on its tail shimmered in the sunlight.

.

"Keep still."

A whispering voice spoke the same words Tomás had when she'd faced a viper on the road outside Cairo.

"Don't move. You've already excited it."

The viper turned its hideous flat, triangle head toward her while arching its back to strike. It launched itself for her.

But a blade slashed.

The viper dropped to the rocks, twitched, arching to slither. The snake's mouth opened, fangs bared, but the head now lay a hand's breadth from its body.

A man landed beside her on the boulder.

"Stay here a bit more. It takes a while for the bugger to know he's dead." Colomb spoke low, his voice rumbling deep in his belly. "A dead snake can poke a snoot full of poison in you. Just to make sure the devil gets what's owed him."

"Thank you. But why did you follow me?"

"Follow you?"

"Yes, from back by the creek."

"I didn't."

"I heard someone."

"Things aren't always what they seem."

He held his sword out, away from his body. His gambeson sleeve fell back, showing that Crux Lunata tattoo. While snake blood pooled and dried under the sun on the next stone, he stood close beside her in silence. She felt his breath on her neck and heard her own breath as it brushed over her lip, as if her soul were unsure whether it was sewn tightly in its casing.

133

Will I die this time, alone again in the wilderness?

This Crux Lunata knight could kill her here, leave her to rot in the sun, and not one of her friends would ever know. *They can't search all of the montaña to find me. And even if they did…*

"A funny coincidence." Another belly-deep rumble from Colomb. "I saw the true Vidal of Valerós slash three vipers with a single stroke once upon a time. On the road near Damascus."

That place in the desert where the Crux Lunata had butchered her uncle Vidal and left Pèire Leteric alive with his grief.

"Do you believe we are guided by saints and angels?" Colomb asked, his voice softer this time.

She closed her eyes. They'd stayed still long enough that the crickets hummed in the heat again. She felt his huge knight's body beside her, even with her eyes closed, like his brother Hugues had stood in the St-Sernin cathedral in Toulouse, when the bishop called her a heretic. But this time, she feared the Beaurain who stood beside her. "I believe God leaves us to stumble along in hopes of heaven, with no magical guides."

"As I thought," he said.

"Why do you ask?"

"You do understand," Colomb's voice rose into registers of challenge, "that if Sebastián of Valerós dies in this war, all of Montcava and Valerós will go to the next older cousin."

"Without a doubt." Her mind raced over every distant connection of cousins, finding no way that led back to a bastard brother of Hugues de Beaurain. Colomb couldn't gain anything by killing her or Sebastián. "The next oldest is Durán."

"The next oldest is Matheus of Girona. Nicolau of Montcava is his true father. That's why Matheus claimed Valerós when the bishops believed Sebastián was dead."

Isabella swallowed a violent *No!* "Matheus is a Crux Lunata murderer who seeks to destroy the king of Aragón."

"That's not true. But it seems that you prefer to let a heretic hold the Montcava estates?"

"Durán is working to protect our domus. He's a true brother to Sebastián."

"And yet, the new Vidal of Valerós isn't Pèire Leteric's son or grandson, is he?" He shifted. "It's safe now. Shall I go first?"

"Wait. I want to ask you. One time you told Durán, 'A scion of Hugues knows how to care for his men.'"

"Òc."

Azure sky above, doves cooing in a hidden dovecote. In that moment, Isabella guessed that Colomb knew only falsehoods about his Beaurain brothers and bastard Beaurain grandsons.

"Hugues had no children."

Colomb tossed his greying lion's main back, laughing at her. "Nicolau and Renoud were his sons. Beaurain cuckoos in the Montcava nest."

"Nicolau and Renoud were indeed cuckoo's spawn, who then bred the bastard Matheus at Xirgú." She stepped back on the boulder so that she didn't have to gaze so far up while speaking truth. "Your brother Esak raped Eloise of Montcava and killed Hugues, his own brother."

"Monkey piss. The children of those men—the ones who hide under the secret cloak of the Confraria de la Crotz—have perverted the honor of good crusaders."

"Honor? Nicolau and Renoud attacked the girl-child sheltered in their domus. Neither claimed their bastard sons, even your own protégé, the man who's out to steal Montcava lands."

"Miquel's son murdered two noble Beaurain sons. Jean-Luc murdered Hugues for his lands."

"Who told you such lies? Your brother Esak killed Hugues. Pedro d'Aragón and Arnau Amalric were there."

Colomb's voice rumbled in his chest. "You dare claim my brother Esak lies?"

"Òc. How did Esak and Matheus lie to you? To persuade you to help with their Crux Lunata evil?"

"My brother Esak says Valerós is a nest of heresy that needs to be wiped clean."

"Yet Pèire Leteric was your friend in the Outremer."

"Who always preached paratge. Which is why I chose to guide Matheus, to reclaim Beaurain honor. But Pèire's offspring—"

"Behave like true brothers. It's honorable that you choose to act for Hugues' sake. But you listened to the wrong brother. If you truly believe in paratge, it's Durán and Sebastián you should join and fight beside. And Felip, if you knew his father in the Outremer."

Not answering, Colomb leaped down from the rock, landing a lance-length past the viper. He held out his sword-free hand, as if he were a chivalry-inspired city seigneur helping his *amor* over muddy cobbles, that infernal grin pasted across his face.

Isabella took three steps back to run and then jumped, landing just past Colomb. One big paw grabbed her shoulder, keeping her from falling. Pain shot from that cracked rib through her torso.

"Steady, now. This bastard might have friends. Perhaps a snaky *bon amic* in the grass?"

Colomb walked away, his long strides leaving her behind. Where the path wound back up into the trees, he called back.

"Simon and the bishops don't like southern women inheriting land. They intend to ask the pope to stop it. But you knew that."

Still cautious of vipers, she stayed ten paces behind him. The wrapping around her chest had shifted in the jump. She reached inside her shirt to adjust it, finding that she'd lost that stone icon from the shepherds' shelter. She regretted the loss, but wasn't about to jump back over the dead viper to look for it. Similar to García the guide, it was one more thing that disappeared in the course of this dusty journey.

It didn't matter. Soon she'd see Sebastián and Yusuf.

Better than icons. Better than unanswered prayers. As good as an apparition of angels.

She tied the damp rag around her face, re-laced her shirt to keep the sun offer her chest, and went to tend the horses.

.

AN APPARITION OF SANCTA MARIA AT LA SOLANA
Testimony of Pascuala, Age Sixty, July 1212

This witness, Pascuala, the grandmother of Salvador and the mother-in-law of Blasco, alcalde of La Solana, had a humble and virtuous servant, Tello, who witnessed the apparition of Our Lady, the Holy Mother of our Lord.

Pascuala sent her servant Tello to fetch the goats for milking. A kindly boy never known to speak lies or blaspheme, Tello returned with the goats, but one kid was missing, and he departed during the midday rest to find the kid at a place in the holm oak forest where he knew that animal liked to graze. The animal wasn't there, but Tello followed tracks along a wilderness trail and found the kid on a ledge high above the river. He carried it in his arms to return home. When Tello gazed down on the river, bright light shone from Heaven, illuminating a woman such that he feared she was on fire and would burn. She lay prostrated on a stone, praying to God, her infant clutched to her breast.

Tello knew this site was the circle where healers in the village collect magical fern flowers on the night before Easter Sunday. To do this, the wise women of the village draw a circle around the royal ferns that grow there and say prayers while standing in the circle. Women in the village keep the fern's spores, which are known by all to defeat demons and grant wishes if blessed by a priest.

It was in this circle that Our Lady lay, praying in the bright sunlight and holding her Holy Infant.

When Tello quieted the bleating goat-kid, the Holy Lady stood and beseeched angels to appear. Tello, knowing himself to be unworthy, dared not speak. The apparition of Our Lady donned Her snowy linen garment while protecting the infant She held.

Tello followed Our Lady from the upper ledge. At the point called Barranco de Las Cabras by the local people, the spirit of Our Lady called to Heaven again, and the Archangel Michael did appear, sword in hand.

Before them, an imp of the devil incarnated, wearing the same form by which mankind first knew Satan in the Garden of All Perfection. The archangel did slay the demiurge, and then did he rise and fly above the trail. Our Lady followed, rising high into the air, soaring with Her immaculate cloak as if flying by the power of the light within Her.

The archangel and the Holy Mother of God, disappeared in the heat and brilliant sunlight. Tello returned to the place where he first saw Our Lady, and there in a crevasse near the rock where

Our Lady had prayed, Tello uncovered an ancient stone, an image of Our Lady cut in the stone as if by magic or miracle, the figure of Our Lady illuminated by flames of burning light, the same way that the sun illuminated Our Lady on the rock.

The Notary, noticing that the boy Tello had bruises on his face and arms, asked if Tello had been beaten by his mistress. The boy, who had been silent in deference to witnesses offered by respected villagers, denied with vigor that his good mistress ever beat him.

"The devil in that viper rose and whipped me," Tello the servant said. "Until I showed the demon the icon of Our Lady."

Sworn by Pascuala, Salvador, and Blasco
as a faithful report of the story of the child-servant Tello
at the shrine of Our Lady at La Solana,
by the Notary of Valdepeñas

13
Rear Guard

Sebastián at Calatrava
June 29, Feast of St-Paul and St-Peter

"YOU LEFT YOUR SHIRT IN Toledo. I saved it for you."

Squinting in the haze of kitchen fires and torchlight under a waning moon, where a lad from the baggage train had dragged him, Sebastián found Taresa again. He hadn't seen her since they were interrupted in Toledo ten days earlier. Now, he talked again with his own angel. She was always so kind to him, so easy to talk to.

"Do you want to sup with me, Valerós? I have cake. Better than the best camp bread. And wine."

Taresa shared a pavilion near the rear, empty because her laundry-women friends were off seeking their acquaintances amid the army camps. She and her friends had made chairs out of baggage and a table out of a food chest. Besides cake and strips of dried goat and bitter Navarrese wine, she offered the kind of solace he didn't dare ask from Pedro. That is, sane company. They talked while the moon crossed Cygnus the Swan, and then Hercules, until it stood above Libra in the western sky.

She said, "You've lived through great danger since I saw you last. Diego Lopez is always the first in any fight. Did you know you'd be in such peril?"

"It's just what we do." He hoped the moonlight didn't betray his pleasure. He'd endured peril, and Taresa admired him for it.

"Will you be in danger when the army attacks Al-Arcos?"

"I won't be in front this time." Sebastián hid his disappointment. "Alfonso gave the front line to his uncle Sancho. As a reward for joining the crusade."

"That's wrong. Everyone knows Alfonso and the king of Navarre have been enemies for years."

"All is now forgiven. Sancho arrived in the dust of the deserting ultramontanos." Sebastián had only just learned about Sancho from Pedro. "How do you know about the feud between Alfonso and Sancho?"

"No one keeps secrets from the baggage train."

"What other secrets do you know?" He felt sure that Taresa teased him, but it was fun.

"Sancho brought only two hundred knights."

"Maybe you know too much in the baggage train."

She shook her head, so her hair escaped her head cloth. She was pretty in the torchlight. "I know Valerós cavalry and infantry are more deserving of honor. Those wild Almogavars that Pedro gave you to lead? They deserve more honor than Navarre."

It was as if she wanted to warm his heart even more than her cake and wine warmed his belly. But he had to defend Diego, because Diego was his general.

"Valerós has only light cavalry. Now that we're here in the midst of the Moors, Alfonso wants to show the famous strength of heavy cavalry."

"Heavy cavalry lost the Horns of Hattin." Taresa poured the last of the wine into the battered tin cup she shared with him.

"No water, bad strategy, and deserting infantry lost Hattin. But that battle happened before we were born."

"Women talk in camp," she said. "About where they've been, and what they've seen. Or what their mothers saw."

"There weren't laundry women at Hattin."

"But there were after the battle. And there's water and laundry women right here." Taresa scooted closer to him.

"Òc. What are you implying?"

"You're filthy, Valerós. Your beautiful red hair! It feels like a dead animal. It's black with dirt."

"Like ten thousand men here."

"But it's only one man that I wish had a bath."

Through the light from the campfires and half-moon, he could see that she clowned, wrinkling her nose. He said, "We haven't found many bath houses out here."

"You crossed rivers."

"And spent our time keeping idiot ultramontanos from letting their horses muddy the streams when we replenished our water barrels. Silly girl, we're in the middle of a war."

"Don't call me silly. I'm sitting right beside you in the middle of this war. It doesn't take more than a moment to wash."

After they bantered more, Sebastián agreed to let her cut his hair. She lit a rush lamp on the make-shift table, then rummaged through her travel pack to find a razor. She sat beside him while she sharpened it.

"You'll cut my throat with that, working in the dark."

Taresa pulled at the buckles of his cuirass until he took it off, then she more than helped him remove his shirt. Before he could get an arm around her, she grabbed a hank of his hair.

"I can see you perfectly well in this light. I used to shave my father. Then my uncle. Sit still while I do this."

"Did they let you run off with the army?"

"They're dead. Now I just take care of myself." Snip. Scratch. "Where are you going when this expedition ends?"

"Wherever Pedro takes his army next."

"Good. I'll stay with this army then, too."

After she'd hacked at his hair with the razor, she fetched a basin of water from the nearby camp kitchens and then lathered his head. The *ka-ka-kratch* sound as she scraped his skull seemed loud enough to wake the dead, but she stood so close that his face was pressed between her breasts, which smelled of lavender and—

She pushed him back, inspecting him in the rush light. "The beard must go too."

"No, the beard helps when I command old men."

"It's filthy. You can start over again. Anyway, you don't need a beard to gain their respect."

"What do you know about that?" He reached out to press her hand away, but she already had his head tilted back, rubbing his chin and neck with soap, that razor hovering too near.

"Don't talk. I know about it because the name Sebastián of Valerós is all over camp. They say Diego Lopez had the Master of Valerós at his side at Malagón. Valerós stands at the right hand of Pedro *le Rey*. The Master of Valerós carries paratge to Andalusia. Valerós leads men to—"

"Enough," he mumbled. Her hand grasped his jaw more firmly.

"You are humble? How sweet!" She wiped his face and head with a strip of linen, then she ran her hand over his now bare head, which tickled.

"It's not sweet, Taresa. *Jhezu del tron*, I'm a soldier. I just do what I'm supposed to."

She brushed the scraps of his cut hair into the basin, and got busy putting away the basin and razor in the rapid, efficient way she did everything. Then she was beside him on the camp-chest, one arm at the back of his neck, turning him to her, the other brushing over his lips, cupping his chin.

"They say you'll be in the kings' chronicles as a hero of this crusade. They say the troubadours will sing of you the way they now sing of the Cid."

"Who are these fools?"

"We heard stories this afternoon, from when our wagons rejoined the army."

He drew her left hand away. "That tickles now."

But her right hand at his neck pressed him to her, and she kissed him, not taking any time to tease his mouth open with her tongue. She tasted of that wine, not bitter now, her breath tickling his bare upper lip as she tipped her head, first one way and then another, dodging his nose with hers, gently sucking the tip of his tongue.

"I like you," he whispered when she released him. "You're the best woman I know."

The hand that he'd pushed away came back to join the other, both hands at his neck, as if holding him so she could devour him, then slipping down to caress his shoulders, her soft cotton shift pressed against his bare chest as she cupped the angled points of his scapula, then ran a finger down his backbone. He shivered.

"And you are the finest man I've ever met."

As if he was born knowing how, he moved her with one arm from where she sat beside him so she stood between his knees. She leaned back from his embrace, tossing her hair, her breasts close to his face. In the dim rush light, he thought she smiled, he hoped with joy. He cupped her buttocks, holding her against him.

"Tonight? This time?" he whispered, afraid to hope.

"Where? Not here."

She settled against his thigh, half sitting in his lap, again rubbing her hand over his bare head. She rested her head on his shoulder.

"The army rides out soon." He sounded like he was begging.

"Òc. I know. To Piedrabuena next. Then to Benavente." Her head and arms felt comforting; the bulge where she had pressed against him felt abandoned. "If you win, the baggage train will journey south to join the army at Al-Arcos."

"We'll win. These Moors don't put up any kind of fight. They shoot a few arrows and then surrender."

"Perhaps at Al-Arcos, we can be alone and get to know each other better." She tipped her head, so much more graceful at this than he was, whatever position she got them into. She brushed soft kisses at his neck. Then wet kisses. Then sucking at the flesh she'd scraped clean at his neck. He tried to bring her closer, dragging one of her hands down between his legs, but so awkwardly that he got his own hand there first. While she sucked a kiss on his neck, he smelled lavender in her hair.

"Know each other," he moaned. "I've learned so much from you."

"Tell me what you learned." She sat up, tugging her shift back into place, sliding off his knee and back onto the camp-chest. He only then heard other people moving near where they sat.

"That the caliph's scouts need only capture a laundry woman to learn what the Christian kings are planning."

She laughed, a throaty sound, the same way she'd laughed on that hillside above Toledo. People spoke nearby, then their voices trailed away. Reaching for the wooden platter with the cake, she broke off a piece. One arm on his shoulder, she took a bite, then fed him, the cake's edge moist from her mouth.

"They tried to make me marry, too." Taresa changed the subject. "My uncle sold me to someone for that."

"People don't sell people in Christendom."

"It's the same thing. A woman is forced to live with a man in trade for property, just like how Pedro is going to make you marry that Castilian senhóreta."

"It isn't like that."

"Of course, it is. I refused. You could refuse, too, Sebastián. I'm waiting for love, like the troubadours sing of."

"People don't marry for love." He shut his lips and refused the cake. When she stopped tempting him with cake, he said, "People only marry for land or other promises."

"I don't mean marriage like kings and uncles force us into. I mean the kind of love that unites two hearts, even if they aren't married. Like in the troubadours' songs."

"I've heard the songs. *Cançós d'amor* are more tragic than *cançós de guerra*. One lover always betrays the other."

"Is your heart so hard? Did your mother not love your father?"

Sebastián, as if rainwater had been dashed on him, pushed her arm away. "I have two fathers. One, my mother hated. The second, she loved with all her heart, but not until after she married him."

"Don't you want that? To grow together in love?"

"When my mother died, my father became a lost soul. I don't have time for that. And I don't care what Pedro needs me to do for the sake of his goals in Aragón or anywhere else."

"But we love each other a little already. If you asked me, I'd vow to stay true, to go wherever you go. We could promise to be true hearts, and we might—"

"*Renrén*. What a chucklehead notion. You're a laundry girl. I am the master of Valerós."

She walloped him with a fist, backed by the muscled arm he admired. First on the ear, so hard it rang like a javelin striking a helmet. Then she smashed his nose, as hard as he'd ever been hit in battle or in arms practice. Blood gushed over his mouth. Surprised, he sucked some in, swallowing as the salty iron tang coated his tongue.

"*Na maliciosa!*" Pain throbbed. He called her malicious. "You know who I am. It's ridiculous to think Pedro would allow me—"

"You never asked who I am. You just think—"

Brass horns called men from their beds, to ride to Al-Arcos.

"Get out!" She heaved his clothes outside her pavilion, standing over him, kicking at him. "Go! You *punxor*. No, you—you—boy!"

■

As the sun rose reluctantly through the thick haze of dust of the eastern horizon, the Valerós force stood still as stones while Alfonso shouted and voices relayed his words through the ranks, translating for those who didn't understand the king's Castellano dialect.

After the last four battles to take citadels held by the caliphate, Sebastián knew the words without the relay voices. Before they seized the minor citadels at Piedrabuena and Benavente, the same words were shouted to stir men to action.

"*Espanya és el Cos de Crist!* We protect the faith!"

"Send the Saracen back to the sea!"

"The Cross belongs in Iberia and Jerusalem!"

Hearts did not beat quickly in Valerós, however, because Pedro had placed them in the rear to guard the baggage train. The best they might hope to encounter would be any Christian infantry fleeing the battle, or a brief fight with dirt-poor Mozarab farmers and *franj* mercenaries paid to combat Christians.

No booty. No glory that day.

No stories to tell children back home.

Back home.

Sebastián steeled his gaze, so the men nearby saw his eyes fixed on Pedro's banner as Alfonso's words relayed to the rear.

Back home where?

Barcelona again?

Join Chrétien at Fontcours in the Toulousain?

Castel-de-Valerós? To become merely the steward of farmlands and vineyards?

How much could Sebastián decide for himself, given that Pedro argued his need for Valerós knights to remain with the Aragón army after this expedition?

Or did Pedro expect him to live on whatever Castilian estates Pedro wanted bound to Aragón through marriage? Not there. Not La

Mancha or Castile or even Aragón. Whatever kind of creature they married him to, Sebastián would either stay in the saddle or go back to Valerós. High in the mountains, where a breeze cools you in summer.

Flies buzzed around him. Flies buzzed everywhere since they broke camp in Toledo. If God had mercy...but didn't Alfonso just say God reserved mercy for all their souls, to bless them for this day's work? If God had mercy, He'd have given men tails, like horses, to swish away the buzzing flies, so the wee beasts didn't crawl in the sweat running from inside one's helmet down the back of one's neck, into the gathered edges of linen, already soaked under cuirass and gambeson. He resisted the perpetual urge to rub at his sore nose.

"Huzzah! Viva! Visca! Vivètz! Desperta Ferro!"

Awake, Steel, indeed. With chores like this, guarding the rear, their steel could take a long nap.

Sebastián roused himself from that unseemly temper, to do as Pedro asked. Time to lead from the rear, to watch Sancho's heavy cavalry take the under-manned garrison at Al-Arcos.

It wasn't a massacre, Father Anselm insisted, if they battled only men arrayed to fight. A massacre includes women, children, unarmed old men. Like Malagón.

Father Anselm, his health improved, rode beside Sebastián that day. By noon, Valerós finished wiping up the deserting caliphate and mercenary infantry. Messengers carried news of victory to the rear. Pennants for Alfonso and Sancho flew at Al-Arcos again. Baggage-train dust rose on the northern horizon.

Sebastián accepted a goatskin flask of water from Father Anselm, after the waterbearers had served the rest of Valerós. He leaned against his horse, which offered paltry shade, waiting for word from Alfonso and Pedro about where his men should camp for the night, hoping that those messages included a promise of booty. Valerós served as Pedro's paid army; they weren't crusaders fighting for forgiveness. And after that many weeks crossing the barren lands of La Mancha, with weeks ahead in the scorching sun, and who knows how long before home, his men needed a reward for their work. As much as they needed fresh water and grass for their horses. And that small force of Almogavars that Pedro had forced on him? He'd heard around their campfire what they most wanted, which was to see real fighting. Just like Valerós knights did.

The dust cloud on the horizon rose higher and moved faster than any baggage train could travel. An army advanced on the exhausted forces resting outside Al-Arcos.

"Caution!" Sebastián shouted to his captains, calling their names, repeating the demand in every dialect used among his men.

The immediate action paid back the time devoted in training. Few words; fingers pointed in command. Valerós infantry was in full armor and saddled, with infantry and Mozarab archers taking their positions. Sebastián looked for Diego Lopez, but saw only two of his own captains, arraying mounted men in preparation for defense.

With no one to consult, Sebastián decided on forward movement rather than passive defense.

"Advance!"

He commanded an advance. The Valerós force ululated behind Sebastián's lead, the men more excited than they'd been while mopping up in the rear of Alfonso's and Pedro's attack.

Until they saw that they advanced on crusaders, their flapping banners with the colors of houses from Toulouse, Montpelhièr, Narbonne, and Foix.

Sebastián held up a hand to halt his light cavalry, stopping an attack on friends.

"*Benvingut al lunfèrn!*" He welcomed the newly arrived captains to hell.

A voice called from the arriving knights. "Why do we want this wasteland? Let the Saracens bake their asses with the devil and a donkey in this hellhole."

Sebastián yanked off the woven cotton rag that was supposed to keep sand out of his nose and mouth. He stood in his stirrups, stroking his horse to keep it calm, and shouted, "*Hola, es Valerós!*"

"*Vivètz Valerós!*"

A cry came from the ranks of the new army, and a figure rode out, galloping to where Sebastián had halted his exhausted soldiers and mercenaries. The rider pulled up on the reins and bounded from the saddle, clasping Sebastián's boot, gazing up to where he sat on his tall horse. White-haired, dressed like a boy.

147

He looked down into the face of the only true angel God had allowed on earth.

"*Hola, fadrin.*" Isabella's face seemed to shine in the late afternoon life. "Now I shall live again,"

PART THREE
"Desperta, Ferro!"

TO MY BELOVED, THE SON OF MY SON,

My dearly loved St-Jordí begs me each day to take action for the love of God in Christendom. But you aren't here with me, son of my son. I beg St-Jordí to intercede with God, to make you well, to bring you to my side. I am in a foreign land, so close to reaping our reward, and yet so far.

Don Carlos's wife, who is our sister in the faith, has failed us in Lérida. Our sister in faith, Petronilla, had promised to aid our work, but her faithless woman's vow has turned to sand. She reports that the woman from St-Féliu has escaped with all her children, including the Cid's heir. Petronilla sent men as far as Barcelona, but it is as if devils or filthy heretics carried that child into hiding. Now we must still find the proper boy-child to rule Iberia under Rome's guidance.

You and I share this belief, that Crux Lunata must supply the new hero of Iberia. We believe in both the prophesy of the Cid and the knowledge that Alfonso and Castile must not steal the royal throne of Iberia. They reek still of the Arian heresy, those Visigoths who resisted the rule of Rome, wading in the filth of heresy which now floods our land.

I need you, my son, and pray for you. But I steel myself every day as it seems I must be the one to raise the sword of the Cid, to remove that unnatural man, Pedro d'Aragón, who obstructs the path of righteousness.

The priests have long said of the Grail, "Those who seek it find it not. It is only found unsought." And yet I believe God will guide you. Bring me the Grail and the sword. And come quickly, for I need your strong, loving self at my side.

— Esak de Beaurain
as God's hand, seeking your sword,
from Al-Arcos

14

The Sword

*Tomás at the crossroads
two days north of Baeza,
July 11, four days before the new moon*

STORKS FLEW OVER THE OLIVE orchards, settling into the stick-and-rush jumbles that made up their monster nests.

Tomás braced to calm his roiling gut, standing with his sword out, as if facing an enemy. Except he faced Rashid, a good and worthy man who wished to be his brother. Or lover.

Loneliness mixed with the foul humors in Tomás's belly.

Both of them had stripped to loin cloths while sparring. Rashid's body glimmered with sweat in the morning sun. For the first time on this side of the Great Sea, Tomás felt the heat. Sweat ran down his back, like a thousand crawling insects.

"I celebrated when Abu Jossep decided to move his army." Rashid performed the defensive motions Tomás had taught him, not noticing that Tomás's hands quivered. "Now he's ill, and we're stuck in this cow town, neither home nor helping the caliph."

When Abu Jossep fell ill, Rashid had commandeered a fortified villa near the foot of the Despeñaperros, several leagues away from the caliph's main forces. Most of the town retreated into the hills, hoping that the army left enough of their farms and houses that they could survive the next winter.

Tomás stepped into a classic feint, wondering if he'd caught Abu Jossep's sickness. Rashid hesitated, as if expecting more from Tomás's attack than the obvious. Tomás touched Rashid's bare shoulder with the tip of his wrapped blade.

"A hit!" Rashid cried, too taken with his thoughts about the army to be ready for Tomás's next move. The hempen canvas wrap on Tomás's sword swished a path through the sweat dripping from Rashid's bare shoulder.

"Now matters are worse than in Baeza." Rashid had energy to both fight and talk. "My officers are so busy stopping deserters, there's no time to plan how best to advance on the enemy. Yet that's what the caliph commands. I'm to prepare this infantry to stand in the front lines."

Tomás motioned for Rashid to attack him. The time he spent gambling at night among the camp's dissatisfied men was paying off, for Pedro's sake. However, Rashid's officers put so much effort into stopping deserters that Tomás hadn't yet found a way to leave with Yusuf and Qasim.

Rashid rushed at the opening Tomás left for him. Tomás's sword clattered to the sunbaked ground. He bowed to his opponent and then wiped his sword and drenched body with the same scratchy canvas cloth. He poured a bucket of water over his head, guessing it would be the last cool moment of the day. His belly tightened on that sharp point of sickness inside.

"You aren't yourself, Tuma." Rashid wiped his sword.

"I haven't been well since before we left Baeza."

"Camp sickness?" Rashid frowned. He insisted on a clean camp, insisting so strongly that some in the ranks called him the Sweeper of Paradise.

"No. Just odd dreams." New and unusual dreams. Isabella came to him at last, her face glowing in moonlight, joyful. She spoke, but he couldn't hear. She motioned for him to follow her, pointing to the eastern horizon. He yearned to run after her, but his muscles were paralyzed. He fell and dragged himself over hard, thistle-infested ground, sharp pebbles cutting into his arms as he pulled his body toward where she waved to him in the moon shadows. "I haven't been able to eat."

Rashid scrubbed at his face with a strip of cotton, then stood still in the sunlight, like a well-chiseled statue on a street in Rome. "All those late nights?"

"How else can I tell you what men are thinking?" Tomás said. And how else could he betray the army's efforts without harming either Abu Jossep or Rashid? That question formed as much of a quandary as the puzzle of how to escape this place.

"That my captains face two kinds of mutiny? Half the army wants to go home, and half are eager to join the caliph right now, willing to desert their own general to join the caliph. You don't have to stay up nights to learn that. I too have eyes."

"I'm still betting that the Christian army goes home before we make it as far as the caliph's camp." Tomás repeated that rumor everywhere. *It seems as if this war will offer no battles, no booty, no glory. They say that anything earned will be taken by the caliph's mercenaries.*

Rashid laughed as he pulled on his shirt and immaculate *sarawil* trousers. "For every other way you tempt me away from the path of righteousness, I am still not a betting man."

They hoisted their arms and other practice paraphernalia and started toward the villa's baths.

"Tuma, I have to tell you—"

Across the way, a cart's tongue crashed to the ground when a burro was unhitched. Rashid glanced around. He put a finger to his lips and stepped closer to Tomás, speaking so low that not even their servants heard. "Our clan is taking Alfonso's offer."

Tomás feigned ignorance. "I don't know what you mean."

"While I've been busy finding traitors and stopping deserters," Rashid hesitated, "Alfonso promised the Rodriguez clan that he will return our old lands to us, from before the first caliphs came to Al-Andalus. If our clan helps the king of Castile to defeat this caliph."

"That's a terrible promise," Tomás said. Since he'd first heard this from Zaheid, he'd wondered how Alfonso could make that promise, since lords of Castile and the orders of priest-knights would gobble up all territory won on this adventure. "The honor of our clan is—"

"Is satisfied only by accepting Alfonso's offer. That's the message my uncles sent me, with a reminder that a man is lost without his clan."

"Do you agree?" Tomás said.

"Where is honor in this adventure? I lose my place in the clan if I don't do as our elders command. The caliph will call for my head if I don't deliver this army to him." Rashid's furtive whisper carried shards of pain.

"My father left Iberia for…" Tomás paused, adjusting the story, "Cairo, because the Rodriguez clan treated our branch as too Berber, as if our grandfathers were savages."

Rashid nodded.

"You need a third way," Tomás said. Another stab of pain pierced his gut. "If you stay with the caliph, you can never be the man you truly are. But worse, you are in danger if you stay."

"Perhaps I should have dedicated myself to the greater jihad before now. Instead I've merely worked to advance my family's ambitions in the caliph's court."

"Regrets do not move the day forward." Tomás sought ways to drive a deeper divide between Rashid and the caliph.

"You freed yourself from the whims of other men," Rashid said. "I see it in how you move, unconstrained, devoted only to the path before you. Do you not have any desires?"

"The *franj* killed desire when they killed my wife," Tomás said. *Though I'm overwhelmed with desire to rescue my son from jeopardy.* "I only wish to—"

They passed Qasim at the edge of the grove where they practiced. Tomás motioned for the Magnificent One to follow.

"We need to convince Abu Jossep to let me move his army forward tomorrow." Rashid caught Tomás's elbow. "When this is over, we'll leave this ignoble land, won't we, my friend?"

Tomás nodded, because it was true, though not as Rashid inferred. "As soon as possible. Now would be a good time."

"Later, when we can go together," Rashid said.

∎

Grander than soldiers' baths in Cairo and Barcelona, the baths in Al-Andalus all offered beauty and comfort, even in this villa on the mountains' edge. In this bath, star-shaped windows let in sunlight. Between each curved arch, brightly colored tile walls added to the tranquility. Alone with Rashid in the tepid bath, Tomás washed while studying his fight partner.

"After this battle? What next for us?" Rashid asked.

The thin, hard fighter slipped under the water, then re-emerged, flicking water from the surface at Tomás.

"I've never worried about 'after' in my life," Tomás said. "I'll just find the next lord with a purse of gold who needs fighters, down the next trail."

"To where?" Rashid slipped through the water, coming to rest beside Tomás. They leaned against the cool tiles.

"Back to Cairo. Or Damascus." Tomás chose far away destinations. "The *franj* still infest that land. There's always work for a fighter seeking good pay."

"You are correct that we can't either of us continue to be soldiers here." Rashid splashed water again, but lazily. Then he grasped Tomás's forearm. "Al-Andalus is for farmers, not soldiers. Look at Abu Jossep. He doesn't want to fight. He wants to inspect his olive groves and listen to a djinni explain his dreams."

"He is owed praise for that. Abu Jossep doesn't want the countryside destroyed for the glory of one ambitious caliph."

Rashid leaned back, staring at the star-shaped windows high overhead, resting his arms on the edge of the pool.

"This all ends before the summer does," he said. "Whatever the caliph or Abu Jossep chooses, we'll be free to leave before the harvest. Won't we, my friend?"

"We should go now."

Rashid stopped Tomás's words with a kiss. With trembling tenderness and unartful longing. Grace. And shyness. A taste of cinnamon and honey on the tip of his cool tongue. The kind of honest kiss that Tomás hadn't known since a time long ago.

Rashid released him. They breathed together, each seeking to know what the other wanted next. Tomás brought Rashid close again, his hand at that knob of bone on the back of that beautiful neck, and instructed with small motions and tiny whispers how a kiss works. He caressed the sharp edge of shoulder blade under the taut, toned muscle of his friend's back. He kissed, lips only. Rashid's hot, eager kisses roamed away from his mouth, kissing Tomás's neck, his ears.

The only tender touch Tomás had known—in how many seasons now? He leaned into that embrace, the sweetness of gentle lips and fingers. Rashid pressed against Tomás, who tipped his friend's head, stopping that flashing smile with another kiss. Their teeth clicked with first-time awkwardness, Rashid unartfully seeking to deepen the kiss.

Rashid moaned. "I want so much."

Out in the foyer, Qasim the Magnificent called out a command for Tomás to present himself before Abu Jossep, repeating every one of the general's honorifics.

Rashid broke the embrace, but Tomás drew him back, splashing in the water.

"I cannot love," Tomás whispered. As lonely as he was, Tomás regretted every gesture since they'd walked into the baths.

"A man?" Rashid grimaced. He struggled out of the embrace. Tomás held him back.

"Anyone. I gave my heart once. It's lost forever. I want you for a brother. I can't make any other promises to you."

With a curt nod, Rashid splashed away. After he rubbed dry with the linen toweling, he glanced back at Tomás. "When we finish here—"

"In the baths?"

"No, when we finish sending Alfonso back to his nest in Toledo. After this battle, I can't stay here, Tuma."

"I understand that you can't respect the way men live here, whether it's your clan or the caliph. Both are a danger to you."

"You see in me what is invisible to other men," Rashid said.

Tomás felt rather that he peered into a clouded mirror. "No man who observes your action could miss seeing the kind of life your heart desires."

Tomás fetched the clothes that Qasim had left inside the archway into the bath. When he dressed, pulling on clean white trousers and a fresh tunic, he faced Rashid, having never intended for it to be like this. "In your true heart, you will always follow the path to righteousness. I'm only a mercenary, a broken cobble in your pathway."

Embracing Tomás again, Rashid breathed in his ear. "You see into my heart because I wish you could live there."

"I cannot love. That only happened in my old life."

Rashid released him. "No? But perhaps two fighters could journey together to Cairo. We can ride as friends, to find new masters."

Just before they emerged from under the final archway, Rashid grasped the top of Tomás's *sarawil*, holding him close. He released Tomás to push open the door to the baths.

"We should leave now," Tomás whispered once again. In despair.

.

Qasim the Magnificent and Yusuf the djinni stood outside the door. One of Rashid's guards called for the vizier's attention, leaving Tomás to walk to the general's pavilion with Yusuf and Qasim.

"Well done, *fadrin*," Tomás whispered. "You convinced the general to change his mind again, to avoid this battle."

"I am honest. I don't want him to go into battle. The angle of the stars indicates that his death is at hand." Yusuf rubbed at his eyes, distressed.

"You are weeping for him?" Tomás considered the old general as kindly enough, but a comic figure.

"He's been so good to me!" Yusuf dropped his voice to a whisper again. "Please let Abu Jossep live. As you promised?"

"I'm not plotting his death." Tomás glanced around. Qasim walked a few paces behind them, too far away to hear. "I merely seek Pedro's victory. Make your general pack up and go home. Perhaps you can save him from the stars."

"His death will come before the new moon. I can't tell him. It's treason here, just like in Cairo, to tell a ruler of his death-day. This isn't a fate you can prevent."

Yusuf broke away and ran for Abu Jossep's pavilion. Qasim whispered in Tomás's ear, having caught up just after Yusuf fled. "The djinni was overcome by fear when he read the stars last night."

"He says Abu Jossep's death is near. That shouldn't cause Yusuf to be afraid."

"No. Yusuf says he shall die on the same day as his father."

"But I'm his…" Tomás stopped.

"I know." Qasim tapped Tomás's breastbone, where that scar was; an enormous familiarity. "You aren't his uncle. That is why Yusuf is overcome with worry."

"We need to be ready."

"To leave," Qasim said. "My mother did not raise a fool."

"I hope mine didn't either."

.

Answering the general's call, Tomás arrived in the courtyard already sweating after the baths and feeling sick. Whatever made him ill was growing worse.

Abu Jossep sat on cushions under a campaign awning, avoiding the morning sun. Yusuf came to his side. The general pointed where he wanted Tomás to sit on an unshaded cushion. Qasim lurked in one corner of the courtyard, opposite where the guards hover at the gate.

"O my djinni, good morning."

"You don't seem well, *Walidi*." Yusuf seemed concerned.

"Indeed, I passed a bad night, my son." Abu Jossep lounged listlessly on cushions, his skin a bright cherry red, as if a fire burned within. "I want to tell you my dream."

Tomás sat as severely straight as if called before his fight-masters in Cairo. He too felt on fire inside

"I galloped across the plain, worried that my horse carried too much with my poor self, my wife, and bundles of goods."

Yusuf said, "You must know that means you carry the weight of the world, *Walidi*."

"For Allah, with Allah's help." Abu Jossep grew excited while he told his dream. "But then my horse was gone. And my wife. And all my burdens. I stood alone on an empty plain with my sword, unable to see my enemies but hearing their horses pounding like thunder."

Everyone dreams that dream. Tomás hoped the "djinni" could turn a common dream into prophecy.

"In this dream," Yusuf said, "you stand bravely alone in your desire to turn away Christian invaders without bloodshed."

"You flatter me, djinni."

"No, my honorable father. I speak truth., as I promised you. You alone have the strength of heart to best defend this land for the people. Not merely for glory."

"I held an old-fashioned sword in my dreams. Like the dagger you wear." Abu Jossep seemed puzzled. "And I stood on two legs, whole again."

Yusuf said, "You held the sword of virtue that will deliver this land from its enemies. *Walidi,* you will understand last night's dream better if I tell you another dream."

"You'll tell me what the djinn dream?" Abu Jossep cried, eager to hear.

"No, I shall tell your own secret dream. One night you rode away from your enemies, seeking safety. Then you soared, flying to the mountain tops. The wind carried you, as a mother carries her child."

"It is so!"

"But you fell, scrambling to fly again. Then you awoke."

"Truly, this is my dream from two nights ago. Do you know its meaning, djinni?"

Yusuf nodded. "It is auspicious for the day of your death. You shall fly to the Garden of the Righteous, without fail."

"Do you see that day in the stars? I beg you to tell me."

At that awkward moment, Rashid appeared on the gravel path beside the pavilion.

"It is not auspicious to speak of death," he said.

Abu Jossep frowned, resenting the interruption, adding to the many resentments he'd shown the vizier in the past month. "We do not tempt fate or Allah. I do not seek knowledge of my death."

The djinni shrugged. "You'll live long, for your day is the same as mine. And I am but a child."

"A child with the wisdom of the sages," Abu Jossep said.

"Can we now discuss this day's business?" Rashid asked. "Do we take the army to join the caliph's forces today?"

When Abu Jossep turned from his djinni to his vizier, pity rather than resentment cloaked his aged, drooping face. "Still eager for war?"

"Just to serve the wellbeing of people in Al-Andalus," Rashid said, "and the caliph's mission to serve Allah."

"Blessed be His name," Abu Jossep said. "Come, my son. Read this new missive from the caliph."

Yusuf nodded, weighed down by the general's arm. The caliph's letter described how the infidels had taken more towns on the frontier but then stopped at Castro Ferral, just beyond Al-Arcos, blocked by the mountains. The caliph begged the general to bring his army to take a place of honor in the front ranks against the infidels.

"It is just as you predicted." Abu Jossep patted Yusuf's hand. "The greediest of the infidels have already turned back to their own homes. Their remaining army is sick from heat and camp life. Yet the blessed men of Al-Andalus remain refreshed."

Tomás had predicted that, not Yusuf. He and Rashid sat with the ill Abu Jossep, who glowed like a sunburned cherry. Rashid recounted the news about how each of the caliph's divisions of mercenaries were to be arrayed.

"Did the caliph chose the best formations to conquer the invaders?" Rashid asked out of genuine curiosity. "You are a more experienced general than the caliph."

Abu Jossep held out his empty palms. "There is no conqueror except Allah."

"Yet you trained the best cavalry in Al-Andalus," Rashid said.

"These infidels do not deserve our best," Abu Jossep said. "As Ibn Mikhail advised, the *franj* never change battle tactics. Heavy cavalry to the fore, infantry and light cavalry on their flanks."

"Let the caliph send his mercenaries to face the paltry infidel army. It shall all be as it pleases Allah." Abu Jossep rose, then faltered while reaching for the crutch Yusuf held. "My djinni says the stars are not propitious now. Our men want to return to their wives and farms more than they want to spill infidel blood. We shall defend our own homes and take care of our own people."

"Leave the caliph's fly-mouthed mercenaries to save Al-Andalus?" Rashid beat one fist against another, sharing the common dislike of the caliph's mercenaries. "How does that honor our forefathers?"

Abu Jossep, leaning heavily on Yusuf, cast his voice as a general does when rallying his troops.

"The caliph and his mercenaries sailed from Tunis, eager to draw infidel blood. But we have lived for five hundred years in the country we received from Allah, where our forefathers built farms and orchards. We seek only to preserve the peace Allah has given us, not the pleasure of butchering our neighbors." Abu Jossep swayed as if dizzy, caught by Yusuf. "Raising our sons to live righteous lives. That's what we owe Allah. And our forefathers."

Leaning heavily on Yusuf, Abu Jossep left the pavilion.

Rashid stood, rigid with fury, mouthing silent imprecations.

160

"Peace, brother." Tomás grasped Rashid's elbow. "Didn't we agree it's best to leave here soon?"

Rashid jerked his arm away. "The worst of it is that I agree with Abu Jossep. But I must do as the caliph demands. Or lose my head for failing."

He was gone before Tomás could say more. Tomás, burning with that fever, went to find Zaheid, with a message for the next courier.

•

Zaheid, leaning on his staff, stood staring up the steep mountains that formed the impenetrable barrier between Al-Andalus and the frontier plains.

"Sacred peaks of the old gods," his giant cousin murmured.

"And I'm more famous than fire on a mountain." Tomás repeated the secret code that first introduced them as Pedro's agents. "But my fire burns more like a sick dog. Can you get a message to Pedro? The general's army is not moving to join the caliph."

"If it were possible to do good for people, you might enslave their hearts." Zaheid fractured his half of the code, then sighed. "But to do good, you must free all slaves, not make new ones."

"What, Zaheid?"

"Our clan has accepted Alfonso's bargain. I wish to take only my boots and walk home to my wife. Like half these men want to do."

"Soon, perhaps."

With a wave to Zaheid, Tomás retreated to the far end of the orchard that climbed the hill behind the general's pavilion, where Qasim had stashed travel goods in an abandoned workman's shed backed up against a rock pile.

Tomás, feverish, needed sleep, to gather energy to travel. Zaheid agreed on a plan that would divert attention near the general's pavilion, allowing Tomás to depart. Qasim agreed on the method to lure Yusuf away from the general's sickbed, where Yusuf spent all his time, singing, holding the old man's hand. Tomás had no qualms about gagging and binding the boy, if needed. He had to trust Qasim's tale of a path that local boys had shown him, winding up the nearby mountains.

Drowsing in the heat of the day, he yearned to separate the burning in his body from his desire to leave here. To be where…

He knelt beside Isabella. At the sacred moment when Pèire hovered between this life and the next. Pèire said, *"How can others trust you if you're just a vagabond and a mercenary?"*

"But I'm not," Tomás protested. "I promised to be loyal to you as long as I walk on God's own earth."

"A loyal man doesn't leave his loving brother behind." It was Miquel, stroking Pèire's head, comforting his old friend one last time. It was so long since his father had come to him that Tomás couldn't choke out a single word.

"He never would," Isabella said. "He's sworn as a bonfraire. No brother will be left behind."

"*Ai, kalila!*" Miquel shook his head. "Look where you are now. Caught here with us, waiting outside Heaven."

"No," Isabella cried. "We are all children of the same father, sharing one heart. Give him time."

Zaheid knelt beside them. Miquel reached out to grip Zaheid's arm, like everyone in their brotherhood greeted each other. Zaheid said, "It's Rashid that kept him here, not just Yusuf."

Zaheid …

Tomás staggered to his feet, shaking with fever. He retched in that rock pile until nothing was left in his sick belly.

"Drink some of this."

Ríma stood over him, holding out a leather flask.

He accepted it, finding his throat parched. It was more of the herbed wine she'd offered him just after the army pitched camp here. He spat it out. "I need water."

"I can't help you then."

By the time he steadied himself, Tomás saw that she held his sword, its blade drawn a hand's breath out of the scabbard.

"Leave that alone."

"I need the Cid's sword." She wore a loose silk robe, perhaps prepared to practice more of her naked witchery.

"Where's your guard Zaheid? You cannot be here alone. You'll get us both killed." His heart beat from the danger. He reached for his sword, but stumbled. She stepped back, out of his reach. That dream and the fever had sucked away even more of his strength.

"You delayed too long." She pressed hard on his chest with the tip of the scabbard, jerking it away when he reached for it. "The Cid's inheritor must embrace fate." She reached a hand over her head. "Yusuf is much more beautiful than you. My scrying shows that he is the inheritor. Not you."

She stretched her lithe left arm higher. Her robe fell open. The dappled orchard light revealed crosses tattooed below her overripe breast. Three crosses. The crescents at each point of the center cross touched the crescents of the cross next to it.

"What are you? A witch?"

"I thought you were my beloved consort, fated to inherit Roderick's throne." She moved farther out of his reach as he stumbled toward her. "But it's Yusuf, not you."

"Keep away from Yusuf!" He glanced around, seeking Zaheid, wanting his help because half the army was likely to come with all the noise she raised.

"You won't act as I command!" she cried out. "The general's time has come. The caliph's time is at hand. Yet you stand in the way of fate. I must act at the time Heaven decrees."

She rammed the heel of her hand at his solar plexus, robbing him of breath, and then slammed the hilt of Tomás's sword into his already throbbing temple.

·

Tomás ran, with nothing like his usual speed, in search of Rashid, finding him in conference with Abu Jossep's ten captains.

"Ríma needs to leave. Now." Tomás bent over for a moment to keep from heaving up his guts again. "Give me five men to travel. Five men and her guard Zaheid will be enough."

Rashid glanced his way. "I've heard Abu Jossep is worse. But there isn't time to cater to his wife's whims."

"Not her whims." Tomás pointed to a corner of the pavilion where they could speak alone. Rashid walked with him to where they couldn't be overheard. "She's a danger to the general. You and

I agree that Abu Jossep has been foolish. But we shouldn't let him come to harm."

"Harm?"

"Our cousin means to hurry Abu Jossep's flight to Paradise."

Rashid didn't ask more questions. "I'll send some of my own men to take her back to Baeza. They can take that false djinni, too."

"No," Tomás said. "He's a comfort to Abu Jossep. You must understand, he's—"

"A tout and a liar. Even if he is your bastard nephew."

"He's harmless," Tomás said. "Let him comfort the old man."

"If you insist," Rashid said. "I'll send men over to the general's pavilion. She can't go with us into the coming battle anyway." He gestured for one captain to join them, gave brief orders, and dismissed the man.

"Abu Jossep just decreed that his army will not march." Tomás again held Rashid's elbow, speaking close in his ear. "Cousin, there is too much evil here. Let's go. Now."

Rashid stepped back. "No, that's not possible."

"It is. We can make it possible.

Rashid shook his head, gesturing to his captains, who watched with impatience. "I have a message from the caliph, Tuma. He's just beheaded two advisors for failing to provision the forces at Jaén. This army marches today or he'll end my life, dragging me behind two horses."

"You're beginning the flag ceremony? Despite Abu Jossep's command otherwise?"

"The caliph left me with no choice," Rashid said. "I hope you'll stand with me. Abu Jossep has been striking cold iron."

Tomás had seen insurrection before. The most dramatic was when the French rioted against the Venetians at Zara, on the way to Constantinople. Nerves twitched. Hair stood on one's neck. Each man checked over his shoulder, constantly looking for what might gain on him. But this wasn't an insurrection. Just a military council quietly discussing the order of the procession.

Tomás's heart beat faster than his sprint warranted. Dizzy from fever, he felt his grasp of all plots and plans slipping away, like the easy way in which Ríma stole his sword.

"I'd best go protect the general." Tomás thought his own voice sounded hollow, as if from the bottom of a deep well.

"Stay, cousin. My men will take care of Ríma. You haven't seen anything like this ceremony in Cairo." Rashid had his hand on Tomás's elbow again. "Watch with me."

The ten captains of Abu Jossep's army each led five garrisons of one hundred men in mixed ranks of cavalry, archers, and infantry. The parade drums beat even louder for the departure ceremony. The deep-voiced drums were borne on mules that seemed undisturbed by the pounding of huge mallets on stretched calf skin. Behind them, an infantry of drummers beat the rhythm on framed hand drums, higher pitched, ear piercing.

Midday sun flashed on the scaled armor of the infantrymen, brass-studded leather of many colors. The *rafraf* tails on cavalrymen's headdresses swayed. Their long mail kazaghand coats and large white shields also caught the sun, the wood whitewashed and rubbed with beeswax.

"It's true," Tomás shouted in Rashid's ear over the thunder of drums and horses and marching boots. "There's nothing like this anywhere I've been."

Rashid didn't answer, distracted by an infantry captain who had joined him, shouting news in the vizier's ear.

"We found ten deserters and two traitors this morning," the captain said. "We hung the traitors, as the caliph commanded. The deserters are now marching behind the mules. Their comrades are charged to watch over them."

Rashid said, "Give the traitors' names to the chroniclers. The caliph will see their families punished after the battle."

"Ah, but one traitor was reported by his clanswoman," the captain said. "That guard for the general's wife. He's from your clan, isn't he? Zaheid of Jaén."

"I need this." Tomás snatched Rashid's khanjar, a knight's shortsword, which rested with other armaments beside the vizier. "Our dear cousin Ríma has wrought evil."

Tomás ran toward the flags that marked Abu Jossep's pavilion, crossing through lines of marching infantry and skirting bowmen, who mouthed curses Tomás couldn't hear over the drumbeat.

.

Tomás stood beneath Zaheid's body, which hung from a post atop the village walls. He closed his eyes, trying to think of a prayer.

What prayer did Pèire Leteric offer when his son Vidal was killed? Thinking of Miquel was no help. Miquel claimed never to have begged anything from God. His mother's prayers were too mild. Isabella? What would she pray? After the heretics were burned at Minerve, she'd never prayed for anything except peace.

"Give his soul peace," Tomás said. "He never asked for more." All those sons in Jaén. The daughters. He'd have to find some way to help them. But if the caliph intended to take revenge, the family needed to get out of Jaén. How to help, when right now he needed to get Yusuf out of—

"Master! She's gone mad." Qasim shouted in Tomás's ear. "She's been saying evil words over the general, and Yusuf too. Come now!"

"Prayers?"

The boy frowned, worried. "No. Spells, I think. When Yusuf dozed, she snipped some of his hair and braided it in a cord that she tied around her neck. Like witches do, to make magic."

"Is she with him now?" Tomás asked. It would do no good to wring his mad cousin Ríma's neck. He quelled the impulse.

"No. Some soldiers came to take her home. But first she left a potion with Yusuf. He's supposed to give it to Abu Jossep if he takes badly ill again."

"You left Yusuf alone? After he's been up all night?"

"He made me fetch you when I told him about Ríma cutting locks from his hair."

Tomás yanked the dagger from his boot-top before Qasim finished speaking. Though dizzy and ill, Tomás ran with Qasim along the edge of the empty camp. Drums echoed through alleyways and cook sites. At the gate to the villa where the general slept, they found Yusuf attempting to lift the gate's bar, frantic to get out.

"She's killing the general," Yusuf cried.

"Come with me," Tomás said. "Where are Rashid's men?"

"Most went to fetch her women and pack the wagons. Two guards left with her."

As soon as Yusuf got the gate's bar free, Tomás dashed to the portico, where two men lay, crimson gore dripping into the granite dust, one slashed in the back, the other at the neck.

Abu Jossep lay on cushions on the portico at the rear of the villa where fountains babbled and bees rumbled in borage. Chanting, Ríma stood over the sleeping general, holding Tomás's sword and Yusuf's dagger, both blades pointed to heaven. One of the general's servants knelt at her feet, his head bowed, his sleeves stained red.

"*Ai*, my love, you've joined me at last," Ríma said.

"Do not kill that man," Tomás said.

"I merely call down blessings on our endeavor. It's time for the new king to free Al-Andalus. Our bodies and souls are God's sword and hammer, my consort. We do this together."

"No, Ríma. Stop." Tomás spoke low, hoping to calm her. Yusuf and Qasim hovered at his side, Yusuf's breath rasping close by his ear. "Abu Jossep doesn't need to die. You don't need to betray Rashid to the caliph."

"Rashid? The caliph will reward him if he betrays our clan. He's dangerous to our family." She smiled sadly, speaking like a parent explaining the moon to a blind child. "We want the old kingdom to rise again. To do that, we must water the ground with royal blood."

"*Jhezu del tron!*" Tomás cried.

Laying Tomás's sword beside the general, Ríma came toward Tomás, one arm inviting him like a lover, the other holding Yusuf's dagger in front of her. Tomás batted at the blade, slicing his hand. She brought the blade up to the gap above his cuirass, where only thin linen covered the lunate scar Petronilla had carved. Ríma drew blood before he could grab her arm.

Startled, he stepped back, stumbling on Qasim and sending them both sprawling in the dirt. She kicked away the short-sword Tomás carried, so that it clattered across stone and into the gravel yard, out of his reach.

"You can't stop fate!" Ríma cried. "Why do you want to?"

"What, my dear heart?" Abu Jossep wakened, if one could call his stupor sleep. Yusuf ran to him, kneeling at his side, murmuring words of comfort. "I'm so thirsty, my son. Is there water?"

Ill and boiling with a fever, Tomás stepped between Ríma and Yusuf. If only he had better defenses than his bare and bleeding hands.

"Father!" Yusuf called. "Be careful. She is a murderer."

While Tomás tried to get closer to Ríma, she circled that dagger, its blade red with his blood.

"Stop." Tomás spoke the command softly, drawing her attention. "Don't kill him. There's nowhere you can go if you do."

"I don't need to kill him." Ríma dipped down to retrieve Tomás's stolen sword from where it lay beside the general. "The old man's heart has been in a casket, ready for burial, ever since I killed his wife and son."

"What did she say?" Abu Jossep whispered. "My dear son, what did she say?"

"You witch!" Yusuf leaped up, moving so fast that he wrenched his dagger away from her before Ríma saw him coming. She lunged at Yusuf, but Qasim dived to shove Yusuf out of the way. They both fell on Abu Jossep, who cried out in pain.

Ríma clutched Tomás's sword with two hands.

"I have the Cid's own sword," she said. "Nothing can stop fate now. I shall be queen."

"You have nowhere to go, Ríma."

She bounded from the portico, running as she shouted back to him. "I'm carrying the Cid's sword. To unite with the chalice. To slay the false king. I go where God leads me."

Following, Tomás stumbled. His stomach heaved with searing pain. He doubled over and vomited. As weak-kneed and stricken as when Petronilla poisoned him, Tomás continued to be sick, heaving, though his stomach was already empty.

"You let her get away!" Yusuf shouted.

Tomás vomited bile.

"So thirsty, my son. Is there water?" Abu Jossep, being helped by Qasim after the fall, mistook one boy for another.

"One moment," Qasim said.

But Yusuf was already at the table. He sniffed a pitcher there, then poured from it into a battered metal cup. Then Yusuf took Qasim's place, cradling Abu Jossep. "Here's almond milk, my father."

"What did she mean?" Abu Jossep asked, so weak, the words were torn from his throat. "About killing my son? You are well?"

"I am well, Abu Jossep. You will be well soon also. Drink this."

"I love you so, my djinni." Abu Jossep patted Yusuf, as Tomás had seen the old man do too many times. "You are my best son."

Abu Jossep couldn't hold the cup. He needed Yusuf's help to tip it up, and then he couldn't swallow. He turned rigid, shook violently, the almond milk spilling down his chin.

Yusuf cried out, a shriek that could be heard over the drums and the parade marching out on the road to Jaén.

•

In the villa's parched courtyard, one of the general's guards had clutched at the trellised bougainvillea, and his blood smeared the villa's whitewashed plaster where he slid down and died. Another guard lay halfway across the stone steps, halfway in the sun-scorched poppies and untended hedge-weeds, his throat like a second mouth, silently screaming his death.

Amid the cushions and carpets when the general held court, Yusuf cried over a rigid, scarlet-red Abu Jossep. Qasim hovered near, a dagger in his hand.

No one alive there but the three of them.

"We need to flee." Tomás couldn't force words loud enough to get the boys' attention.

Then Rashid appeared, alone. He paused at the courtyard gate, stunned, and then he began to shout.

"Murderer! You fiend."

At Rashid's cry, Tomás tried to walk to him, swaying like a drunk, sick coating his boots.

"No, lord," Qasim said. "That witch did it. And she poisoned my master. Her men did that." He pointed to the dead guard near Yusuf.

"You demon!" Rashid had eyes only for Yusuf. He took up his short-sword where Tomás had dropped it.

"Father!" Yusuf, pinned under Abu Jossep, shouted to his father for help.

"He can't help you. You killed him," Rashid said. "The general isn't your father. Never was."

169

But Yusuf and Qasim both looked to Tomás.

To tell them what to do.

To save them.

"Father, help me!" Yusuf called again, this time in Catalan.

"Father?" Rashid faced Tomás, who stumbled while trying to reach both boys, his boots turned to lead, his stomach filled with hot brass spear points, his head stuffed with poison-soaked cotton.

"Dear brother, it is not as it seems." Tomás choked out the words, then doubled over to heave again. "Ríma caused all this."

"You call me brother?"

Rashid had his arm up to strike Tomás when Qasim came between them, lashing at the vizier with Yusuf's dagger. Behind him, Yusuf struggled out from where he cradled Abu Jossep.

"Get back!" Qasim shrieked, his voice breaking.

"You upstart slave!" Rashid hissed, swinging with the flat of his blade, knocking the dagger from Qasim's fist. Yusuf snatched up his dagger, rising up under Rashid's guard to slash the man's thigh.

"O my brother!" Tomás caught Rashid as he toppled, both of them falling into the gravel beside the portico. "Ríma brought all this down. Not these boys."

"A woman? You betray me and blame a woman?"

"Come away with me, Rashid. The caliph will kill you for Rodriquez clan sins. Let's ride out like we agreed, as brothers."

"Master." Qasim tugged at him to stand. "We must go now."

"This wound isn't mortal," Tomás said. "I'll come back for you after this is over."

"You betrayed me. You cannot love because you are a traitor." Rashid managed only a whisper. He had his hands on Tomás's neck, choking him. The same position they lay in mock battle a week ago. To resist that hold, which Tomás had taught him, Tomás had to hurt him.

But Yusuf knocked Rashid at the temple, hard, with the hilt of that dagger. He yanked Rashid's turban off and unwound it quickly.

"Qasim, help me bind the vizier. Father, you must make yourself well enough to ride."

"Let's hide him in the villa." Qasim tore a length from Rashid's turban and used the longest piece to bind Rashid's hands behind him, and then stuffed a smaller piece into Rashid's mouth. "Then he can't call the army down on us."

"You're lucky I'm here with you, Father." Yusuf tugged at Rashid's bindings to ensure they were snug. "It's good that I'm not tucked safely at home when you needed me."

Rashid shrieked behind his gag. No telling how long until servants or someone found him.

"I didn't betray you, brother. The caliph wants you dead." Tomás struggled to stand, the courtyard whirling about him. "I'm trying to save you. I swear on our grandfather's honor."

15

The Grail

"FEELING LEFT OUT, SENHÓR XIRGÚ?"

Colomb dismounted and stood beside Felip while that shaven-headed soldier released Isabella and then embraced Chrétien, shouting, "Bonfraire!" Next, the soldier had a stranglehold on Durán. "*Benvingut, mon fraire!*" Isabella hung close by the whole time.

"You've grown tall." Chrétien said.

"*Òc.*" The young soldier laughed. Up close, he proved to be only a boy. And the youthful image of Isabella. "Hurts like the devil to stretch bones so quickly."

This was the son she'd lost, who made her glow, happy in a way Felip had never seen before.

While Felip pondered that look of beatified joy, another soldier dismounted and dropped his reins. He wore the gambeson and tunic of a secular priest. He pulled off his helmet and rushed past Durán and the others, his arms wide in greeting.

"Senhór Colomb! You here?" The man spoke the common tongue with a Norman inflection. "Angels have rained blessings on us."

"Anselm?" Colomb broke into the first truly joyous smile Felip had seen from him. "You, a priest?"

They gripped each other's forearms, then gazed at each other and embraced fully.

The priest released Colomb. "I could weep for joy, seeing a true comrade here in this stinking country."

The joyous quartet, who'd been lost in their family reunion, stopped to watch that priest and Colomb as they gathered the reins of their horses and ambled away, talking and gesturing, stopping to embrace each other again.

"Who knew Colomb had friends?" Chrétien asked.

"He didn't recognize me," Isabella said.

"How could he?" Sebastián laughed. "Your white hair? Those clothes? A better disguise than you managed in Cairo."

"Who was that?" Durán asked.

"Father Anselm is the Valerós priest. He crusaded in the Outremer with Pèire Leteric before he was a priest." Isabella mused, thinking of her grandfather as a mercenary working for lords of the Crusader States across the Great Sea. "Colomb said he too rode on crusade briefly with Pèire."

"Father Anselm might convert Colomb from the Crux Lunata heresy. If anyone can." Chrétien clapped his hands. "A useful priest, just when we thought every goat in town died."

"Crux Lunata heresy?" Felip said it aloud, pondering the idea. As viciously as these Montcava and Valerós people spoke of that order of knights, he thought of it as a rivalry with Matheus. And a desire for a different king. "Heresy?"

Chrétien became solemn. "Lying and murdering to gain power while using the Lord's name. If you prefer."

Sebastián studied Felip. "I'm Sebastián of Valerós. Welcome."

Durán said, "Master Sebastián, meet another Montcava cousin we found along the way. This is Felip of Xirgú."

"Xirgú?" The boy flashed white-hot, angry enough to set Felip on fire, if lightning and burning fields hadn't done that already. "The man who's out to steal Valerós?"

"No." Chrétien clamped a hand on Sebastián's shoulder. "It wasn't Felip."

He whispered in Sebastián's ear. The boy stepped back, studying Felip. The anger emptied from his face, and he grasped Felip's forearm, where the crossbow bolt's burn hadn't yet healed.

"*Benvingut*, Senhór Felip." Sebastián spoke in a Catalan mountain dialect. "Xirgú rode with my great-grandfather. Now you ride with me, bonfraire. When the world is chaos, you will always have your brothers."

While Felip pondered the miraculous way that burn on his arm had turned the boy into an ally and friend, Sebastián leapt into action, shouting for his captains to guide the new arrivals to water for their horses and a place for their men to rest. "My captains will help with all that you require. Then we can—"

"*Bon vèspre,* Valerós!"

Sebastián halted, his golden eyes catching the late-afternoon sun.

Fifty paces away, a herald in scarlet and yellow called out Sebastián's name. "We came to thank Valerós for its work today. But we're interrupting. You have guests."

Chrétien held his hand in the air, a formal greeting he seldom rendered. Durán imitated him and said, "The count of Foix prays for the health of the king of Aragón and sends you his best men."

Trailing behind that herald, an armored figure stood, draped in magnificent silks, a circle of gold around his helmet. Felip stood straighter, since that silk-clad figure must be the king. The herald advanced on their band.

"I'm touched that you came all this way." Taking Durán by the hand, the herald said, "*Ai,* the seigneur of Montcava! Didn't I predict that you'd be of use one day?"

Chrétien pulled back the hood of his chainmail, cast off his arming cap, and shook his long blond hair free. "*Bon vèspre,* Monsenyor. It's good to see you, bonfraire, even in this stinking wilderness."

"Chrétien?"

"It's me. Ramón-roger of Foix asked us to be useful."

The man in the crown, silks, and glorious armor was ignored. That tall herald was the king. Why was he forever the last to know what things meant? It gnawed at Felip's core.

"Monsenyor, this is Felip of Xirgú." Durán motioned Felip forward, so they all stood in a half-circle before the king of Aragón, as if this were an ordinary conversation with their captains. Felip bent his knee the way that Durán did. Chrétien didn't bow at all.

"You're Xirgú's son?" Pedro put his hand on Felip's shoulder, a touch Felip had never dreamed might happen in this life. "*Benvingut,* seigneur. We're happy you joined us."

"M–my brother is seigneur, but– he's injured. I'm j–just a scribe."

"We need all manner of men here." Pedro glanced past Felip, suddenly grey under sunburned skin. "A ghost?"

"No, Monsenyor," Isabella said. "We came to warn that—"

"This is Vidal." Chrétien interrupted. "Of Valerós."

"*Ai, benvingut*, Valerós!" Pedro greeted her the same way he'd greeted Durán, gripping her forearm as if she were a man. His face twitched with emotion, shifting from grimace to a broad smile while he regarded Isabella in her scribe's clothes. "Arnau Amalric sent me a message. If Vidal of Valerós appears in my camp, I'm to send him to the bishops for judgment about murder and heresy."

The clerk at the king's elbow said, "But Monsenyor, your message to the archbishop insisted that there is no such person."

"Have I ever lied? Dissemble, yes. But bold-faced lies? It would be a sin."

The clerk seemed doubtful. Isabella said, "I came because—"

A high-pitched shriek rang behind them.

"Senhór Sebastián!"

Fortuno ran toward them, having escaped from the rear ranks where the Norman captain Thierry kept the lad.

"You left me behind! Where's Yusuf? I have to tell him about his brother Quelo." The lad stumbled, surrounded by armored men.

Chrétien snatched him up, arm and sleeve covering his face.

Fortuno uncovered his mouth. "Did I do a bad thing? Forgive me. I didn't speak Don Tomás's name. Since he's dead."

The child wiggled free and ran to embrace Sebastián, who lifted the lad onto his shoulder. "*Benvingut, fadrin.*"

"Where is Yusuf?"

Isabella clutched Pedro's wrist, her chainmail jangling.

"Tell me." Her voice creaked, as if the dust from their hard ride corroded her throat. "How did Tomás die?"

"Die?" Pedro frowned. He again gripped her elbow in a soldier's greeting. "Tomás is alive. Wherever did you get such an idea?"

"Sancta Maria!" Isabella, in a passion, seized Chrétien and buried her face. But her body shook with only a single shudder. Perhaps some might call it a sob.

Chrétien, too, clouded like a thunderstorm about to spew the wrath of God. "A lie? We believed a lie?"

Pedro clasped Isabella's shoulder, the same way Durán did when offering comfort. "Tomás is alive. Though I'm not sure how to find him at this moment."

When Chrétien released her, Isabella smiled at the king of Aragón.

That's the only apparition Felip had ever seen. The woman he knew disappeared. Gone was that creature of worries and pain and hard work. This new woman was ablaze from an inner fire, glowing such that Felip understood why they painted a golden corona around figures of saints. The etching of agony that her face wore, even in sleep, was gone now. She seemed magnificently innocent, and no older than her son, who hovered nearby. Felip believed that he'd seen what true redemption looks like, though that was blasphemy. When Isabella spoke, her usual rasp had softened, warmed.

"That makes life seem…more promising, Monsenyor."

.

The king's camp aides arrived and began pitching a temporary pavilion at the side of the clearing. Like his friends did, Felip gave his horse to one of his captains and cautioned Fortuno to stay with Thierry and the Montcava men. He then followed the king, offering a silent thanksgiving that his friends trusted him and invited him on this day's adventure.

The commotion seemed to give Isabella a moment to collect her feelings. Like dawn breaking over the mountains, her joy from when she'd first greeted Sebastián grew brighter. She clung close to Sebastián and Chrétien, who was slow to let the fire of his anger die. Then Chrétien seemed to come back to himself and grinned in his usual teasing way.

They crowded together under the temporary pavilion.

Chrétien, Durán, Isabella, Sebastián. Felip.

The king and his clerk Doménec, who kept staring at Felip.

"Your messenger found us outside Girona," Chrétien said, "with a letter saying Tomás died in Barcelona, and asking me to tend to his affairs."

Pedro glanced at his clerk, frowning. "What happened?"

Being in the presence of a king was new to Felip, but that king's frown seemed fearsome to behold. Yet the clerk, a priest and not just a scholar, lifted his shoulders, not seeming concerned about censure. Doménec said, "We're so far from the scriptorium now, I cannot tell you who erred or why."

"You came all this way to ask me how Tomás died?" A deep line pierced Pedro's brow.

"No, we're here to warn you," Isabella said.

"It's why the count of Foix sent us," Chrétien said.

Pedro laid his sword and scabbard on the ground, then sat on a campstool that an aide had unfolded. "If it's about dwindling supplies and blistering heat, I already know."

Felip had never met a man as magnificent as Pedro d'Aragón. The lords and churchmen in Girona never appeared so grand. It was not that the king dressed extravagantly. He just moved more gracefully than other men do. Pedro listened to each person speaking as if that person were most important to him in the world. Chrétien described what he and Durán had learned about Crux Lunata, and why they'd undertaken this journey:

Matheus's plot with Crux Lunata.

Maria's assassination plot and magic incantations.

"That's your story?" Pedro unbuckled his grieves, refusing an offer of help from his clerk. "My wife and some southern seigneurs and a few Churchmen want me dead? That's not news."

Although the tent where they met was only a sunshade with no sides, Felip found the conclave crowded and confusing. Doménec the clerk wore a portable desk around his neck and kept busy writing. The aides had spread carpets on the dirt, where the newcomers sat cross-legged around Pedro, with Durán and Sebastián on either side of him. Isabella's hand rested near Sebastián.

That left Felip beside Chrétien watching Durán to see how to sit and what to do with his hands. He endeavored to do whatever Durán did; Chrétien seemed too at ease to serve as a proper model.

Durán said, "The Crux Lunata and other orders also took a significant portion of the provisions intended for your returning army. But yes, they want you dead."

"I've endured two dozen attacks since the crown of Aragón came to me." Pedro dropped the unbuckled grieves beside his scabbard. "That's why another man wears my armor."

"Which many people know," Chrétien said. "That disguise no longer protects you."

"The count of Foix's list of conspirators? It's all preposterous." Pedro pointed to the letter Durán had given him. "Did the time he spent in prison in Urgell scramble the count's brain?"

"There's a glut of abbots, priests, and bishops here who intend to speed your way to heaven." Isabella held the packet of letters she'd stolen at St-Pere and Girona, which Pedro returned to her after reading them.

Speaking only to the king, Doménec said, "Those same men knelt with you and Alfonso at mass this morning, swearing before God that we are all united."

Pedro tapped a finger on his knee, which Felip guessed indicated impatience.

Durán said, "The Crux Lunata took gold and horses from your subjects to pay for their journey here."

Pedro scoffed. "Every seigneur here mortgaged his household to come to Iberia. That's how crusading is done. I'm still paying my father's battle debts. How is this different?"

Excited, Felip knew this answer. "Th–they also took land. The laws your father laid down f–f–forbid any lords from giving p–property to the Church without the k–king's permission."

Pedro smacked his knee. "Who?"

"Ch–Ch–Xirgú, for one. M–my brother."

"And your wife, Monsenyor." Chrétien spoke without one note of the teasing with which he plagued Felip.

"And half my Montcava cousins. Though not this one." Durán tapped Felip's wrist.

"No." Felip hated saying it. "M–my brother made me give my lands to the Church."

"That land will come back to your keeping, Xirgú, I promise you." Pedro glanced at his clerk. "Make sure it's on our list of chores when we return."

"The names that Ramón-roger sent you," Chrétien waved the count's letter. "They have all given portions of their land."

"None of them are real military men." Pedro stared up at a corner of the pavilion's shade. "What do they think will happen when I return home?"

"Their leaders' idea," Isabella's voice was as raspy as the friable gravel of the plains, "is that you won't come home."

Chrétien said, "We believed that Colomb de Beaurain was recruited as an assassin."

Pedro denied that with a shake of his head. "Colomb is a good man. Crude at times. But worthy."

Durán said, "I saw him plotting with Matheus and your wife."

"But I believe they enlisted Colomb with lies," Isabella said. "You might learn more about your enemy by asking Colomb."

"Where is he?"

"He greeted Father Anselm and left with him," Sebastián said.

"I shall speak with him later." Pedro shifted his long legs. "So, bonfraires. You came to warn me that the Church is paying a passel of inexperienced knights to—"

"And your wife," Chrétien said again. "She's paying, too."

Pedro continued. "To stop me from battling the caliph."

"Òc, to ruin your enterprise," Isabella said.

"Why ruin what the pope wants done in Iberia?" Pedro stood again to shrug off his chainmail. "Alfonso and I have toiled for years to build and provision a united army."

"The count of Foix says the Church doesn't care one fig about Alfonso," Chrétien said. "Your enemies don't want you to come home a hero, bonfraire."

"No more territory for Aragón. No booty or glory for your knights," Isabella said. "And best if you are dead."

Pedro weighed this argument with his hands, but did not offer an answer.

"Leaving all of the south," she continued, "to be divided between Simon de Montfort and María of Montpelhièr as regent for your son."

Pedro closed his eyes, perhaps mouthing a prayer. Then he stood, kicking aside the discarded arms at his feet. "Chrétien and Durán, take Marcos and Cebrián from my guards and find out which of my captains are loyal. Prove that Ramón-roger's list is correct."

"Òc, Monsenyor," Durán said.

Chrétien rubbed his hands. "A little music around the camp-fires, dice with noble knights while chatting."

"Be discreet." Pedro repeated the word in Latin and Catalan. "If you know what that means." He turned to Sebastián, who had been silent through the story. "Valerós is now my guard. Give my thanks to your men for work well done today and move them to my camp in the morning. I'll send apologies to Alfonso and Diego Lopez, since I need you more."

Sebastián offered a formal farewell and departed, with a quick smile to Isabella.

"Senhórs," Pedro pointed to Durán and Felip. "All your men will serve under Don Sebastián." He stood, apparently dismissing them. "Send Colomb and all your captains to me after prayers tonight."

Daring the limits of his courage, feeling that cup hidden for so long inside his jerkin, Felip asked, "What about Crux Lunata magic? Do we worry about that?"

"María's spells?" Pedro mocked the idea. "Magic emblems? Prayers said backwards? I've heard about it for years."

Felip reached into his jerkin and then unwrapped the weight he'd carried from the St-Pere monastery. "Their plot involves magic, for which they seek the Grail. My uncle Lorenç claimed this chalice is key to your defeat."

"A magic cup!" Chrétien laughed, of course. "Lovely glasswork. Naxos, isn't it?"

"Sancta Maria! You stole Lorenç's wine cup?" Isabella winced as if in pain, likely from her battle with Colomb. "That's why they're still hunting us."

"What is it?" Durán asked.

"The abbot at St-Pere had relics from the Holy Land. All fakes," she said. "Pèire Leteric claimed that's what every man brought home from the Outremer."

"This is an important relic," Felip insisted. "Lorenç received this from a dying crusader." His uncle Lorenç had many faults, but Felip didn't believe he was a liar.

"Lorenç claimed it's the chalice from our Savior's last supper, taken from the Saracens by El Cid." Isabella didn't hide her disdain.

"But this one, like the other hundred fakes, doesn't glow or do miracles. And who knows how it traveled from Jerusalem to Valencia and then to Girona?"

Felip held the cup out for Pedro to examine, since it deserved solemn attention. "My uncle Lorenç promised Arnau Amalric that he'd carry this chalice to Andalusia."

"As part of the Crux Lunata plot against you, Monsenyor." Isabella reached for the cup, but Felip kept it from her.

"Monsenyor, your enemies believe it carries power from God," Felip said.

"It's why Arnau Amalric wants to find me," Isabella said. "To find the Grail. They say this chalice will reunite Christendom."

Pedro frowned. "Arnau's message claims that Vidal of Valerós left murdered priests behind at St-Pere."

Felip hoped to explain. "The abbot at St-Pere had an accident with a sword."

"*Ai.*" Pedro, head in hands, tugged at his hair. "At least they can't blame Don Tomás this time."

"He died in a struggle with Tomás's sword, Monsenyor." Isabella offered her open palms in a gesture of innocence. "The sword they believe came from the Cid."

Chrétien laughed, as deeply cynical as Felip had ever seen him be. "When they unite those two magical objects, God will free them from your sinful tyranny, Monsenyor."

Pedro laughed, too, choking on his efforts to suppress it. He tried to speak, but laughed again. He held up a hand for patience. "Excuse me. Tomás took the Cid's sword to Andalusia with him. The one Miquel gave him. At least, that's what the caliph's vizier demanded of me."

Isabella crossed her arms. "That's ridiculous."

"Exactly." Pedro still laughed. He took the goblet from Felip and handed it to his clerk. "Doménec, put this away. We don't want anyone hurt by broken glass. And don't any of you speak of magic. My captains will laugh themselves to death. I need every single body at arms."

"Don't drink from that thing," Isabella said. "Lorenç was also fond of poison."

The king's clerk carried away that burden, leaving Felip to regret humiliating himself before the king of Aragón by repeating his uncle Lorenç's foolery.

Isabella said, "If you'll excuse us, Monsenyor, I'd like to find Yusuf and spend a few moments with my sons."

"Yusuf isn't here." Pedro said. A dark look of confusion crossed his sunburned face. "He's in Barcelona with my cousin."

"No," Chrétien said. "I searched for him there. People say Yusuf left the same day Sebastián did. And your cousin is in Lérida with Petronilla."

"I saw Yusuf when..." Pedro groaned. "He overheard my false quarrel with Tomás, when we convinced the courtiers that I had banished him."

Isabella was the only one who wasn't frowning. "Yusuf must have followed Tomás. They're together. God granted them grace at least this one time."

Pedro ran his fourth finger along the deep worry line in his forehead. "Senhóra, take a moment with your son and his brother." He pointed to Durán. "When you are rested, I want to hear your tale."

•

That left Felip alone with Chrétien.

And the king of Aragón.

Who said a dozen words that changed Felip's tumultuous life.

"I knew your father, Xirgú. He rode with mine to take Teruel, on the road to Valencia. My father said that Justí de Xirgú incarnated everything a wise and honorable man should be. Justí was well regarded among all men."

A lump lay siege to Felip's ability to speak. He soldiered past it. "Thank you, M–Monsenyor."

"You are a scribe? Is that what you said when we met today? Will you work in my court? A king needs superior scribes. The Church can't steal away every good man."

As if again struck by lightning, Felip stood before the king, bees stinging his fingers and toes again.

"Perhaps you long to be a soldier." Pedro again put his hand on Felip's shoulder. "Yet I believe that Justí de Xirgú would see your scribing as honorable and crucial to our cause."

"How else will our children's children know who the real heroes were?" Chrétien interrupted that magical moment.

"My very thoughts," Pedro said. The clerk Doménec reappeared and seemed to distract him. "I'm thinking of—"

"How Simon de Montfort's tale about the burning of heretics at Minerve reached the pope before yours?" Chrétien, using a tone familiar to Felip, intended to provoke Pedro.

But Pedro squeezed Felip's shoulder and ignored Chrétien. "First, Xirgú, record what happened at St-Pere monastery. Write how the abbot Lorenç died by his own treachery. Tomorrow, Doménec will share his work with you. He's preparing a missive to send to the pope after we defeat the caliph."

"O you blessed optimist," Chrétien said.

The king's clerk reappeared from his chore with the chalice and listened to Pedro's new request to supply the seigneur of Xirgú with what he needed to write letters for the king. Felip focused on receiving what Doménec shared. Good iron-gall ink, a packet of quills, and a traveler's writing desk. Doménec, with a roll of his eyes, silently shared Felip's discomfort at Chrétien's casual intimacies with the king. Doménec was a well-made man, with ink-stained fingers that revealed he shared a vocation with Felip, who determined that he'd be far better off watching how Doménec deferred to and served the king of Aragón than anything he might learn from Chrétien.

Chrétien began a new topic. "In Barcelona—"

Holding up a hand for Chrétien to wait, Pedro sent Doménec on another errand. Felip dipped his head over parchment and his pen into the inkpot, and then he began to write the story of misadventure at St-Pere monastery.

"I received your message that Tomás was dead. People at his villa spoke of him as a dead man." Chrétien sat on Doménec's deserted camp-chair, hands on his knees, which touched Pedro's while they talked. Felip grimaced at that rude gesture. "But the food in your city is as fantastic as my mother's succulent meals. The streets though... your city must have been built by goat herders a thousand years ago."

"No worse than any other city. Tomás and I arranged a quarrel, and I pretended to banish him. We needed everyone to believe there'd been a drastic severance between us. His servants likely consider him dead. But I didn't send you a message like that."

"Where is my brother? We know he'll ride into any storm you ask. Was Andalusia his idea?"

"No, I bullied him into going. It seemed like the right thing. Tomás was worthless, sunk in grief over losing Isabella."

"Another faulty story. Aren't there too many now?" Chrétien pounded one fist against another. "But perhaps worse, you sent his wife to live in Lérida with your cousin Petronilla. The laundry-women's baggage train might be safer."

Pedro bounded from his camp stool. "No, I asked that Dolç be sent to a convent outside Barcelona. She'll be safe until I returned."

Chrétien, an insolent hand on the king's chest, pressed him back to the chair. "She never made it to any convent. She's at the royal house in Lérida. With her girls and the infant. She named him after Miquel of Morella."

Pedro swore that he'd been compromised by donkeys and goats in unclean ways. Felip stayed busy, as if he were used to such talk, though he'd been travelling with Chrétien, so perhaps his skin was thickening.

Chrétien tapped the front of Pedro's cuirass. "You made him marry her."

"It seemed best. He was a lost soul. But I asked the Church to annul it. And it's approved by now. What worse mischief can the devil beget?"

"I don't know about the devil, but Petronilla dotes on Dolç's tiny babe, who's as beautiful as Yusuf, though born too young. Therefore, I left an old friend to watch over Dolç."

"Thank you." Pedro swore again. "Petronilla had a tiff with Tomás in Barcelona. She can be cruel when she thinks she needs revenge. Who knows about this?"

Chrétien circled with a finger, indicating the three of them. "Durán. Isabella. And little Fortuno. Who knows about Dolç here?"

"Sebastián. Every seigneur from Barcelona. Let's send Vidal of Valerós to the rear of the army. I shall speak with her."

"*Òc*," Chrétien said. "Perhaps 'Vidal' can learn how the bishops intend to kill you. If they don't kindle a pyre for our favorite heretic."

"Find her a new name. Since the archbishop is seeking a man named Vidal."

"*Òc*. We'll produce yet another Montcava bastard that the count of Foix sent on this adventure."

Doménec reappeared with a message for the king. With one deft motion, Pedro dismissed Chrétien and Felip.

When they walked away, Chrétien kicked a fist-sized rock out of the pathway. "Doménec gets what he wants when long-haired black goats rule Jerusalem."

"He seems to do whatever the king asks." Felip considered the great care that clerk took with that chalice.

Chrétien halted, hands on his hips. "That's my point, Xirgú. You can't possibly think they're lovers. Tomás says Pedro never lowers his guard in his court or household. It won't happen in Doménec's wildest fancies."

Dismayed, Felip followed when Chrétien strode off again, humiliated once more because he didn't understand the world. Chrétien rattled on.

"I'd wager my armor that Doménec exercises those fantasies every night. You have more of a chance with Isabella than that mooncalf does with Pedro. Which is less than none."

"But the king…" Felip stopped in the sandy yard beyond the king's pavilion, struck by new awareness. Not like Saul on the road to Damascus. Rather, like King Solomon in Ecclesiastes, Felip felt the futility of it all.

Chrétien came back to Felip, not with a tease on his tongue, but seeming concerned. "Xirgú? It goes well?"

"We rode here, through all that hell, to warn the king. And he laughed at us for being fools."

"*Ai*, no, bonfraire." He touched Felip's elbow with what seemed like kindness. "Pedro believed us. We scared him."

"But he laughed."

"I laughed too. Doesn't mean we aren't serious. Pedro's busy reordering his entire camp for safety's sake. And we too have work to do." Chrétien stopped dead in his steps. "Jove's pissing monkey be damned. My brother is alive."

Chrétien grabbed Felip around the waist, lifted him, and danced a dozen steps before letting him go.

"He's here on earth!" Chrétien shouted, startling everyone around them. "He's not burning in hell! Tomás lives!"

16
Wayfarer

Dolç in the Pyrenees, Serra del Montsec
July 11

DOLÇ AND HER MERCENARY FRIENDS skirted villages on their travel through the mountains. From the first encounter, villagers weren't happy to invite in visitors, because bands of home-going soldiers had brought dysentery to their town. Her own girls were no longer ill, and Dolç didn't want to expose them to illness on the road.

One of Jacques's friends proved to be an uncanny scout who warned them whenever other travelers were coming, quickly spying any bands of mercenaries going home from the Andalusia expedition. Jacques' friends had a method. They hid Dolç and the girls in the trees before encountering other travelers and then negotiated safe passage. The many unhappy returning mercenaries required caution, Jacques insisted. But each time Dolç and the girls scurried up a narrow limestone ravine and hunkered in the trees, she watched below and saw only hungry, tired men.

"May the sweet baby Jesus and his Holy Mother guide and protect you," Jacques invariably called in greeting. "We see you're coming from Hades. Where might home be?"

However wary a traveling band might be—their swords and pikes and javelins in hand—this greeting gave them pause. They asked a similar question. "You sound like a Norman who's traveled far."

"Oui. My mother's pure Norman. My papa was a traveling man like me. You sound like a man straight from the Pays de France." Or Burgundy. Or Pays de la Loire. Or Aquitaine. After settling where they all came from, Jacques next asked, "Did the king of Castile steal all the promised booty from you, too?"

From that question, Dolç learned new invectives in the French tongue, though none as creative as what she remembered when Don Tomás lived in her villa.

Jacques agreed with their dissatisfaction. "It was that way when we chased the Angevine king John." The good cheer disappeared from his voice. "The priests promise forgiveness of sins and talk us into mortgaging the whole countryside to go on crusade." ¹

The travelers always agreed. "Then they shall send us home empty-handed."

"It's not like our fathers' and grandfathers' day," Jacques said. "When a man could find glory and gold in crusading."

At each encounter, after grousing about the unfairness of kings, the band of travelers would decide that Jacques and his men were like them, scavenging the countryside, with nothing to contribute and nothing to steal. And they rode on, leaving Jacques and his mercenary friends tending their horses.

Senhór Chrétien had entrusted her family's safety to a magician. That bandy-legged soldier Jacques turned every challenge into a friendly discussion of the ways of kings and the travails of true fighters.

The haste to scamper up a ravine and hide became a pleasant break from the tedium of riding the mountain trail. Rather than strain to overhear yet another encounter with thin, sunburned men in a hurry to be home, Dolç watched a flock of birds under the trees across from the side of the ravine when she cuddled with the girls, whispering for their silence, calming their restlessness.

A dark-purple mother capercaillie scratched in the undergrowth. The bird had the unmistakable scarlet spot of naked skin above its eye and the half-chicken, half-pheasant shape of the creature she remembered from her childhood. Busy teaching her chicks to hunt under the shelter of an ancient spruce tree, the mother paid no regard to the humans hiding across the ravine. The chicks wandered into the dense undergrowth, attracted by whatever luscious bug or berry might be found there.

The mother hen perked up her head, startled, and then urged her chicks up into the branches. Comical, inelegant fliers, they made many attempts to reach higher branches. The mother, short and plump bodied with round, useless wings, beat the ground, the noise thundering in the ravine as if to warn off attackers. She lifted off the ground and glided briefly, a whistle through her feathers echoing in the ravine. Then she dropped down to nudge a recalcitrant chick to take flight to a higher branch.

Dolç felt for the awkward mother, hustling her chicks into safety but unable to take flight up through the trees like songbirds. She quieted her own brood, who clung close, the girls' hair smelling resinous from dashing through brush and low pine branches. Quelo rustled, swaddled deep in her robe. She guided him to latch on, calculating how many weeks until he learned it for himself. So very tiny still. Too young.

Directly over the ravine, crows cawked and complained, diving, chattering, circling, and then attacking, the way a roving band of mercenaries might.

Three dogs sniffed their way up the limestone creek bed of the narrow ravine, the uncaring target of the crows' diving attacks.

■

Shouts echoed up the ravine, single-word oaths in French and Catalan mountain dialects.

The two shaggy Pyrenean sheepdogs and a large, dark mastiff perked their ears. The sheepdogs stood at attention, alert to the commotion below, while the mastiff still wandered up the creek bed, pausing to look back at its friends.

The shouts continued, punctuated with screams of steel-on-steel and the *thunk* of what must be wood on bone. Dolç, her heart beating loud enough to summon the mastiff, whispered to the girls to be still. Quelo, perhaps feeling her wildly beating heart, squirmed and sighed the tiniest squeal of distress. She mashed Quelo into her breast, forcing him still, then helping him latch for comfort.

The mastiff's ears perked, aimed for where Dolç sheltered in the ravine, huddled over her brood like a frightened hen. The dog whimpered, drawing the attention of the sheepdogs, who couldn't decide which way to go. At last, the shaggy pair bounded down the ravine toward their masters.

The mastiff stood, catching its footing in the limestone scree in the empty stream bed, its eyes intent on the place in the trees where

Dolç had only her own body to protect her children. A piercing howl from another dog far down the ravine snatched away the mastiff's attention. It dropped its head and then loped after its friends.

The sun, directly overhead when Dolç and the girls first scampered up the ravine, shifted to the west, and the shadows on the east face of the ravine grew longer and longer, the colors of the trees changing from a thousand shades of green to greys and purples. She begged the girls, in breathless whispers, to be patient, that their hunger wouldn't last forever, that there'd be another meal soon. She taught them long prayers she'd learned from her mother, whispering the lines together, breathing the words instead of speaking them.

At last Jacques appeared, along with another of the mercenaries. They lifted the girls onto their shoulders. The littlest one wrapped herself around Jacques' middle. And they all picked their way down the dry creek to the trail.

"Who was it?" she asked when the trail was in view. "More crusaders going home?"

"Just wild mountain bandits, ma dòmna. Do not worry."

The rest of their band held the horses, all packed and ready to travel as if the party were setting out from their morning camp. The horses stamped, uneasy. Dolç called the girls' attention to the magnificent sight of a bearded vulture circling high in the sky while she shaded their view of the dark stains on the trail.

When they'd ridden a good long way from that place, she dared to ask, speaking in her own tongue.

"The dogs, too, Jacques?"

"Of course not, ma dòmna. They've gone off home, wherever that is. Who'd want to hurt a dog that never done no harm?"

Jacques dangled an amulet before her, wanting her to take it.

"Look what I found, ma dòmna. A wolf's tooth. The best amulet for a wee baby's safety. Can he wear it? My own mama would give her eye teeth to protect her children with such magic as this."

She draped it loosely over Quelo's neck, tucking it safely, not asking where Jacques found it.

17

The Icon

WITH THE SLIGHTEST GESTURE, PEDRO waved off the captains who followed him and walked with Isabella to the meager shade of a snaggled holm oak. Aromatic gum-rockrose covered the nearby hills, blooms nearly depleted in the summer heat, but enough left that they could make into tea for the dozen men complaining of stomachache and worse. Further down the valley floor, the alder, willow, and ash trees offered more shade. But the two of them stayed under that one ragged holm oak, a shout away from Pedro's followers. Pedro motioned for her to sit under the oak and then sat beside her, stretching out his legs.

"Are you furious with me?" Pedro tilted his head to her, more than curious. "Like when we first met?"

"No, I'm overcome with joy, Monsenyor."

"Tomás had a new wife. Who I forced him to marry," Pedro said. "To preserve lands from Simon de Montfort."

"I know. And she has a child." She threw up her arms the way Pèire Leteric did whenever surrendering to the precarious ways of heaven. "Monsenyor, remember how I was once married to two men, one we thought was dead? All I care is that Tomás is alive."

"He was consumed with grief, believing you dead. Where were you, ma dòmna?"

"A woman found me, one of the many people Simon de Montfort has chased into the hills. Rubea of Castel-St-Jean. Do you know her?"

Pedro clenched his fist, muscles knotting along his jaw. His breath rasped. "I knew her husband. He held that castle for my father and grandfather." Unclenching his fist. "I never met his wife."

"Widow. When I met her, when she rescued me, she lived in a cave deep in the forest. She'd swept out the bones left by wolves."

"Why there? Why didn't you seek Chrétien in Toulouse?"

"I was too ill to travel for a long time. And remember why we left the Toulousain? The Church has already tried twice to condemn me as a heretic. I need to avoid Simon's predators. When the Crux Lunata murdered my rescuers, I took refuge in the monastery at St-Pere de Selva."

"They have no daughter house." Pedro's blue eyes pierced for truth, like when they'd first met in the heat and dust outside of Minerve and she'd sold him Valerós knights as mercenaries. "You played the same trick as when I mistook you for the Master of Valerós. Traveling in a man's garb?" He wagged a finger.

Isabella ignored the scolding. "I've lived through strange times, Monsenyor."

"Why did you come here, ma dòmna? You could have sent a message with Chrétien. Especially since the evidence you brought," he made a gesture of despair, "means little unless I personally carry it to the pope."

"Can you give it to a bishop you trust?"

He laughed, but didn't answer.

"Monsenyor, Chrétien met your wife María in Narbonne. Did you know she's gone to Rome to seek a divorce?"

"Mercé Dèu!" Pedro hissed in horror. "I hate to think of the lies she intends to tell."

"You persist in begging God's mercy, Monsenyor. As if we could be sure of His help."

"Yes, I do."

"I have a gift for you." Isabella slipped the painted icon from inside her jerkin, close to her heart. "It was made by one of the women who healed me. I want to pass it on to the next man beset by devils."

He examined the crude painting of St-Maria in flames of glory, holding the chalice with which she caught the Savior's blood.

Isabella said, "Her name was Blanca. She made images of the Holy Mother so that when you feel darkness all around, you can touch these flames to light your way."

"St-Maria? On fire? I thought the Good Christians didn't believe in saints."

"We don't. They don't."

Pedro blinked, catching that slip. "Have they called you heretic so often that you joined them?"

She stroked the stone in his hand.

"She was the strange daughter of a seigneur's widow. Simon's heretic hunters hounded them from their homes. She lived in a cave, its walls covered with paintings like that."

"From the early people in these lands?"

"No. Blanca painted endlessly. A priest who saw the paintings at her mother's domus was shocked to see St-Maria drawn larger than Our Savior. He declared the family hereticated and harassed them into the mountains."

"It happens. That's why I sent Master Guillem home to tend to affairs at Valerós." He closed his hands around the icon. "God has been kind to me. And I'm happy that He saved you. Thank you. I shall cherish it."

"Can you save the south from this terror, Monsenyor?"

"*Ai, òc*, ma dòmna—"

Before Pedro could answer, one of his captains called to him.

"Later, ma dòmna. We shall talk more." Pedro nodded to her and then returned to his people.

■

After morning chores, having slept better than she had for a year, the scribe Miró, who used to be Vidal, stood for mass with the entire camp. The priests scattered in a ring around the camp, singing the ritual words simultaneously, so that where any man stood, he heard one thread clearly along with the echo of others to either side.

Because she needed to avoid most of those priests, Isabella lingered at an edge, away from her friends, that cotton rag tied around her face to block the sun and sand.

Eyes closed, swaying from standing so long in the sun, she listened to ten thousand men breathe together in prayer, louder than when she'd heard French invaders pray together on the plateau outside Minerve. Here on the edge of the crowd, Isabella listened to the plains, as she had on the ride across La Mancha. In the distance, hobbled horses nickered, happy for the days of rest granted the men. She listened, hoping to hear the wind from the mountain over the muttered prayers.

After the priests lifted the Host to heaven, Isabella slipped off to an oak grove, away from the throng. She sat under the dappled oak canopy, the red glow of the sun shining through. She formed his name in silence, a habit she struggled to break at St-Pere.

Tomás.

Not in purgatory. Instead, he walked in the orchards and pastures on the other side of those mountains.

Here in camp, everyone wiped sweat and dirt from their eyes with balled fists, so they all looked hollow-eyed in spite of deep sunburn. With dirt always hanging in the air, many men did as Isabella and tied strips of linen over their mouths and noses to keep from breathing and swallowing dust every moment. Isabella had begged Durán for a clean strip of linen, since they both knew one of his shirts was in shreds from hand-to-hand practice. She wrapped it over her mouth and nose.

At work again in the scribes' open-air pavilion, she and Felip breathed dust kicked up by the coveys of priests in chainmail that passed by every few heartbeats. She glanced up whenever a knot of warrior-priests paused in front of the pavilion. Not a single familiar face passed, certainly no one from St-Pere. None stopped to stare at Miró, the itinerant scribe from the Toulousain employed by the seigneur of Xirgú.

She and Felip recorded captains' reports about how men proved their valor as the united armies of Castile, Léon, and Aragón together with other knights of Christendom worked to conquer Piedrabuena, Benavente, and Al-Arcos. The two scribes chose poignant words to describe the valorous conquests of mighty cities, not goat-herders' compounds with penetrable stone walls atop modest hills.

The kings and their captains claimed the army was made up of fifty thousand men. Felip had walked with Isabella early in the morning to a rise near the camp. They tried to count.

"I guess ten thousand," she said.

Felip said, "Maybe fifteen thousand."

"If you count the laundry women, times ten," Isabella said.

Back at work, Felip wrote *Juliol VI*, and then recorded the fantastical numbers of men that the captains reported. While Felip recorded troop reports, Isabella recorded men's reports of apparitions of saints before and during the battle. Or while standing guard when they camped at night on the journey across La Mancha.

"I hate wasting good ink on these stories," Isabella said to Felip when they were alone. "These daydreams clutter the story of the army's real actions."

"You don't believe in the appearance of saints?" Felip set aside his pen, querying her in the friendly way they used to talk in the cold days over last winter.

"These saints seem to appear when it's most convenient to the witness. It seems to be popular on this journey, since the locals aren't selling splinters of the True Cross. Or table scraps from Our Lord's Last Supper."

Buried in his work, Felip said, "You think it's f–foolish that I carried away Lorenç's c–cup."

"No. You kept others from snatching it up."

A man in Castilian armor stood before them, fingering a scrap of metal that flashed in the midday sunlight.

"I'm sent by Father Anselm to tell my story," the man said. "I have been blessed by an apparition."

"Please sit here, señor." Isabella indicated a stool beside the work table. She understood most Castellano dialects, but couldn't express herself as well. This promised to be an interview riven with misunderstanding. "My name is Miró. I will write your story."

The man cocked his head, listening. He wasn't as tall as she was, perhaps the height of her grandfather, but he was a robust man, used to the saddle. He hadn't shaven for a month, and his hair, unwashed for many days had coiled into knotted locks. When he sat down, he began twisting one of those locks, while the other hand worked that piece of metal, a silver cross, over and under his knuckles in a wave of worry.

"Shall we begin?" She had a clean parchment and fresh quill, ready to write his story.

He again tipped his head, listening, like one trying to identify the call of a bird in the early morning. "You are from the mountains? Or near the sea?"

"I've lived many places," she said. "When I was in my cradle, my mother sang in Catalan. Tell me your story."

He didn't wait for her prompting questions, didn't even say his name, but began telling his story like a man in a trance. No inflection for excitement, no raised or lowered voice to express amazement. Just staring at the dirt in front of him, and repeating a story he must have told to several priests.

"St-Martín stood beside me at the blackest moment, when Satan's dark angels whispered and called me to follow them. The air smelled of charred wood and burned meat. Fires smoldered all around, the smoke acrid, so that every breath filled my body with the foul winds of perdition. Flies buzzed in the heat. I brushed them away from my face, and they crawled on the backs of my hands. I wanted to run away, but everything I'd learned at the hands of my father and uncles held me in place, though this was a horror they had never endured."

He spoke so slowly that Isabella kept up easily while writing each word. He paused, still studying the gravel.

"At what place?" Isabella prompted, having left that line to be filled near the top of her parchment.

The man looked up, blinking in surprise, as if the greatest simpleton in the world questioned him "Malagón, of course."

"St-Martín appeared to you?"

"He stood beside me, making it suddenly cool amid all that heat." The man began again, twisting a lock of hair, twirling that silver cross knuckle to knuckle, staring at the bare ground. "He whispered my name and handed me his cloak, the half he cut for the poor man. 'Cover the woman,' he said to me. I knew it was St-Martín when he spoke. I laid the cloak down to cover that poor woman who had been…"

The man stopped. Tears ran down his bristly, sunburned face. He dropped one lock and began twisting another.

Isabella ceased writing, not wanting to prompt him. Beside her, Felip also stopped his work, listening to the man who had met St-Martín.

"The woman had been killed." The Castilian resumed his story. "St-Martín said, 'She is with God,' but I could not tell whether she was Christian or another sort of believer in the God of Abraham." He stared off again for several heartbeats. "Then, as I passed through that place of death and perdition, I came to the body of another woman. St-Martín again gave me half his cloak to cover her, saying once more, 'She is with God.' And so, I did as he asked. Until I came to the church in that town. I stood with him for a long time before the altar, because he loved me more than my brother ever did. His golden armor shone in the darkness, and he comforted me. And then other men came, and they took me out into the midday sun, where I couldn't see the saint. And they gave me water."

"Did you tell your story then?" Isabella asked.

The man shook his head. "Later, Father Anselm said a mass, and after that he made me tell my story. Then he made me tell it to other priests."

"Tell me, *mi amigo*." Isabella spoke wretched Castellano.

"I want to do as St-Martín did. I want to bring the infidels to true belief. But without the sword."

He ceased his rhythmic fidgeting, crossing both hands before him. The story seemed to be done.

"What is your name?" Isabella asked, prepared to write it at the top, where she had already written *As told to Father Anselm of Valerós and the scribe Miró at Al-Arcos*.

"Diego Lopez de Haro, the second of that name, after my father."

The man who led one of Alfonso's armies. Who was said to be Sebastián's mentor.

"Will you walk with me, señor?" Isabella laid aside her pen. She touched him gently on the shoulder. "Let's talk in the shade of the trees."

He rose and walked silently by her side, away from the others.

"You have no reason to hear me." She struggled with the Castellano tongue. "But I too have walked among the angels of death. I've heard the cries of the dead, both saved and damned, calling out in terror, begging mercy."

Diego stopped beside her, a river of tears falling unchecked. "I can't stop their voices. I see that woman's face…"

Isabella grasped his shoulders, hoping she imitated how Father Anselm must have tried to offer comfort. Then she stepped back to reach into her jerkin.

"In the darkest caves of despair, I found this." She held out the silver-encrusted saint's finger, which she'd taken from Rubea's cave. When he didn't reach for it, she placed it in his palm, then lifted his other hand so that he traced the silver etching.

He rubbed at it for several moments, then looked up. "Why are you offering me comfort?"

"My hopes are now come true, greater than anything I could have asked God in prayer. It's your turn."

"But why?"

"Because you and I must still live among men. Perhaps this will help you do the work you are called to."

They walked back to camp together.

"*Adios*, señor scribe," he said when they reached the scribes' pavilion. He placed that silver cross he'd been twirling in her hand. "Perhaps it's your turn to hold this."

·

"I've brought a letter for you, ma dòmna."

Pedro's voice pulled her back from daydreams. She rose from her scribe's work and offered him a proper greeting. Behind him was that rugged row of mountains the army couldn't penetrate, the Despeñaperros.

He handed her a folded scrap of parchment, where she read scratched Latin in heartbreakingly familiar bad handwriting.

> 'X fold less than told.
> Farmers go home to their fold.
> Rex promises lands of old.
> Clans prefer their homes, not gold.'

"Who is Rex? You?"

"Alfonso of Castile. He's my partner in this endeavor for peace." Pedro glanced about, checking whether anyone might overhear. "Tomás says the caliph's army is much smaller than claimed, and the locals are deserting."

"What about the clans and gold?"

"Alfonso promised several Mozarab leaders their old lands if they ally with him." Pedro reached for the message. Isabella handed it back, though she wanted to keep it, because Tomás had touched it. "Ma dòmna, I don't know how safe he is. A week ago, the caliph killed several of Alfonso's Mozarab agents. And then launched a search for more spies."

"Monsenyor, why did Tomás go into Andalusia? This adventure," she pointed to the mass of tents, "was our destination last year. Tomás and Sebastián wanted to march with you."

"Tomás was diminished without you." Again, the piercing blue eyes. "He needed to be out in the world."

"Ai, òc. Sebastián came on this expedition alone, leading an army out in the wilderness."

"As he was raised to do. But Father Anselm is with him."

"And that Castilian general you left him with? Diego? I wrote the story of his apparition. He is seriously disturbed."

Pedro tapped the bonfraire scar on her wrist. "You have every reason to be proud of Sebastián. But I didn't come to argue how the world was arranged while we thought you dead. I came to ask you to perform a service."

"Before or after you rescue my husband?"

"I pray for his return. The same as you do."

"I no longer pray to God for anything." When Pedro blinked, startled, she added, "I pray. I just don't ask anything in return. What do you want from me?"

"My own rescue. From those who seek my destruction."

"It's why I came all this way."

"After this expedition completes the last battle—"

"— and after we find Tomás."

He continued. "The first message to the pope must come from me. Not Alfonso or the other kings."

"What can I, your favorite heretic, do for you?"

"My relays are in place. Fresh horses are ready. Two ships of mine rest in Valencia harbor. Four parties of the fastest riders, each taking different roads, will carry the story to Valencia as soon as the outcome of the battle is known. I need the best riders from Valerós."

"Did you ask Sebastián for men from his ranks, Monsenyor?"

"I know the best riders. Sebastián. Chrétien. You. And you three have the skill to travel while avoiding the kings' roads."

"After the battle, I'll be searching for Tomás."

"For the few days it takes you to ride the first leg to Cuenca, I'll do everything to find him. Will you please accept this task?"

"Thank you for pretending I have a choice. It's two years since I rendered our castles and our services. I must do as you ask."

"You are now not so mercenary as when we first bargained?" Pedro's smile twisted into that familiar warm, wry grimace.

"I cannot say no to you. However, they say that the army must give up and go home within days. Is it true?"

"There's still hope." A twitch of a smile. "I gambled everything on this quest. And if Innocent doesn't hear directly from me what this gamble won for Christendom, then it will be many long seasons of torts in Church courts to reclaim land in Toulouse and nearby counties."

"And skirmishes with Simon to protect widows from his pyres? You know he'll light new fires as soon as Innocent lifts the ban on fighting. It is as the count of Foix claims. The seigneurs of the south need you to lead."

"I thought all your noble southern seigneurs abjure the idea of kings." Pedro grinned, repeating the argument they'd had outside Minerve. "Does not every lord in Toulouse and Narbonne and Foix insist that his independence is God given?"

"Whether people know it yet, Simon leaves us with few choices. That's why I rendered Valerós castles, so you'd protect us. Praying doesn't seem to be sufficient."

"I intend to keep the promises I made to you and to Tomás."

Beyond Pedro's shoulder she spied a pair of griffon vultures in the dusty blue sky. The pair floated, white-headed, their yellow bills visible in the sun, broad wings soaring high above the army camp, which was ripe for scavenging. Pedro followed where she pointed.

She said, "The griffon lives as long as many men, they say. Even over forty years."

"Pray God grants us lives at least as long as His vultures."

Her eyes strayed up the mountainside where Pyrenean oak and stone pine grew, almost like at home. At Valerós.

18

Communion

THAT MORNING'S MASS WAS PRIVATE, with only scribes and priests. Since Felip remained over-excited about scribing at the king's command, he spent more time watching the clerk Doménec than attending to the bishop who said mass for them. And Felip watched rather than listened, because the periodic thunder in his ears still caused words to boom and fade no matter how closely he tried to attend.

Doménec seemed more like Felip than any other man he'd met, both of them dedicated to a life of letters and happily serving a remarkable king. Doménec bent over his prayers, reminding Felip of how transcendent he'd been through each day's litanies when he first began life at St-Pere monastery. Doménec, a fine-looking man, bowed to God, his eyes not darting around. A man made for life in service to God and Church in exactly the way Felip had failed. The silly aspersions Chrétien cast on that clerk made no sense. Doménec raised his eyes to heaven when the Host was raised, tears streaming down his cheeks, glistening in the early morning summer light.

Felip too glanced up at heaven, but all he saw was a griffon vulture teetering high above. No heavenly hosts. If there was any way that he moved that seemed as holy as Doménec, it was because Felip still felt stabs of pain from the lightning. He shrugged away the hurt, remembering that moment for being as close as he'd ever come to God. In this camp, even amid this flock of priests, God didn't feel so near.

The priests scattered to their daily chores, blessing the stinking crowd of Christian soldiers who filled the camp, stretching as far as a man could see amid all the dust raised.

The sight of Doménec's devotion sent Felip to his scribe's desk in the pavilion, intent on showing his own dedication to the mission with which Pedro had entrusted him. The task held so many pleasures, including once more working beside his friend Vidal, now called Miró.

"It's nice when a servant brings ink and parchment the moment you ask for it," Isabella said. They kept busy in the scribes' pavilion, in a corner away from Alfonso's priests and scribes. "No pounding oak apples and grinding minerals. No scraping and stretching hides."

"I should not be enjoying this as much as I do." Felip felt more like himself than he had since entering the St-Pere monastery. "Poor Durán has to worry about the sufficiency of beans and water for Xirgú and Montcava men. While we j–just...."

"We just ink our pens," Isabella said. However, she glanced up whenever another drove of armored priests passed by, undoubtedly checking for familiar faces. It made Felip look too, so he remained distracted.

Then a prancing horse stamped near the pavilion. It was Colomb on his big black gelding, its face hooded in Beaurain blue with a field of golden stars.

"Off! Before I chuck you down!"

A woman slipped off Colomb's horse, then sprawled, ducking in fear of the horse, though Felip knew from experience that Colomb always had perfect control of his horses.

The woman crouched in the dust and faced them.

"Serena Taresa!" Felip cried her name in shock. "Whatever are you doing here?"

Colomb said, "You, Xirgú, are to care for this chit we found in the baggage train. Pedro d'Aragón commands it."

He tossed a bundle at Felip. Isabella, being closer, went to help Serena to her feet. Serena threw off Isabella's hold on her arm and then shook her skirts, her loose hair whipping in Isabella's face.

"I'm fine," she hissed.

"Peace," Isabella said in Catalan. "You are safe here."

Colomb spoke only to Felip. "Are you man enough to restore Xirgú honor? Can you do right by this woman?"

Felip felt the hairs stand on his arms and neck, bristling like the spines on a hedgehog. "I am Xirgú. I hold my family's honor."

"Then fix what your brother tried to ruin." Colomb flicked his flywhisk in Isabella's direction. "Pedro *El Rey* says you are called Miró of Toulouse."

Isabella glanced up, standing closer to his huge horse than Felip ever dared. She nodded.

"Like a changeling!" Colomb exclaimed. "Who'd believe that anyone in God's creation could cut Valerós out of the heart of a man?" Colomb drew out the last word, sneering. "Even with the sharpest knife?"

Colomb nudged his horse, easing away from the pavilion, and disappearing before either Isabella or Felip might ask questions.

Serena Taresa stood smiling at Felip, like how she used to flirt on feast days. "We must indeed be guided by angels. Here's the friend I'd most want to see in the world."

"What are you doing here, Serena?" Felip repeated the question, flummoxed.

"Laundry, like most women in camp. But now Pedro *El Rey* says I must do what you tell me."

"I am amazed," Felip said. "How did you come here?"

Isabella watched them, so she must have seen the brazen way Serena Taresa moved toward Felip. His thoughts in disorder, Felip hoped Isabella guessed that this was the woman he'd spoken of when they shared secrets at St-Pere.

Serena said, "I ran away from Matheus. He was cruel and crude to me. What are you doing here?"

"I left the monastery to join the crusade."

"Then we're both runaways." She stepped closer. Her breasts rose and fell under the rumpled shroud of a tunic that she wore. "I wish you'd never gone away. You should have married me, not Matheus."

"You m–married Matheus?" Felip stepped back, shocked, as if lightning struck again.

"No, *renrén*. I ran away and joined the women from Girona who followed the army."

"Serena! How your family must worry!"

"My uncle is all that's left, and he's not himself. That's why Matheus got our land so easily. Matheus doesn't want me, just my father's land." She touched Felip's hand. "Why did your brother send you away? I missed you so, *mon amic*."

Felip glanced at Isabella, who watched them intently. "I wanted to go. At first. But a monk's life wasn't for me. I left to come here."

"Isn't it wonderful?" She traced the fingers of Felip's hand. "Pedro d'Aragón brought two friends together, guided by angels."

If God granted Felip wit, it emptied itself when Serena Taresa stood so close.

Isabella spoke, uninvited. "Pedro is not God's agent. He just needs to protect his seigneurs. What does he want Felip to do?"

"It's so humiliating," Serena said, her chin in the air. "Colomb saw me in the laundry camp and dragged me to the king of Aragón, who scolded me for risking my family's honor."

"I'm s–sorry, Serena, but the king is right."

She didn't listen. "I told him that my uncle sold me into slavery, but Colomb just laughed at me."

"How awful for you," Isabella said.

"Then Pedro told Colomb to bring me here. He said, 'Xirgú understands honor. He'll marry you.'" Her nostrils flared as if the word disgusted her. "What arrogance! Just because he's king, he can make me marry Matheus."

"Pedro meant Felip," Isabella said. "Felip understands honor."

"*Ai.*" Serena Taresa stopped, still as a post, so surprised that her mouth remained open for a moment in her pretty way.

"And Pedro wants women of the south married," Isabella said, "so Simon de Montfort and the French invaders don't steal their land, like Matheus has tried so hard to do."

"Would you ever marry a man because a king or a lord forced you?" Serena Taresa asked Isabella, though Felip didn't see how she could tell that Isabella was a woman.

Isabella said, "Before Philippe Augustus sent invaders to our land, no. I tried hard to refuse when my grandfather cautioned me to marry. He wanted me to protect my lands from French crusaders."

"And now?" Serena Taresa asked Isabella again, which Felip rather resented.

"Now we need every strategy that Pedro and his allies can muster. If I were you," Isabella pointed at Serena Taresa, which seemed rude, "I'd thank God it's Felip that Pedro chose as your protector."

"I don't need a protector." Serena Taresa had her hands on her hips, the same as when she used to argue over games at home. Her obstinate posture provoked Felip more than what she said.

"Running away with the laundry women, Serena Taresa?" That bothered him most. His mind couldn't yet ponder Pedro's command.

"Matheus gave my land to the Church to pay for this crusade," she said. "Therefore, I too should receive remission of my sins and passage to heaven. Washing soldiers' linen is small penance." Serena whispered, "Don't you think I'm as brave as a knight, coming on crusade alone?"

Before Felip could answer, another visitor arrived at the pavilion.

"Miró? I'm seeking a scribe from Toulouse." A voice carried from beyond a bevy of passing priests.

Isabella, barely protecting the ink from spilling and destroying her work, rose and ran from the pavilion. "Father Anselm?"

"It is you." The man grasped her hands the way soldiers greet each other. "I didn't see you when Chrétien and the others arrived. Colomb didn't tell me you were in that little army. But now, well, come the next mass, I shall shout that I do indeed believe in the resurrection of the body."

Isabella put a finger to her lips. "Best to avoid pious jests."

The priest laughed. It was that secular priest, the Norman who had greeted Colomb as an old friend when they arrived in camp. He wore a simple linen tabard over chainmail. "Where have you been? And why must I call you Miró?"

"It's a long story."

"But I hear that you were indeed saved by the grace of God."

She hesitated. "Some might tell it that way. My escape and rescue were harder than I ever understood 'grace' to be."

While they chatted, seeming to forget the rest of the world for a moment, Serena Taresa and Felip regarded each other. She reached out and took his hand in hers, which left a streak of ink from Felip's finger along her palm.

"You've marked me now," Serena Taresa whispered. "I'm yours. Pedro says so."

"Who'd believe it?" Felip blurted.

"Òc, who'd believe it?"

The priest had his arm on Isabella's shoulder, as if she were another soldier. "Come break bread with me. In the Valerós camp, where we can talk. Colomb managed to find better victuals than we've had for weeks."

"Colomb is a friend of yours?" Isabella hesitated.

"We rode together in the Outremer. He tells me that you mistook him for an enemy."

"He's Crux Lunata," she said. "We thought Maria of Montpelhièr might have hired him to be Pedro's assassin."

"Impossible. All Colomb cares about is his brother Hugues's legacy. From his stories, I believe Colomb enjoyed riding here with..." The priest paused and glanced over at Felip, where Serena Taresa stayed close by. "With your little army."

The priest steered Isabella toward the path, but she stopped him. "Wait!" She pointed to Serena Taresa and Felip. "Pedro has commanded that these two should be married. Can you do that?"

"W–what, now?" Felip had been busy staring at Serena Taresa. Bees buzzed in his hands, his toes, his nose. Her eyes flashed in a glance toward the priest.

Isabella held out her empty hands, looking like a shepherd surrendering to the fate of heaven. "Your king commanded."

Her priest-friend examined Felip and Serena Taresa closely for the first time, having been so intent in conversation with Isabella. "Taresa from Toledo?"

"Serena Péletier," Felip said, "from Girona."

"Who'd believe it?" The priest's brow wrinkled, quizzical. "We shall need one more witness."

•

It happened so fast, Felip's heart barely kept up. Doménec came with a written command from Pedro and agreed to be the other witness.

207

"The master of Xirgú is of age." Father Anselm studied the message, which was Pedro's command that Felip de Xirgú take legal charge of Serena Taresa. "The bond this woman's guardian signed promises her to the seigneur of Xirgú."

The priest went on to ask for the couple's confession. "Confess, so that you might enter marriage with all sins absolved."

Serena Taresa sat with the priest on the far side of the scribes' pavilion, but she didn't lower her voice, so both Isabella and Felip heard what she confessed.

"I have been willful with my superiors. At times, I fell into the habits of those with whom I worked, taking the Lord's name in vain and speaking oaths."

Felip had deep concerns about what to say to a priest, since Isabella—Miró—had warned him on more than one occasion to temper his confessions. Yet this priest seemed to be Isabella's trusted friend. When Felip's turn came, he sat before the priest, hands in supplication.

"I departed in haste from the house of God," Felip said, "without awaiting a b–benediction, because I lusted in my heart both day and night. I longed too much for the world and to serve God on this crusade."

The priest prompted for more, but didn't sound censorious. "You disobeyed your abbot?"

"No." Felip once more lied in confession. "My abbot released me. He had absolved me already of sins of both thought and deed. But I didn't wait for the formal leave-taking."

"And since that absolution?" the priest prompted.

Felip hesitated. He believed it likely that God saw how he'd sinned every moment of each night and day. How to describe that so a priest might understand? "I was jealous of other men, for being knights, for understanding the ways of war better than I. On occasion, I lusted after women, including another man's wife."

"Did you act on your lust?" The priest asked mildly.

"Never. And I didn't know she was married." Felip also didn't know Isabella was a woman then. "I bring a pure body to this marriage, as the temple of God."

The priest accepted Felip's claim that he had nothing else to confess and so absolved his sins. Privately Felip promised God that he'd confess all the rest another day.

"Is all well under heaven?" Felip whispered in Serena's ear as they waited for the priest. He unstitched a fold in his gambeson to retrieve silver, since a wedding requires thirteen coins, and all his wealth was otherwise out of reach. "You ran away so you didn't have to marry. Now you're with Xirgú again."

"You aren't your brother," Serena whispered back. "Just promise not to hurt me or make me do evil."

Then they stood before Father Anselm and made promises, the kind Felip had never dreamed he'd do in this life. Seized with joy, Felip repeated what the priest insisted they say. After the couple rose from beneath the pall—Felip's gambeson—the priest declared them married in the sight of God and Man.

Then they signed the contract of marriage, which Isabella had been writing while Felip and Serena Taresa were confessing and making vows. Felip wrote his name more carefully than ever in this life, signing as seigneur of Xirgú.

Doménec signed as witness. The priest bent his head to study the contract and then asked for a quill and signed his own name and added all the traditional details.

> Done in the field before the castle at Al-Arcos, newly joined with Christendom under the kings of Castile and Aragón. Made and affirmed by Felip of Xirgú, son of Sibilia of Narbonne, and Serena Péletier, daughter of Raimunda of Girona. Consented by Pedro of Lérida, Xirgú's seigneur. Written by the hand of Anselm the priest on the eve before the Christian armies rescue the fortress called El Castillo del Ferral from the Saracens, the eleventh of July, in the sixteenth year of the reign of Pedro II, King by the Grace of God of Aragón.

"What happens next?" The priest seemed curious.

"J–j–just…"

Felip's heart beat so hard, the ceaseless noise in his head loud as a drum, that he didn't know the question wasn't for him until Doménec answered.

"Part of the force will take Castro Ferral tomorrow."

"Not the whole army?" Father Anselm asked.

"Too small for that," Doménec said. "There's barely enough land for a base. It will take a miracle for the army to cross the mountains."

The priest turned grim. "And then we go home?"

"That's what most say, those who know." Doménec shrugged. "No food. Unhappy men. No way over the mountains that doesn't lead straight into the caliph's two hundred thousand men."

Serena Taresa pressed against Felip. Warm. Soft. She whispered, but Felip couldn't make out her words over the pounding in his ears and the thumping of his heart.

"What next?" Felip whispered. "We need to find a place for you to be safe."

Doménec's voice carried back. "The kings have now accomplished the best that can be hoped for. See the sheer face of the mountains? There's no path over. It's an impenetrable wall. We're trapped by land and logistics. No glory for anyone."

"We craved so much more," Father Anselm said.

"We wanted a miracle, but God has not blessed us with either an apparition or a rescue." Doménec departed with Isabella and her priest-friend.

"I can be happy anywhere." Serena had stopped whispering. "Doesn't the seigneur of Xirgú have his own tent?" She ran a finger down Felip's cheek, stopping at his mouth. "Now that he has his own wife."

"Y–yes, I do." At that moment, Felip found the camp to be the happiest, most comfortable place he'd ever been in this life. He just had to evict the scribe Miró and the camp-boy Fortuno from his tent.

.

"You've brought a woman here? What work of evil is this?"

The little priest who accosted them seemed so blind, Felip wasn't sure how he identified Serena Taresa as a woman. Especially since there were plenty of priests around, so that he can't have identified her ragged skirts as different from a cassock.

"This is my wife." Felip added an honorific to salve the priest's feelings. "Monsenyor." Though Felip didn't know whether this priest merited any honorific at all. That encounter reminded him how much he did not like to be scolded and judged by some priest so ancient he couldn't possibly remember what it's like to be strong and able to run in the sunshine.

Felip and the little priest argued about the appropriateness, and then he agreed to move his tent out of the conclave of priests, which meant that his wedding night was delayed by the need to strike a tent, gather his pack and Serena's, and traipse across the way in the dark, to pitch a shelter amid the Xirgú men.

Who weren't ready to sleep and found great joy in toasting the couple and jesting about their lord's new wife and what Felip was next to undertake.

Serena, good-natured as ever, accepted the toasts and insisted that she and he must sing with the men, the way they would if they were in the Xirgú feast hall back in Girona, in their old world, now far away. At last they lay beside each other in Felip's tent, yet the calls and jests pursued them long into the night until the captains demanded peace and silence. Waiting for the camp to go quiet, exhausted in the midst of that noise and joy, Felip drifted to sleep and was immediately lost in a dream, that he was back at St-Pere, reading a gorgeous manuscript, murmuring the Latin words aloud as he ran a finger over the ornate leafing on the opening initial, imagining how Vidal's hand formed those letters, stroking the soft goatskin vellum.

"'Who shall feast and abound with delights as I do?'"

Felip jerked awake, his hand on the soft skin of his new wife's thigh. She cupped her hand over his.

"Shh." She whispered in Felip's ear, tickling the little hairs and making him shiver. "We have angels to protect us."

The whole while that Serena chattered, perhaps as nervous as Felip felt, she had one hand up his jerkin, the other slowly untying his linen undershirt.

"Do you believe that?" Felip ventured to nibble at her ear, getting used to this idea that she belonged to him, that this was not another of the lonely dreams he'd clung to in that cold monastery.

"Aren't I a testament to the power of heaven?" she murmured, "I've come so far under the protection of angels. Where have you come to?"

They were a world away from that cold, lonely monk's cell in St-Pere, or from Felip's Girona bedroom, where he hid in fear of his brother. He had so much he wished he could tell her. That he lived in a world where God spoke in a flash of lightning. Where the air was hot and heavy, pressing at his chest. How he heard echoes of God's thunder in his ears, but he also heard wind from the mountains stirring in the tops of nearby stone pines. That while he lay beside the other half of his soul, the heavy air that whispered in the pines also carried the sighs and groans of tens of thousands of men, each suffering a shared hardship, but also sighing as a massive prayer to God, who is a mighty God, for whom men choose to suffer hunger and deprivation while seeking the glory of heaven.

But he couldn't tell her about that. She breathed sighs on his neck, then kissed him in a deeper way than he'd ever dreamed. Each breath came hot, comforting, provoking, beyond what he imagined.

"*Eu vos amor.*" He whispered it, not sure where he'd ever heard the words, but he spoke them with the same silent, stunned thunder that deafened him when lightning struck that iron cross.

She stroked his brow, then the ridges of his ears. The same way that the wings of an angel might tickle your shadow in the midday sun. He shivered.

He couldn't say the rest, how his heart overflowed, a rippling stream at spring flood, running into a new valley, never to return to old ways.

PART FOUR
Las Navas de Tolosa

ALL BLESSINGS UPON YOU, MY DEAREST WIVES.

I am a prisoner, and I fear all is lost.

I am held here at Al-Arcos and it is just before the new moon. Yet I go unnoticed among my captors, and I have procured this pen and this rag of scraped parchment, which are my sole comforts. And I have hope that the guards between where I am held and where you live in peace are so lax that I shall find a messenger to bear this tale to you.

Abu Jossep commanded his army to march from Baeza, and I accompanied his court with great joy. Then along the way, the general fell ill and hesitated once more. While the general dithered, ever more ill, the vizier Rashid al-Aziz took command. The parade drums beating, our hearts soared as the army began to march forward, to join the caliph in Jaén.

At this joyous news, I was swept up with Abu Jossep's wife's convoy and her determination to join the caliph ahead of the full army. We rode hard, harder than I've known in this life, and late at night camped in the fringes of the mercenaries who will first greet the infidels if they march from the frontier over the road into Al-Andalus.

I had barely laid my head down, my blanket thrown over my saddle, when we were roused, cautioned to silence, and then urged to mount and ride again. In the dark, I asked how long until we might sleep.

And found that I rode with an armed band of Rodriquez clans-men, traveling through the pass to Al-Arcos to join the king of Castile. I could not turn back in the dark. Come dawn, I could not undertake the ride home alone.

At daylight, you might guess the first thing I found when I took off my *jubba*. A long hair on my coat. Yes, a sign that I have been bewitched.

Here I am, miscast into the small force that guards Ríma de Rodriquez, who calls herself a Visigoth queen and consorts with infidel priests. Entirely by accident I am alone in a strange and hostile world, with only Allah to guide me.

Do not think I have deserted you. Do not give credence to any report that I have betrayed the caliph. I am a prisoner seeking a way to come home to you.

— Ibn Jafar, The Poet
From the frontier,
serving Dar al-Islam in captivity,
two days before the new moon in midsummer

19

Penance

Tomás in the Despeñaperros,
July 14, the day before the new moon

"I'M SORRY TO LEAVE MY burro behind. We have only Al-Malik, the king, to carry us away."

Qasim was the first to break the silence. Tomás leaned heavily on both boys while they hurried to where the Magnificent One had tethered the horse. Qasim tied bundles of food and water onto the horse. Tomás strained to move from where Qasim had propped him, but his muscles refused any command.

"You've been poisoned, Father," Yusuf said. "Ríma gave you the same potion that killed Abu Jossep."

"We need more water," Qasim said. "More food. But this is as much as I could stash."

"You did well, *fadrin*," Tomás said. "Let's go to Baeza. There's no other way out of this valley without embracing the caliph's army."

"We go over," Qasim said.

"Over what?"

"The Despeñaperros," Yusuf said. "To join Pedro's army."

"There's no road."

"Not true," Yusuf said. "Qasim met two shepherd boys the first night here."

"It's as you taught me, master. A clever boy finds all ways out. Just as you said."

Tomás refused when Qasim insisted that he mount the horse. "I'm too ill to travel. You two go find Pedro's men. Tell them what you know."

Yusuf shook his head. "Not without you."

215

"I can hide for a while. I'll make my way later and join you again in Barcelona."

"No," Yusuf said. "We stay together."

Tomás was sick again, so sick that his ribs felt bruised from vomiting. It took a moment before he could argue again. "I've ridden in a dozen campaigns. Please listen to my wisdom."

"Why?" Yusuf said. "You didn't listen when I told you Ríma was dangerous. You let that woman defeat you."

Tomás's arguments seemed to be weakened by fever. "I want you to be safe, *fadrin*. Go now with Qasim."

"No, Father. If I were ill and had to stay, what would you do?"

"For the sake of what I promised Pedro, I'd go find him."

"I think not. We'll do what you would."

"Master," Qasim said, "both greater and younger, we stay together. Mount now, please."

.

Tomás in the mountain pass
July 14

Tomás sipped at water, of which they had too little, though he longed for more under the burning intensity of the sun. They'd started at midday, and by late afternoon, he felt that he'd ridden a thousand leagues. Yusuf and Qasim took turns riding behind him while the other boy walked. They stopped frequently for Tomás, who needed the greatest possible purge under heaven.

As with the path of righteousness, the track proved narrow and rocky. And steep. A goat might find it difficult to choose the way. Sheep would need a shepherd. Myrtle and wild olive trees crowded the path's edge, rock rose crept over the stones, hiding the path. Qasim found markers, though, where his shepherd friends had told him to look, at each point where the trail seemed to die out or forked in too many directions.

"You didn't kill him," Qasim said.

"He looked dead." Yusuf's voice sounded hollow.

"He won't even bleed to death before someone finds him."

Yusuf said, "I killed a man once before."

Through his own haze and pain, Tomás heard battle-shock in his son's voice. Qasim must have heard it, too, because he slipped off from where he rode behind Tomás and walked beside Yusuf.

"Young master, at the next turning, let's rest."

"We must keep moving." The flat notes in Yusuf's voice betrayed his exhaustion. "I did it just before you came to Cairo to fetch me, Father. One of my mother's protectors. He was hurting her. He would have killed her."

Sparrow hawks and kestrels floated on the late-afternoon updrafts from the narrow valley. Rock thrushes hopped in the tumbled stony sides of the trail.

"The servants," Yusuf spoke low, "claimed a *franj* slave did it. And so, another man died too."

For the first time Tomás understood Yusuf's refusal over the past year, never wanting to learn to fight, accepting Sebastián's dagger only after being badgered to take it.

"Let's rest for your father's sake," Qasim said. "We need to get him out of the heat of the sun."

Qasim won that argument.

Not far from the shelter they found, Qasim discovered water. While Al-Malik browsed the undergrowth and rested, the other three huddled in the shade of an overhang. Qasim kept making both Tomás and Yusuf drink. As the sun set, Tomás imagined a breeze stirred.

"We need to be back on the road," Yusuf said. "They must be seeking us."

"I'll pack the horse." Qasim left Tomás lying atop a burnous, still so weak he could barely sit on his own.

Yusuf stretched out beside him. "Boys in my school in Cairo all wanted what they couldn't have. Boys from the city wanted horses. Boys from the country wanted to run free, shoeless. Ugly boys wanted beautiful girls."

"What did you want, *fadrin*?"

"I just wanted to be with my father."

Qasim called them to travel.

"Now I have that. Please don't die, Father."

■

217

Cistus scrub with shriveled, sun-dusted blossoms crowded the narrow trail, which was more a goat path than a road. In the moonless dark, they trusted the horse to pick its way along the ridge through slate and greywacke sandstone.

At one point, where Qasim again found water, the Magnificent One defeated all of Yusuf's arguments, and they agreed to rest until dawn. The two boys huddled beside Tomás on one burnous, the other one covering the three of them. Perhaps the boys slept in spite of Tomás's shivers and tremors. When Al-Malik nickered, just when the black cloak of night began to lift, the boys rose and silently began to fill their water flagons and pack the horse.

Just as the sun broke the horizon, a pair of kestrels soared upward, repeatedly screeching *klee! klee!* On the ledge above where the boys walked, a lynx stared down at them, its black tufted ears thrust forward.

"See," Qasim nudged Yusuf. "The little cat wants to know if we're dinner."

He'd been diverting Yusuf by pointing out every beast and tree, insisting that he knew the names of all creatures. Tomás, still sunk in a haze, listened, wondering if a Valencian city boy did know the trees and animals, or if he just made up names.

"It's just one oak after another," he said to Yusuf, who asked about a particular tree. "Every tree doesn't need its own name."

"Yes, it does," Yusuf said.

"What for? Its mother can't call for it."

"Science," Yusuf said. "If a good medicine could be made from one, you want to know which one. You have to give each kind its own name."

They paused at breakfast for only the moments it took to gnaw at dried bread and dates stolen from the villa's kitchen when Qasim and Yusuf left Rashid in the cellar. At the edge of the matorral on the rocky edge of the Despeñaperros, both boys glanced up at bearded vultures soaring overhead. Their mouths fell open as they gazed upward, the way children do. Then they stood to look over the trail's edge, where one of the vultures dropped a bone. The bird swooped down, its wingspan wider than either boy was tall, and snatched at the dropped bone, tugging and then swallowing marrow.

They trudged through the morning at a constant rhythm. Ride, walk, rest. Ride more. Midday, when Tomás felt as though the sun had dried all water from his body and set his blood to boil, Qasim called that it was time to rest. He'd torn his turban to give Yusuf half the length of green silk, so they both had covers to keep the sun off their heads, with a length left to cover their mouths to keep out the dust. Yusuf had slit one of the linen food bags after their breakfast and wrapped it to cover Tomás's head, who still felt the sun searing his uncovered and sword-cut hands. He couldn't fold them under his shirt, because he needed to grip the saddle, still too dizzy to sit upright on his own. But the continual abrading of the sword-cut kept him from drowsing into sleep.

After they unpacked the horse to rest near a mountain meadow, an ibex darted over the rocks, fleeing. The horse bolted, losing its footing.

When it was over and there were no more tumbling rocks, when Al-Malik was calm again and the boys were catching their breath, Tomás once again vomited nothing but water from an empty aching belly. Qasim determined that the horse was too lame to continue.

"He cannot even follow us on a lead," Qasim said. Tomás caught the quiver of the boy's lip as he delivered that judgment.

"There's water here," Tomás said. "He'll be well."

"And more grass than he's seen on this journey." Yusuf touched Qasim's elbow. "It will be like Paradise for him until we return, after we find Pedro."

That same gesture as when Rashid took Tomás's arm. As when Tomás grasped his friend's elbow and told him one lie after another.

"It's downhill now," Qasim said after leading the lame horse to what he believed was the sweetest grass. "We'll make it to the end of the trail before dark."

They walked on, two boys propping a dazed and poisoned knight on a trek through slate scree, downward, toward the frontier, away from Al-Andalus.

In the greatest heat of the day, in the dusty haze that had settled over Tomás's mind, they rested again. He couldn't make out all of what the boys said between them. Qasim's voice seemed easiest to understand.

"I haven't found a marker since we kissed Al-Malik goodbye."

"But it is to be hoped that you left markers." Yusuf's lighter voice.

"My mother didn't raise a stupid son."

"My mother didn't raise me."

"Alas for you."

·

"He can't walk. And we can't carry him further."

"And there's no water."

The hot air hummed in Tomás's ears. The air shimmered close by as well as on the horizon. Yusuf swabbed Tomás's lips with a damp end of green silk.

"She's a witch. A bad one. She put a spell on him."

"She's less a witch than I am a djinni. She isn't that smart." Yusuf's voice sounded close by. Tomás tried to see. A hand brushed against his head. Yusuf cradled Tomás in his lap.

"Back home, there was a boy I worked with on the docks."

"You loaded ships?"

"*Aiieee,* unloaded. The hardest work I found. But lots to glean if the rats didn't get it first." Qasim sounded farther away. There wasn't enough shade for them to all sit close to each other. "But this boy on the docks, Idris, he said women steal your jizum and take your soul with it, and they capture it in their secret place."

"Nonsense." Yusuf snuffed. "Your own mother would call you a fool for repeating such babble."

"What do you know about those secret places?"

Skree!

A predator's call echoed across the hillside.

"A golden eagle?" Yusuf asked.

"Likely. Is he better at all?"

"No, he's hotter than before. We have to keep him out of the sun. He's burned and parched."

"You are too. Your skin looks like ash."

"Yours looks like cinders scraped from a village oven."

"Yours looks like spent charcoal, bleached in the sun."

"You are powdered bone."

The boys stopped talking. The air hummed. The heat wrapped around Tomás's chest, crept down his lungs, and lay smoldering inside him.

"The cuts on his hands need to be washed and bound."

"We can't spare any for that. It's best if I go find water."

"I'll stay with him. Will you go forward? Or back?"

"Ahead. As the boys on the other side told us. Walk toward the horizon. Keep three hands' breadth to the left of where the sun rises. Watch for the sheep skulls that mark the trail."

"Hope those boys know more than your friends on the docks."

"If you forget I ever said that, I promise to come back for you."

Yusuf laughed.

Tomás, shifting to keep from slipping into a dream, tried to remember if he'd ever heard that laughter before.

.

"I'm carrying the Cid's sword. To unite with the chalice. To slay the false king."

Ríma had Miquel's sword. Which wasn't a hundred years old.

Another angry woman with spells and knives. Carving lunate crosses. One burned and stung on his chest, even though that sweet woman Layla in Almería had covered it with more stitching.

He probed in a fog of memory, whether he'd ever known a woman that mad. Ríma had already rained blood across Jaén province. Off now to find—what? More clannish aunts to shelter her? To help her kill a caliph so she could be queen?

Not caliph. A false king. Alfonso? Who was that king in Léon?

In his dream Tomás wrote a report to Pedro. A mad woman seeks a king to slay in Iberia. She has the Cid's sword and...

A lunate cross under the pendulous curve of her breast.

Crux Lunata. Here in the wilderness. She wants...

He stirred, trying to wake.

Pedro. Bonfraire!

"Beware!" he cried.

.

Yusuf sang. First it was the same haunting songs from Cairo that mesmerized men in Abu Jossep's court, each song sadder than the last.

Women mourning lost sons.

Did Numa mourn him? Or did Chrétien convince her not to worry? Or had she ever stopped mourning Miquel?

Women mourning lost warriors.

Did they not have songs in the Outremer for warriors mourning lost women?

That song about the bird in the early morning.

Tomás felt rain falling on his face. Thinking heaven had been merciful, he tried to open his rime-caked eyes.

Yusuf wiped at his face with that silk rag.

"I'm sorry, Father. Don't weep. We're only waiting for Qasim to bring us water."

Then Yusuf sang the old songs that Chrétien had taught him when they brought Numa to live at Fontcours.

▪

"Just a moment, Father. Let go. It's all right. Just for one moment. I have to see who it is that's coming."

▪

"Stay with me, *fadrin*, where it's safe."

Tomás called after his son, heard his words die in the night air.

That was how it came to be that even Yusuf left him there alone in the wilderness, whispering words that sounded like promises. But he left. Tomás was more alone than he'd ever been, more alone than he'd been during that awful nightmare when his father died, or was it just as alone as he'd felt when bashing stones into the pit of bones where he'd buried Isabella, as if this was what God had always intended, that he end up alone in the wilderness, no brother or son or cousin or lover for him to betray or fail or hurt beyond healing, and no bonfraire, not a single one, so that unlike his father's final days surrounded by the ancient knights who'd been his brothers-in-arms, Tomás lay here, thirst swelling his throat closed, so that he couldn't cry to God for mercy, even if he believed God would grant him mercy.

If only this night were silent, instead of all the sounds that came near and then deserted him again.

The whistle echoed in the rocks. A chamois seeking its mate?

Hooves trampled in the narrow valley. Sheep don't roam at night. Roe deer? Too high in the mountains for wild black pigs. No acorns to feed on here. A wind wafted up from the valley. Or a lynx came to sniff his ear. One or the other.

"No fear, *fadrin*. Your brother will come. And your son."

"Father, are you here?" Only Miquel called him *lad*.

"Patience, *fadrin!*"

"Are we in heaven, Father?"

"No, why would you think this is heaven?"

"You left me at the heretics' pyre in Minerve. Because you loved that woman and comforted her when she died. I thought you were in heaven with her. Did God send you to me?"

Miquel snorted, that familiar half-laugh that came whenever he judged his son ignorant. "I tell you again. God does not care what fools like us get up to."

"Where do we go then? When God frees souls to wander away from living men. I want to find Isabella."

"You need to stay and do your work. Keep your promises to your sons. Your brothers."

"Brothers? There's only —"

"Chrétien. Pedro. Rashid. You owe Rashid your life, a new life, before you can be free to roam."

"To earn my way to heaven?"

"No, *fadrin*. You need to make sure your honor doesn't rot with your bones."

Tomás roused, as if this was a dream. But no, his father Miquel comforted him again, the way he had when Tomás lay in that pit of torture on Cyprus. Miquel held his head, wiped his brow, chided Tomás to be strong, to do as he was taught. "Patience, *fadrin!*"

Animal voices called to each other.

"*Silencio!*" Miquel put his finger on Tomás's lip, warning him not to cry. "Wolves? Feral dogs?"

The yapping increased, echoing. There must be another narrow canyon nearby.

"I'll make sure you are safe, *fadrin*."

Miquel's voice trailed off into the night, like Yusuf's when he left. Only the sounds of animals calling to each other.

Everyone had left him.

Shaking to clear his head, Tomás tried to sit up, to check what was around him. Miquel wasn't nearby. He wanted to weep, but there was no water left inside for tears. Nothing to swallow except his swollen, hot tongue.

The birds had long ago ceased their twilight racket. The plodding steps of a large animal echoed up the trail.

More than one.

What would it be, wolves or bears who came to gnaw his bones and scour what remained of his betraying soul?

Or a ghost, best of all, her ghost would come walk with him to whatever was on the other side.

20

Despair

ONE OF THE GREATEST PLEASURES of Felip's scribing work was the opportunity to daydream, listening to the faint calls of birds in the mountains and not the laboring noises of the camp. The time he spent over the battle history for the king of Aragón allowed him to remember, repeatedly, every detail of his wedding night, to savor it over again, with no guilt about what he owed to God. The sweet way in which Serena kissed him, though they were surrounded by too many sleeping, groaning men to ever...

Isabella's warrior son appeared, breaking Felip's reverie.

"Pedro sent me to explain the planned battle array, so you can write it now and add details later."

The boy-soldier Sebastián seemed ready to do battle, his nostrils flaring red and white. Felip glanced past him, trying to see what might have ignited such a heat in the boy so early in the morning.

"I don't think there's a rush for that." Felip didn't even lay aside his pen. In spite of how his life had changed the previous night, he'd returned to the scribes' pavilion just after dawn, faithfully discharging the duties with which Pedro entrusted him. Serena remained safely in his tent, whispering a promise to bring him a midday meal when he'd kissed her goodbye. "All the priests say we're going home. There's no way over the mountains. There's no food for either knights or foot soldiers."

"Pedro says we'll find a way forward." The lad snapped at Felip, who couldn't think of one thing he'd done to offend this bonfraire. Weren't they all supposed to be brothers? Chrétien (of all possible defenders!) made it clear when they first met Sebastián that it was Matheus who transgressed against Valerós, not Felip.

"Tell me what Pedro wants me to write." Felip saw that Sebastián wanted to complete his task and be gone, so he took up a new quill and inked a starting place, following where he'd been listing all the lords from Navarre who appeared in the past few days, after Bishop Arnau commanded the king of Navarre to abandon his previous alliance with the Moors.

Sebastián folded himself up and sat cross-legged, leaning against a travel chest. He spoke rapidly, almost too fast for Felip to write.

"'As the kings Pedro and Alfonso agreed, Castile will be in the center.'" He coughed and spat. "You should write this as if it already happened, because—"

"That's what Pedro asked me to do," Felip said, speaking as respectfully as possible, because Sebastián still seemed ready to blow the sparks of his anger into a burning pyre at any moment. "He wants to send messengers to the pope as soon as there is good news."

"Pedro says you are to write, 'At Alfonso's left hand, the troops of Aragón are placed with their king Pedro of Lérida. At Alfonso's right hand are the knights and troops who traveled from León and Portugal under Sancho of Navarre.' Did you get that?"

Writing quickly to keep up, Felip nearly wrote Sebastián's question. "Yes. I'll ask you to repeat if I—"

Sebastián hurried on, reciting. "'At the forefront are the best of the knights together with knights of the holy orders, including the Hospitallers, the Templars, the Knights of Calatrava, and the Knights of the Lunate Cross.'" He breathed heavily, like a man who'd run a far distance, and then he spoke through clenched teeth. "'This line of noble knights was led by the great general Don Diego Lopez de Haro, who seized Malagón from the Saracens.'"

The boy bounded up, pacing like a caged dog. He snapped his fingers, then clenched his fists. Felip waited for more, his pen poised, afraid to ask what prompted this passion. After a few heartbeats of this outburst, Sebastián leaned against that camp-chest again, and resumed dictating the words Pedro had sent.

"'The kings stood with their forces aligned behind their noble knights. Behind the kings, the archbishops aligned their infantry, with militias from Nantes, Toledo, and Narbonne.'"

That must be what had set a fire of passion in Sebastián. Felip wanted to show that he understood how much this coming battle meant to Sebastián. "You'll only be in the second line, protecting the king? You m–must be d–d–disappointed."

"No, *renrén.*" Sebastián responded with utter disdain, calling Felip a fool. "Alfonso stays back and watches. Pedro fights. We shall be in the vanguard. The orders all dislike each other and fight only for their own glory. And Diego Lopez doesn't have enough time to teach any of them to listen to him, except for the Knights of Calatrava. The whole array is to make Alfonso and the archbishops look good for the chronicles, not to...*Ai*, don't write that down."

"Of course not. I'm not stupid."

Sebastián snorted. "That's what my mother says. She's always so kind."

Having exercised enough patience to last a summer's worth of new moons, Felip intended to put a stop to the boy's rude anger. "I don't know how they do things where you were raised, but in my father's domus—"

A clatter of chainmail and boots halted at the edge of the scribes' pavilion. A ring of knights in Calatrava colors stood to one side. Another handful of knights in Aragón house colors formed a defensive half-circle, their backs to Pedro, who stood in their midst.

Spying Sebastián, Pedro motioned him to come to his side.

Leaving Felip in peace to daydream again.

.

Sebastián at the mountains' edge

Sebastián, taking his place at the king's right hand, felt peace at being called away from that usurping scribe. Pedro, not looking Sebastián's way again, said, "Don't make me run after you like an errand boy." Pedro had that friendly tone he used when he meant business. He wasn't speaking to Sebastián.

"We need food. It's that simple." It was Alfonso, the king of Castile, whom Sebastián had only seen with the archbishops during mass.

This king was old and stooped, as if his long white beard weighed him down. The age difference between the two kings was more than a generation, and it showed in the energy of the conversation.

Pedro smiled at Alfonso in a chilling way, his eyes like ice. "Ah, but my good friend, we cannot turn this force loose to ravage the countryside. After victory, we can't rule these people if they've been robbed and left to starve through the winter."

"Castile has battled Saracens for centuries." Alfonso folded his arms, stern, shrugging free of Pedro's embrace. "Our knights know how to travel this land quickly, taking only what they need."

"*Si*, we praise your *razzia* and *cabalgada*, in and out with booty in the blink of an eye. However, foot soldiers are another matter," Pedro said. "Arnau Amalric promised all these men remission of their sins to get them here. But only our provisioning plans will get them home again."

"Which is the greatest reason why we need to treaty now with the caliph," Alfonso said. "We will try again next spring. Now that we're united with Navarre, perhaps Aragón need not exert itself next year."

"We have no strength with which to treaty," Pedro said. "We must fight. We took too little territory on the frontier this year. Arnau and Rome won't help you build a new force next summer. They won't grant indulgences again for this adventure. The pope has other fish to catch, in the rivers of the Holy Roman Empire."

Alfonso said something in the Castellano tongue that Sebastián didn't understand, but then said, "We don't need Rome. As I say to Arnau, we are independent. I am the defender of the faith in Iberia."

"*Mi amigo*," Pedro sounded conciliatory, "I want you to succeed with all my heart. But we must seize this opportunity now. Navarre and Léon wouldn't be here if the pope hadn't threatened to excommunicate them. The Knights of Calatrava are Cistercians. Arnau heads that order, so you can't even count on those knights next year. This is our moment. We cannot turn back."

The men, half Aragón, half Calatrava, had waited quietly in the bright sun. Now they stood utterly still, waiting to hear an answer.

"The moment," Alfonso said, "has passed for this year. The caliph moved his hordes from Jaén and sealed the pass through the mountains. We try again next year, as Castile has for generations. If I am not here, then my son will try. And then his son. It's not defeat to wait."

Alfonso called a go-with-God farewell and that ring of Calatrava knights moved with him as he departed, like a swarm acting with a single mind. They left Pedro behind with his knights—and with Sebastián wondering why he'd been summoned. Once the area outside the scribes' pavilion cleared, Sebastián saw a dozen Valerós men, also there to guard Pedro. He joined his men.

The king of Aragón looked around as if just then recognizing where the argument had carried him. He greeted Sebastián with a raised hand. Doménec spoke quietly to Pedro, who shook his head. The king glanced into the mostly empty scribes' pavilion and stepped inside. Sebastián followed when the king motioned for him to come along.

·

Felip at the king's command

"Senhór Felip, how goes your work?"

With Doménec at the king's elbow and Sebastián behind him, Pedro stood where he could read what Felip had written.

"You must add an 'M' to each of these numbers," Doménec pointed to the written tally, which already inflated the size of the Christian forces by twice the number of men in the camp.

The king's hand once more rested on Felip's shoulder.

"Xirgú, thank you for your service to our ward from Girona." The king's voice resonated like a soothing melody. "And what you do here is as important and honorable as any sword or lance that will be raised in our coming battle. You show true paratge. Your father would be proud."

"Has every goat in town died?" Sebastián cried in crude backcountry Catalan. He stomped away in the same white-hot heat as when he'd first appeared that morning.

Then he jerked back at the opening passageway.

Serena stood at the edge of the pavilion. She held a bowl of stew—more water than beans, as that's what everyone ate now—

which she'd promised to bring Felip when they parted at dawn. Sebastián stepped back as if struck, seeing her there. He said something, then walked a wide ring around her, as if she had a disease that might be catching, and walked away toward the Valerós camp.

Felip hadn't guessed before then that Sebastián felt about women in the same way as Chrétien and Durán. But then, he'd just met this lad. How could he guess Sebastián's inner workings?

Pedro made polite, brief conversation, congratulating Serena Taresa on her marriage, then bid her farewell.

She watched the king depart. "He promised that the Church will restore my land."

"We just have to live through the summer so he can to restore order at home." Felip spoke as if he possessed deep knowledge, though he was only repeating what Isabella said.

"The king said he'd only do it if I married. That he'd leave it to my husband to punish me for running away and putting myself in danger." She turned her beautiful face on Felip, like a light shining on his soul. "No one knows how frightened and furious I was about that. Until I found out it was you." She put her finger to his lip so that he couldn't speak, though he was too filled with feeling to make his tongue work. "You won't punish me, will you?"

After a moment, he found his voice. "For what? For being braver than most men? For refusing to have evil thrust upon you? My brother should never—"

She shushed him again. "I could grow to love you."

"Will you sit by me while I scribe for the king? Tell me what Sebastián said to you."

"He said, 'May God protect your husband.'"

"He seemed to say more than that."

"He also said, 'Congratulations on finding true love.' But he doesn't know that you and I are only old friends." She kissed Felip's forehead, and then broke his heart, declining the invitation to sit by him. "I have to return to the baggage train and help my friends pack. Everyone in the priests' pavilion and all the women in the baggage train say we're going home tomorrow."

∎

Late into twilight, Sebastián studied his bonfraire friends who had gathered around a small, smoky fire to ward off mosquitoes, each of them staring into the burning brands while Father Anselm spoke. Isabella—now the scribe Miró—had joined them, sitting by Durán and Chrétien. Colomb huddled near Anselm to listen.

Felip hadn't come when called, being too busy with Serena Taresa. Too busy enjoying what Sebastián once thought had been his. Back when she was only a laundry girl. Serena? Was any woman ever so misnamed?

Father Anselm lowered his voice, which caught Sebastián's drifting attention. "What do you fear most in the coming days?"

Sebastián started to answer, as the youngest one there, ready to be taught. But Colomb snorted at Anselm's suggestion. "Only a priest who fought thirty years in the Outremer could ask such nonsense."

"Ah, I presume you practice the common fallacy." Father Anselm reclined in front of the fire, propped on his elbow. "As many did in the Outremer."

"What fallacy?" Sebastián asked, willing to have his beliefs adjusted by someone who'd seen real battle.

"That you won't be among those who die in the foray," Isabella said. "Just as Pèire Leteric taught men to think."

Sebastián yawned. He'd never considered death a possibility.

"Before I die, I will revive the Beaurain family honor," Colomb said. "I can't do that if I let Moors and Saracens butcher me. So, no. I won't die in this battle. But I am following a well-reasoned plan, not treasuring a fallacy."

"I already died once." Isabella had been fiddling with a silver necklace in her hand, very much like that silver cross which had obsessed Diego Lopez. "Not doing it again now. Tomás is out there somewhere, so I will stay alive until I find him."

Chrétien had stretched out like Father Anselm, his hands behind his head, watching sparks from the fire drift up on the smoke and head toward the stars. "I fear that I've dragged Durán to one end of the earth where he doesn't belong."

Seeming stunned, Durán asked, "Why would you think that?"

"You've claimed it quite enough," Chrétien said. "There's no point in fighting these people. It goes against what you believe as a Good Christian."

"It's too late to worry about that now. I've come this far, might as well go on. What I fear ..." Durán paused. "I fear losing Chrétien. And any of you, too. But mostly I fear being alone again."

"I promise not to get lost," Chrétien said. "Just call out 'Vivètz Valerós!' and I shall be there."

"What inane foolishness." Colomb rose, hovering over the circle lit by the campfire. "When it starts, when the fight comes close to you, you'll be so scared you'll want to shit yourself. My friend Anselm is lying if he won't admit as much."

After Colomb had tramped away, Father Anselm spoke quietly. "What I fear is that there's slim chance of any battle occurring. The streams all have traps set, the kind that kill and maim men. That means we can't use the creeks for passage through the mountains." He shared what he'd learned among the priests.

Durán said, "And the only road through the mountains leads us straight into the caliph's arms."

"With no good options for either surprise or battle array," Chrétien said. Sebastián shook off his meditation on jealousy and resentment, hearing Chrétien say what everyone thought. "It's time to pack for home."

"No!" Isabella, who wasn't even a soldier, jumped up as if there were some action they could take right then.

"Peace, Master Miró." Chrétien tugged at her shirt sleeve.

"Honestly, the priests and the orders have predicted this for weeks," Father Anselm said. "We're out of food. There's no way forward. The choices are home or mutiny and desertion."

"But Tomás is still in Andalusia."

Sebastián seized his mother's hand. "We'll find him. After the army has turned around and the caliph has forgotten about all of this. We know how to travel where we aren't wanted."

A pair of nightjars *whirred* in the nearby bracken, carrying on as usual while the army pondered packing it all in. Like every summer for five hundred years.

"What we need," Chrétien said, "is an angel or djinni to appear and lead us through the wilderness. Else, this adventure is over." He stirred the smoky fire, making embers crackle and leap at him.

Too much like Sebastián's first foray as the Master of Valerós had been: a little noise, a lot of smoke, not much heat. Nothing laid on raw and then taken up cooked.

The whole lot of them, all bonfraires, shuffled off to find their bedrolls. Staying by the smoky fire, Sebastián closed his eyes, imagining what the next day would bring, when he had to stand in front of his men and announce that all they'd get from this adventure was their wages and a few more months of plain beans. There wasn't even enough salt to get them home, unless Pedro's provisioners knew where to find the saltlicks that wild beasts use.

■

Durán in the Valerós camp
July 14, before midnight

Too hot for more than touching fingers, Durán lay in their bivouac tent, the canvas flung open but not catching a hint of breeze from the cooling mountainsides.

The modest fortress at Castro Ferral had been taken by the unified army, and now everyone waited for what possible action the army might take next. Thousands of men camped below the insurmountable Despeñaperros, stuck with no passage into Andalusia that didn't lead straight to the caliph's massive army.

Chrétien and Durán, like most other men in the camp, spoke softly of what was most important in life.

"It's simple. I'm not a complicated man," Chrétien said, causing Durán to giggle. "*Chícharo*, in any of the ways my mother prepares them. Especially in hummus. Garlic, olives, onions. Done up in oil with sesame paste."

"Garbanzos? That's all you wish for? Well, if it's to be simple," Durán said, "then it's how my mother cooked broad beans with pimentón and onion. A nice, thick stew is like the comfort of rocking in safe, warm arms."

"No rocking tonight," Chrétien said. "Too hot."

"I meant my mother, may her soul have found consolation and a new and better life."

"Hmm," Chrétien said. "I'm sorry you lost her."

"If we can ask for anything, then no lentils, please." Durán wanted to change the subject. "We ate enough lentils on the journey here to last me till next Candlemas."

"Let's forget simplicity," Chrétien said. "Roasted lamb with cardamom. Spooned out on my mother's flatbread, straight from the oven, when it's so soft you can fold it."

"If she's going to cook for us, then I want Numa's chicken stew, the way she does it with cream and garlic and mushrooms, those little crinkled yellow ones we picked for her last fall. With lardon chunks the way she makes them. So crispy."

Chrétien spoke sternly. "You're a rotten incarnation of a Good Christian, eating all those innocent animals. Who can tally how many transmigrating souls you've gobbled up since my mother's been feeding you?"

"It's best when we can find cane sugar for her. Then she fries up that special bread with cinnamon and—"

"Shut up, *baquelar!*" Someone nearby shouted in Catalan. Others echoed the same command with rude words in several dialects.

Durán laughed. Chrétien touched his lips to silence him, then traced the edges with his finger.

"Dates wrapped with bacon," he whispered.

"Strawberries with almonds," Durán whispered back, knowing Chrétien's weak spot.

•

Sebastián in the Valerós camp

Sebastián sat alone by the dying fire, everyone else having escaped to their tents or bivouac shelters. He poked the embers, too aware of the whispers from a nearby tent, that warm voice he couldn't hear now without burning, humiliated.

He couldn't mention it to a soul, how he felt betrayed when Pedro gave her to another man to marry. It wasn't as if she'd made a promise or owed him another thought after she'd chased him out of her tent, back when he believed Serena Taresa was a sun-burnt laundry girl. It wasn't as if Pedro should have recognized that he could protect her, once people knew the laundry girl was a senhór-eta of Girona. He didn't have time to take care of more men than Pedro had assigned to him.

Sebastián needed the kind of advice that only Tomás could give him. Chrétien would laugh himself sick. Durán would not under-stand. It wasn't the kind of problem you could take to either your mother or your priest. He needed to forget that he'd ever wanted Taresa the laundry girl; he'd deny ever coveting the woman who had married Felip, the master of Xirgú. Or Pedro's scribe, or what-ever the fellow was supposed to be.

He'd forget, the same way they were all supposed to forget they'd come all this way only to turn around and go home without a battle. Or booty.

"Senhór Valerós!"

Sebastián glanced up from the fire, sunk in thought. Bernart, one of Durán's captains, stood at the edge of their ring. Sebastián finally roused himself to ask his business.

"A ragged mestitz goatherd asks for the Master of Valerós. He's a kind of a madman, though he's only a boy. He says the same words over and over, as if he learned them."

"Give him crusts and honey and send him on his way," Sebas-tián said. The whole lot of soldier-beggars would all be on their way back to Aragón come morning. "You don't need my counsel to care for starving beggars."

"The goat-boy asks for you by name, Senhór Sebastián. Says he has a message from your brother Yusuf."

Sebastián's heart beat with too much hope as he listened to the message. Forgetting that Felip had the faithless Taresa in his tent, Sebastián ran to find Isabella, shouting Miró's name. He kicked at Chrétien's tent, his boot colliding with one man's backside.

"Rise, bonfraires. Yusuf says we have to rescue Tomás!"

.

Sebastián had practiced with his men, and now they proved it: an army can get on its feet quickly and move in near silence when it must. Father Anselm and Colomb knew that truth, from their time in the Outremer. Pedro d'Aragón knew from years of raids at the frontier. Instead of shouting orders to be echoed back through fifteen thousand men, the leaders whispered commands that the men whispered through the ranks.

Instead of riding iron-shod horses over the rocky trail, they tied leather wrappings around the horses' hooves and then led the horses instead of riding, the knights and their sergeants quieting any beast unhappy about the tramp through the dark.

They'd spared a couple of burros for riders. Yusuf and Qasim, exhausted, rode burros at the front of the line, where Sebastian marched near Pedro. Yusuf and Qasim knew the way forward—how cow and sheep skulls marked a narrow path through the Despeña-perros that the caliph himself didn't know, only a handful of shepherds who'd shared the knowledge with two curious boys. Sebastián marched near his brother, trailed by Isabella and the others who were seeking Tomás along the trail.

The cares of yesterday—to go home without real battle, to leave Tomás in Andalusia, to have to coax starving soldiers into action—had dropped away. Excitement twittered in Sebastián's chest with each step. Angels guided their feet among the native cobbles that otherwise might twist men's ankles and sprain horses' legs.

His brother Yusuf was a hero, though concerned only about recovering Tomás. And Yusuf's secret path over the mountains meant that angels from heaven still dangled before Sebastián the promise of action, to engage an enemy in real battle.

An animal barked and then howled somewhere out in that black wilderness. Another answered farther off.

But at that moment, these marching men were the wolves out on a hunt. Valerós, Aragón, Castile, on the way to surprise their prey. Masked lanterns cast more shadow than light, fifteen thousand pairs of eyes peering through the dark.

21
Reunion

Bonfraires in the Despeñaperros
July 15, new moon, at midnight

"GO WITH THE ANGELS, FADRIN."

Miquel knelt beside Tomás, laid a cool, ghostly hand to his son's head, and wiped a damp rag across his lips, then dribbled water onto his tongue.

"Angels, Father?"

"It's your only hope. They never helped me, but you still owe your life to your brothers, so maybe angels will come for you."

"Are there angels?"

"Tell me I didn't raise a fool."

"No angels?"

"Tomás! No!"

.

Isabella in the Despeñaperros
July 15, after midnight

Isabella shoved past Chrétien and Durán, slipping the leather flask of water from her belt as she clambered among the boulders, and then dropping to her knees, broken stones bruising through her leather leggings.

"Tomás! No!"

His name ripped from her throat as she trickled water over his lips, then lifted his head to drip water into his mouth, his head cold with sweat. In the dark, she couldn't see if he moved, so she lifted him. He offered no resistance, like when you cradle the dead.

That screaming voice of a death angel again, the same as the sound in the forest swale, and when Nicolau killed Tomás but he didn't die. The burning rush from her spleen to her heart.

"Tomás," she repeated his name like a prayer, feeling at his neck for his heartbeat. "Don't be dead again."

She grasped his beard to open his mouth, finding it wet because he hadn't swallowed.

Drip more water.

He gagged, then swallowed.

"Isabella?" Tomás whispered her name like a ghost word.

"Òc. You're safe now, my love."

"Are you a ghost? Or an angel?"

Her soft laughter, muffled among the boulders, rocked his body in her lap. She jerked away the turban he wore, dripped more water on his head, and rubbed at it, her fingers scratching across his shaved head. "I'm the queen of Jerusalem."

"We have to keep going," Chrétien said. "I'll carry him."

"No," Sebastián said. "Don't be a hero. We'll make a litter."

Tomás stirred in her lap. "If I'm alive, I can sit a horse."

"We aren't riding. We're sparing the animals and marching."

"What for?"

"We attack the caliph tomorrow, thanks to your son Yusuf and your slave Qasim."

"He's not a slave."

His words sounded so dry, she wetted his lips again, dripped more water for him to swallow.

·

A half-dozen Montcava mercenaries had left the trail with Isabella and the others when they'd stopped to find Tomás. They all rejoined the line of marching soldiers, now far behind Pedro and Sebastián. The men traded off carrying the litter that bore Tomás over the trail. Wherever the trail was wide enough, Isabella walked beside the littler, her hand on Tomás. When she had to trail behind, she made them stop often to give him water.

Feeling his pulse under her hand again, how could she not have always known in her bones that Tomás lived? The dark nature of the world hid the truth, presenting one falsehood after another. *My eyes lied to me at that massacre in the swale.*

But her heart, belly, and sinews should have known, should have cried out the truth. *No need for ceaseless prayers to heaven. He's only as far away as the other side of this dark world.*

The dark nature of the world...*and when did I begin to think like a Good Christian?*

"Where have you been? In heaven?" He croaked each word. Not the melodic lilt she was once used to. She wetted his lips again.

"Enduring Simon's harrowing of the south. I shall tell you in the morning." Like everyone else marching the narrow trail, they could only whisper.

"Where's Yusuf? And Qasim?" He sounded desperate.

"At the front of the line with Pedro and Sebastián, finding trail markers. How did they find us?"

For a long and jolting time, Tomás didn't answer. She offered water again.

"One turn of good luck," he said at last. "The only one this year."

When he next whispered, he said, "Is there a priest near?"

A jolt of a question. "Do you need to confess?" *Don't die again.*

"No, I need a purge. I was poisoned. Do priests know medicine?"

"I'll tell the men to pass word to find one."

She laid her hand on his chest just to feel his heart beat. Or she grasped his wrist to feel his pulse and his breath across the back of her hand. After letting him drink, she kissed his fevered brow and then tasted his sweat on her upper lip for long moments after. Better than honey and milk.

"Is your hair white? Did I dream that, *kalila?*"

"Òc. I had a hard time last year. It's over now."

The rhythmic thump of leather boots on a rocky trail beat like the heartbeat of an enormous animal.

In the dark, traversing the unseen rocky ground, passing back whispered warnings about changes and blocks in the trail, Isabella tried to judge whether the ascent was over and the army was descending into Andalusia, or whether her heart had wings now and flew above the long trail of men in the mountains. Her nose told her that the forest was mixed pine and oaks. In gaps between boulders, the trail was crowded by cistus scrub. The parade of men seemed to be descending into another matorral, but it wasn't light enough to distinguish one tree from another, though she often smelled the resin of stone pine.

Awake so long into the night, she dreamed while walking.

No, it was last year's nightmares departing, dissipating into the starry, starry sky.

The bloody swale, forgotten.

The weeks moribund in Rubea's cave, neither dead nor alive, forgotten now. No more sleepless nights weeping.

Her lost friends, killed for loving God the wrong way and for sheltering her. Those friends walked free now in heaven. Or wherever the Good God of light placed the innocent lost ones.

Freezing and coughing in the monastery, grief dulled by the time she spent copying the gospels. And that particularly fine fortnight she'd spent copying an ancient scribe's rendition of Ecclesiastes.

All the travail dissipating on the hot night's breeze.

She had everything. They just needed to do this one chore—fight a battle—and then they'd ride home with Pedro and free Valerós.

"*Eu vos amor.*" Tomás whispered. "Is there more water?"

．

Felip in the Despeñaperros
July 15, before dawn

"It's like in a *canço d'amor*," Serena Taresa whispered.

She'd walked over the mountain at Felip's side, though the captains all declared, "No women!" She'd appropriated his second-best linen shirt and someone else's leathers, and when Felip protested, she pointed to Isabella in their company, and then proceeded to march through the dark mountain passage without complaining.

When Isabella and Chrétien departed from the trail to rescue Tomás of Morella, Felip and Serena Taresa also paused along the trail with the Montcava mercenaries. Felip whispered to Serena Taresa what he knew of the lovers' story, how they'd found love, escaped heretic hunters, lived through a siege—and then believed each other dead. But were now reunited.

Neither Felip nor Serena Taresa needed to contribute help, so Felip stood beside the woman he hoped to make his own true love and watched a love story by lamplight.

The lamp Chrétien held shone on Tomás, the man they rescued, a wreck of a soldier, half naked among the boulders, having thrown off the burnous covering him. When they roused the man, he gazed up, where the light from Sebastián's lamp illuminated Isabella.

Purely transfixed. The way scribes draw the saints in the corner of a manuscript, to show their ecstasy. What a man looks like when an apparition appears.

"*Kalila?*" The man's words were as dry as the mountain scree where he lay.

"It's me. I'm here," Isabella said. "You're safe now."

"Saved?"

Chrétien and Durán bound Tomás onto a makeshift pallet, a blanket stretched between two lances. Then they rejoined the thousands of men marching over the narrow mountain pass. Felip and Serena Taresa stayed close to their friends, as silent as the captains commanded everyone to be.

Yet whispers flew back to Felip on the mountain air, like the whir of a hummingbird in the garden, or a cat petted on his grandmother's lap.

"Don't die, Tomás."

"*Ai, kalila,* it's you. In life?"

"It's me. I'll always come."

"I heard angel wings and believed it was you."

"You know I'm no angel. You called me your favorite sinner."

"I did? Was it a lifetime ago?"

"*Òc.*"

"I need water from your hands, *kalila.*" Tomás whispered when they began moving again after one stop.

"You need a physician. I'm sorry water is all I have for you."

"It's enough. It's more than I ever expected under heaven."

"*Eu vos amor.*" She'd whispered it as often as Tomás did. "We have the world now. That's enough."

■

Isabella in the Valerós camp
July 15, at dawn

Isabella heard the screech, gazing upward to follow the sound.

Overhead, when the sun broke through after dawn, an imperial eagle circled, perhaps curious about what prey it might find in the river of men that broke through the mountain trail.

Above the valley where the army was to fight, men halted and bivouacked. Set beans to soak and field-bread to rise. Waited for the kings to tell them what to do next. Durán, Felip, and Serena Taresa went in search of where the Valerós, Xirgú, and Montcava men were setting up camp.

Isabella found a place with shade and less rocky ground, and commanded the Montcava litter-bearers to leave Tomás near a tree. After they departed seeking the rest of the Montcava men, she checked again. His heart beat was stronger, his face a human color. When she wetted his chapped lips, he roused, awake.

She folded up beside Tomás, bone-tired but intending to stay awake and watch over him until a priest or physician could be found. Chrétien, silent as a sprite, sat beside her. The shadows deepened. Two boys hovered over her.

"Yusuf!" Even bone-tired, she sprang up to embrace him.

"*Hola*, Mother. I'm happy to see you." Yusuf breathed the words into her hair. He was so much taller. "Why is your hair white? Touched by an angel?"

"Nothing so grand."

"Mother, this is my brother Qasim. He saved us."

She released Yusuf to grasp the forearm of the ugliest or most beautiful young man she'd ever met. "Thank you, Qasim, with all my heart."

Too tired, all of them, they sat on the ground beside Tomás, who had again fallen asleep.

"I shall watch him, ma dòmna." Qasim said *my lady* with such a deep accent that it sounded like other words entirely.

"I'm called Miró, the scribe. Please think of me that way."

"Tomás often told me about you," Qasim said. "You should rest. It's my job to watch him."

"But you walked that trail twice without sleep. Get some rest for yourself."

Qasim folded his arms, leaning against a pine tree so that he sat erect. "It is what he pays me to do."

In the end, when Durán appeared and woke them, all four had fallen asleep, their heads resting on Tomás's shoulders, his belly. She clasped Yusuf's hand, who held Qasim's, who clutched Tomás's forearm with his other hand. Chrétien lay prone, Tomás's head resting on his belly.

"Can you let me up, please?" Tomás begged, rousing them. "I'm much better." He had his hand on Isabella's head, who bent over him to offer water.

22

Holy Orders

"PEDRO WANTS YOU."

Durán nudged Yusuf where he lay beside his father and mother and that slave boy, all sleeping under a pine tree. And Chrétien, too, had deserted him for the sake of his milk-brother's company. Durán, bone-tired from helping set up the Montcava camp, smothered fleeting jealousy. The world proved extraordinary and surprising, and he didn't need to ask more of it than he had. Instead, he was happy that Chrétien had found his brother again.

Isabella bolted upright, scrambled to find her bota and urged water on Tomás. He drank, then tried to rise from where they'd been nursing him.

"No, not you, Don Tomás," Durán said. "Pedro wants Yusuf to report what he learned living so close to that general."

Tomás reached for his jerkin, which had been Chrétien's pillow. "Pedro? He's in danger. We need to warn him."

"Of course he's in danger," Durán said. "There's a battle about to begin in the valley."

"I mean the danger from Crux Lunata." Tomás struggled to keep standing.

Isabella touched Tomás, which seemed to calm him instantly. "We know. It's why we are here. Pedro allows only his closest guards and Valerós near him."

Seeing Isabella and Tomás together again, it was so obvious that the swordsman cared deeply about her. Durán felt happy for them, but what he most felt was a bone-deep need for sleep, a decent meal, and diversion from what everyone was preparing to do that day.

"Yusuf!" Durán called again. "The king wants you."

The boy sat rubbing his eyes. The other lad with him, Qasim, who'd led the army over the mountains, was awake even faster and pulling on his boots while Yusuf shook himself.

"We're going together." Tomás poked through the pile of gear. "Where's my sword?"

"That witch Ríma took it." Yusuf said. "Remember?"

Tomás repeated a string of slurs, the same words and accent as Durán had heard from Chrétien over every upturned tin mug or misplaced boot for the past two years. The kind of curses that always made Chrétien's mother turn her head, smiling secretly.

Isabella swore, too, in Catalan dialect, insisting that Tomás lie back down, but he'd already found his leggings, jerkin, and boots and demanded that Qasim help with his chainmail since he, Qasim the Magnificent, was Tomás's servant, not Yusuf's, and he damn well better do as he was taught if he expected to carry home to his mother more than one rotten burnous and a pocketful of fava beans.

"And where's Al-Malik? What have you done with my horse?"

"That horse died years ago, Tomás. Lie down. You're feverish."

"It's a different damned horse, and I'm fine."

"Well, then." She rustled in the pile of gear. "Here's your other sword. Will that do?"

Tomás stopped raging, swept her in his arms, and kissed her with the kind of passion that Durán only knew from—

"Ah, family reunited," Chrétien murmured beside him, his breath tickling the back of Durán's neck. Warm. The breath of life. "Wonderful, is it not?"

"Master," Qasim called for Tomás's attention. "Your king promised that his men will find and rescue our Al-Malik. Be patient."

"Yusuf," Durán said, remembering his mission, "Pedro wants to talk to you."

"He can talk to all three of us," Yusuf said, slipping an arm under Tomás's shoulder. Qasim appeared on the other side, helping Tomás to walk, while Tomás insisted that he and all the cat-wrestling monkeys on this mountain side were just fine. "And we still want a physician. My father needs a henbane purge. He was poisoned. Wolf bane, I think. And he needs a salve for the cuts on his hands."

"Father Anselm is with Pedro. And here, *mon fraire*. I brought bread from camp. Eat on your way to the king."

When they set off, Chrétien followed, saying something to Tomás that caused Yusuf to grab Chrétien around the waist and pound his head on Chrétien's chest. Tomás had his head in his hands, tugging at his hair, then he too embraced Chrétien.

Durán shouted to them. "Pedro wants Yusuf. Now."

They set off again, glancing back at Chrétien, who called after them. "Jacques is with her in Lérida. Dolç is safe."

Isabella loitered beside Durán, watching the scene too. She said, "News of his other wife and child, don't you think?"

"They aren't married. Pedro annulled it."

She waved a finger, shushing him. "Imagine the burden Tomás feels. I know how he worried until we found Yusuf in Cairo to bring him home with us."

∎

Durán in the kings' pavilion

Durán stayed just outside the kings' pavilion at the top of the ridge. He hadn't been called into the conversation, where Yusuf and Qasim answered questions from Pedro and Alfonso, the king of Castile. Tomás was inside with Chrétien, who couldn't seem to tolerate being more than an arm's reach from his brother. Pedro and Alfonso, the king of Castile, were questioning Yusuf for details.

"It's called a *nava*." Yusuf's voice carried across the pavilion. "Several of these wide valleys run among the hills. Since God's creation, rain and floods have washed dirt from the mountains to create these plains."

Yusuf stood formally before the kings in the tent, but seemed wholly sure of himself. The heretical thought danced in Durán's mind that young Yusuf was like the child Jesus before the Pharisees at the temple. He'd known the lad for only a fortnight before Tomás and Isabella and their sons rode off to be massacred on the road to

Barcelona, but it took only a moment with Yusuf to recognize that he was a scholar wise beyond his years.

While Yusuf talked, Durán watched the morning light flicker across Chrétien's face, the shadow of pine boughs jittering in a light mountain breeze. Chrétien hadn't been so happy since Tomás appeared in Toulouse with their mother in tow. But it wasn't just Tomás of Morella who made Chrétien happy. Like the whole rest of the world, Chrétien was excited about the battle at hand.

With everyone else, Durán watched from the top of the hill as the army settled into units, absent the baggage train, which they'd left back at Castro Ferral. The entire force remained up on the hillsides and in the upper narrow valleys, under the shelter of holm oak, cork, and stone pine. Ash trees and willows lined the creek sides. Below, in the vista that Pedro's pavilion commanded, a plain opened up at the foot of the mountains, where a small stream ran west to east. People were departing the farm houses that edged the valley, some with push carts, most on foot, children in hand or tied to their mothers' backs or mounted on the shoulders of fathers and older brothers. They headed south quickly, few even pausing to look back up the mountain to the north where the army rested and waited.

"Donzel." Pedro held Yusuf by the shoulder. "You will remain here behind the line. If a retreat starts, you will be in the forefront, headed with the priests and scribes back over the trail you found."

To the south, from the direction where the farm families had fled, the first of the caliph's riders appeared, mounted on horses, calling out to the Christian forces sheltered in the trees.

Men on the Castile side of the camp shouted back. "*Dios ayuda a Santiago!*"

The ultramontanos, most at the rear of the Valerós camp, cried, "*Dieu le veut!*"

The Aragón army and other knights from the south called out, "St-Jordí!"

Sebastián's troops bellowed, "*Desperta, Ferro!*"

"What are the Moors shouting?" Pedro asked.

"It is the Takbir," Yusuf said. "It means God is great."

"We aren't here to debate that," Pedro said.

The talk drifted to numbers of troops and where the caliph's greater army was camped.

"Then we move into battle formation now." A voice behind Pedro spoke. It was Sebastián. Durán had paid too close attention to Chrétien and missed that his brother was there with the kings.

"I'm not sure of that." Alfonso of Castile shook his head. "Our men are exhausted from travel. How do we know this news is any kind of truth?"

"Because I've been in Baeza all spring," Tomás said, "alongside one of the caliph's viziers. The men down in the valley here are a smaller force from Baeza and Úbeda. They were camped a few valleys over. The greater army doesn't have time to get here within the day."

"Baeza?" Alfonso said. "Is Abu Jossep across the valley? We've met in the field before."

"Abu Jossep is dead." Tomás's voice trailed off. In a few moments, Tomás and Chrétien left the pavilion and headed down to where the Valerós and Montcava men were camped. Their departure left space around Pedro and Alfonso. Before his guards closed that space, Colomb appeared behind the king, along with the ugliest man on earth, Arnau Amalric.

·

Durán believed he was thoughtful, careful to act. And therefore, perhaps he was the most surprised of everyone to find himself between Colomb and Pedro, nose to nose with his great-uncle but no weapon in his hand.

Colomb's eyes widened, astonished, but he stepped back only to grasp Durán by both wrists.

"*Hola*, Beaurain. Glad you joined us."

He released one arm but held Durán at his side with one hand. A quick glance and Durán saw that his uncle wasn't armed. No one in the room carried a weapon except the kings themselves. Pedro stared at Durán and Colomb, but Archbishop Arnau Amalric and everyone else listened to Alfonso, who seemed to be used to delivering sermons while others waited for as long as he chose to speak. "Our bishops and priests have preached the holiness of this effort, with bells ringing to command all men to think of what they owe God. But this isn't a pilgrimage. Not the way popes have been sending men to the Outremer since our grandfathers' grandfathers' time."

While still grasping Colomb's arm, Durán glanced past him, seeking Archbishop Arnau, but that man was intent on what Alfonso was saying and hadn't seemed to notice Durán.

"I honor your work," Pedro said to Alfonso. "You are the man others must seek to witness *imitatio Christi* in the flesh."

"Your liege lord Innocent does not see it in the same way." Alfonso folded his arms in challenge.

"But I do." Pedro's mellifluous voice seemed to stroke Alfonso, like pacifying an over-roused cat. Durán understood the words *imitatio Christi*: the imitation of Christ. But he didn't know what those words had to do with what these men were discussing, which seemed to be that they should turn around and go back after walking all night over that mountain pass. "We must let flow the passion your example has built in our men."

"We send out our best knights, the Templars and the Order of Calatrava. We steal their standard and return over the mountains."

"And take back a few frontier castles on our way home?'

"*Si*." Alfonso nodded vigorously. "We will have a better season for the chroniclers to record than Castile has known since I was a young man."

"I didn't mean that as an actual suggestion," Pedro said. "We brought knights prepared for a real battle, not mere raids as if we were all Almogavars."

"You disparage our Almogavars?" Alfonso's voice rose. "They are the hardest and best of fighters."

Pedro held up a hand for peace. "No, I'm arguing we need more than raids. We must give battle with our knights in formation, prepared to show all the strength of Christendom."

"Yet our supply trains are depleted." Archbishop Arnau spoke. He stood near Alfonso. "We fear the kind of supply failure that led Norman lords to go to Constantinople instead of the Holy Land. We need to determine what's best for the unified Body of Christ."

In Durán's ear, Colomb whispered, "Let's go, *fadrin*. Kings in parlay? Not for you and me."

Outside the pavilion, Durán asked, "What are they doing?"

"Convincing Alfonso of Castile that we came here for a battle."

"Didn't we?"

Colomb had his hand at the back of Durán's head and locked them together forehead to forehead. He whispered, "What were you about in there? Have you gone mad, *fadrín*?"

Durán crossed his arms, putting that much space between them. "The Crux Lunata seek Pedro's death. I thought you were the assassin. They promised death by this new moon."

"No, lad. The Crux Lunata seek only to destroy heresy."

"You are as wrong about that as you are about your brother Hugues and all the Beaurain brats."

Colomb's shoulders rose, like a man prepared to defend against his enemies.

"Hugues was a great man." Durán hurried into the truth. "But you already heard what's true from...Vidal. Hugues didn't father bastards. Your other brother led you astray. And the Crux Lunata seek to murder Pedro. They'll use you if they possibly can."

Once again, they were nose to nose, Colomb's nostrils flaring with anger, his eyes wide and staring, the yellowing edges watery with fury. "What proof, bastard?"

"Esak told me himself. He claimed Sebastián and me as his grandsons. When he held Hugues as a prisoner in Béziers."

A voice interrupted their quiet, personal ferocity.

"Beaurain?"

Colomb stepped back. "Monsenyor?"

Arnau Amalric had followed them from the pavilion, that archbishop who wanted Durán burned on a heretic's pyre.

"We haven't had a chance to talk." Arnau stopped when he recognized Durán at Colomb's side. "You!"

"You've met my nephew, Durán of Montcava." Colomb had his arm around Durán, is if they were affectionate uncle and nephew. "He's come here as the master of the forces sent by the count of Foix."

"The man Matheus of Xirgú condemned?" Arnau's wide mouth compressed into a thin, hard line. The same unforgiving judgment Durán had suffered in that tiny airless room in Narbonne, when he'd been forced to give an oath.

"Matheus was mistaken," Colomb said. "I've traveled with Durán these many weeks. He's as much an inheritor of the Beaurain sense of duty to Jesus and a Christian life as I am."

Arnau stared in the way great men do. He was used to forcing his will through a glance from his cold eyes and a thrust of his hard chin, as unforgiving as the priests in the St-Sernin abbey in Toulouse, taking poor people's pennies to say prayers for them.

"*Benvingut*, Beaurain!" Arnau said. "Welcome to our enterprise of peace." He then lost interest in Durán and returned his attention to Colomb. "You are joining our camp now, with our brothers of the Cross?"

"No," Colomb said. "I'm staying with the men of my domus, with my brothers of blood." He had his hand on Durán's shoulder.

Arnau offered the repetitious blessing about being protected by God on paths of glory that Durán heard from the priests who wandered from camp to camp, offering blessings to huddled men who would prefer more bread and extra beans. Then the archbishop returned to the kings' pavilion.

"Who'd believe it?" Durán murmured without meaning to share the thought with his uncle.

"See what you made me do?" Colomb said. "I had to lie to the archbishop just now. He sent me to ensure you're a good Catholic."

"I have never lied to you or asked you to lie for me," Durán said. "And you know I have a sense of duty."

"Are you fighting tomorrow if the kings decide to take to the field for battle?"

"No. I break faith with myself whenever I swear an oath. And I swore I would not raise arms against another man."

"Do you want to check the horses with me?" Colomb asked. Durán felt it was an invitation to join in Colomb's greatest pleasure. He regretted declining.

"Another time? I need to find my friends."

"*Bon vèspre.* Let all be as it pleases God."

"*Òc*," Durán said. "It will be, soon or later."

•

Durán sought Chrétien, who of course was with Tomás. They were outside Pedro's pavilion, taking advantage of the view from that ridge of the gathering Saracen forces at the south end of the valley. Isabella, a few spear-lengths farther than she'd been from Tomás since they'd found him, was on the other side of the pavilion, deep in conversation with Yusuf.

"Our cousin will be out in front." Tomás pointed to a clutch of men atop the hillock that blocked most of the southern end of the valley. "Even though the caliph prefers to sacrifice farmers first, rather than his own knights."

"Which one is he?" Chrétien peered into the distance, shading his eyes against the late afternoon sun.

"The tall one in white. Up close, you'll see a vizier's insignia. It's a broach at his collar that looks like this." He drew in the dust with the toe of his boot.

"How else to recognize the man?" Chrétien said.

"He resembles our father more than you do."

"And you want him spared in the battle?"

"From both Christians and the caliph's own guards, who will likely try again to assassinate Rashid. If you find him, bring Rashid to Pedro, who's probably the only one who can save Rashid's life. I owe Rashid what I owe my own brother."

"You don't owe me anything," Chrétien said.

"But I did once." Tomás held out his hands in a gesture like prayer, which Durán had never seen him do. "I owe him for the same sins of affection and betrayal that you once warned me about with Pedro."

Chrétien softly repeated a string of oaths, condemning Tomás but not in the same way as for bootlaces and cold porridge. "I'd rather be a dust-eating priest choking my chicken in a hermit's cave than be your brother. You're like the assassin of a dark god, piercing hearts. You piss in the wind and never learn."

"Òc," Tomás said. "That is all true."

"Durán, *cor dolç*." Chrétien stopped swearing suddenly and stirred to leave. "Let's find Felip. We need to join Sebastián and go to work. Enough lounging around at the pleasure of kings and priests."

"I didn't intend it to be that way." Tomás called after them. "I love him but it turned out…"

Durán lost the sound of Tomás's words, hurrying to catch up with Chrétien and find Felip.

■

Felip at Las Navas de Tolosa,
July 15, before twilight

Two people, one tall, one small, came down the path toward where Felip worked in the hastily erected scribes' pavilion.

"*Bon Dèu!*" Serena cried. "It's that little priest who complained about us being in your tent the night we married!"

She leaped up from the camp-chest where she'd been sitting and gathered the tin bowl she'd brought for their shared breakfast, preparing to depart.

"We've c–confessed and have nothing to worry about from p–priests," Felip said, joking the way they used to, in the easy, friendly days of life in Girona.

"You, perhaps. That priest acted like I was vile, as if he'd stepped in a barnyard."

"Surely not. He's—"

But his new wife disappeared, slipping away silently. As soon as she was gone from his side, Felip again felt the lightning-borne bees in his fingers and toes. The censorious little priest stood at his side, squinting in the same nearsighted haze that he'd shown previously. His little nose wrinkled up, trying to see, which Felip guessed was what Serena interpreted as disdain.

"You need to write a contract for this woman." The little priest commanded Felip's service without either greeting him or asking his name. "A barraganía contract."

A tall woman stood beside the priest, but she was veiled, so Felip couldn't judge either her face or her position in society, though it was a nice veil. And she wore handsome tooled-leather boots.

The priest shook his finger at Felip. "Can you write that?"

"Yes, but Pedro d'Aragón asked me to finish this letter."

"The archbishop commands this greater need. Church over kings." The priest's voice rose, ready to dispute the issue.

Felip yielded. "If you dictate, *mon senhór*, I shall write quickly."

"It's a contract between Don Carlos of Toledo and Ríma de Rod-riquez, a widow."

Felip got busy with a new quill and fresh parchment, inscribing the text that the priest recited. A barraganía contract for a nephew of Alfonso of Castile. Not marriage, but more than concubinage. Felip mused while he wrote, because it seemed the Church accepted certain arrangements in Castile that were forbidden elsewhere, in this case a secular union between a widow and a married man, framed with enough law that children wouldn't be bastards, because the woman served as barraganía, not concubine. The contract united land between the man and the woman, allowing for children if the man's real marriage was childless.

The woman spoke, her voice from behind the veil surprisingly deep, like a man's. "I did everything. Mixed his hair with earth from his footsteps, then burned it to powder and got him to eat it."

"Woman's magic," the little priest sneered. He quit hovering over Felip and went to stand over the woman, who had taken a seat on a camp-chest. "Is that a talisman around your neck, Senhóra Ríma?

"Best known charm on earth and in heaven," the woman said. "The hair of the man-child. I can still call him to me."

"Under the banner of what saint?"

"St-Hermenegild, whose own faithless father chopped off his head. And my ancestor Roderick, who should be made a saint for all he did to resist the Saracens."

"You repeat heresy only to provoke. Like a child." The priest scowled in her direction. He seemed quite blind.

"And yet I am victorious. I alone brought you the sword. And I am the Rodriquez clan leader now."

"Will you complain and demand a better solution for your future life than this barraganía?"

"This contract is fine for now. It gives me safe haven in Toledo. And Don Carlos is close to the king. He is as aspirational as I am."

"You mean ambitious."

"God wants peace and unity in Iberia," she said. "Do you con-sider that ambition? Isn't it what you seek?"

"Senhóra, I don't care a fig about Iberia. I consign that entire wilderness to you."

The little priest left her side and returned to Felip.

"Here are the final terms you must write." He spoke slowly, as if Felip might be dimwitted. "The couple shall live together as one as long as they are able, sharing the land and family honor each brings. Any children born of this agreement shall inherit all, divided equally among them."

The woman interceded. "But the oldest shall inherit his father's divine rights."

"You need to get a male child from him first." The priest scoffed. "You haven't succeeded so far."

While Felip worked, the two ignored him.

"I am victorious. I came here on my own, leading men from my clan." She seemed to be a haughty person, quite proud of herself. "We claimed a place at the edge of the caliph's camp, then crept away in the night."

"You weren't alone. You had your men to protect you." The little priest didn't seem to want to concede anything to the woman.

"We rode for two entire days," she said. Felip compared her claims to Serena's exploits. His wife had crossed all of Aragón and La Mancha without a contingent of men to guard her.

"Enough bragging, senhóra. Do you have it?" The little priest interrupted, tapping a foot, impatient.

"Indeed." Rustling within her light cloak, the woman produced a sword, its crosspiece tied to a homemade baldric, which she slung over her shoulder when she presented the treasure to the priest, who inspected the blade closely, holding it close to his nose to study its inscription.

"This isn't the right sword, you silly whore."

The priest chucked the sword so that it crashed against the travel chest beside Felip and clattered to the ground.

"I took it from him myself." The woman removed her veil. Auburn hair tumbled loose. She might be considered pretty by some men, but Felip considered her to be rather bug-eyed. "It's been in my possession since I rode away."

"The blade we seek has a sign like this at the cross piece." The priest toed an image in the sandy floor of the pavilion.

At the mention of a sword, Felip sat erect, then slumped so that he didn't draw attention, hoping they'd continue to ignore him, because he desperately wanted to hear their quarrel.

"*Ai*, his bastard son had it." The pretty woman turned pale under the sunburn that crossed her face like a crimson mask. "The blade you want is on the other side of the mountains."

"Where is he? And his son?"

"Dead. They were likely butchered for murdering the general."

"That filthy mestitz bastard is finally dead?" The little man's glee was unseemly for a priest.

"*Hola*, senhór!" Fortuno cried out, that small boy Chrétien had brought from Lérida. His voice rang across the scribes' pavilion. "Where is Master Miró?"

"Look what we have here," the tall woman said. "A mestitz son."

"A camp brat?" The priest wrinkled his nose, trying to see who'd come in.

"What's your name, little boy?" the woman cooed in accented Castellano baby-talk. "Where are you from?"

Fortuno seemed uncertain, glancing between the priest and Felip, who shook his head. After Fortuno was found to have sneaked his way into the tramp across the mountains, Chrétien had ordered the lad to stay with Yusuf.

"She asked your name, child." The priest spoke in an Aragón dialect, but with a heavy Provençal accent.

"*Ai*. I am Fortuno of Morella. I serve with Valerós in Pedro's army. We are going to defeat the Saracens."

"*Deus occulte!*" the priest cried. *God works in mysterious ways.*

"Would you like honey and bread?" The woman cozened Fortuno in baby-talk. "Come with me, and I'll give you sweets."

"My master says I'm to stay with men now. I'm not a baby." Fortuno glanced at Felip again, who looked as stern as he could. The boy ran from the pavilion.

"Sign the contract, Senhóra Ríma, before chasing after that child." The priest bent over Felip's work, inspecting every letter, his old-man's breath drying the ink so that it didn't need to be sanded.

"Before Alfonso changes his mind about giving you to his nephew. He can't make up his mind about much these days. We'll have to produce miracles to get that doddering king to do more for us."

Felip considered what he'd heard. More people sought a sword than Matheus. These people had to be discussing Isabella's husband and son. Felip needed to find Isabella and tell her what he'd heard.

But just after his querulous visitors departed, Serena Taresa reappeared. Even wearing Felip's shirt and borrowed leggings, no one would mistake her form or voice for a man's. Yet it was hot, and no amount of begging would coax her into borrowing Felip's cuirass for protection.

"I've brought bread and cheese," she said. "The bread's fresh from this morning, but the cheese is this side of moldy."

"I'll close my eyes." Felip received the food from her work-worn hands with gratitude. "I have all else I've ever dreamed of. Good food can wait. Coming from your hand, it's like honey and milk."

"Don't go to battle," she said, with far more passion than sharing bread warranted. "Stay with the scribes."

"That's what Pedro asked of me, but my men—"

"You can't help me in this life if you're dead. I'll be here with you tomorrow. When they sound the retreat, we'll go back together."

"Retreat? We won't—"

"Oh, you blessed innocent!" She scolded him, but was nice about it, stroking his hand. "Don't you know what the kings are saying? There's no chance of victory. Their knights will each take a tilt at the Saracens, and then we run."

"Xirgú!" Durán stood outside the pavilion, calling Felip's name. "Come meet with the captains. We are to be with our men tonight. Sebastián insists we must show them courage. Your wife should be with Miró."

Chrétien, behind him, tapped his sword hilt with impatience, waiting for Felip to say farewell to his wife, who instead said, "I'm coming too," which launched a small dispute.

"Can we get to work?" Chrétien said. "To do what we came here for?"

Without waiting, Chrétien started down the path toward where their men were camped.

Before following, Felip retrieved that discarded sword, intending to return it to Isabella's husband.

As they set out, Durán said quietly, "I came to protect my family." Yet Chrétien heard. He slowed up, waiting for them.

"And here we are now," Chrétien said. "Nothing left but to do our best. Xirgú, Montcava, both of you. Follow Sebastián tonight. He's our master and there's no one here who can better show how to care for men before battle."

"How do you know?" Felip asked, still unsure about a youth like Sebastián being a captain of men, given his own struggles with leadership over the journey through La Mancha.

"Because he was taught by the man my father admired most in the world. Come, bonfraires. This is what we were made for."

"Perhaps it's what you were made for," Durán said. "God made me to sell cabbages in the marketplace. I'm only here for my brother."

Felip followed, Serena Taresa at his side, preparing for his first adventure as a crusader before battle. Tired, hungry, worried, Felip paused only to retie his bootlaces.

Then he became eager to go to work when they entered the camp, seeing Durán, Chrétien, and Isabella embracing Sebastián.

Felip motioned to Isabella, to tell her about the little priest who couldn't find the sword he wanted, but he couldn't catch her attention, and then she disappeared from sight when the Master of Valerós began to speak. Those words stole his attention, because Felip now had two vows to keep, his new vow to Serena Taresa, and the deeper vow to these friends who made him their bonfraire.

While Sebastián shouted words to stir the hearts of the Valerós camp, the captains roared the words back through the ranks during pauses. Serena Taresa rocked on her toes, the way she did when overexcited when they played together years before.

"This the most thrilling night of our lives!" She yelled in Felip's ear to be heard over the shouting captains.

Felip nodded, though the most thrilling night of his life had been the night they married. The next night after that, he'd marched through a steep rocky hell, silent, but with his wife at his side. Amid shouting men, he seized Serena Taresa's hand and joined in the excitement, though he believed the most thrilling night of his life lay ahead, when he could be alone with his wife.

On this third night after he married, Felip walked with his fellow captains among stinking, nervous men, speaking words to rouse their passion and strengthen the steel in their spines. Felip with Durán roamed through the night, following the Master of Valerós, who was warmly welcomed among each camp when he congratulated and praised men, and told them that this was what they trained for, that they'd be victorious over the Saracen before the sun was next at mid-heaven.

Felip and Durán took turns repeating Sebastián's words, finding they were cheered as if the words were their own. Late into the night, his throat raw, Felip felt a gloved hand on his shoulder.

"*Ai*, Xirgú!" Colomb whispered in his ear. "You woke up among true crusaders, who made you their brother. So, my friend, God answers prayer, eh?"

It took a moment, since Felip recoiled whenever Colomb came near, to hear that Colomb wasn't tormenting him this time, that the knight meant what he said.

"*Òc*." Felip said, answering truthfully. "I am blessed among men, to be with these new brothers.

23

New Moon

WHEN DURÁN WOKE, THERE WAS just enough predawn light to see Chrétien buckling his armor.

"You're going to battle."

"*Òc.*"

"The plan was, you were going to be in Pedro's bodyguard." A safe place, that was the plan. With the king.

"*Òc.* I'll guard Pedro when he sneaks onto the battlefield. You know he will. Sebastián needs me."

"Sebastián needs you?" *I need you to be safe.* "You're going to fight because you want to."

"*Òc, cor dolç.*" Chrétien had that crazed happy look, so rare since this journey started. "This army has nothing to eat, nothing worth drinking. Might as well fight."

.

Sebastián's frightened horse skittered like all the others when the Moors' distant drums began to beat at dawn. He whispered and cajoled to reassure the animal while he studied the valley below. The battle was to be fought in a bowl that opened between the mountains, its fields plowed and leveled, with pines and oaks lining the bowl, offering protection to the priests and kings behind the battle line.

The Moors had the advantage of the rising ground at the south end, while the Christians were arrayed in the flat center of the valley. The Valerós forces, on the left with the Aragón knights, formed the vanguard, positioned to stop any incursion by the caliph's cavalry.

Diego Lopez, who rode his charger back and forth in front of Castile's line, shouted to the priest-knights and Alfonso's heavy cavalry, words that didn't carry this far. Around Diego, the united army waited, the whole of knights and infantry now arrayed exactly as Alfonso and Pedro had commanded.

The king of Castile intended to give all the glory to the Knights of Calatrava, the Templars, and the best of Castile's knights.

The night before, Tomás had said, "Let's hope those knights find glory and not slaughter. To go against the Moors' array, you need infantry with bows and light cavalry with spears. Castile's generals should know this after years on the frontier."

How unfortunate that Tomás was missing this day's battle. An excited happiness vibrated in Sebastián's veins. He was here at last, in the vanguard with the Valerós knights and Aragón fighters ordered to engage the Moors' flank. Light Catalan cavalry and fierce Pyrenees bowmen. Not a siege this time. A real battle.

A voice shouted nearby. "*Vivètz Valerós!*"

Chrétien rode into the front ranks, armored and happier than Sebastián had ever seen him, as if he was ready to sing, not fight. He called to Sebastián, "Tomás is with the knights surrounding Pedro. They don't need me. Let's go get some glory, bonfraire."

With Chrétien beside him, Sebastián found it easier to wait, even after lingering a day while the kings dithered. His private grousing through the spring (about Tomás's absence) was gone. Bonfraires side by side.

"Feel your sword arm hardening?" Chrétien said. "And yet easier to move than ever? So, Master of Valerós, check your bones. Are you ready?"

"*Òc.*" Sebastián kept checking. The nervous fear he felt in the Toledo riots? The valley here wasn't the tunnel of blind, unfamiliar city alleys. He knew where to direct men, where he belonged. His bones just wanted to move, wanted to hear the generals' command to go forward. But like the Toledo alleys, this valley was filled with men. The birds and local people had disappeared. No smoke from kitchen fires rose from the riverside houses. The pines and holm oaks stood still, no breeze swaying the branches.

Horses stamped and whinnied, blowing the unrest they sensed in their riders and their own fear of the pounding drums.

Iron-and-hide shields clattered against javelins and lances.

Feet stomped an impatient tattoo in the sunbaked dust.

The devil's own thunder echoed up from a hidden curve in the valley, advancing closer, like a summer's onrush of thunderheads.

Masking the sound of marching boots.

The knights' horses could no longer be heard, except for cries of fright or pain rising above the thunder.

Weapons swung overhead among the army arrayed across the valley, jutting up to match the thunderous rhythm.

The famous drummers of the caliph's army appeared from that bend in the valley. Their drums reverberated across the valley, then echoed back, as if two swarms of drummers pounded together, converging behind the Saracens, who arrayed in three wings similar to the kings' united army. Their front line was exactly as Tomás had reported: infantry in Saracen scaled armor and a very few men mounted as light cavalry, each with a large white shield that dangled three tassels. Behind these skittering troops were two lines of Azgaz bowmen, the ones Chrétien said not to fear, whatever rumors he'd heard, because they were the kind of mercenaries who run off if there's any sign that the day wasn't going their way.

"Faithless snakes!" Sebastián said, having learned from the ultra-montanos to hate deserters.

"Seems smart to me," Chrétien said. "They fight in order to be paid. No use losing your hide. Best to live for another payday."

Atop a hill across the way, the one now surrounded by the caliph's forces, men scurried to erect a pavilion. The Moors' incessant drums grew louder, drew closer. A covey of men mounted the hill and settled under the red tent. From this distance, Sebastián made out a solitary figure seating himself, having set his shield and weapons down. A white horse minced near him. This must be the caliph, the most exotic of figures discussed in Christendom, who wanted to be the new Saladin. Neither fat nor thin, short nor tall, the figure in white had nothing to distinguish him except the manner in which men stood in deference to him. One tall man stood close by, sheltering him with a parasol.

The exotic scene around the caliph became more dramatic when a hundred black men, all chained together, marched to the top of the hill and formed a ring about the caliph's pavilion. A captain, head-to-toe in immaculate white, chained together the first and last of the black men, creating a wall of human flesh glistening in the morning sun, surrounding the caliph in his blood-red tent.

Sebastián shifted in his saddle. Beside him, Chrétien shifted too, seeming as relaxed as when he sang before wine-laden soldiers. Sebastián shrugged inside his chainmail, wishing to copy that cool, focused determination.

Seeing the signal from Diego Lopez at the center front line, Sebastián raised his hand in a two-fingered V. His captains did the same. They'd practiced this more than any other bands among the united forces. The experienced Valerós knights were paired with the less experienced riders and infantry. The kings had arrayed their forces to look like the three-wing battle formation used since their forefathers first conquered Jerusalem. However, the Valerós infantry would never flee, as happened too often elsewhere, because Valerós knights were right there with them.

Or so every captain hoped.

A line of light skirmishers sallied forward from among the Saracens' front line. The caliph's army had finished waving its flags and was preparing to fight.

Sebastián checked the Valerós line along his side and farther back. Men's eyes flashed in the bright sun, most mouthing prayers or talking to themselves. Time to do what his grandfather Pèire taught and make sure men are shouting, not fearing what comes next. Sebastián raised one hand again, this time elbowing the soldier beside him to lift the Valerós standard. He shook that two-fingered V signal emphatically, commanding the men's attention away from the Moors' pounding drums. He bellowed the cry.

"*Desperta, Ferro!*"

Cavalry and infantry alike beat their javelins, spears, and bows against the ground. The men repeated Sebastián's cry and then shouted back, "*Vivètz Valerós!*"

Sebastián felt his heart beat in time with the drummers from hell. To his left, Diego's front-line cavalry danced nervously, their horses frightened by the drums. At the rear of Castile's infantry, men parted for priest-knights in white tunics bearing a huge red cross.

"Advance, bonfraire!" he called to Chrétien. "*Desperta, Ferro!*"

Chrétien flashed a grin. "Don't get killed, brother. All the rest is vanity."

·

Durán with the Aragón royal guard

A nose-burning stink of sweat and male funk and the acid tang of battle fear filled the air. Durán stood behind the shuffling, sweating mass that swayed in the morning light, multitudes eager and anxious to move ahead. The long-time plan: Durán would remain at the rear with Chrétien and Tomás, commanded by Pedro to serve as the king's guard.

Instead, Chrétien had armored himself while laughing at Durán's anxious question about how to live through the day. "*Don't be a target. Or if you are, be magnificent.*"

At the front of the Aragón flank, amid the Pyrenees and Catalan fighters that the other generals disdained, Sebastián waved a hand and commanded, his words shouted back along his ranks.

They're just men.

Durán liked men, but not so many, not so close, not armed and screaming battle cries. No reason to fear. This wasn't the backstreets of Toulouse. This crowd wouldn't turn and beat him. They all swayed, ready to move forward.

Tomás began to explain the battle array. Durán waved for silence, then saw that Tomás spoke with Isabella, now Miró in chainmail, whom Pedro had insisted should remain in the priests' pavilion.

"The caliph is atop the hill between those olive groves. Do you see the red tent and banners?" Tomás pointed. Isabella took advantage of the press of soldiers to stand so close to him. "The caliph believes himself holy and always holds the Quran, one he copied himself. The ring of slaves around the pavilion are set there to protect the caliph with their lives."

"Do they have more mounted knights than us? Alfonso was frantic, consumed with those numbers." Isabella was as intent as Tomás, studying the field.

"No. Only on the flanks. The caliph's generals intend to send those mounted riders out to overwhelm our front line."

"That's not seventy thousand men," she said.

"And we do not have thirty thousand men, which is what the caliph expects of us."

"Sancta María," she exclaimed. "Do the saints indeed answer prayer? Or did God Himself send a bonfraire to Sebastián's side?"

Chrétien was on his horse, riding into position with Sebastián.

"It's just Chrétien doing what he wants." Tomás grinned. "What's Pedro going to do? Punish a knight for fighting in a battle?"

The distance from where Durán stood and where Chrétien rode with Sebastián at the forefront seemed wider than this valley. Of course, that's what Chrétien would want to do. Off to kill people, as he was raised to do.

Tomás was still teaching Isabella battle strategy. "This is how Christendom arrays for a battle. Alfonso's knights are down in the center, Sancho is over there, on the right. The knight-priests are in the middle of the main force of those knights."

"That's what the kings fought about yesterday? Whether Pedro or Sancho is on the right? But now? *Aiieee!*" Isabella grabbed Tomás's arm, then seemed to remember to be Miró the scribe.

Durán gripped his own arm, agitated. Chrétien and Sebastián galloped out, Valerós knights around them, engaging a clutch of the Moors' knights riding out from the flanks of the Moors' array.

"Stop worrying," Tomás said. "There'll be more skirmishes like this before the battle begins. Look, their challengers are already retreating to regroup."

Except Chrétien was on the ground at that moment, in hand-to-hand battle with a knight of the caliphate as broad as Chrétien was tall. But that was only a moment. Then Chrétien was again on the horse that Sebastián led up for him.

Tomás crossed his arms. "I always fight alongside Chrétien. And I promised Sebastián last winter that we'd be in this battle together."

"Don't sulk," Isabella said.

Durán squinted to discern the people below. In the center of Castile's forces, the rows of Christian infantry and knights parted. An archbishop from Toledo came forward on horseback, surrounded by Calatrava knights, their surcoats white in the morning sun. The figure riding with the archbishop carried an enormous red cross. It was Arnau Amalric, the archbishop who persecuted Durán in Narbonne. Then the contingent of priests was lost from view amid the mass of Christians forces moving forward to meet the caliph's army.

But not in the orderly ranks in which they'd been arrayed.

Instead, the well-ordered rows of knights and infantry turned into a mob and charged the Moors' front line. Many of the infantry became trapped for a moment among circling horses, but then broke free, infantry attacking moving horses, thousands of men suddenly engaged in massive combat.

Durán had come here, deluded, thinking it would be like a street fight in Toulouse, but bigger. And all the knights around him on the journey across La Mancha talked about honor and glory and service to God. But below him, it was merciless slaughter, unlike anything he'd imagined.

"Valerós is pushing into their flanks again. Their fourth sortie." Tomás spoke close by Durán, who watched the riot at the center of the forces. Where Tomás pointed, the caliphate knights on the flanks were being pushed back, with Valerós in the fore on Aragón's side of the field, fighting the caliphate knights back up into the rocks and trees above the valley. Repeatedly, Valerós knights broke free of one engagement, rode up the side of the valley into the tree line, and then reappeared farther up the valley, emerging from the trees to attack another clutch of lightly armored caliphate knights, driving them back and out of the battlefield.

At the center of the valley, the writhing mass of bodies screamed and bellowed. The luckiest of the fallen knights' horses ran for the tree line. The enormous red cross and the shining-white tunics of the priest-knights were lost in that mass of men.

"Let's go." Isabella nudged Durán.

"I'm not fighting."

"No, we're picking up the fallen."

.

After making their way along the left edge of trees, Isabella led Durán near where the Aragón forces were fighting. For the greater part of the day, Durán worked like a field laborer with Isabella, carrying men from the edges of skirmishes who fell and yet still breathed. Durán's plan to avoid killing anyone worked well. Probably most saw him as another captain, taller than most, who moved through the ranks with a shield and quarterstaff, finding the gaps to step through, shoving men out of his way who weren't his own.

Isabella and Durán caught and calmed horses, returned them to unhorsed knights. When they found fallen Montcava and Valerós men, they dragged them out of the field, or at least out of the way of the mounted knights. A handful of times, their burden stopped breathing and departed this life before he and Isabella could gain the safety of the tree line, where they left their burdens with the unknightly Churchmen who watched the battle from safe vantage points above the field.

"God bless you, my son."

A Churchman offered the blessing and handed Durán a leather flask of water after Durán laid a bloodied infantryman at the monk's feet. The broken leg and bleeding arm of the infantryman didn't look like a blessing from God.

But Durán drank the water. Over that monk's shoulder, he caught sight of a coterie of Christian knights with Crux Lunata insignia break from the melee and gallop toward the left rear and Pedro's pavilion. The press of Aragón infantry pushed back against a Castilian line that was trying to evade the melee, which forced the Crux Lunata knights back and into the Aragón vanguard. With a hand wave—Durán was convinced he watched Matheus of Xirgú—the Crux Lunata knights rode toward where Sebastián was rallying Valerós infantry.

Another knight, taller than the rest and riding a black horse, intercepted their charge, slashing at the Crux Lunata leader. Sebastián, meanwhile, had spurred his horse to ride after a fleeing band of Saracen knights.

"They aren't returning."

Isabella jostled him, pointing. She'd been watching another side of the field and pointed up into the trees to the left of the caliph's pavilion. "The Moors, I mean. The knights that Valerós has been driving into the trees. They are not returning to the field. Their infantry is deserting. Why isn't that red cross moving forward?"

"Because," Durán pointed to the rear of the Castilian array, "Alfonso's men are deserting too."

∎

Felip with Alfonso in the kings' line

Those infernal drums echoed through the whole valley, making it hard for Felip to cool his heartbeat the way that Chrétien taught. Blood pounded in his ears, but that had been true ever since the lightning strike. Felip didn't believe he was afraid. The army would retreat before the enemy reached the line of priests chanting pleas for God's blessing.

The scribes, including Felip, worked busily, huddled near the Castilian priests and archbishops, everyone in chainmail. The scribes knew their assigned duties: to record for the kings what happened on the battlefield, which knights found glory through victory, which went to find heaven's reward.

Alongside where the scribes worked, the bishops buckled sheaths at their waists and watched the battle as if prepared to join in. But not one of them had their aventail laced correctly, or even laced at all, or had their swords truly available for action—oh, save one knight beside the archbishop of Narbonne who looked prepared.

None stood in the ready way that Chrétien had beaten into Felip within two days after they'd met.

But when Felip caught himself entertaining those thoughts, he wondered when Chrétien's voice had become his inner guide about fighting and fear. But then, the teasing had stopped after that night when they became sworn brothers.

The morning of the battle, Felip stood alone in a crowd of strangers, away from his friends. Pedro had requested that someone hear and record what happened in this pavilion, amid many of Pedro's foes, including a handful of Knights of the Lunate Cross and Arnau Amalric, the archbishop of Narbonne. What Pedro requested wasn't as dramatic as asking Tomás to spy in Andalusia, yet Felip now lurked amid foes, invisible amid all the functionaries perched above the battlefield.

That clerk Doménec appeared, carrying messages between Alfonso and Pedro. Felip raised a hand in greeting, but Doménec didn't seem to notice him. Everyone's attention turned to the field.

Below, the first lines of the unified army had entered the field. Knights against knights, rows of archers, infantry ranks. From the kings' and archbishops' perches on the hill, it was relatively easy to see factions of the army move, though not easy to identify individuals. It should be easy to differentiate Christians from their Muslim enemies, though Tomás had warned that the caliph's army included Christian mercenaries. Felip spied the Valerós banner amid a line of cavalry and infantry shoving through Saracen infantry. The entire scene was an unholy mess, with the mass of men surging and retreating and rolling ahead again like waves seeking the shore. Screams rose above the pounding of those drums, men shoving, thrusting, plunging ahead, some falling, others trampling.

A world of which Felip knew nothing, though Chrétien's voice banged inside his head, along with that bell that continued to ring, offering advice about how to see the battle.

Scanning the field below, finding the Valerós flag again, Felip sought helmets or horses he might recognize. Sebastián stood by his banner, his horse gone now, his hand raised in a sign that commanded a forward thrust. That line of Valerós men moved again, like a storm wave battering the Saracen infantry, which retreated as the force moved over them.

Elsewhere on the field, the wave of human flesh retreated as Saracens pushed against Navarre cavalry or Castile's infantry.

"My eyes are too weak. What's happening?" a voice nearby asked. "Are we retreating?"

"It appears so, Monsenyor."

Curious, Felip turned sideways in the mass of scribes, finding the small priest who had forced him to record that odd barraganía contract. Which Felip failed to find Isabella and tell her about.

Now, that little priest stood quite close to Alfonso, the king of Castile, who was a tall, high-colored man with hanks of white hair that sprang free from its tie-band and hung limply around his face. Like the others, the king's aventail was unlaced, and he held his helmet under his arm while he conferred with advisors and the bevy of

Cistercian monks clustered around him, all clad in spotless white in the midst of this filthy field.

"No one is winning at the moment." A deep voice rose from amid the advisors. "It's going both ways."

"Don't hold out false hope," a thin voice cried. That little priest again. Beside him was Arnau, the archbishop of Narbonne. "Let's be honest with ourselves and learn the truths God teaches today."

Pedro had instructed him to record everything. Though Felip understood only half of what these men said, he wrote rapidly.

The king of Castile and his lords were weeping.

Alfonso stood ten feet away, but he was so wrenched with passion, he might as well be weeping right in Felip's ear.

"Rodrigo Jiménez, vos y yo aquí muramos!"

Rodrigo Jiménez de Rada. A name like a jingling bag of coins. Felip penned the archbishop's title, not just his name. And wrote in Latin, so the words seemed less shameful. *Archbishop, it is here we die!* Then Felip wrote the rest of the king's despair over the morning battle. The Knights of Calatrava annihilated. Diego Lopez de Haro and the military orders encircled by the caliph's cavalry.

Now Bishop Arnau proclaimed that the Christian spearmen were retreating.

"Deserters!" Alfonso exclaimed.

Bishop Jiménez consoled him, insisting that God answers prayer. But that little priest kept yammering on, urging Alfonso into despair. "In truth, your front-line cavalry and archers are retreating. The day shall belong to Mirammolin."

"It's as I've feared since the moon emptied. As I dreamed for the past fortnight." Alfonso meandered in frustrated dismay.

"The devil-damned caliph has brought out his reserves," Archbishop Arnau said. "Though it seems early in the day for that."

"Those ill-bred farmers and merchants are fleeing. They're running back to Toledo." The little priest seemed to gloat, though Felip guessed that it was merely the normal tone of that high, scratchy voice.

"The day is lost," Arnau said. "We need to get our kings to safety. Our brother Doménec, can you carry a message to Pedro?"

"Sancta Maria, Reina del Cielo, nos muestran gracia!" Alfonso fell to his knees, pleading for St-Maria to show grace. He had a dagger

in his hand, its point near his own throat. "I failed you, Madonna, and your Son. Worse than when I lost Al-Arcos. Oh, infamy!"

Felip sprang forward, not thinking in that heartbeat, since the old man appeared ready to hurt himself. But Felip collided with that wall of white-robed priests. Those nearest to Alfonso—the little one and Bishop Arnau—stepped back, giving the grieving king room rather than coming to his aid.

This is the blasted moment. Squeezed among priests and scribes, Felip believed he was watching the doom that Isabella and Durán had whipped them across La Mancha to prevent. *The Crux Lunata gets what it most wants. Here was Pedro's defeat in battle.*

And Felip could do nothing among those gloating enemies.

"No, Monsenyor." Bishop Jiménez spoke calmly. Everyone else in the pavilion was over-excited. "It is here we live and conquer!"

Alfonso stopped, the dagger still in his hand. Trembling.

"Look, there." Bishop Jiménez pointed down the field. "Sancho's line is closing on the right side. And that line of knights and infantry from Aragón on the other. Those wild-men that Pedro boasts about. The ones who trained half his knights."

"Filthy forest savages," Bishop Arnau sneered. "You saw them in Toledo. Slashing and screaming as if the devil has their tails. The devil probably does."

"They aren't even knights of Aragón." That little priest added to the disparaging of Valerós, though Felip knew the man was too near-sighted to see the battlefield, for all the gloom and despair he'd bandied about that morning. "More like bandits from sheep farms in the Pyrenees."

"Call them savages if you like," Bishop Jiménez said. "They forced Saracens' light cavalry off the field while we stood here in despair."

"I'm not so sure." Bishop Arnau stared down at the quarter of the field where the archbishop of Toledo pointed. "Your hopes blind you."

"Who's blind? Half the caliph's infantry has fled. Victory is our destiny today."

"Do you think so?" Alfonso got to his feet again, now seeming touchingly wistful.

"Send our reserves in now," Bishop Jiménez said. "Let's not have Aragón go to battle alone. Are you coming, Alfonso? You'll feel better on the field."

That archbishop, the one from Toledo, helped Alfonso buckle his helmet.

"What we need to do," Bishop Jiménez said to Bishop Arnau, "is to get our crimson cross upright on the field again, to help our men remember what they're fighting for."

Bishop Arnau also buckled on his helmet, standing for a moment with his hands on his hips, glaring at the little half-blind white-robed priest.

Though from where Felip stood, it looked like the bishop glared at Doménec, who set off on a trot back to Pedro's camp.

Which was where Felip wished to be. With all these men departing for the field, there wasn't anything to overhear. Felip followed Doménec, with every expectation that he'd find Isabella at Pedro's pavilion, so he could tell her about that little priest.

•

Durán near the caliph's pavilion

Your back foot!
Shield up!
Thrust now!

Chrétien's voice rang in his head, repeating calls from training. This was the hardest work Sebastián had ever done. It wasn't like Toledo, where he fought men but hoped not to do serious harm. He checked his shield the way that voice reminded him.

The real Chrétien was a few horse-lengths away, his voice not distinguishable in the melee. A significant arc of Valerós fighters moved through the caliph's footmen, many of whom fled when Valerós came within a pike's reach.

Chrétien brought his sword down on the shoulder of a Saracen knight who thought he could swing faster. The man dropped to the ground, drenched in his own gore, howling, but not dead. Chrétien kicked the man's weapon away and stepped over him.

Sebastián, his latest target fleeing with four others, raised his fist, and forced two fingers into a V as he again shouted, "*Desperta, Ferro!*"

Valerós men screamed the words together, shrieked the way Chrétien taught, and shouted *Awake, Steel!* Again, the soul-curdling mass of men pursued the retreating light infantry and the Saracen foot soldiers who fled both their captains and the encroaching Christian fighters.

With Chrétien shielding him, Sebastián glanced around for a heartbeat. The Valerós wall appeared as it had when they trained. Faces he recognized and expected, though stretched with the work at hand. Those Mozarab bowmen, whom Pedro had sent to Sebastián's camp, now took their position behind the Valerós front line, stopping when their captains called, to nock arrows and loose them in an arc into the midst of Saracen infantry. With each flight of arrows, Valerós shouted Arabic words that Father Anselm had taught. *God wills it!*

Below, the Castilian knights and infantry let out a roar, shouting *Sangre de Cristo Jesús! Sancta María!* That massive blood-red cross seemed to be on the move again.

The Saracen infantry roiled, like a whirlpool in a river running over rocks. Men couldn't turn back fast enough, shoving and crashing into each other to get away. The Saracen captains shouted, but the fleeing men did not look to their captains any longer. They wanted to go home. Not face a wall of death-screaming steel.

Once more Sebastián, taller than the men around him, raised the V signal, directing Valerós toward the hill holding the caliph's pavilion. He shouted until his voice went raw.

"*Vivètz Valerós!*"

Boots stomped, throats shrieked Valerós cries in unison, as loud as the Saracens' infernal parade drums. A wall of men stomped forward. Since this mass of men moved at a wave of his hand, and Saracens fled as they came, Sebastián led them over the field, intending to silence those infernal drums.

More Saracens fled ahead of them than Sebastián had men to pursue. The Valerós line wove its way ahead, slashing at any who came near, whether infantry or light cavalry. Instead of weaving around the caliph's mound to encounter the drummers, Sebastián crested the hill with fifty Valerós knights and infantry behind him.

The fleeing Saracens parted before them, like waves running around boulders in the sea.

Valerós stood on the left of the caliph's circle of chained slaves. Across the way, men in the colors of Sancho of Santiago also crested the hill. Inside the chained wall, those remaining were in sheer panic. The parasol was gone. The caliph's throne was empty. The chained men in the rear formed only a stumbling obstacle to the caliph's fleeing bodyguards.

Sebastián shouted, "Run, fools! You're free!"

Chrétien, who loved drama, appeared, his eyes flashing behind his helmet's nose guard. He swung a mace he'd picked up from the field, shattering the chains between two shrieking guards. He shouted at the men in Arabic, which Sebastián understood enough to guess.

"*Run! Your master has deserted you.*"

Across the circle, where the caliph's white-coated guards fled, Tomás fought against the deserters, pushing them back, shouting in Arabic to fight. As if the united army didn't have enough Saracens to kill that day.

But why would Tomás leave Pedro's side? He said he'd never leave Isabella again.

Whatever Tomás was doing, it was time to rout these lingering Saracens and then return to the mountain tree line where Pedro had assigned Valerós to fight.

Sebastián once more cried, "*Desperta, Ferro!*"

That fighter could not be Tomás, because he did not turn at the sound of the Valerós battle cry.

24

Hereticated

Dolç at La Seu d'Urgell
July 16

HIGH IN THE MOUNTAINS, clouds clung to the glacier-covered peaks and relieved the heat of summer. After so many days on the trail, and nights finding shelter safe from both animals and men, the travelers came to a place where the river they'd followed was joined by a second river. In this high valley, people had endured long enough to build both a castell high up the hill and a cathedral with several churches. La Seu d'Urgell seemed to be as old as Narbonne, and from the size of its cathedral, its old counts had grand notions of their place on God's earth.

Jacques agreed that, for one night, the travelers could spend silver to sleep in real beds and eat hot food at an inn, food that didn't taste of burning pitch and made with lamb instead of their usual daily fare of rabbit or other trapped vermin. Rather than join the men at the inn, Dolç begged to be left alone with the children for a moment to go to church.

Inside the cathedral complex, she found the church of St-Miquel. The girls chattered at the idea, touching Quelo's head to tell him they were in his church. On the back wall of one alcove an image of the Virgin had been painted on the plaster, the infant Savior in her arms, crowns of gold circling their heads. Sancta Maria had such a look of peace that Dolç tarried there, her exhausted children happy to pause in the cool stone shelter, each of them calling out another detail in the image. They clung to Dolç, of course, even the oldest not venturing further than a single step while holding a fistful of Dolç's robe.

Which was filthy. They all were beyond dusty, their clothes stiff from trail dirt and smelling of horse sweat. But Jacques insisted that it wasn't a good time to pause for a real rest. "Why do you want a laundry?" he'd asked, puzzled. "We'll all be dirty again before we're a flea's hop away from this town."

A priest appeared in the alcove where Dolç and her brood rested. He called a blessing and asked her name in the local Catalan dialect. When she turned to answer, her eye caught the frieze on the opposite alcove wall. St-Sebastián, tied to a tree, arrows piercing him, his blood pouring from each wound. Not what her overly-tired daughters needed to see. But she could only guide and guard so much. At least they sheltered safely on sacred ground at that moment.

"St-Félíu?" The priest repeated her domus name when she answered him. "That isn't a family name from these parts."

"My homes are in Narbonne and Barcelona," she said.

"Is your husband here? Why so far from home?"

"He's fighting Saracens in Andalusia with Pedro d'Aragón." It was a lie, since Tomás was no longer her husband and Chrétien claimed he was dead. But the priest was asking whether she traveled alone and why she was here. How little to tell the first friendly person she'd met on this journey? "I'm traveling to join his brother's domus while awaiting his return."

"Alone, ma dòmna? How brave."

Quelo chose that moment to shriek as if in pain, his terrified cry echoing from St-Sebastián's alcove throughout the church. She shifted him, but couldn't wrestle him onto her breast without reaching into her robe, which didn't seem appropriate in front of the priest, however wild she'd lived while traveling through the mountains.

A hand in a leather gauntlet seized her shoulder.

The girls screamed, though she'd taught them better.

"Let us have peace in the house of God," the priest intoned.

Two hands grasped her shoulders, forcing Dolç to turn around. She faced Baudoïs de Montpelhièr in chainmail, dressed in a priest-knight's white gambeson. Her children huddled even closer, clutching at her, so that she couldn't move.

"You have stolen that which is to be the salvation of God's kingdom on earth." Baudoïs, aventail laced over his face, loomed over her. "In the name of Jesus Christ our Savior, I condemn you for heresy."

Days before, back in that ravine, hunted by a bandit's massif, Dolç thought how trapped a woman was when protecting so many children. Unable to run, unable to rise and fight without exposing herself to more danger.

Not even able, like the plump capercaillie in the ravine, to fly up into the safety of higher branches.

"You are mistaken, senhór." The best Dolç could manage was to imitate her cousin Petronilla, who always sounded haughtier than any other woman under God's heaven. "You see us here, offering thanks to God for all His blessings, in a house built by the most holy Catholic Church."

"But not seeking forgiveness for your sins." That colorless priest who'd greeted her turned from benign to malign in the flicker of an eye, his mouth set in disdain, his forehead creased with deep disgust. He turned his back on her, speaking only to Baudoïs. "Take her to the nuns' dormitory. It's the only space we have to hold women."

Baudoïs seized Dolç's left hand, jerking it behind her. He reached for her other hand, as if to bind them together. But Quelo cried, once again disturbed by her heartbeat.

"You must let me console my child."

He relented, wrapping the cord he'd intended to tie her with so that her arms were pinioned. The girls, roused from shock, were weeping. They too needed her to hold them.

"Make your brats shut up!" Baudoïs commanded with a shove.

"They are children of God, saved by our lord Jesus Christ, and blessed in baptism." Dolç spoke softly and evenly, using the same tone as for calming her children. "You are frightening these infants for no reason. Which is beastly in the sight of God."

Baudoïs laughed. Having seized the neck-edge of her robe, he pushed and dragged her toward the big wooden doors of the church. That priest nudged his way in front of them and pushed the heavy, creaking door open.

Outside, lightning circled the valley where she'd only moments before enjoyed how mild a day it was because of the clouds. Jagged forks stabbed at mountain tops. Deeper flashes illuminated the dark clouds. It didn't rain here, but the thunder echoed close by, the charge in the air crawling across her arms, her neck, into her hair. Her oldest girl cried out at the next crash of thunder.

Quelo, first startled, then angry, wailed more than you'd think a tiny body could manage. She struggled to comfort him, but couldn't move, and so the poor thing cried his heart out.

At the foot of the steps leading up to the church, Jacques stood alongside another man, and a dozen armed men stood behind them. She recognized Jacques's tall companion with the bearing and dress of a southern lord as a man who had been at her wedding. Her first wedding.

"Bon día, Senhór Ramón-roger." She dipped her head, since the bindings didn't allow any other honorable greeting.

"Have all the goats in town died?" The count of Foix seemed amused, which she found reassuring. He spoke mildly and yet loud enough to be heard over Quelo's complaints. "Whatever is the king of Aragón's cousin doing in these mountains?"

Rather than answer, she called her children's names. "Go stand with Jacques, please. Do it now."

The girls ran, peering from behind the bantam-sized Norman soldier, but then were hoisted onto the shoulders of the men they'd rode with through the mountains, each girl wrapping her arms around the neck of her savior.

"I'm traveling to Senhór Chrétien's domus in Toulouse," she said. "But our journey has been interrupted."

"Ma dòmna, I'd shame myself as a Christian if I didn't offer you shelter." The handsome count, perhaps older than her own father, seemed to attend to no one but her. She didn't see the gesture that caused the men wearing his house colors to surround the knight who held her hostage.

Baudoïs stiffened, grasping her robe even tighter, jerking her close to him. Quelo cried again.

"In the name of God, and for the sake of my brother-soldier and cousin Pedro d'Aragón," Ramón-roger spoke mildly, as if asking for salt and bread, "release this woman."

The priest piped up. "She has been condemned as a heretic and is in the hands of the Church for judgment."

"How sad." The count didn't seem sad. "The bishop of Urgell will be disappointed to learn how easily you are deceived."

"But this is a man of God!" the priest wailed.

"He's a man who lied to you, Father. A deserter from the kings' enterprise in Andalusia. A ruffian harassing this good woman." Ramón-roger dragged his gloved finger down Baudoïs's tunic. "Wearing a cross doesn't make a man holy."

The count's men moved closer, weapons drawn. Baudoïs released her at last, so she could again cradle Quelo and offer him true solace.

●

Later, in the enormous comfort of the count's rooms at the castell, she calmed the children, got them to eat bread and cheese, and settled them to nap on cushions in the rushes. Then at last she could ask.

"How did you know to find me?"

Jacques looked to the count first, but answered. "At the stable, we asked about other visitors. At the inn where we sought bread, cheese, and wine, we learned who was in town asking questions."

"And my men," Ramón-roger said, "are always just as active, letting me know what strangers came through the gate today."

"All that worry in the woods," Jacques mused, "when it's town we have to fear."

"Now, ma dòmna." Ramón-roger settled in beside Dolç, pouring wine for both of them from a stone jug. "How did you come to be pursued by the Crux Lunata? I thought you married a seigneur in Narbonne, with five merchant ships and a spice-trading business."

"That poor man died," she said. "The doctors said apoplexy. For my safety, Pedro married me to his friend, Don Tomás of Morella."

"For safety? Tomás of Morella?" Ramón-roger exploded in mirthless laughter, rousing the girls from their naps. "*Jhezu del tron*, what was Pedro thinking?"

"That good man died too. It seems Pedro's enemies are interested in Don Tomás's child, so his brother Chrétien suggested that—"

"*Ai*, ma dòmna!" Ramón-roger sobered. "We can't have you wandering the countryside with the Crux Lunata chasing after you."

"We are going to Toulouse," Jacques said, "to wait for Chrétien and Senhór Durán to come home from Andalusia."

The count of Foix threw his head back and laughed. From the looks of others around him, this was a familiar behavior, so it appeared Dolç was the only one who found no humor in the current state of affairs.

But Jacques asked, "Senhór, do you not agree that the Master of Montcava should be her protector?"

"Durán?" The count considered the question, then shook his head. "I can ask only so much of that man."

"The king of Aragón is my protector." Dolç had to speak for herself. "Who is the master of Montcava to care for me?"

The count sobered. "Indeed, both men shall step into service if…when the expedition in Andalusia is over. Meanwhile, I shall serve Pedro as your protector."

Ramón-roger then rose and left them, instructing his steward to make the appropriate plans.

"Thank you, master Jacques. I am grateful to you."

"It is my job and my pleasure, ma dòmna."

"Who is Durán? I thought Sebastián of Valerós was the inheritor of Montcava."

"Sebastián asked his brother Durán to act as steward for Montcava. He's Chrétien's *bon amic*. A good man."

She knew so little about Tomás's family. "He's another child of Isabella of Valerós, like Sebastián?"

His eyes widened. "No, a child of Isabella's husband."

Jacques was busy with the steward, so she couldn't ask more. Though she wondered what *bon amic* meant.

She changed the subject. "Is there a chapel in the castell where I can thank God for deliverance?"

"Not sure you are delivered yet, ma dòmna. It's still a long road to Toulouse."

25

Salvation

Felip with bonfrariers at Las Navas,
behind the Aragón line
July 16

ALL DAY FELIP PRAYED WITH every breath, every heartbeat, in the way that the old monks at St-Pere insisted men must, but that Felip never before understood. At St-Pere, Felip begged God to make Himself known. But here, Felip watched God guide the day and no longer harbored doubt. He prayed with gratitude, after first beseeching protection for his bonfraires.

From the priests' and scribes' pavilions high on the ridge, Felip commanded a view while safe from the dangers below. He had cautioned Serena Taresa to remain near the priests' pavilion.

Yet he abandoned his safe scribe's post when the king of Castile took to the field, making a well-reasoned decision to run behind the rear flanks to reach Pedro's pavilion. His portable desk banged his back as he ran, bruising his shoulder and throwing him off balance. At least the clang of battle drowned out that bell that rang in his head.

In the gap at the rear between the Castile and Aragón ranks, a crowd of men ran toward Felip. But it wasn't the Castilian rear guard that Bishop Jiménez intended to call forth. Instead, spear- and bow-bearing infantry swarmed toward him, the injured and tattered men who'd been in the center of that maelstrom. Pushed aside and battered as they ran past, Felip found himself in front of a mounted knight who led a second horse.

"Time to fight, Xirgú."

Of all people Felip least wanted to encounter in hell, Colomb de Beaurain appeared, handing over a spear, which Felip caught by instinct. Tossing Felip the reins of the second horse, Colomb boomed, "Do what your father would!"

Felip mounted, clumsier than any time he'd climbed on a horse since he was six years old. Colomb reined his horse close by, studying Felip, who wore only a chainmail shirt. No protection for arms, legs, or head.

"W–What?"

"We are stopping this retreat."

Colomb raised a long red banner—a man's shirt, bloodied—and shouted, "On your father's honor! Rally to the king!"

Then he shouted again in a host of dialects. Castellano, Aragónese, French, Catalan.

Felip rode beside Colomb, no more than a spear's length apart, shouting the Lord's name, calling for courage, insisting that the battle was won and booty to be had. Together, they herded men, the way they'd herded panicked sheep in that mountain vale.

When men struck out at them, Felip calmed his horse to keep it from hurting the fleeing foot soldiers, then he helped to block and herd the men back to their positions. Other captains appeared and joined in a mounted effort to send panicked men back onto that bloodied field.

While they worked, Felip had no moment to pause or rise up in the saddle to see what happened on the main field. Then a roar rose from the crowded field.

Sangre de Cristo Jesús! Sancta María!

Men's voices in unison rose above the clang and screams, so loud that the fleeing herd looked back to see. Then they began to shout, the words echoing to the rear where Felip rode with other captains to stop the deserters.

"The holy cross goes forward!"

"The caliph is gone!"

These desperate men glanced around, looking to each other for reassurance. With the captains, Felip took up the cry.

"The day is the Lord's! Join in the victory."

A dozen more shouts, throats raw, and then the herd turned, running again to the battlefield.

"Run for booty, you bastards," Colomb shouted. He reined up near Felip again. As the throng rushed away, he spoke in lower tones. "If you won't run for honor."

Colomb swung an arm, clattering chainmail across Felip's back. "You, Xirgú! You did a man's work! Earned a man's honor!"

This praise came from Colomb, the man thought to be Pedro's assassin. Yet Felip felt a deep warmth, a balm flowing through his soul, unlike any benediction or declaration of forgiveness for sins.

"You rode a horse into a battle," Colomb said, "and led men to fight as they must. Your father would be proud."

Colomb rode with him to Pedro's pavilion, where Felip needed to return to the work the king had charged him to do. Yet when he reached the pavilion, none of his friends were there, though Felip expected to find Isabella and Tomás amid the king's guard. Most of the guards had departed for the battlefield.

Felip unloaded his desk from his bruised shoulders, found a camp stool, and prepared to work. Pedro watched the battle from the other side of the pavilion, but he greeted neither Colomb nor Felip or even glanced their way. Doménec, who worked nearby, glanced at Felip but didn't seem to recognize him. While Felip prepared his pen, he failed to smother the pride in his breast. *I saved deserters for the king. Like a knight, a captain of men.*

"*Hola!*" Colomb called to the king, who turned and waved. The figure wasn't tall enough to be Pedro.

"Where's the king?" Felip asked.

"Below."

Where that man pointed, it was impossible to differentiate one Aragón knight from another. "Pedro's in the fray at the left flank where Alfonso wanted him. The king of Castile hasn't even reached the edge of the maelstrom."

"Why would Pedro put himself in that much danger?"

"He's made that way." Colomb glanced at Felip. "I knew your father in the Outremer. Justí de Xirgú was the most honorable of men. A great man."

"Thank you for s–saying so." Felip worried his pen point, needing to return to the task of recording the events of the battle.

"Justí saved my life one day," Colomb said. "And in the next battle, he lost his while fighting to protect other men."

"Another day, I'd like to hear that story." Felip had to sort his thoughts between the praise he'd received from Colomb and the weeks' long fears that Colomb was a Crux Lunata assassin. "You do know that Matheus was sired by Nicolau of Montcava? That he's not Justí's son?"

"Òc, he's the spitting image of my old uncle. Makes him Durán's brother, doesn't it? Not yours, *fadrin*. Still, I owe you, for the sake of Justí's honor."

"You don't owe me anything," Felip said.

Colomb said, "My work—my family's honor—I tried to lead Matheus when I found out he was a Beaurain. I failed both Renoud and Nicolau. Now it's only me left. I alone am responsible for reclaiming the Beaurain name."

"Why not leave it to Sebastián and Durán?" Felip's audacity surprised him. "They seem to have inherited your brother's courage."

Noise blocked any possible answer from Colomb. Castile's ranks shouted back their king's words. Felip bent over his scribe's work, needing to write fast to keep up with the changes in the day's events. He sharpened his pen and translated the Castellano words to Latin.

"Kill, not seize! Bring a prisoner, you die with him!"

Once again Felip watched where Pedro's guard fought, hoping to discern which might be the king of Aragón. Nearby, a contingent of Crux Lunata knights bashed through the center melee, riding for where Valerós knights fought ahead of the other Aragón knights.

"If you want to serve honor, perhaps you can stop that." Felip pointed to where a knight who might be Matheus swung a sword at other Christians. "Are they after the king of Aragón?"

"Sweet angels singing in heaven!"

Colomb voiced several invectives in the common tongue as he ran for his horse and then rode off toward that contingent of Aragón knights. Felip strained his eyes, looking for Tomás among the Aragón guards. He must be fighting alongside Pedro, whatever armor the king chose to wear. That was the plan for the day, for Tomás to remain near the king.

Those Crux Lunata knights struggled with men who shrieked *Desperta, Ferro!* That cry came from Pedro's fiercest contingent.

"Which man is Tomás?" Isabella stood near him, anxious.

"Which is the real king?" Felip asked. He watched while Colomb seemed to hector those knights, sending them back to the real battle. "None of them is Pedro. Colomb will think I misled him."

"*Aiieee!* Felip!" Isabella's cry startled him. "That sword you carry. Where did you get it?"

He'd failed to give it to Tomás earlier and had worn it as if it were his own. "A woman and a priest carried it to the scribes' pavilion, but left it behind. The priest said it wasn't the magical sword he wanted. I thought Tomás would want it back."

"*Ai, mon amic.* Tell me the whole story. You might be a hero." While she listened to his story, she took the sword from him, buckling it over the weapons she already wore.

∎

Sebastián at the caliph's pavilion

From the caliph's hilltop, Sebastián saw one crowd running up the hill while another ran down. In the whirl, he continually checked whether he was to protect or strike the next man who ran past. Beyond what Sebastián had seen at Malagón, the field below was filled with fallen bodies. The day's heat, roiling up from the valley floor, carried the stench of butcher's offal.

Just outside the chained circle of the caliph's protectors, Chrétien bellowed again in Arabic.

"Run, my friends! You are free."

Each man was as least as tall as Chrétien, twice as wide, half-naked, and sweating in this hilltop inferno. They seemed to be shouting prayers. Chrétien yelled again.

"Calling on Jesus won't save you. Flee!" Chrétien swung his mace again and broke another link in the iron chain, still shouting in Arabic. "Alfonso says no prisoners. They'll kill you!"

More than half the chained slaves stood still where they'd been chained, continuing to shout prayers. A horde of Sancho's men, the latecomers from Léon, poured through the gap in the circle, intent on seizing whatever the caliph left behind, and then running after the retreating Saracens, thirsty for blood and booty after the morning's frustrations.

Sebastián, taller than all but Chrétien and the huge slaves, saw over the helmets of the fighters at the edge of the slave-circle where Tomás pushed back the retreating guards. Sebastián paused midway, confused for a moment. Chrétien urged the chained black men to flee, and Tomás urged the Saracen guards to fight. Sebastián dodged the booty-mad men from Léon, seeking anyone else from Valerós, then signaling Benito and the mercenary Thierry to follow him. He called to Chrétien, shouted for Valerós, and motioned for his men to join Tomás.

Two spear-lengths away, Sebastián shouted, "Let them run, Don Tomás! The Léon butchers want to kill them all."

When Sebastián was a spear's length from Tomás, a Saracen guard of high rank—his snow-white linen tunic and gold at his shoulder meant that—lunged for Tomás's back, long dagger out, intent on murder.

Sebastián swung, his sword striking deep into the attacker's shoulder. On the other side, Chrétien hamstrung the attacker. While the struck-down man cried out in agony, Tomás swung his sword around to attack his saviors.

Sebastián shouted, "Tomás! Bonfraire!"

Only it wasn't Tomás.

As much like him as Yusuf, but not Tomás. A bit taller. Finer featured. Seeing the mistake at the same moment as Sebastián did, Chrétien parried the new attack while shouting in Arabic.

"Rashid al-Aziz?"

The Tomás-like Saracen fought back—if they'd watched from a distance, his sword work would lead any fool believe it was Tomás—but he wasn't prepared to handle two larger men at the same time. A flicker of a glance from Chrétien showed that he, too, was not prepared to kill Tomás's twin. While Chrétien had the man's attention, Sebastián bashed his sword's pummel at the twin's temple.

Proving once again that the inventive Moors did not have good helmets.

Chrétien caught the man as he fell.

"Great work, Valerós! Look at his badge. It's the grand vizier Tomás wanted us to capture and protect."

"Alfonso declared no prisoners." Sebastián hadn't hesitated all morning, but did now.

"And yet Pedro is our king and knows the value of this hostage."

"He's injured." Sebastián pointed where a deep cut in the man's arm dripped over Chrétien's chainmail.

"Let's get him off the field. Grab his sword. Perhaps it's magical, like Tomás's."

Chrétien heaved the captured vizier over his shoulder and started down the hill. Sebastián snatched up the man's dropped sword, grasping it with his left hand, his right hand holding his own sword ready. The man's pommel was worked over in silver, shaped like a pine cone.

But he had only a few heartbeats to consider it. The second wave of fighters, men from Sancho's flank, were taking trophies. Sebastián spotted two men under his command, a pair of Almogavars, taking an ear from a fallen slave. He interrupted them, then rounded up all the Valerós men on the hilltop and commanded them back to their position along the ridge, protecting the Aragón knights and stopping any advance from Saracen light infantry.

When Sebastián caught up with Chrétien, their captive began to rouse. Sebastián bound the man's hands with a leather thong from his belt and used another to tie his feet, so that Chrétien didn't have to bear a struggling man.

"Kill me now!"

Their captive bucked. Chrétien grasped him more firmly.

"We just saved you from an assassin," Sebastián said, wary of whether the wiggling man might unbalance Chrétien. "Not so we could kill you ourselves."

"Your kings are killing hostages. Why wait?" The man spoke in accented Castellano.

"I'm Pedro's man." Chrétien spoke in Arabic. "I take what I want. And I'm betting my brother doesn't want you dead."

"Your brother?" The captive persisted in Castellano.

"Tomás of Morella. I'm betting you're Rashid al-Aziz, the man Tomás calls his noble and valiant cousin. My brother asked us to find and protect you."

At Tomás's name, their captive lapsed into Arabic, swearing oaths as mighty as any Tomás ever had, calling God's wrath down on Tomás's name.

"You must be one of those Christian Mozarabs," Chrétien said. "I've never known a good man of Islam able to describe my brother so accurately."

As they picked their way across the battlefield, now populated with scavengers seeking any goods the dead had to offer, Chrétien began to sing a blasphemous old crusaders' song, "*Seinhos, aujas, c'aves saber e sen.*"

> 'While the dogs slept,
> I dreamed I was in heaven,
> saying you are in the wrong, God.
> Try a different attack.'

·

Durán at the caliph's pavilion

After midday, the field stunk like the abattoir in Toulouse, what Durán thought of as the smell of sin, with an extra tang of fear, especially from the horses, whose gambesons and caparisons were drenched through with sweat, stained with blood.

"*Kill, not seize! Bring a prisoner, you die with him!*"

The Castilian heralds cried across the battlefield, the words echoed by captains and then shouted by the masses.

After midday, Durán's resolution not to kill any man didn't matter to either the God of Light or the God of Darkness. All around him, men busily called on God's name while butchering whoever came near. All the Saracen units ran in retreat, headed for the tree line, dropping the weight of battle gear and moving rapidly away from the pursuing Christian knights and infantry.

Catching sight of Valerós knights ahead, Durán pushed through until he was near the caliph's pavilion, the throne now empty, overturned. The ring of chained slaves had been breached, perhaps so the caliph could escape. But most still stood braced to fight instead of running away, each a head taller than Durán and blacker than Tomás, further sunburned to crispness and nearly naked. Each had a shield and a short sword, but no other armor. For a final guard, they were ill equipped to fight mounted, armored knights.

But with a few slaves freed, and the caliph and his advisors gone, they fought only to protect each other, while each freed man worked to free another from chains. Over the screams of horses and men, and the clash of steel on steel, the sound as Durán drew near was stone on iron, freed slaves finding the weak points in iron links to free their brothers.

The pounding of the infernal drums had lessened and moved off, sounding now from only one place in the valley. The other beat continued, the trampling of men and metal clashing, a counter tempo of horses shrieking when injured. The grunts of men still fighting, the soul-shivering screams of men struck or trampled.

The sun now burned so hot, it was as if the heat could be heard, waves of it rising off the field, adding to all the other noise. Captains shouting. Sebastián's voice rose nearby, above the others.

"*Desperta, Ferro!*" Awake, steel!

The Valerós and Montcava men responded, their voices rising together as they stomped and slashed through the field.

"*Vivètz Valerós!*"

Durán fetched away two broken Valerós men and returned, stepping through the gap in the ring of black slaves, who shouted in a language he didn't understand. The pavilion within the ring, where the caliph had been, seemed deserted of the silk-robed men who'd watched over the battle earlier. Behind him, outside the ring, the men of the two armies writhed in mass, like vermin on a carcass, several horses seeking to run, reined back, rearing while the knights slashed at their enemy.

Scanning the quarter where Valerós men fought, Durán sought Chrétien, spying him near Sebastián, the two of them carrying Tomás. Then the field seemed to take order again, laid out once more in the way Tomás had explained. But a few Montcava men were behind the line of chained slaves. Sancho's knights and a band of priest-knights had ridden through the gap, three with Crux Lunata gambesons. None saw that the chained slaves were closing the gap, trapping them. Durán bashed with his quarterstaff through the fleeing caliphate mercenaries, seeking any Montcava men who needed saving.

Inside the ring, it wasn't Chrétien and Sebastián trapped there, just those Crux Lunata knights and a couple of priests, the tallest of whom proved to be Arnau Amalric, sheltered behind the knights, standing where the caliph had been in the pavilion, his sword gone, his thigh sliced. Bleeding, though perhaps he wouldn't die.

"We need to get you out of here, Monsenyor." Durán looked around for another assistant, at the same moment that the Crux Lunata knights burst back through the ring of slaves, rejoining the battle. The two priests remaining should never have taken to the battle, too old, too small, and now too frightened to assist.

"Your sword! Give me your sword!" Arnau demanded.

"I don't carry one. Let me get you back to the kings' pavilion."

"How?" Arnau, close to panic, glanced about, sweat flying as he twisted his neck. His gaze came back to Durán as he squinted in the sun. "You're that Beaurain bastard who's a heretic."

"I'm the seigneur of Montcava, and I'm about to carry you to safety." Durán shifted his shield to cover his front, and then prepared to hoist the archbishop over his shoulder. The injured man was tall, but not fleshy. Durán had to make it only through the ring of slaves and then dodge a knot of fighting Moors to reach Christians who might help.

"We can't leave the cross behind." Arnau seemed to be in the habit of commanding, even with gore seeping from his thigh.

"And I can't carry you if you intend to pour all of your blood on my head." From under his own chainmail, Durán pulled at his shirt hem, using his knife to slice a length of it. Without asking or telling, he bound the strip around the archbishop's thigh.

Arnau ground his teeth while Durán worked, then sucked in a breath and said again, "We cannot abandon the cross."

Durán pointed to the two old men in priests' cassocks. "You must bear it between you." Then he judged the packets of caliphate knights and the chained slaves between where they stood and the closest Christian safety.

Don't be a target. Or if you are, be magnificent. Chrétien's goodbye. Who now fought in another quarter of the field.

"You have chainmail under your robe?" He pointed to Arnau as he asked. "Monsenyor?"

"Òc."

"Then give me your robe." Durán didn't wait for an assent and began helping his enemy Arnau out of that robe.

"Why?"

"We shall manifest magnificence." Durán draped the robe on the cross, only able to do it because he was as tall as the crossbeam. "Come, Monsenyor. I'm not St-Cristòfol, but I have an idea how he carried his burden."

"Blasphemy!" Arnau sputtered. His indignation seemed to divert him from his pain when Durán hoisted him onto his shoulders.

The old men determined between them how to manage the weight of the cassock-swaddled red cross. Harangued by Durán in a way he'd have loved to harass complaining priests on the streets of Toulouse, they set out through the widest of the growing gaps among the fleeing slaves.

"Those Saracens will kill us." Arnau's voice rasped, his mouth too close to Durán's ear.

"They're running away. And half their mercenaries are Christians. Can't you hear those slaves screaming Jesus's name? There, again. Hear it?"

Arnau didn't answer.

"And your soldiers are murdering them." Each word puffed out with the work of carrying a large man on his back. He shifted the archbishop to rest more weight rested on his hips.

"Alfonso's men have the enemy running." Arnau pointed out the obvious, that the men moving past them were Castilian knights and infantry, not the enemy. "This country will now learn to praise God with proper prayers."

"You want people to praise God at the point of a sword?" Durán felt he might laugh, but he could barely breathe and talk, bearing this weight. "Wherever did Jesus say that? What good do you do, killing people for God?"

"We are called to battle for the risen Christ." Arnau shifted, causing Durán to stumble. He steadied his burden before answering.

"We are called to love God with all our hearts. And to love our neighbor as we ourselves long for God's love."

Towering over the cross-bearers, Durán shouted commands to redirect their passage, away from mounted Moors or any infantry, off toward Aragón's side of the field. A half-dozen times he warned Arnau not to struggle, that he wasn't helping. The archbishop argued less as they crossed among bodies and pockets of fighters who fell away at the sight of the cross. Men shrieked as they passed.

A ghost! The Holy Spirit!

Un fantasma!

Un fantôme! No, le Saint-Esprit est parmi nous!

Una aparicion! L'Esperit Sant es entre nosautres!

While Durán persisted in his work, afraid that if he paused he couldn't go on, the weight he carried stopped fighting, stopped breathing imprecations in his ear. He carried an unconscious, if not dead, man into the priests' pavilion at the far end of the field. Other men rushed to help, so that his burden was lifted without Durán having to bend or lose his grip.

Durán straightened. The pain in his muscles rippled down his back, cramping for a moment, then settling into fire. When he moved again, the skin of his neck and back complained, having been rubbed raw by chainmail shifting under the burden of Arnau's weight.

"Look at our men!" A priest nearby pointed across the valley, where Christian knights rode hard after fleeing Saracens. "They shout with joy, bringing the Cross back to this land."

Durán followed where the priest pointed, but it was such a swarming mass that the priest couldn't be pointing to anyone in particular. He said, "I believe they are merely shouting for joy over the abandoned Saracen supply wagons."

∎

Felip in the kings' line

When Felip returned to the scribes' tent, Serena Taresa joined him. She helped prepare ink for the coming days' work. Felip had finished and dispatched the day's final message—*We all lived!*—when Durán came to the pavilion carrying the archbishop of Narbonne, the man who had caused Valerós and Montcava so much trouble.

It took a moment for others to recognize Arnau, but then five priests rushed forth to attend him, lifting him off Durán. Others helped the two cross-bearers and asked after their wellbeing.

Only Felip ran to relieve Durán.

"Bonfraire, you are injured!"

"Merely tired." He glanced down where Felip stared. Durán's chainmail was drenched through with blood, the tail of his shirt crimson, his leather leggings soaked in red and caked in dust. "It's not my blood. I have to return to where our men are fighting."

"May the Lord bless and keep you!"

"Why should God keep me? And not the others?" Durán sounded bitter, which wasn't like him. "Men are being butchered here."

Bishop Arnau had roused and called for Durán. "Montcava! I thank you for your service. I understand now that you stand on the correct side when Christian men battle for God." He shrugged off the administering priests and held out his hand, in the way that men of the south offer a sign of peace and honor. Durán took the man's offered hand.

"Do you mean, Monsenyor, the battle in our own lands? That's not Man fighting God. It's ordinary men caught in the middle between kings and Church."

Astonishingly, the bishop nodded, as if accepting Durán's notion. "My life is given to the idea that the Church and the pope know best how to do what God commands. Kings serve best when they support that command."

Felip feared that Durán, in this dark mood, would speak even more heresy. Yet Durán said only, "And not one of them cares about me. That's why I do only what I owe every man, the best possible goodness. And I do it always. As Jesus guided us to do."

Again, the bishop listened to the words without censor. "I'm grateful that you saved me, Montcava. The Church thanks you, since you made it possible for me to carry on my duties, to do what God requires of me."

Durán said, "I saved you because it's my duty to any man. Not because you're a bishop. I do not believe that you owe God more than I do. Or that I owe you more than I owe my own brothers."

Felip's ears burned at this heresy, sure that Durán was undoing whatever goodwill he'd earned by saving the bishop. But the two men were again shaking hands.

Durán said, "I need to be back with my men. There's still work to be done on the field."

One of the scribes called out, "Seigneur Xirgú, will you write the story of the Holy Spirit appearing? The miracle of the apparition that saved the battle and the archbishop? Your writing is the most handsome among us. And the story must go to the pope."

"He's writing the day's events for Pedro d'Aragón." Durán stood with his hands on his hips, looking obstinate.

"No, I finished that," Felip said. "Chrétien came with Tomás and Isabella to fetch copies for the couriers. They've already left camp on their ride."

Durán's face darkened, even more than the day's coating of grime left him as stained and bloodied as men who'd fought in the battle. Durán left without another word, so Felip returned to his work, both to describe the apparition (which was, of course, no apparition at all) and to begin the report of the aftermath, though he was hungry and had no idea when there was to be food.

Felip's hands tingled with lightning bees. Yet inside, his heart throbbed with joy.

We all lived.

His bonfraires had served valiantly on the field. They'd trusted Felip enough to make him their brother. And he'd done his job when called to duty. Even his nemesis Colomb praised him, praised his friends. He'd never dreamed that he'd be delivered into the world of honorable crusaders.

As the sun dipped toward the horizon, the king's standard flew on the nearby pavilion again, so Pedro had returned from the field. Tomás, Chrétien, and Isabella were safely on the road to deliver the story of victory for Pedro's couriers to carry to the pope. The pope would soon read the story of how this unified army won the day, written by Felip de Xirgú.

Serena sang softly. A crusader hymn from the Outremer.

'We bathe in the spirit, evening and morning,
Doing what reason says is right.

We choose to be washed in spirit.
It is the true remedy, to be washed in spirit
Before we journey to our death.
We shall dwell in castles and not in low places.'

As shadows grew long, armed men who hadn't pursued the fleeing Saracens began to sort bodies on the field, taking trophies, stripping dead men of their swords and spears, rolling the many defeated Saracens into piles at the foot of the hillock where their caliph had reigned earlier that day. Many fewer Aragón men were being carried to the center of the field where Christian bodies were being gathered.

Before dusk, the crows came.

And their cousins, the ravens.

A bevy of priests set out, carrying lanterns, snaking their way down to where the Christian dead were being laid. Their prayers echoed in the valley, carrying up to where Felip worked beside Serena. On the caliph's deserted ground, one pyre was kindled, and then another. Ten fires. Felip had written only a dozen lines of the apparition story when the smell of the pyres drifted up the hillsides.

He closed his eyes, repeating the words one does for the dead, while he heard Isabella tell again about the pyre outside the city of Minerve. What it smelled like when Christians burn people who call on the name of the One True God.

To offset the coming twilight, Felip kindled a rush light and then kept working, the way his friends and the Xirgú army continued to labor on the darkening field below. Then Colomb appeared again.

"Come, seigneur. We must attend our injured men."

Felip said, "Sebastián has charge of my men while I work for Pedro. And Durán is tending the injured."

"Your men need you. Sebastián's playing king's courier, and that damned heretic can't do what must be done now." Colomb plucked the quill from Felip's hand. "We shall find our injured. Any suffering man who is beyond saving, we deliver him to God. Durán can't do that. We'll get Anselm to join us."

Felip paused, but Serena Taresa was behind him and pushed him forward. Colomb stepped in her way. She motioned him aside. "I go where my husband goes. Xirgú's work is mine."

"Pedro sent you to the rear, senhóra. The field isn't for women."

Before Felip could argue, Serena said, "I helped deliver dying men to God after the riot in Toledo. It was called women's work there. I am not afraid."

PART FIVE
The Way Home

CHRONICLES FROM THE FRONTIER

Our caliph, called Al-Nasir, the Eagle, sat on his shield in front of his pavilion. He cried out amid the fury of the battle, "Allah speaks truth. It is the djinni Iblis who lied." He remained faithfully in place until the infidels came for him, having slain the ten thousand noble men who were his guard.

A vizier, mounted and armored, cried to the caliph, "Allah has fulfilled His will, O Commander of the Faithful." The vizier gave up his horse to the caliph, declaring, "Ride now. For your own salvation." Al-Nasir rode forth.

The slaughter of our Muslim faithful continued into night until all who remained had died. The infidels' swords drowned in our blood, while not even one thousand of theirs salted the earth.

I shall make my way home to you, my beloved wives, as soon as the roads are clear and I can free myself from the bondage in which that witch Ríma holds me. Perhaps I shall arrive before this message reaches you.

> — Ibn Jafar, The Poet
> At sunset, 16 July 1212
> From the place called Las Navas de Tolosa

.

I, Felip of Xirgú, scribe to Pedro d'Aragón, appeal to all my brethren who shall copy this work. You must be diligent as you work, to copy faithfully and correct your errors. While we wait for our Lord to come again in Judgment, you must transcribe this appeal

297

in your copy. I beseech you, for this is a true account, these final words written in haste to tell the world of Christian victory.

We have seized victory for Christendom in the face of overwhelming Saracen numbers, thanks to the grace of God, the firm leadership of Pedro *El Católico*, and the valor of the civic militias and the knights of Aragón, Navarre, and Castile. Knights serving Pedro d'Aragón broke through the ring of slaves who guarded Mirammolin, and so the caliph of Córdoba has fled. His mounted mercenaries abandoned their infantry in the face of our greater forces. I end this account here, because couriers to Rome are departing to carry the joyous news of this victory. More details shall follow soon.

— *Felip de Xirgú*

·

On this day, the victorious knights of Castile, León, and Navarre seized the Mirammolín's pavilion, his standard, and its tapestries, which shall be delivered to our blessed pope, Innocent III.

The forces led by Alfonso of Castile fought under the banner of the Holy Virgin and her blessed Son to advance the Cross in Andalusia. It is as our bishops proclaim, "In the careful way a mother protects her son, Castile protects the faith." With thanks to God, Christian losses were few, but to our kings' great dismay, most came from the orders of knights who so valiantly led this battle. You see below the roll of names of those knights and lords who gave their lives or were grievously wounded carrying the Cross to the Saracens.

We thank God for the valor of the knights and militias of Castile, and the mounted knights of the kings of León and Navarre. Those valiant men are seizing booty from the Saracen, such that our captains believe two thousand burros will be needed to carry it away. God has provisioned the army of the righteous with the Saracens' seized supply wagons. The great king Alfonso shall pursue conquest of the Saracens' towns of Úbeda and Baeza, whose army now lies slain in the place called Las Navas de Tolosa.

— *Esak de Beaurain*

26
Promise

Bonfraires below the kings' pavilion
July 16, twilight, after battle

"DON'T GO."

Durán's voice croaked, as if he'd been scarred inside by battle. He found Chrétien in the ring of men from Valerós who stopped people that sought to approach the king's pavilion.

Chrétien was in a hurry. "We're doing this errand for Pedro. We'll be back in a few days. This is what Isabella talked about, making sure Pedro comes home a hero."

His spirit numb, his nose fouled by the bonfires, Durán begged. "Let the others do it. Sebastián and Tomás and Isabella. Stay here and help me deal with the Valerós fighters. I can't do that on my own."

"You have Colomb and Felip to help you. And you need to help Felip with Colomb." Chrétien wasn't listening to what Durán was saying. That he didn't want to be alone. "Please take Tomás's cousin Rashid to Pedro, please. Consider it a bonfraire duty."

Rashid interfered before Durán could beg again. "My family won't ransom me. And the caliph ordered me to stay on that hill. He won't ransom me either."

"Alfonso forbade ransoming hostages," Chrétien said. "But we're taking you to Pedro. Tomás said the caliph has been trying to kill you since the new moon in June. We are your brothers now." He spoke to Durán. "Find Yusuf if you need help with the tongue he speaks. You'll find him with Pedro's fawning clerk." He snapped his fingers, impatient, trying to remember the man's name. "You know who I mean. Doménec."

"I can speak for myself." Rashid was fluent in the king's dialect, accented but correct. "And I refuse to be taken before any king with my hands bound like a common slave."

Durán accepted the tether from Chrétien, not knowing how to hold it, never having had another man on a leash. "Don't go. I need your help here."

His own voice sounded pathetic. And had no effect. Chrétien was gone, merely touching Durán's arm in farewell.

Rashid said, "Are we both betrayed by Tomás of Morella? That's what you call him?"

"I'm merely annoyed." Durán studied Rashid, who somehow, wasn't as grimy as any other man on the battlefield, though blood stained his slashed right sleeve. Rashid scowled, but what Durán saw was an extraordinarily handsome man. What Tomás must have looked like before Renoud of Montcava destroyed his face. "Tomás claims you as a brother and wants us to take you to Pedro."

"He's gone, isn't he?" Rashid laughed, without apparent humor. "Tomás won't face me."

"Tomás is doing a chore for Pedro." Durán sobered, finally hearing what Chrétien had said, that the chore with the couriers was part of what Isabella talked about. "He asked us to save your life."

"Tomás betrayed me. And your...*friend*...left you to go with him." Rashid's voice broke on the word *friend*. "It seems that you know betrayal. I pray God will guide you to let me go, to let—"

"Shut up!" Durán lost patience and then reeled back his temper. "Forgive me! I'm tired. I pray to be home in my own bed, but I have no hope that God answers prayer. We're seeking Pedro now. Not angels or apparitions."

Rashid was quiet for a moment. When Durán pulled the tether close, so that Rashid walked alongside him, the man said a few words in his own tongue, and then spoke again in the common tongue, seemingly devoid of passion, carefully listing all he had lost. Each step up the hill carried one more complaint from Rashid, who had a slight limp though Durán couldn't see the injury.

"I bowed to my uncles' wishes and served the caliph. Though I preferred the longer and harder path. I bowed to my aunts and prayed in secret the way they taught me. Even though they barely call me a Rodriquez." Rashid paused.

Durán jerked on the tether to prompt him forward, which also prompted more words from the man.

"I bowed to my caliph and did as he asked, to serve a general who didn't want to fight. I have no army of my own. No home. No children or parents. My horse is gone to infidel invaders."

When Rashid paused once again, Durán tugged harder. The words continued, still without passion.

"My caliph wants me dead. And I'm left on earth because the man who betrayed me—in ways I could never imagine—wants me alive. Am I to beg this king for mercy? Or should I ask for a knife in my gullet? Why am I—"

Durán jerked up hard on the tether, mashing Rashid's hands between them, his lips a finger's width from Rashid's elegant nose.

"You think God tested you beyond endurance? The lords of my land want me burned on a pyre. The family I sacrificed everything for just left me here alone. I promised God never to shed blood, and then God gave me a man who kills as his way of life. And you think life has cheated you? Tomás called on us to save you, so I have to save you or damn my soul. *Calla, per l'amor de Dèu!*"

"What is that word, *calla?*"

"It means close your fly-specked mouth. Stop speaking." Durán dragged Rashid along on the trail to Pedro's pavilion and began a litany of what Chrétien might say. "It means I'd rather eat dust or chew raw tripe or be a priest rather than hear one more word from you. I'd listen to a race of lepers singing with the adulterous sister of the God of Darkness before I'd ever listen to you complain about being alive."

Where the newly beaten path arched up to the king's pavilion, Rashid stopped again. Durán tugged to keep him no more than an arm's length away.

"Come up."

"I won't be hobbled like a horse."

Tired deeper in his bones than he'd ever been in this life, Durán slipped his knife from his belt, a pathetic, dinged-edge dinner knife, and cut the bonds at Rashid's wrists and let the infernal tether fall beside the path.

At the king's pavilion, one of the guards was a Catalan man Durán had met before.

"Cebrián, this is a man Tomás asked us to rescue from the caliph. Pedro knows him and would want to hear what he has to say."

All Cebrián cared to discover was whether they carried weapons, and while he was removing Durán's dinner knife from his belt and feeling perceived bulges in his chainmail, Rashid again spoke behind him.

"You love that man who captured me? He is your life?"

"Òc," Durán said as they entered the pavilion. "All of it."

•

Felip at the scribes' pavilion
July 16, twilight

"Xirgú? I'll take that letter straight to the couriers."

Doménec the clerk encountered Felip and Colomb on the pathway and begged for the papal letter that Felip had written for Pedro.

"Senhór Chrétien came for the letter earlier." While Felip answered, Doménec studied Serena Taresa in the fading light, clearly mistaking her for a boy, while Colomb motioned to hurry them along. "It's already on the road to Valencia."

Doménec looked startled. "I didn't know. Esak said…" He shifted a package from one hand to the other, then hurried toward Pedro's pavilion without finishing his thought.

Colomb frowned.

Without saying why, Colomb took a fork in the path to follow Doménec. He called after the clerk.

"Are you Esak's man?" But Doménec didn't seem to hear.

Torches and lamps burned outside and in the pavilion, so it was nearly light as day. Outside, it was like the first market-day before an early Easter. Men of all sorts scrambled to be in line for entrance to the pavilion, argued and boasted everywhere in the clearing around the pavilion. Servants scrambled to respond to shouted commands, and guards called for caution. It was like a holiday.

Except for that appalling odor from the battlefield, which carried up to this ridge where the pavilion had been pitched and hung in the evening shadows, even though mountain winds blew down into the overheated valley.

Felip and Serena Taresa were jostled by over-joyous captains and their knights as they hiked up the ridge to where the king was, the royal banner flying over the pavilion.

As they approached the opening to the king's pavilion, Yusuf stumbled, getting in Colomb's way. He held Fortuno by the sleeve.

"What did you do with my dagger?"

Fortuno wiggled, trying to escape. "That queen gave me three silver coins to show it to her. She just wanted to see it."

"What queen?" Yusuf, furious, shook the boy, who finally managed to escape. Colomb reached for the fleeing Fortuno, but missed. Yusuf pushed through the crowd, pursuing Fortuno into the pavilion.

Colomb bellowed, "Esak de Beaurain!"

In the milling herd of priests and bishops who'd all been last-comers to the battle, one man faced Colomb. That censorious little priest who forced Felip to write that odd contract.

"Not now, brother."

The priest disappeared in the holy crowd, too small to be spotted among the taller armored and mail-clad priests. Colomb strode up to the guarded opening of the pavilion, spoke to the Aragónese soldier there, and then deposited his weapons where the guard pointed and went inside, not looking back to see if Felip and Serena Taresa followed him. Felip indicated to the guard that they were with Colomb and entered behind him.

Inside, Pedro was talking to a man wearing the colors of Castile. "Alfonso can send messages to fetch his baggage train. But mine stays on the other side of the mountain. Aragón is going home tomorrow."

"We have the opportunity to take Baeza." The Castilian held up his finger, as if in warning. He spoke in that blurred way they all did.

"Alfonso deserves glory," Pedro said, smiling in that cold way he had whenever Felip saw him with those lords of Castile. "Aragón cannot go farther this year. It's a long journey for us to go home."

The Castilian lord spoke more, but not in Castellano. "*Dum calidum fuerit, debetur cudere ferrum.*"

It was Latin: *Strike while the iron is hot.*

Pedro answered: "Neither God nor a king can ask more of my men this year." And then softer, he repeated an old proverb in Latin, *"Defuncto canis est melior vivendo leone."*

A living dog is better than a dead lion.

The Castilian lord departed rather abruptly.

"Ah, Xirgú!" Pedro glanced at Felip, who was following Colomb de Beaurain. "They say you performed well on the field today. How are my papal missives?"

Felip knew God saw the excess pride he felt. "Your letters are on the way with your couriers, Monsenyor."

Behind Pedro, a huddle of priests parted and Matheus appeared, a dagger in his hand.

Felip leaped forward to stand between Matheus and Pedro with nothing in his hands but the sting of lightning bees. His gift from God.

■

Durán at the king's pavilion
July 16, after sunset

Durán pushed his way into the pavilion, Rashid at his heels.

Inside, Colomb bounded for Pedro.

At that same moment, Felip also ran for Pedro, shouting, "No! On our father's honor, no!"

Then Colomb had his arms around the king. And Felip lay on the carpet at Pedro's feet.

A boy—no, that woman Felip married—charged across the room, screaming curses. She tore at the face of the man behind Pedro.

Matheus.

Pedro's assassin.

Colomb nudged Pedro aside while seizing the knife from the king's belt. He lunged for Matheus, who thrust that girl to the ground, kicking her while swerving away from Colomb.

"Àvi!" Matheus shouted. "Do God's will!"

Another tussle rose among the crowd of bishops. Qasim and Yusuf pressed their way into the pavilion, both shouting.

"Watch out!" Yusuf screamed. Qasim cried, *"Desperta, Ferro!"*

Esak de Beaurain advanced, a dagger in one hand, that cup of Felip's in the other, marching to Pedro, who hadn't yet regained his footing or a weapon.

"Stop!" Durán shouted a warning. Colomb shoved Matheus to the ground and advanced on the little priest, holding Pedro's knife, ready to strike.

"Is it you, brother?" Colomb's shout silenced the crowd.

"You perverse animal!" Esak spat the words in a farmer's vernacular. He had eyes only for Pedro, as if the rest of the pavilion were empty. "St-Jordí, deliver us from your iniquity."

Durán shoved his way toward them, crying to stop Colomb while stepping in front of Pedro. "No, no, uncle! Not your own brother."

Yusuf ran for Esak, shrieking words in a tongue Durán didn't know, dodging between Colomb and Esak before Durán could intercede. Then Yusuf stepped back. That dagger Esak carried was now in Yusuf's hand, dripping.

Esak fell onto Colomb, who began sobbing quiet curses. One of Pedro's guards held Matheus, wrenching his arms behind him.

Durán knelt by Felip and checked his wounds, the same way he'd checked men's bodies on the field all day. Except now his hands were so cold it was hard to move his fingers, and his heart beat in the searing fear that God meant to take this good and innocent man in just moments. He blinked back tears while he cradled Felip, holding him up so the man could breathe better.

Like a winded horse, Colomb sighed and leaned against Durán, Esak still in his arms. But Esak was already gone to bargain with God over where his soul might next be consigned to struggle.

"You bloody mad fool." Colomb scolded the shell of flesh that had been his brother. "And your pet? Where's your pet?"

Behind them, the archbishop pushed his way between Yusuf and Qasim and then stared with revulsion where Durán held Felip and Colomb wept over his evil brother.

Felip stirred in Durán's arms, tried to speak, calling on God in Latin. "D–D–Domin..." He choked on blood and couldn't finish.

Dominus vobiscum? The words that priest in Toulouse spoke when giving Durán's mother a basket of bread husks?

"*Ai*, bonfraire, be at peace," Durán murmured. "All will be well." Blood flowed from Felip's nose and mouth. Durán wiped it away with his tunic sleeve. How had that goodwoman consoled Durán's mother on her last day? Never looking away while Felip stared up at him, Durán spoke the words as he best remembered them. "*Dolç fraire,* you are the temple of the Living God, who says, 'I dwell in you. I will not leave you without comfort.'"

Felip tried to speak, like a parched man wants to ask for water. How had Durán never noticed the deep beauty of Felip's eyes before this moment? Long lashes. Deep pools of soulful searching. He blew softly on Felip's face, the way a mother shushes a frantic infant, and then began to say the words. "With my breath, receive the Holy Spirit. God sees in your heart and blesses you."

The next words were about sin, but sin didn't matter now. Felip was most of the way gone to God. And he'd never had a chance to sin enough that God could bother to keep count.

Durán spoke louder, as if Felip had wandered away, but still needed to hear, to be consoled. "God is here at your good end, my dear brother. This world will pass away, but you shall abide forever."

He knew the next words because he still heard his mother whisper them. Felip now scarcely blinked, still staring at Durán, who had to say the words for him since Felip couldn't speak. 'Because you long to do the will of God, receive the power of God." He blew softly in his friend's face again.

Noise exploded in the pavilion, but Durán cared only for Felip. "God keep you, bonfraire. *Parcite nobis.*"

Under all the noise, Durán listened to Felip breathe. Until he was gone. For the second time in this life, Durán held a hand and saw a human spirit leave its body behind and rise.

The swirl and noise came back again. That woman Serena, not weeping, cursed in ways he'd never before heard from a woman. Wild with fury, she allowed only Yusuf to touch her, listening to what he murmured in her ear. Arnau again asked Pedro if he was injured.

"Bonfraire?" Pedro's voice broke.

"He's gone to God." Durán's words poured from his mouth like sand.

"This is heresy!" A priest near Arnau shouted, his face choleric, his fists clenched over his head.

"Be still," Pedro said. "A good man has just gone to God."

"Prayed over by a fiend, a heretic." The angry priest persisted.

"A man called on our Lord and Savior to receive a soul known to be devout and right with God." Pedro's face was dark with fury.

"You condone heresy!" that priest cried again. He turned to Arnau, who clutched the cup Esak had carried into the pavilion. "Monsenyor, I beg you to intercede for God here."

"Stop it!" Durán rasped, like the groans of injured men on the field below. When he could choke out sensible words, he shouted at Arnau. "All this blood! And you keep crying God's name! It's the God of Darkness you call on!" He pointed a finger at Arnau, seeing for the first time that his hand was crimson with Felip's blood. "You claim to love God, while you seek to kill a king."

"No!" Arnau seemed stunned, as if Durán had struck him with that crimson hand.

"Yet here's your priest, your friend, with dark magic in his hands. You are Crux Lunata, just like him."

"No, we only want—"

"Why do you think Crux Lunata wields its goat-piss magic? You all seek to kill Pedro and seize his power."

"N–no."

Arnau stuttered a denial. Like Felip stuttered. Durán clutched his friend closely again. "And your Crux Lunata fools aren't even good at it. All they managed was to murder an innocent."

In the swirl of soldiers and priests, Durán searched for friends, Felip still in his arms. Yusuf and Qasim embraced Serena, who was ghostly white under her sunburn. Pedro, one arm on Yusuf's shoulder, placed his hand on Serena's head, but she batted it away. She still seethed with anger, not crying.

Matheus was gone.

Colomb had disappeared.

And so had Rashid.

27
Duty

SEBASTIÁN LET HIS HORSE DO what it wanted while he jostled along in the saddle, never before as tired and sore as on that ride. He'd taken a bad cut on his arm near the end of the day, and there hadn't been time to attend to it before riding out. His arm throbbed and his rear end had taken to quarreling with his saddle. Such a simple chore for Pedro, yet so painful.

Other than Chrétien's bantering, which served to keep them all awake, the only other sound was the plodding clop of horses finding their way in the dark along the king's road. Chrétien coughed. He'd been coughing since the ride began, which resulted in repeated offers of water from Isabella. He said, "Tomás wasn't supposed to come on this jaunt, yet he's doing better than any of us."

"It's easy to see why," Sebastián answered. "My father spent the battle napping in Pedro's pavilion while the rest of us worked."

"And my brother managed to get himself carried over the mountain when the rest of us had to walk across." Chrétien coughed again. "My brother does have his crafty ways."

Sebastián laughed at every one of Chrétien's jibes. "And my father has certainly been eating well. While we've been starving, he's fat as an Easter lamb."

"They don't have Easter where my brother's been," Chrétien said. "But it's true. He's as fat as I've ever seen."

"*Ai,* Senhór Chrétien, you didn't see him after we spent a month on Cyprus, eating your mother's cooking."

"Let's not talk about Numa's cooking," Chrétien said. "I'm starving now. How soon till we finish this chore and go home?"

"The last marker we found was just before dawn." Isabella had most likely been counting, to estimate distance. "It can't be long before the rendezvous marker."

"Hope there's a stream clean enough to wash." Chrétien dropped his teasing of Tomás, probably because he hadn't roused a response from his brother. "I'd like to see what set up housekeeping under this chainmail, nesting in the dirt from yesterday's festivities."

"All I got out of yesterday's clash was the return of my father's sword." Tomás spoke, having been quiet since they found the last pile of stone trail-markers. "That, and everyone coming out alive. Sebastián especially fared well. From where I was on the ridge, your fighting form looked quite good. Pèire Leteric would approve."

For a long while, only the horses beat an answer. Then Sebastián spoke, the words he'd been longing to say since twilight.

"I did it."

"Excuse me?" Chrétien said. "I didn't hear."

"*I did it.* I called commands, and men did their work, the way we trained them. They lived through the day. And we won the hilltop."

"Pedro asked for that to be recorded in his letter to the pope," Tomás said. "That Valerós made the caliph retreat."

"'We lived through the day, chased the caliph away,'" Chrétien sang. "We must demand of the count of Foix that he write a *cançó de guèrra* so people remember us."

"I didn't think we'd be heroes," Sebastián said. "The Castilian generals call Valerós men savages. They say we're no better than wild Almogavars fighting on the frontier, living in caves."

"Because their only efforts each summer are to capture a flag. And then lose it a year later," Tomás said. "Five hundred years of swapping flags with Saracens."

Silence again as the horses picked their way along the road. Then Sebastián declared what he'd been thinking, from even before they'd found Tomás. "Pedro assigned some of those men to me, those Almogavars. They don't play flag games. They strike the unguarded. Strip booty and then hide in the hills where they can never be found. It's what we have to do to defeat the French invaders."

Isabella said, "I didn't enjoy my time in the hills, hiding from heretic hunters."

"You were alone, Mother. I'm talking about leading warriors to fight. No more enduring sieges. We defend from the terrain that those fat French knights don't know."

"I'm not sure," Isabella said. "We need Pedro to bargain with the pope and the bishops."

"We need to fight," Sebastián said. "I'm taking any of the Valerós men, and others Pedro assigned to me who want to keep fighting. We'll go with Pedro to Toulouse, which is where he's headed next. To bargain like you want him to. When that fails—"

"No," Isabella said. "Pedro won't fail. Yesterday's victory will matter to the pope. It's a greater victory for Christendom than Ricart Coeur de Lyon and Philippe Augustus won outside Jerusalem."

"Then I shall say *if*." Sebastián conceded only that word. "If Pedro's bargaining with the bishops does not succeed, then Valerós will serve like the Almogavars. We'll fight and hide in the hills. Only we fight the invaders trying to take our lands."

"*Ai, fadrin*," Tomás exclaimed. What he meant, Sebastián didn't learn. For the sun broke the horizon at that moment.

Isabella called attention to the stone markers by the road.

Chrétien repeated his desire for a clean stream and a bath.

And they rounded the bend to find four bodies stacked across each other, stripped naked, amid a murder of crows screaming for their breakfast. Sebastián spurred his horse first, scattering the crows, shouting and waving his spear to keep the birds away.

Tomás and Chrétien dismounted and turned over the bodies.

"Saracen?" Chrétien asked. "Christian?"

"Mozarab," Tomás said. "This one is Pedro's man. I saw him once in Baeza."

"These are our couriers?" Isabella hadn't gotten off her horse, which she held at a distance, since it wanted to dance away from the travesty.

"*Òc*." Tomás glanced around, scanning the hills. "We have to ride on. We need to find the next courier rendezvous."

Sebastián said, "They weren't killed here. There was no fight. It's too open for a massacre."

"Why leave them naked?" Tomás said.

"Booty?" Sebastián asked. "If any of yesterday's mercenaries or Saracens escaped along this road—"

"They didn't," Chrétien said. "The caliph's army fled through a different valley. We rode north and east. Perhaps they were killed by some of the Almogavars Sebastián admires."

"No," Tomás said. "These are more likely to be Almogavars who work for Pedro. They were killed by Christians."

"How do you know?" Chrétien asked. "They're naked and dead. No armor. No horses."

"I feel it in my gut," Tomás said. "We need to ride to the next courier rendezvous. And we need to pick up the pace."

"Our horses are exhausted," Isabella said. "And we can't leave these men for the crows."

"We must ride on," Tomás said. "Perhaps we'll have to ride all the way to Valencia."

Isabella slipped off her horse. "Our horses need a rest. Let's pile stones, and then find a safe place off the road to sleep a bit while the horses rest."

Tomás seemed inclined to argue, but then he said, "Only as much rest as the horses need. Then we ride for Valencia."

·

Sebastián heaved as many boulders as his friends, though his slashed arm was now on fire and stiff from the night's ride in filthy gambeson and chainmail.

Because Chrétien had complained most, he had to walk forepoint in a search for an off-trail resting place, while Isabella and Tomás slashed tree limbs to mark the trail for later, when they'd return to the king's road. Sebastián brought up the rear, responsible for spying whatever bandits might pursue them the way the king's couriers had been done.

They found a stream and enough grass for the horses. Too tired to argue, Sebastián let Tomás and Chrétien quibble about how open the small valley was and whether that left them more or less prone to ambush. Instead, he and Isabella hobbled the horses downstream and dumped travel packs in the shade of the valley's single oak tree.

Still arguing with Tomás about the safety of where they chose to rest, Chrétien peeled off his armor and linen and slipped into the valley's summer trickle of a stream, emerging soaking wet, his hair in long white tangles down his back and shoulders.

"Who's next?"

"Sebastián, you go," Isabella said. "Tomás and I weren't in the melee yesterday. We'll stand guard"

He didn't need more prompting, eager to strip like Chrétien had and hoping the mountain stream might put out the fire that burned in his arm.

When he came up wet and half naked, having removed his shirt to wash it, Isabella cried, "*Ai!* Sancta Maria!"

Sebastián glanced where she pointed, where rubbing at that cut on his arm had made it bleed again, which he thought seemed like a good idea. Then he remembered how much she hated blood.

"Your blood will turn to poison," she said.

"It's Chrétien who should stitch him up," Tomás said. "You still carry a needle and silk, eh, brother? There's a bota of wine in my pack."

Chrétien poked at Sebastián's cut. "Hold still, *fadrin*. I can't stitch a monkey."

Sebastián did as asked, pouring wine over the wound to wash away blood whenever Chrétien muttered that he couldn't see. Sebastián mostly felt bad about subjecting his mother to that sight, though she kept her eyes averted while Chrétien stitched. When Chrétien finished, he and Sebastián stood guard while his mother and Tomás removed their chainmail and splashed water on each other.

"Your hair is growing out. It's so red!" Chrétien pointed at Sebastián. "It's easy to see that you're a Beaurain now."

Isabella looked away, as if this wasn't something she wanted to hear. Still wet, she rummaged through her travel pack, producing two small loaves while chattering about what they needed to travel.

"We should have brought extra clothes. And more food."

"We're supposed to be on our way back by now." Tomás still studied the broken hills that opened into the little valley.

"I'm going to check the horses." Isabella tugged on her chainmail first, leaving her gambeson with their travel packs. Sebastián pondered his own pile of clothes and armor and the prospect of climbing back into that stinking shell with his injured arm. As she walked along the creek, Isabella called back before disappearing around the bend where the horses were hobbled. "Eat now. We'll ride if the horses are rested."

"*Ai*, food!" Chrétien cried. "Have we ever had to subsist so long, grubbing like turnip-chomping heretics?" He bit at the thread close to Sebastián's elbow. "There you go, *fadrin*. Not my prettiest needle work, but not so ugly that it'll stop women from loving you. Now, after a nap, we'll find rabbits and—"

Behind Sebastián, Tomás spoke softly. "I suppose you want to kill me, cousin."

That twin, the mistaken man on the caliph's hilltop, stood prepared to attack Tomás. He held an unsheathed sword in one hand, the other held a spear like Saracen knights favored. But now he wore an Aragón soldier's surcoat, like the one Tomás used to wear.

"Indeed." The man's face was twisted in a rictus of disgust. He was more like Yusuf than Tomás, since Tomás's face was so damaged. He uttered a stream of words, which Sebastián understood as Arabic.

What happened in the last two heartbeats while he and Chrétien were more than an arm's reach from their own weapons?

∎

Tomás on the Cuenca road
July 17, midmorning

Rashid had his sword at Tomás's throat, and he faced Chrétien and Sebastián, ready if either or both of them advanced on him.

Tomás spoke, feeling the blade at his Adam's apple. "Pedro d'Aragón's colors look good on you, cousin. Did Pedro convince you to work for him?" He felt a wave of hatred from Rashid, as if that sword had already been thrust through him. "How did you find us?"

"Ríma said I'd find you dead on the Cuenca road. She's in the king of Castile's camp, laughing at me." Rashid scowled. "She said her protector would get revenge before I could."

"Her protector?"

"The little priest your lover killed," Rashid pointed to Chrétien, "when the priest tried to kill Pedro. The resulting chaos made it easy to slip away."

"Durán? He killed our grandfather?" Sebastián, astonished.

Chrétien, his hand on Sebastián's shoulder, squeezed, warning him to be quiet. "We are too many for you, Rashid."

Tomás, though believing that he'd be dead if Rashid wanted to kill him, spoke softly with that blade near his neck. "Join us. Begin the next adventure, the way we agreed when chasing those burros."

"Is this your other clan?"

"Not a clan. This is my brother and my son."

Rashid's eyes swept over Sebastián. "I can't believe that."

"Stepson. Join us, Rashid."

"You betrayed our clan. You betrayed me."

"I worked to betray the caliph. Not you. I believe—"

"Believe?" The word burst from Rashid. "You are a fly-mouthed *batini* who believes nothing."

"I believe as my father tells me. He says I owe you a new life, that I'm your servant until—"

"You spread lies," Rashid said, "like vermin devouring a carcass."

"Our father is dead." Chrétien stood and pulled on his chainmail, which distracted Rashid, who still held his sword close to Tomás.

"Miquel visits me." Tomás could have batted away Rashid's sword, but he deserved to be at Rashid's mercy. "He was with me on that mountain before you and Isabella came."

"Like an apparition?" Chrétien motioned for Sebastián to pull on his chainmail, frowning at what Tomás said.

"No, apparitions aren't real." Tomás spread his arms, making himself even more vulnerable to Rashid. "Miquel says I have to care for my brothers. He named you, Rashid. He insists I owe you my life. We are—"

At the clattering racket, Sebastián and Chrétien jumped and reached for their swords, still scrambling for bucklers when javelins rained on the clearing.

A swarm of Christian knights descended on them, like armored carrion-eaters. More than a dozen men.

And the intruders already had Isabella, her hands wrenched behind, cap pulled off, her chainmail gone, her linen shirt torn. That silver cross tangled from a chain around her neck. Her sunburned face glowed, the angriest Tomás had ever seen her.

.

Isabella and her friends stood in the clearing like the five points of a star, a dozen or more Crux Lunata knights in a circle around them. Her friends had been seized, each held by a pair of knights.

The monster who hunted her had found her again.

"*Bonjorn*, seigneur Matheus," Chrétien called. "I've never seen you so early in the day. How's your dog?"

Matheus still glanced between Tomás and another newcomer, who must be that cousin Rashid, dressed in the surcoat of Pedro's guard. "Two of Pedro's lover-slaves?"

"Matheus of Xirgú?" Tomás said. "You're that man who keeps trying to murder my wife."

"You three," Matheus pointed to knights behind Tomás. "Ride now to let the others know we have won."

"Still tupping Hélène de Beaurain, Seigneur Matheus?" Chrétien asked. "You prefer your auntie's flesh to a wife?"

"What did you win?" Tomás asked. "Esak is dead. Pedro's alive and knows your crimes."

Chrétien taunted again. "There's no hope for Crux Lunata in Christendom."

"And God despises murderers," Isabella said.

Matheus slapped her so hard that she recoiled in pain.

"We hold the Grail and the Cid's sword." Matheus pointed for one of the knights to bind Isabella's hands. "And we have two of your sons now. Which means that the Cid's line belongs to us. We are victorious."

"No!" Tomás screamed as though his heart had been torn apart. The men who held him pushed Tomás to the ground.

"*Òc*, your Mozarab whore Ríma holds that aberration you call Yusuf and your brat from Morella." Matheus grinned, the way he had when he entered the clearing in the Pyrenees where he'd murdered her friends. "They're on the road to Toledo today, to live with a prince in Castile. And one of our knights has your infant."

"No, Tomás." Chrétien spoke softly. "As I told you, Jacques has Quelo and Dolç. They are safe."

Matheus laughed at him. "One mercenary against all of Crux Lunata? No, the Cid's line will rule Iberia again in this generation. Pedro gained nothing, even if he lives to crawl back to Lérida."

One of the knights had emptied all their travel packs, holding out Pedro's letters once he found them.

"We'll need a fire." Matheus pointed to two of the knights. "A big one. After we burn the letters, we have heretics to destroy."

"Burning those letters won't stop anything," Tomás said. "There are four more courier parties on four more roads."

"All dead, like the men you found." Matheus shrugged. "Now, to business. I am commanded by the fathers of the Holy Church to seize you, body and soul, in the name of the Father, the Son, and the Holy Spirit. And to purge from you the repeated sin of heresy, until fire shall burn away the evil you have brought to this world, leaving only that which God alone shall judge."

"Don't we get to say our creed?" Chrétien said "To prove we are good children of the Church? That's the way it worked every other time you people tried this on my family."

"In addition to heresy," Matheus said, ignoring Chrétien, "our fathers in the Church add the sins of murder of a consecrated priest of God and theft of the Grail from its holy vaults."

"You can't prove any of those lies in a Church court." Isabella spoke so sharply, she could spit blood.

"There won't be a Church court," Matheus said. "We are Knights of the Lunate Cross. We have the blessing of our Church fathers to try, condemn, and rid the world of you heretics. Now."

The first fire had been kindled, and Pedro's letter to the pope began to burn, with that acrid odor of torched animal hide. Matheus increased his bruising grip on her arm. "Now, false woman, true heretic. You shall again watch your tribe destroyed."

She closed her eyes, willed God to stop her ears.

"No, *putana*." Matheus pawed at her face, poking at her eyes. "Watch. You will see them go to judgment. Watch it all until your own time comes."

28
Solidarity

ALL NIGHT AND INTO THE morning, Pedro was scarcely an arm's length from Durán. First, he called for a clean tunic for Durán and offered a basin for washing his hands.

"More water!" Pedro called. "Your face, too."

Then the king, with his guard, accompanied Durán to tour the Valerós camp, where they left Yusuf, Qasim, and Serena in Father Anselm's care.

Torches lit the camp, where most men had rags tied over their faces to block the smoke and the smell. Pedro congratulated the men from Foix and Montcava, and consoled Xirgú men (though most barely knew Felip). Repeatedly, Pedro told each band of men that Aragón and Valerós forces would pack after midday rest to go home.

"None of your men will sleep tonight," Father Anselm said, when Pedro bid that priest good night.

"The battle is over," Pedro said.

"But you leave them only until morning to take booty from the field," Father Anselm said. "They won't sleep, and their horses and burros will be weighted down with booty, so they'll have to walk half dead out of this valley."

Pedro seemed thoughtful, then turned to the circle of Aragón and Valerós captains standing nearby.

"Take men now to make sure Aragón seizes its fair share of the caliph's supply wagons. And make sure the Almogavars get a share before they disappear into the hills."

Pedro kept Durán at his side when he visited Alfonso, seeking at dawn to offer prayers of gratitude with the king of Castile and his late-arriving cousins from León and Navarre. By then, Pedro had acknowledged his captains' messages, and agreed that his army couldn't be ready to march by midday. The Aragón force would remain another night.

"See what Sancho seized!" Alfonso greeted them like an over-excited child. His pavilion was stuffed with booty from the caliph's hilltop piles of tapestries and flags. The caliph's scarlet-dyed tent. "We shall send these to His Holiness in Rome, don't you think?"

"*Si*," Pedro said. Not distracted by the booty the priests and lords exclaimed over, Pedro continued in Castellano, which Durán struggled to understand. "Cousin, help me make sure that Aragón gets its fair share of the caliph's supply wagons."

Alfonso, astonished, said, "They'll come with us when we drive into Andalusia."

"It's a long road home," Pedro said. "Aragón needs to depart. We leave the remainder of this season's glory for you to seize."

Before the priests prayed, Diego Lopez came to Alfonso's side to announce the losses. Durán, tired to the toes of his filthy boots, feared that at any moment he'd close his eyes and not be able to open them. He concentrated to understand the Castellano words.

"The Saracen losses are over a hundred thousand men. Those that lived are now running to Jaén and beyond."

"God is good!" a priest cried.

Another shouted, "God is great!"

Diego held up his hand for peace. "We believe our own losses number fewer, perhaps less than two thousand, but the count is not yet complete."

More praises to God and shouts to deliver all souls to heaven. Durán stirred, only to keep himself awake. Why had Pedro kept him so close at hand all this time?

"It was our priestly orders who led the attack," Diego said, "and those orders suffered our heaviest losses."

While priests called blessings, Diego reported names, none of which meant anything to Durán. More dead strangers among thousands and thousands and thousands littering the field and…

"May God the Father and the Son receive Pedro Gómez de Ace-vedo of the Order of Calatrava. May Sancta Maria, the mother of our Lord, comfort the soul of Alfonso Fernández de Valladares of the Order of Santiago."

The names and words and blessings turned to clatter and clamor, so that Durán could not say what the Castilians discussed. At his side, Pedro murmured, "We'll sleep soon. You look dead on your feet." He glanced past Durán, then said, "Bad choice of words."

Durán looked where Pedro glanced in the dawn light. Three boys followed Doménec, one of the boys leading another by the hand.

A fatigue-thought drifted by, and Durán grasped it, wondering where the boy Fortuno had got to. He was last sent to the scribes' tent, out of the way of battle. But if the boy hadn't behaved, then where would he have...

The thought of the scribes' tent brought his exhausted mind back to Felip, and he again felt Felip in his arms, seeking comfort. Cross-ing over.

Durán brushed at his face. It did nothing for that lost man, to be weeping. The prayers and recitations seemed to be ending. He couldn't listen to prayers without again seeing innocent Felip strug-gling with his last breath to speak God's name. *D–D–Dominus...*

"... and wipe heresy from the face of Christendom."

The word "heresy" brought Durán back from muzzy thoughts to find that shrieking accuser from the night before again pointing at Durán. *Don't be a target, be magnificent,* Chrétien said. Well, Durán had failed at that. Was it late enough in the morning that Chrétien and the others might be returning to camp? In time for this debacle?

"Leave him alone," Pedro said. "He worked hard for Christen-dom yesterday. He saved men with no thought for his own life."

"You heard the filth that came from his mouth last night."

Pedro raised his voice. "I heard him call on God the Father, the Son, and the Holy Spirit to comfort a friend who was dying. A friend who risked his life for my sake."

"We cannot excuse heresy!" The priest was choking on his own anger. "We are called to wipe away abominations to God. How can you, anointed by our own pope, defend perfidy? These people eat their own children."

"Peace." Arnau Amalric stepped from further back in the ranks of bishops. "This man saved my life yesterday. He spoke to me only in the words our Savior taught, to love God with all our hearts."

Pedro nodded. "I need to tend to my men. My best wishes to you all, for another day that shows the glory and blessings of God."

He signaled his guards, a couple of whom seemed as exhausted as Durán felt. They gathered near Pedro when he left the king of Castile's pavilion. Pedro had his arm around Durán, who woke enough from that haze of fatigue to understand and feel gratitude for why Pedro kept him close all night.

"But why are we even here?" Durán hadn't meant to say it aloud. But Pedro was nodding, as if they agreed about something.

"God put me here to work for his people," Pedro said. "With this victory, I can now dominate Simon and heavy-handed Churchmen."

"Dominate." Durán repeated the word, forcing himself to take one step and then another to keep moving as he followed Pedro, though he only wanted a quiet place to sleep.

Then it came to him, like an answer heard in a dream.

Not *Dominus vobiscum.*

Felip was not calling on God as he died.

Doménec.

Felip was trying to say Doménec's name, the clerk who'd slipped away moments ago, leading Yusuf by the hand, along with Qasim and Serena, dressed as a boy.

·

High notes from Fortuno's voice echoed among the tents.

"She says that I'll be a king. And Don Tomás is dead. And so is Senhór Chrétien and even Sebastián. I might as well go with her."

'They aren't dead." Qasim's voice, thundering, accented.

"She says they are. And Pedro will be soon."

Yusuf's voice. "They aren't. Even if they were, you have to stay with your domus. We are your family."

"She promises to be my mother and make me king."

Durán thrashed through the maze of tents to find the voices. Pedro and his guard followed.

In a small clearing amid the priests' tents, Fortuno sat on a camp-chair. "And she gave me honey and biscuits. And sausages."

Yusuf and Qasim glanced up at Durán's arrival, Yusuf's eyes flickering past him to where Pedro had stopped. Fortuno followed where they were looking but, of course, he didn't recognize Pedro, who wore no insignia.

One person stood still as a statue. Doménec.

Durán, his insides boiling, pointed to the white-faced, startled clerk. "You betrayed us."

"I never."

"Felip tried to tell me. You were in this, with my grandfather."

"Your grandfather?" The clerk seemed to collect himself, stood taller, like a man ready to fight back. "You? You're a heretic and a bastard. I'm a man of the Church. How could I be connected to your nest of heretics?"

"Esak de Beaurain. The man you stood with in the king's pavilion. The man who killed my friend. And who tried to kill Pedro."

Doménec was sputtering an indignant denial when three knights clamored through the maze in the priests' camp.

"It's done!" one shouted, coming into the clearing. "All dead! All destroyed! As God willed it!"

Durán didn't see it, but Pedro must have signaled what he wanted, because half his guard moved to encircle the three arriving knights, who all wore Crux Lunata colors.

Pedro's voice hummed behind him. "Are you people no good at secrets without Esak?"

But Durán didn't hear more. He kept asking, "Who's dead? Who did you kill?"

"No one." One of the knights bared his teeth. "Fleeing Saracens have slain stray Christians."

The only one of the knights who showed any fear, the youngest of them, no more than a donzel. He spoke in a rush while Pedro's guards stripped him of weapons. "The king's messengers to the pope. All of them. We were commanded by the priest to do it. To save Christendom from heresy."

"My master!" Qasim cried, while Yusuf shouted, "Father, no!"

Durán found that the heart doesn't break, it shatters.

∎

The ground stayed in place, so he could walk, one foot in front of the other.

But when Durán glanced down, a gulf lay before him, deeper than the Great Sea, broader.

Crows complained in the trees, clattered up in a black cloud, occluding the sun, then settling in the pines again. Complaining.

And cawking inside his head.

He couldn't swallow his thoughts.

Because a wraith had hold of his throat, choking him, scolding, promising to throw him into that abyss that lay just before him, that he could see if he glanced down.

He followed Pedro, his eyes fixed on the back of the man's sun-burned neck. The man leading him through the perilous horde of priests who had sprung from their tents and pavilions to watch them pass by.

"Christian?" It was that shrieking priest again, who wanted to spurn and burn Durán. "Christian? You say Christian?"

But all Durán heard was Chrétien.

Chrétien.

Chrétien.

∎

At a word from Pedro, Serena hoisted Fortuno onto her shoulders and went with Qasim to find Father Anselm. Two guards brought Doménec and the Crux Lunata donzel to Pedro's pavilion. The king threw everyone else out, and then pointed to a corner where he wanted Yusuf.

"Not a word from you, *fadrin*," he said to Yusuf. "Go where I say and do as I ask, just this once."

Durán seized Doménec's arm. "You traitor!" He jerked the man close, wanting to see into the soul of the man who destroyed all hope. But all he saw in Doménec's eyes was animal fear.

"Don't murder a Churchman, please," Pedro motioned for Durán to come to him. "That's how Count Raymond got into so much trouble in Toulouse."

"I don't want any more blood on my hands." Durán ripped at Doménec's sleeve. "I want to find—"

The Crux Lunata tattoo, high up the clerk's forearm.

Pedro said, "What honest bishop can we find to listen to the story you will tell me, Doménec?"

Yusuf stirred. "I shall write for you, Monsenyor." He seized the clerk's own desk and had a pen in his hand before Pedro nodded. "You were anointed by the pope. I was taught in my lessons that you don't need a priest present when judging, because whatever you say is witnessed by God."

Yusuf was also staring at Doménec, his eyes like a cat who wants to pounce on prey. Otherwise, Yusuf showed no emotion. Durán covered his own face to hide grief, which doubled when he thought of Yusuf, now without either a father or a brother or a mother.

While Pedro asked questions, Doménec stood in the middle of the pavilion, two of the king's guards close by. The frightened Crux Lunata donzel recited what he knew in detail.

"The priest in our town, together with the master of Crux Lunata convinced my father that the way to salvation and the honor of good men was to join these knights. To restore the Church's power in the heart of Christendom. My father gave land and gold and made them promise to keep me as a knight."

For Durán, that recitation was like listening once again to Felip's tale about salvation and crusade and going to Andalusia for paratge. They all believed they were doing God's will. For the love of God, they murdered and betrayed, hoping it led to the eradication of heresy in the south.

"But the part about killing my messengers?" Pedro said, speaking so quietly that his voice could barely be heard over the croaking crows still stirring in Durán's head. "And about Esak's effort to kill me? I take it that Esak de Beaurain is the master of the Crux Lunata."

"No, only our spiritual leader. Matheus of Girona leads us."

"*Ai*, Doménec." Pedro sighed. "What am I to do? You lived by my side all this time and wanted me dead?"

"No, Monsenyor! They didn't tell me about killing a king." Doménec called out in a passion. Durán felt that torrent wash over him, and then found all his own grief and anger still seizing his muscles, smothering each breath. This clerk had lost nothing, while Durán had lost everything. "I was asked to keep you free of evil, to keep heretics and their defenders away from you."

"Then you're a fool as well as a traitor." Yusuf again disregarded Pedro's insistence on his silence. "You helped kill my father, my brother, my mother, my uncle."

"If you want to continue working for me," Pedro pointed a finger at Yusuf, "you will refrain from speaking my thoughts ahead of me."

∎

After an eternity, Pedro sent everyone away, consigning Doménec and that Crux Lunata donzel to his guards. Father Anselm came to claim Yusuf, Qasim, and Serena and took them away. Then Pedro sat alone with Durán in the shade of the pavilion.

No one crowded them, which left enough space for a man to breathe. Fewer men present than any time since...when? Durán couldn't remember when at least a hundred men weren't watching every move he made, every word he said.

"What will you do with Doménec, Monsenyor?"

"Give him to Arnau Amalric, I suppose. I have no power to punish a Churchman."

"But they let Esak free after Hugues died."

"They did." Pedro mused on this. "Do you want him to die? For revenge?"

"No." Whatever Durán felt, it wasn't blood lust. "I'm sick of men dying. But it's you that Doménec betrayed."

"If I send him with Amalric, he'll be free again. If I send him to Rome, he won't be punished." Pedro laughed. "And maybe he'll join with my wife to plan more problems for me."

"Then you'll keep him?"

"Perhaps the bishop in Toledo can find a use for Churchman who creates problems. They do things differently in Castile." Pedro handed Durán a clay mug of wine.

"What are we doing?"

"The plan," Pedro said. "Taking the Aragón forces home. Eat breakfast with me, and then join your men. You'll have to lead all of Valerós now, too."

"Breakfast?" Durán still couldn't swallow. The wraith's long fingers still clenched and clawed at his throat.

·

The next day, Aragón forces broke camp and took the king's road around the mountains, riding their horses instead of leading them. The caliph's forces had abandoned the road and its environments. The army had no impediments on the main way to Toledo, and that first night out, every man enjoyed extra provisions from the seized Saracen wagons.

Except Doménec, who had been left alone on the road before sunset, with only water, bread, and a blanket. And a command never to appear in Aragón in this life.

In camp, the men sang *cançós de guerra* and *cançós d'amor* until late in the night. Everyone sang.

Except Durán, Yusuf, and Qasim, who laid their bedrolls out under a thousand stars, away from the others, and wept.

The sound of those men's voices soothed after a while, but Durán still couldn't find the country of sleep. He spent too much time under the stars listening to the songs, weeping because he did not hear Chrétien's voice.

It was very late in the night when Durán realized that Fortuno's voice was also missing.

29

Atonement

"WE HAVEN'T EVEN HAD A DECENT breakfast." Chrétien chivvied the knights surrounding him. "It's an uncourtly breach of good manners, a truly unfair scuffle you've proposed here. A leprous goat shows better manners to his cuckolding ladylove."

One of the knights slapped at Chrétien, who dodged and offered only his shoulder as a target.

"You curse the Holy Spirit," Matheus said. "We are here on earth as God's judge."

Tomás kept checking the numbers. Fifteen men arrived, three left. Then two got busy scavenging wood and kindling a fire. Tomás stood with four friends. But one, Isabella, was bound. And by some miserable lapse, the moment of bad judgment that must never occur, Sebastián's and Chrétien's chainmail lay on the ground, discarded while they tended yesterday's wounds.

Sebastián, with that gash down his sword arm.

Chrétien remained close enough to Sebastián to protect him, and they'd at least been able to grab their swords.

Two Crux Lunata knights had come between Tomás and Rashid. They'd disarmed Rashid, who was also injured, blood staining the red silk sleeve of his surcoat. Yet Tomás included Rashid in his numbers, since his cousin must want to survive this day.

While Tomás figured the odds and determined where each and every weapon in that little valley was held or cast aside, Chrétien got a hand free. And waved.

That odd backwards summon, like the farewell wave of an untutored infant.

But Tomás had no room to move, to make the first tripping and thrusting attack. He shook his head at Chrétien, because it wasn't possible. But Chrétien stepped into the feint and attacked.

And Rashid followed immediately, just as Tomás had taught him, knocking the man between them to the ground, seizing a sword and piercing him.

"Tuma!" Rashid tossed that sword to Tomás, who found it to be longer and heavier than what he was used to, abrading the cuts on his hands, unhealed since Ríma's attack.

Sebastián's eyes flashed in the heartbeat it took him to imitate Rashid's initial move. Sebastián's first move toppled the man closest to Chrétien, and then he passed the fallen man's weapon to Chrétien.

Tomás forgot that they were too few for the number of attackers. Instead, he fought with speed and force, to make up for every mistake since that swale in the Pyrenees where he'd last lost Isabella.

Forget that they were still too few. That Chrétien and Sebastián and Rashid were bleeding. Rashid bashed at a sword that wanted to take off his face. The ploy, Chrétien's invention for two men on eight, required Tomás's rapid help, which kept him on the other side of the clearing, away from Isabella.

His hope rose when he grabbed a buckler that one of the attackers had dropped.

Rashid fought viciously and aggressively, his lunge-and-recover speed better than he'd ever shown in practice.

Sebastián fought back to back with Chrétien, the two of them against five men.

And Tomás saw in the first moves that these knights had trained for horseback and neglected to learn footwork.

Rashid clashed with a knight who parried with the edge of his sword and who was surprised that Rashid countered with the flat of his blade and then took the man's hand off.

Two men fighting Sebastián bashed at him wildly, but he stifled first one and then the other, leveraging his weight and blade. In a heartbeat, one lay on the ground and the other was backing off.

That peaceful creek side now stunk of dying men, blood, and that tang of frightened sweat. Men screamed, groaned, and grunted. Sebastián again shouted yesterday's battle cries. Chrétien laughed in that mad way he did in battle, when they were all going to die. Then he hamstrung a man and thrust his dagger through a gap in chainmail, up into the man's groin.

Yet no one was making it to Isabella. She struggled with Matheus, who growled, "You animals are anathema to God."

Someone was shouting, first in Provençal, then in a Toulousain dialect, and then Catalan. "Stop! In the name of Our Savior. This is not God's will!"

Matheus stood with a shocked look, staring at the knife in his shoulder. He let go of Isabella and tried to pull out that knife.

Colomb strode into the melee, a sword in one hand. He shouted, "Vidal of Valerós!"

"I thought you saw the truth." Isabella struggled out of the bindings on her arms and hands.

"I did. *Vivètz Beaurain!*"

Colomb tossed a quarterstaff her way. She caught it and then stepped exactly the way Chrétien taught her, attacking the man closest to Matheus. Colomb stayed near, fighting off any attacker who came close to her, a broad smile on his face.

"I failed the real Vidal," Colomb shouted to Isabella. "I'd die rather than fail again."

Once more, Tomás failed to be the knight who saved her.

Tomás and Rashid had only reduced their work to two against five, the pair of them now fighting back to back, just as they'd trained together. He had to concentrate with that many blades, and how fast he and Rashid had to move, so he couldn't even look away to see how well Isabella fared.

Tomás could not get free to help when Matheus grabbed the sword of a fallen comrade and advanced on Isabella again.

But Sebastián stepped between them, receiving a blow with the flat of his blade and then pushing back with all his strength. He held Miquel's sword.

Though Matheus was larger, he stumbled before recovering. He advanced on Sebastián again. He was a better fighter than his comrades, half of whom were dead or dying. He shouted as he fought, calling down the wrath of God on them.

"My blade is the key to hell and death."

Lunge.

"You corrupt the faith of men."

A cut from Sebastián.

"You spew venom, hostile to Christ."

Chrétien screamed high and loud enough to chill living bones. "Sebastián! Make him shut up."

Matheus laughed. "This boy? Born of a slut heretic?"

Sebastián assumed a classic stance, ready to do as Chrétien commanded.

"*Ai*, Valerós!" Colomb shouted. "You can't kill your own brother. Give the fight to me."

Matheus stepped back, distracted. "Uncle?"

Colomb advanced on them, stepping into the gap between Sebastián and Matheus, attacking with his long sword. Matheus sliced at the inner gap in Colomb's chainmail, piercing his thigh.

"He's not my brother." Sebastián shielded Colomb when he collapsed, then struck back at Matheus with perfect timing, disarming him, kicking him to the ground. "My father is Don Tomás."

Sebastián had his sword at Matheus's throat. Matheus gazed up at him, his aventail shifting away. "I command you all. Crux Lunata must tear these heretics from God's earth."

"I saw you murder my mother last year." Sebastián plunged his sword into Matheus's throat. Then ripped it free.

Rather than answering Matheus's last command, the remaining knights fled. Chrétien and Rashid walked among the fallen, dispatching anyone who moaned. Tomás finally reached Isabella.

Sebastián stood over Matheus. "He isn't my brother, Senhór Colomb. You did not have to warn me or interfere."

Colomb sopped at the blood from the cut on his thigh. "Durán called that to me last night when Matheus attacked Pedro."

"Because Esak killed Hugues?" Isabella asked.

"*Òc*, Master Vidal. I wanted to do for Sebastián what his brothers did for me."

"*Ai*, no!" Isabella cried. "Durán killed Esak?"

329

"No," Colomb said. "Yusuf did."

"*Per l'amor de Dèu!*" Tomás again failed to be there when Yusuf needed him.

Colomb didn't seem to hear. "All Durán did was say heretic prayers over Felip in front of a gang of priests."

•

"It was an honor to fight with you at my back." Tomás reached out a hand to Rashid.

Who refused it.

"*Ai*, cousin. Do you not yet see?" Tomás clasped his hands, begging. "You stood with me, ready to die for these people, my family. I'd lay down my life for you, too."

"Did every goat in town die? And now we're forced to eat mouse droppings?" Chrétien scoffed at Tomás and then turned his attention to Rashid. "Don't you have a brother? Brothers don't do what you want them to, more often than not."

"My brother died," Rashid growled.

"See what I mean?" Chrétien said. "Mine died several times, and yet here I am again, hauling his monkey bottom back from hell. He can't have done any worse by you than he has me."

"You scrofulous vulture!" Tomás protested. "Stay out of this, Chrétien."

"He stole my honor," Rashid said.

Chrétien laughed, throwing his head back so that his long hair streamed out around him. "Did you never have to lose your honor to protect others? It's what a brother does."

Rashid said, "Tuma deserted me. And dishonored our family."

Chrétien said, "Once? Twice? He deserted me a dozen times because he prefers women when there's a choice. He leaves his children to go work for the king of Aragón. He left his wife—"

"Because he thought she was dead." Isabella interrupted. She was helping Colomb with his injuries, pausing to check fallen knights to tear away strips of linen for bandages. "Tomás never betrays. Though the whole truth cannot always be known at any moment."

"What do you know about betrayal, boy?" Rashid sneered, not liking the interruption.

"I am that wife," she said. "One of them, at least. The one he thought was dead."

Tomás, to save his own honor, said, "And I must thank you, Senhór Colomb, for saving my wife just now."

Startled, Colomb turned to Isabella. "That's who you are?"

"Òc." She offered her hand. "Isabella of Valerós."

"And what Durán said about you knowing Hugues?" Colomb was asking Chrétien.

"My brother and I spent a month in a dungeon with him." Chrétien answered while checking the cut on Rashid's arm, signing with his fingers that it needed stitching. "Hugues taught us courage. Tomás kept us alive."

Isabella said, "And your brother Hugues showed me great kindness once, Senhór Colomb. When Renoud had me on trial for heresy in Toulouse."

Another moment when Tomás had failed her. For all the relief of rescue, he was not finding joy. Chrétien had a needle and thread out of his jerkin, not waiting for Rashid to refuse or to start arguing with Tomás again.

His attention on Isabella, Colomb spoke rapidly, like a man having to explain himself. "The moon touched that lad as soon as he crawled free of his mother's loins."

"I noticed." Chrétien stripped Rashid's surcoat and inspected him for more cuts.

Colomb said, "I never thought Matheus capable of true evil. Until last year, when Hélène told him he was a Beaurain. The devil lit a bonfire in his soul."

"You think he had a soul?" Chrétien prodded one of Rashid's cuts to make it bleed again, then poured water over it from a bota.

"I stuck close since All Saints, hoping to guide him." Colomb couldn't stop talking. He should be flinching, given the firm hand Isabella was taking with his injury. "After he met Esak, Matheus was eaten up with ambition to take back Beaurain glory."

Isabella said, "He was filled with too much of Esak's bile about Pedro and heresy and had none of Hugues' honor."

"Òc." Colomb said. "I cannot calculate how to repay what I owe all of you for the evil he wrought."

"Nothing," Isabella said. "You helped save us."

Colomb burst into tears. Then he choked on the words as he explained. Tomás guessed battle shock. "But I didn't keep him from killing his own brother. Like Durán and Yusuf saved me. Poor Felip." Colomb then told the previous night's story with greater clarity than Rashid had. Meanwhile Isabella made him strip his breeches so she could wash that long sword wound.

"Esak poisoned Matheus with his notions of God's will," Colomb said. "I see that now. Esak destroyed your brother in a different way, but as surely as he destroyed mine."

"Can we agree, please," Sebastián said, "to stop calling Matheus my brother? He was just a faithless monster."

"Can we tend to the horses?" Isabella asked. "And see if we can glean provisions left by these knights? We can argue about everyone's honor on the road home."

When they were back on the king's road, Chrétien cantered close, kicking Tomás in the shin, then reining in his skittering horse. "You talk to Miquel? You see him?"

"Since that dungeon on Cyprus. But not since Minerve."

"But you saw him again in the mountains?"

"Òc."

"What did he say about me?"

"Just that I have to keep my promises to you."

Chrétien nodded, then cantered up to ride alongside Colomb. He shouted back to Tomás. "When you see Miquel next, kick his ass. I want to talk to him too."

That left Tomás riding beside Isabella, who smiled.

"Long story?" she prompted.

30

Crossing Over

WHEN THEY RODE THROUGH THE gates at Lérida, Pedro asked Durán and Yusuf to meet in the council room after they settled. Somewhere between handing over care of his horse in the stable and finding space in the guest barracks, Durán lost track of Yusuf. He tarried with Cebrián to eat sheep's cheese and flatbread in the king's guards' barracks.

When Cebrián had to take his shift in guard duty, Durán followed him to the council room. Durán had just opened the door when Yusuf shoved past him and raced into the council room.

"Where's Dolç? Where's my brother? Chrétien said we'd find them here in Lérida."

Pedro glanced up from where he read messages at a heavy, dark table. "They tell me she left in early summer for Barcelona. Which is where I wanted her to be. She'll be safe there."

Durán had a hand on Yusuf's shoulder. "She's with Jacques. We know she's safe."

"Are you ready to work?" Pedro asked.

Without answering, Yusuf sat at a scribe's desk, took a breath, and masked the anxiety he'd carried into the room. Pedro handed him one of the messages he'd been reading.

"Alfonso has declared himself the king of a new Spain," Pedro said. "He's so happy about it that he's made peace with Navarre and León. Even let them keep castles they stole from Castile."

Yusuf, reading faster than most people, had already devoured the message. "Alfonso conquered Úbeda and Baeza. Those poor people."

Alone with Durán and Yusuf, Pedro revealed more passion than he'd shown when everything was lost after the battle, complaining about Alfonso's strategy.

"'Imperishable glory in the kingdom of heaven!'" Pedro shouted the words. "That is what Alfonso's bishop claimed this was all about. But what did that doddering king do? Grab land and booty. Destroy whole cities."

Yusuf said, "The scouts say the caliph is running home to Tunis. The pope must see how you helped victory in Iberia."

Pedro glared. "Are you mollifying me? We lost. We lost everything I worked for, hoping to prove Aragón can lead in Christendom. Alfonso has claimed all glory." He rose and paced. "The chronicles Alfonso has sent to the pope will declare that Portugal's two hundred men did more in battle than Aragón did. Men who showed up two heartbeats before the melee began will have their names unrolled before the pope as true heroes."

"*Òc*, Monsenyor." Yusuf took up the parchments Pedro had signed, then laid out more on the table. "After you spent five years provisioning, training, planning, preparing."

Pedro paced, still angry. "The magnificent performance of the Aragón fighters on the field? The pope will hear from me too late to grant credence to the genius of Aragón in battle."

It was as if Pedro exploded with the same burning anger Durán carried every moment.

"And what did Alfonso's infernal bishop say this was to be?"

Pedro wasn't asking a question he wanted answered. Yet Durán had been there, had heard the words, had puzzled the meaning with no success. He repeated what the bishop said.

"*Imitatio Christi*."

Pedro stopped pacing, stock still, like a man who'd been dashed with cold water.

"God put me here to do this work. How did I fail? Trusting where I shouldn't? Not believing all your warnings? Too confident that victory would give me strength to fight Simon de Montfort?"

"You didn't fail anyone." Durán had been locked in his own anger, doing his best to comfort Yusuf and Qasim, and never for one moment considered what Pedro must be enduring.

"Monsenyor, you only failed to remember that we can't understand what heaven intends." Yusuf said. "Like trying to capture water in your fist."

.

After midday, Pedro had them all in his chapel—Yusuf, Durán, Serena Taresa, Father Anselm. It was forty days.

Forty days since the battle.

Since the Aragón army departed north.

Since his couriers to the pope had all been lost.

Pedro had requested a private mass from Father Anselm, which wasn't meaningful to Durán.

But afterwards, Pedro brought them all up to the rooftop. Even here in Lérida, he seemed to keep Durán near. And Yusuf had taken over Doménec's former duties. Pedro begged them to come up, ostensibly to check the army camp from above, counting men to see if the captains' reports were correct. Yusuf, who seemed to have the eyesight of an imperial eagle, was especially good at this, and so Durán had drifted off to stare out over the village and farmlands that surrounded the city of kings.

Near Durán, Father Anselm had provoked the usually silent Serena Taresa into conversation. Father Anselm said, "The king commands me to ask whether your marriage was consummated."

Serena Taresa scowled. "The king can leap at the moon. My husband is dead. Under his own laws, a widow is independent, not the king's business."

Anselm said, "Pedro commands you into union with the Master of Xirgú. Since we lost Sebastián, it's Durán who will receive Xirgú."

Durán swallowed, having expected this would be the next command passed to him.

However, Serena repeated oaths that must have been learned in the baggage train. "Am I once more landless and passed as the king's reward? Pedro promised to get my land back from Crux Lunata."

Anselm persisted. "The king needs you to marry again, for the sake of paratge and the future of our lands. Durán understands."

"Do we have to do this now?" Durán felt for the woman's grief, and truly did not want to discuss the politics of what it meant to take his brother Sebastián's place as Master of Valerós. "It's been only weeks since…" He still couldn't say the words aloud.

"It's the contract that matters," Anselm said. "Serena Taresa can return to Girona as steward there. You'd never see her after—"

"I'm not marrying a heretic," Serena Taresa said. Pedro must have heard, but he didn't look their way. "They claim a woman must be born as a man to gain salvation. And I like cheese. And sausages."

Below, a guard shouted up into the battlements. "Monsenyor, the scouts say a band of Moors approaches. From the south."

"There!" Yusuf pointed to the horizon.

"Men lost when the caliph deserted them?" Pedro speculated. "New emissaries?"

Durán had to look twice, unlike Yusuf, but he counted five figures on tired, slow-moving horses. Three wore the scaled chainmail and light surcoats of caliphate knights, two of them dark as Ayyubid cavalrymen but one with shocking white hair that glistened in the sunlight.

The other two were much taller, one with bronze sun-bright hair, dressed in Beaurain house colors, and the last one, in an ill-fitting Saracen surcoat, sat tallest in the saddle, his long blond hair streaming loose in the afternoon wind from the mountains.

"Truly wonderful." Pedro blinked and blinked again against the sunshine and wind. He had his hand on Serena Taresa's shoulder. "*Ai, ma dòmna*, it appears that your husband will be Sebastián of Valerós."

"But you made Sebastián marry a Castilian witch." Serena Taresa shaded her eyes, peering down the king's road.

"Diego Lopez broke the contract when Sebastián died."

"But he's not dead, Monsenyor." She tipped her head up to smile at Pedro, the first time any of them saw her smile.

"Let's ride out to greet them." Durán bounded up and ran.

Pedro caught up with him on the stairs, shouting. He had to repeat twice before Durán made out the words.

"This is sweeter than victory!"

•

Sebastián made it to the courtyard of the king's residence several paces ahead of Tomás and Isabella, so he embraced Yusuf, who seemed delirious, bouncing with joy. Sebastián, of course, couldn't match paces with Chrétien, who embraced Durán. Yusuf released Sebastián, calling to his father.

"Father!"

Yusuf tackled Tomás, clutching him around the neck, then the waist, then his neck again. Qasim hung close by, happy, and happier still when Tomás shook his hand and then squeezed Qasim. Behind them Pedro greeted Rashid, a formal handshake and quiet words that couldn't be heard over the noise of reunion.

"Where's your new brother?" Tomás asked Yusuf, who was now embracing Isabella.

"They've all gone home to Barcelona," Yusuf said. A flash of emotion crossed Tomás's ruined face. It had been a repeated theme on the journey here, to find Dolç and resolve how to live with wives and sons. Yusuf saw that look. "I was disappointed, too, Father. But Pedro says they're safe."

Sebastián clenched Durán when his brother finally managed to let go of Chrétien. Hot from the road, Sebastián shed his surcoat.

"This is yours, Durán."

"Colomb?"

"He died on the way here. A week ago. He was wounded rescuing us. We asked help from every herb-witch we found on the road. But it turned poison." Sebastián pressed the coat on Durán. "He wanted you to have this, for his quest to revive the Beaurain name."

"You keep it." Durán embraced Sebastián again, heat and sweat and all. "I'll never wear chainmail again. I honor Colomb and his passion for the House of Beaurain, but I don't need a knight's coat."

"He had one more thing he insisted you have." Sebastián rummaged inside his jerkin and then pressed a jangle of metal into Durán's hand. "He said you should always call—"

That collection of silver on a tether from many days' coin toss, picking partners for midday sparring. Durán clutched it close.

"Pedro's head."

.

At that night's feast, Sebastián endeavored to devote himself to each conversation in the room. But it had been too many months since he'd eaten anything except dried bread and beans, so his trencher and the platters that servants passed took most of his attention.

People had exhausted their need to embrace each other and weep, but Pedro insisted on a long prayer, praising God for their salvation. Taresa stood across the table from Sebastián, staring at him through the long prayer.

Sebastián didn't repeat the prayers Pedro demanded, only stood silently, hoping he looked respectful. The truth? They were saved by their own swords, not delivered by angels. But Sebastián wasn't about to argue the point because angels seemed to have delivered this feast.

Stuffed eggs, with brewed salt and quinces.

Since it was harvest season, there was also quince paste with fresh farmers' cheese.

Roasted lamb with cinnamon and caraway.

Raised bread, from that morning's baking.

A fried flat bread with rose syrup.

Buttered cabbage.

A potage of harvest foods with vegetable marrows, wild celery, pot herbs, and olives.

Durán and Chrétien had disappeared and now were late to dinner. Sebastián glanced around, assessing whether there'd be enough food left or whether he should hoard a bit for those two. Then they slipped onto the bench beside him and got busy saying yes and no to what the servants offered.

"This potage has your name all over it, Durán." Sebastián nudged his brother, who looked wistful, lost in dreams, and had to be poked twice before accepting the potage and heaping it onto his trencher.

Nearby, Pedro had Rashid seated on one side and Tomás on the other. At Pedro's prompting, Rashid had told the story of what happened among the caliph's army in the days leading to the battle.

"It took a half day for our messages back to the caliph to be believed," Rashid. "That must be added to your chronicles to explain the wonders of how that battle unfolded."

"You were introduced to me in Barcelona as one of the caliph's most trusted viziers." Pedro offered to pour wine for Rashid, a gesture that Sebastián recognized as how Pedro managed intimate conversation. Rashid held out a hand to stop him, but caught Tomás shaking his head. Rashid settled his hand in his lap and accepted the wine. "Why didn't he believe your messages?"

"Al-Nasir was unhappy when I returned from Barcelona without having persuaded you to keep your army at home." Rashid sipped at his wine, frowned, then sipped again. "He sent me to the frontier to persuade Abu-Jossep to move his army. I took too long to achieve that. Then rumors flew that the Rodriquez clan had accepted Alfonso's offer to restore their old lands if they helped Castile."

Tomás interrupted. "The caliph was sharpening a knife for you before the clan rumors began."

"How could you know that?" Again, Rashid seemed to tussle with the idea of sipping his wine.

"Common sense," Tomás said. "And Zaheid's spies."

Sebastián had heard this argument between the two cousins repeatedly, perhaps every third day over the journey back from the frontier. The issue was never resolved, Sebastián believed, because Rashid refused to admit that everyone in his world had betrayed him.

Since he didn't care to watch this hash refried again, Sebastián waved to a servant who carried a loaded platter of cardamom-spiced chicken. And then was surprised at what Pedro said next.

"We began the year, each of us living in a different world. And now we are alike, you and I." Pedro reached out, almost touching Rashid's hand where it rested on the wine cup. "I too have been betrayed where I most trusted. For a moment, I lost sense of why God put me here. What will you do next?"

Rashid sipped wine again. This question hadn't been resolved in the long discussions on the journey to Lérida. Rashid refused Tomás's repeated invitation to come to Valerós with him.

Pedro prompted for an answer, not accepting silence. "Perhaps you can find a taifa general to serve."

"I'm sure that way is closed to me."

"If Alfonso is rewarding the Rodriquez clan, perhaps he has a place for you in Castile."

"You are kind to consider it," Rashid said. "Please do not think it rude, Monsenyor, but I'd rather die in the wilderness than ask a favor of a king because I have Rodriquez blood."

Pedro said, "At least the caliph isn't a problem for you now. He's gone to Tunis, and his mercenaries are scavenging their way toward the Great Sea to sail home." He also sipped wine, pausing to regard Rashid over the brim of his cup, a gesture that meant Pedro was pushing for more than a man might be ready to give. "The men who worked for me in Andalusia have rescued their families. They helped your cousin Zaheid's family travel to Morella, where they are safe."

Rashid seemed uncertain. "Surely you don't think—"

"Think you seek safety? No, *mon amic*. You need work. Come work for me. I need a captain for the Mozarabs and the Moors who deserted the caliph and followed me north."

"Monsenyor." Rashid rattled his cup so it clattered on the lye-scrubbed wooden table top.

"I can't find superior generals like you in the hedges of my own country."

"Lead men to fight my own people? Like that traitor you call El Cid?" Rashid shook his head.

"No, I'd never send you into Iberia." Pedro again almost touched Rashid's hand, hovering over it. He put down his wine cup and reached to take up Rashid's other hand, studying it. He'd seen the mark, where Chrétien had branded Rashid on their journey to reach Pedro. "*Ai*, bonfraire! I shall grant you a landed title in one of my counties, with five hundred men to command. Not as lofty a title as grand vizier. But you'll find it interesting. We shall launch a defensive campaign next year in the heart of Christendom."

Rashid hesitated, that wine cup shaking in his hand.

Pedro said more, words that sounded like Arabic.

A smile twisted across Rashid's face. "I believe what you mean to say is an old proverb. 'You need a brother. Without one you're like a person rushing to battle without a weapon.'"

"Indeed, bonfraire. What say you?"

Rashid pushed his cup aside and held out his hand to Pedro. "Another proverb. 'I'm already drowning. Why fear getting wet?'"

Pedro grasped his hand the way bonfraires do. "*Benvingut.* You'll make Sebastián happy, too, since he's likely tired of commanding whatever band of strangers I push his way."

The sound of his name roused Sebastián from the frenzy of feasting he'd indulged.

"What next for you, Master of Valerós?" Pedro asked Sebastián. "Going home?"

"No, I shall follow you to Toulouse, Monsenyor. Half of our Valerós band remains willing to travel in your service."

"Easier band to manage now?" Pedro tipped his wine cup in Sebastián's direction, which indicated that it was a real question.

"I've only just walked through the camp to say hello." Sebastián wanted to defer to Durán, who still looked only at Chrétien, missing most of what happened around him. "My brother has done most of the work."

"Durán got that herd of motley strangers shouting for Valerós in unison." Pedro persisted. "Did any stay with the army?"

Durán finally awoke to the questions. "The Catalans and Toulousain mercenaries stayed. The others found their way home when they heard Sebastián had died."

Pedro folded his arms, thoughtful. "Do you think any can be recruited again to fight in Roussillon or Toulouse?'

"Not any ultramontanos," Sebastián said. "I assume the Almogavars went back to their lives on the frontier, since I didn't find any when I walked through camp today."

"Are you ready to take command of an Aragón squadron? Lead if we confront Simon next summer?"

Pedro's question caused a certain hot joy to bloom in Sebastián's middle, the part that hadn't been stuffed at the feast.

Before he could answer, Pedro said, "Your life spent as a commander for Aragón? I'd like to offer you that."

Sebastián had just speared a slice of quince paste, and it hung over his trencher. "I'm honored. And I'll join you for the coming summer. But I intend to fight like the Almogavars do, but for the sake of my own land. And my neighbors."

"We shall see. Meanwhile, I need you to take a wife. The mistress of Xirgú."

"I'm a warrior," Sebastián asked, "not a househusband. I shall live my life like Pèire Leteric."

Serena Taresa, who sat across from him, glared at Sebastián, as fierce as when she'd thrown him out of her tent. "You don't want a laundry girl?"

"You should have told me who you were."

She folded her arms, prepared to spar. "I'd never have gotten beyond the Girona city walls if anyone knew who I was."

Father Anselm said, "We can take Serena Taresa and Yusuf to Valerós until—"

"No one takes me away," Serena Taresa said. "I shall stay with my husband."

Pedro had his hand on his chin again. "You liked life with the baggage train? Perhaps you'll like skirmish fighting in the mountains."

"And I'm staying with my brother Sebastián," Yusuf said. "Also, the king needs a personal scribe he can trust."

"O Magnificent One," Tomás called to Qasim, who sat beside Yusuf at table. Something had happened since Sebastián first met Tomás's servant, because he now sat by Yusuf's side, like another son with a place at the table. But then: Qasim did show the kings the way over that wild-dog mountain. "Your bond ends at the next full moon. What will you do?"

Qasim glanced between Yusuf and Tomás.

"Come home with me, Qasim." Tomás beckoned. "We'll fetch your mother from Valencia and shelter her at Valerós."

"No, master. You have knights riding with you. Yusuf requires my protection. Especially since he now holds a dangerous position."

"Working as my scribe?" Pedro glanced up, surprised, from where he was absorbed talking with Rashid.

"There have been bleak outcomes," Yusuf said.

Serena Taresa glanced up, looking fierce as fire. "Doménec, his last clerk is rotting in hell, I hope."

.

At Lérida, one morning after a glorious breakfast, Pedro's army prepared to march to Urgell, to winter in that valley. A small band of

Aragón knights and Valerós bordoniers split from the main army, following the king's road to Barcelona and then for home.

Sebastián tarried, saying goodbye to Father Anselm and Isabella, who were joining the Valerós band.

Yusuf and Tomás talked quietly between them, saying goodbye. Tomás held out a dagger for him. Yusuf took it, said thanks with a grin, but then passed it to Qasim.

When Tomás turned back to join Isabella, Pedro and Rashid were there, both offering him a bonfraire embrace. Rashid held onto Tomás for a long moment, then nodded, and strode away with Pedro.

Sebastián kissed his mother goodbye. "Will I see you in Toulouse come summer?"

"If Pedro makes Simon's heretic-hunting grounds safe for me." She hugged him again. "I'm happy that you have everything you wanted as a soldier. Pèire would be pleased."

"Except Pedro forced me to marry a woman I can't forgive." Sebastián blurted it, regretted it. Isabella blinked, surprised.

"What did she do that's unforgiveable?"

Words ran, more than he intended to say. "She promised to be true. She said we could refuse fate. But then she married the moment Pedro ordered it, the first time. She just runs from—"

"Sancta Maria with all the perpetual virgins." Tomás grabbed the back of Sebastián's neck, turning him around until they knocked foreheads. "Why does any woman who did a brave thing to protect herself ever need your forgiveness?"

Isabella had hold of Sebastián's wrist, over the bonfraires' sign. "*Òc.* Perhaps Serena Taresa has wisdom to share that you can't find elsewhere."

One of the captains called his name, so Sebastián said a hasty farewell and then had to attend to his men. He left Lérida riding in an honor position in Pedro's guard with Chrétien, Durán, and Rashid. They paused on a crest, spying the band with Tomás and Isabella just before they disappeared along the road. Taresa cantered up alongside Sebastián.

"It's like a *cançó d'amor,* isn't it?" She was once more, *per l'amor de Dèu,* dressed as a boy, still swearing she'd go wherever her husband did. "Except your mother is the hero who saved the knight."

Rashid said, "Will we see them again?"

"God alone knows," Pedro called to them.

"And no God, Light or Dark, ever reveals the future," Durán said. "At least, not in a way we can understand."

"But if you know how to play the odds," Chrétien stretched to punch Durán's shoulder, "you can win more often than not."

Pedro motioned for Rashid to ride alongside him so they could talk, which they'd been doing endlessly after dinner and at breakfast, ever since Rashid arrived at Lérida. At Pedro's marshal's signal, they all moved up the road.

Chrétien burst into song then, joined by men from their ranks. He sang a *cançó d'amor*, the one about the shepherdess who tricked the evil hedge-priest that had seduced her.

31

Heart Springs

Ibn Jafar, poet to kings,
Toledo, at the vernal equinox

ALL BLESSINGS UPON YOU, MY DEAREST WIVES.

By the grace of God, who we praise endlessly, I am alive and well. I have a new position in a royal house, a position that promises to keep us all in greater comfort than you and our children ever believed could be ours.

As you must have heard in Jaén, Al-Nasir has fled Al-Andalus for Tunis. And the king of Castile has taken the frontier cities of Baeza and Úbeda, since their local defenders were defeated in battle. It is a blessing from heaven, then, that Ríma de Rodriquez took me with her, is it not? If I'd remained in Baeza, I would have watched infidels tear down the walls, destroy farms and orchards, and carry people away as concubines and slaves.

The rumor here in Toledo is that taifa generals from Jaén and Granada have led their men to the frontier, hoping to retake Ferral and the other lost citadels. But the Christian militias resisted, though we hear rumors that camp sickness is now sending home the forces from Castile and Leon. All of Toledo is excited, preparing a victory festival to celebrate its returning heroes.

But I must explain to you how the doings of kings and generals now affects your two lives, blessed among women, and I, who live with you here humbly on earth.

By God's grace, I now serve Señor Carlos of Toledo, who was made vizconde after the battle. He worked as an emissary to the Aragón crown before this battle. He now serves Alfonso's own

345

daughter, Berengaria, the woman who will be regent on the sad day that Alfonso of Castile departs this world.

I am kept busy each day, chronicling the doings of the multitudes from across Iberia, including militias from Segovia and Avila who came to the battle with Sancho of Navarre. As I write each story, I describe numbers which, if believed, mean that the roads to the frontier were so crowded, the last man had not yet left his house before the first man in the militia's column crossed into Al-Andalus.

But if God has granted the Christian militias the glory of victory here on earth, who am I to deny the glory they seek to claim in the chronicles?

My next news shall strike you with amazement. When I close my eyes, I can see you clutching each other's hands in surprise. The crucial work given to me is to create a poetic record of the lineage of the Visigoth kings, whose current heir is Ríma de Rodriquez.

Yes, the bruja you condemned in the solitude of your own courtyard has indeed wrought magic, the result of which is that you are now invited to live with me in a king's house.

What I'm commissioned to write is the true chronicles of the lost Visigoth kings and their new-found heirs. The story is in the style of my odes that are so popular in Córdoba and Seville, a bit old fashioned in word choice and rhyming in a way that reveals fabulists' tales to be true.

My first ode celebrates Rodrigo Díaz de Vivar and his heirs. You remember him from my grandfather's stories, the traitor who left Dar al-Islam and brought Valencia into Christendom? This ode makes it clear that Ríma is not only carries Rodrigo's bloodline but is also a direct heir.

And I'm already at work on another ode, in an even more archaic style, which describes how Ríma and her clan are the direct inheritors of the old Visigoths who reigned in Iberia until the first of our forefathers came and claimed this land for Dar al-Islam.

It's clear from my sponsor's instructions that Vizconde Carlos shall treat my odes as ancient writing newly found. You, my darling wives, are not shocked by this, are you? None of us cares about the deceptions that Castilians and other Christians play on each other. Further, I shall tell you the story that I know, not the one I am paid to write.

Ríma came to Toledo directly from that battlefield, where she became the Vizconde Carlos's contract bride. It's a strange notion that only Castilians could invent, where she shares the property and bed of the vizconde, and any children shall be considered Carlos's legitimate heirs. And unlike what did not occur with her previous two husbands, Ríma is already said to be carrying Carlos's child. However, she isn't called Vizcondesa, only "ma doña" in the slippery tongue of Castile.

The actual vizcondesa just arrived in Toledo from Aragón. She's a cousin of the king there, so you see that I'm lucky to have a sponsor who cultivates important connections across royalty in this part of the world. The vizcondesa is called Petronilla, a name that sounds like broken rocks to my ear, and she's childless, with a disposition that makes Ríma seem sweet-natured. Petronilla was clapping and shouting at the news she'd become a vizcondesa, but her celebration turned to shrieks of dismay when she learned that Vizconde Carlos now sheltered a contract-bride. But Carlos seems to know how to manage his women.

It's not a peaceful household, though, for these women don't possess the secret that you two have of living in harmony.

There's also a child that Ríma claims is hers. I'm paid to record that he is a direct descendent of the traitor Rodrigo, who's called El Cid here and hailed as a Christian hero. Only I know that the child isn't even Ríma's, so that the true nature of his forefathers hardly matters. The lad is to be married today to an infant niece of the king of Castile, though he's only the age of our oldest two girls. He's a sweet boy who's now a favorite in the royal household, in part because he sings like an angel.

I work each day in a grand scriptorium. One of my scribing comrades is a good-natured, handsome man who is charged with writing the chronicles of one of the Christian orders who led the defeat of the caliph this summer. No, it is not the famous Knights of the Order of Calatrava, because many of those men fell in the first wave of this summer's battle, so their order is in disrepair.

His chronicle describes the heroic doings of another of tedious band of infidel priest-knights, which I believe is called the Knights of the Lunate Cross. I'm still uncertain about how all these Christians are related, but these knights are ruled by Vizconde Carlos here in Castile. I've read some of this clerk's writings, and this order often calls on magic for its doings and blames the Evil One for their failings. The vizconde, therefore, must be comfortable ruling over that bruja Ríma now that she is his contract-bride. But to live here, under the protection of Ríma's contract-husband, I must cease to call her bruja. That clerk, who's called Doménec, which means "belonging to the Lord" in a Christian tongue, insists that Ríma and Vizconde Carlos indeed hold magical objects from God, a chalice and a sword, which are locked in a chapel that I have never seen.

You might think from my story that I live in an upside-down world. But in this New World, I wear silks, dine on fine food, and roam comfortable, beautiful rooms that are all my own. And I hastily assure you, I am neither forced nor inclined to pray in the way my Christian sponsor does.

The messenger who brings you this letter is charged with managing all the business necessary to bring you and our children to Toledo. He will discharge any debts that you may have incurred after the caliph sent me to Baeza. You will travel in a grand merchant train to this city. My new sponsor has promised to ensure every comfort for your journey.

When you come, you shall live in a palace, and our daughters will play with children who will be princes and kings. However, it is the same here as in other noble courts we have known. As the proverb says, like bees they carry sweet honey in their mouths, and in their tails poison.

I await you both, with empty arms and a full heart.

> — *Ibn Jafar, The Poet*
> *From the king's residence,*
> *serving at the command of Vizconde Carlos of Toledo,*
> *in honor of Doña Berenguela of Castile,*
> *at the first sighting of the crescent moon before the equinox*

.

"Thank you, Master Jacques, for being so good with the children."

Dolç had been ill for five days, begging Jacques to stop many times. She'd suffered so many embarrassing times in the bracken along the trail. Camp sickness was what the mercenaries called it. She knew what that meant. The children had to keep away from her, sleeping in a circle of soldiers who cajoled them to sleep with songs and outrageous tales.

Jacques made her drink water, though Dolç scarcely had the strength to lift the goatskin bota. But Quelo needed milk. And as ill as she'd been, Dolç still found her breasts engorged, sometimes had to wake Quelo and beg him to feed.

"It's funny to be this far in life and play nursemaid for children," Jacques said. "Have to remember what my own mama did for us."

"Are you settled now? Will you have a wife and children of your own?" She prodded Jacques to talk, to distract her from the effort to keep upright as the horse jolted along, from worry about the children, who rode safely in the arms of their soldier-guards, and who chattered and found new adventure on this endless trail.

"A wife? No, ma dòmna, I'm a mercenary."

"Don't you believe that's why the Lord put us here, for the sake of children and family?"

"Never thought of that." Jacques pondered it. "No, I believe what I'm paid to believe. I guess since Durán pays me, now I believe in what you people say about domus and honor. What's the word?"

"Paratge." Dolç clung to her horse as it lurched in an effort to climb a new hill.

"That's the word. But I wasn't born to that way of thinking. In the old days, we just sold our personal honor to the next master, back when Chrétien and Tomás were happy to live the mercenary life."

"Out in the wild like this? Don't you long for a clean bed?"

"What? No." Jacques seemed to laugh to himself. "Mercenary life is for men who don't fit, who don't need a house and cows and those troubles."

"But you are so good with the children."

He didn't seem to hear her. "Mercenary life is for men who don't crave a woman to run things for them. Or any other daily lover. When you go that way, then you can't be a mercenary anymore."

"Will you be hired away when Senhór Chrétien comes home?"

Jacques denied that. "We're stuck with each other now. In Toulouse, we'll all be guarding children and mothers. And we won't fight any more. War will be over when Pedro wins against the Saracens. He'll kick Simon de Montfort all the way north of the Pays de France. Children can play as they please."

She drowsed in the heat of the midday sun, feverish, dreaming of the courtyard where she played when her father gathered his soldiers and rode away on crusade and never returned. "Come inside, *mainada*," her mother said. *My little girl.*

"Papa left us alone. Who will take care of us?"

"You and I are crusaders' children, *mainada*. We shall take care of each other."

•

"We are home, ma dòmna." Jacques, speaking close to her ear, roused Dolç from her malaise. "*À la maison. Eh bien, pour l'instant.*"

"Mama, it's so beautiful!" Her oldest daughter, excited, called out from where she and her guard rode far ahead of Jacques.

At the sound of his sister's voice, Quelo stirred, instantly groping for milk, latching hard onto her sore breast.

Jacques spoke the words he used to calm and control his horse. They'd stopped, and when Jacques handed her down from his saddle, one of his comrades received her and then helped steady her so she could stand. The girls were hopping about in anticipation. Dolç tried to stand the way her mother had taught when meeting strangers. Her effort to straighten her gown and cloak were feeble. His horse given over to another of the mercenaries, Jacques came to her side.

He hailed three figures in the yard outside the domus, which was a tile, brick, and plaster manse larger than her own house in Narbonne. After some scurrying and more hellos shouted, a woman emerged and hurried toward them. Erect, stern-looking, clad in black like the women in the marine quarter at Narbonne, but of a lighter complexion, grey-and-russet hair escaping from her veil, she hurried to meet the band of mercenaries who had descended on her domus.

"*Hola! Adieu! Salut!*" Jacques shouted in several dialects.

"*Benvingut!*" The woman who answered welcomed them in an odd accent that Dolç last heard when Chrétien left Lérida. "Where's Chrétien? Durán? Why are you home from battle before them?"

"Chrétien asked me to care for these wee waifs, ma dòmna," Jacques said. "For Tomás's sake."

The woman peered at the bundle Dolç held, then wrapped her arms around Dolç, taking all the weight from Jacques.

"You'd best come in out of the sun. You look more than half done for, *mainada*." She called Dolç *little girl* the way her mother used to. "You are home now."

•

WHERE CAN YOU BE, MY DEAREST WIVES?

> I, your own Ibn Jafar, remain your husband. Yet the merchant train has arrived in Toledo from Jaén without you. How my heart aches not to see you brought to me. Are you using the silver I sent to make other arrangements? Whatever the confusion, it will be spring before I can again gather sufficient coin to pay agents to bring you to me.
>
> I miss you both so, and the children, and long for you to join me in this interesting life.
>
> And I'm anxious to see our children because of the furor here over a missing child, which makes my heart beat so, wanting to know our own children are safe.
>
> That child of Ríma de Rodriquez that I told you of, the heir of the traitor Rodrigo? I had completed all the records under Ríma's command, including a document that Christians create, called a baptismal record. I'd made three copies of the marriage contract, wedding the boy to the king's niece. When I was there, helping the child to sign the name Rodrigo on the contract, he whispered in my ear, "I'm called Fortuno, you know. My father said I was to be his fortunate son."
>
> But it seems he is not so fortunate, for the boy has disappeared!

351

The search through all of Toledo and beyond was extraordinary. And then Vizconde Carlos received a formal letter from the Conde de Foix, declaring that he held the young child as a hostage, a surety bond to protect against any incursion by Castile against his friend, the Condesa de Urgell. The child is now sheltered in the household of one of Foix's seigneurs in Toulouse.

I witnessed the formal presentation of that letter. The vizcondesa laughed. Ríma shrieked in anger, but never wept. The vizconde merely shrugged and passed the letter to me, with instruction to write an answer: *Por lo que va, por lo que va.*

It's hard to find a translation in words that make sense in our world. The vizconde offered a careless surrender to fate.

You can imagine how I worry now, when you did not arrive with the merchant train. I worry about our children, and about you, my dear wives. I include my last dirham so that you can pay a scribe to write and send me your message, to tell me of your plans to come to me. My heart scarcely beats, waiting to know where you are.

— Ibn Jafar, The Poet
From the residence of the king of Castile
at the command of Vizcomde Carlos of Toledo

·

Durán at Le Seu de Urgell
September 10

Durán, Yusuf, and Chrétien served as audience while Pedro and the count of Foix sat in conference in the count's house in Urgell, plotting other people's futures.

"Nice of you to reward Durán for doing your spiritual chores on our enterprise of faith." Pedro nodded to the count of Foix. "But I need him as the seigneur of Montcava for coming battles with the Church. It will be a season or two before he can play grandee on his fief in Urgell."

"Whose land do you need to protect?" The count yawned. "With or without heirs?"

"I'm not leading armies or fighting anymore," Durán said. "It's against what I believe."

"We aren't discussing battlefields. You need to marry for the good of all southern seigneurs," Ramón-roger said. "I'll order your wedding coat myself. If I remember that correctly, you like blue velvet best."

"It's a good color on him." Chrétien said.

"And Yusuf," Pedro said.

"Blue isn't as good on Yusuf." Chrétien frowned. "A deep gold or bright yellow, I think."

"Monsenyor?" Yusuf seemed lost, as if he'd just awakened upon hearing his name.

Pedro said, "As Tomás's heir, you need to protect all he had, the way Tomás did for me. We shall find a bride for you."

"I'm too young," Yusuf protested, looking first to Chrétien and then Durán for consolation, but Durán felt his own turmoil. No, perhaps he'd best admit to panic.

"Only half a year older than your father was when you were conceived," Pedro said, chiding Yusuf. "But let me consider this. I don't want to make a mistake."

Pedro had a hand on his chin, staring at Chrétien while he pondered whatever was on his mind. Chrétien tied and retied the string of his shirt collar, which Durán recognized as sign that Pedro had unnerved him. Durán was across the room and so couldn't reach Chrétien for reassurance. Instead, he clasped that bunch of coins tethered at his belt. The ringing coins caused Chrétien to look at Durán before answering Pedro.

"No, Monsenyor. If you think I must take Dolç," Chrétien said, "that's impossible. By Church law, I cannot marry my brother's widow, or whatever she is, since you had their marriage annulled."

"That particular reward belongs to Durán." Pedro seemed pleased with himself. "More land for him, more land protected for the south."

"Monsenyor?" Durán stammered, as ready to protest as Yusuf had been.

The count of Foix laughed, one hand on Chrétien's shoulder. "I told you last winter, Senhór Durán. We shall not let Philippe Augustus steal the south through the bedroom."

"Oh, perfect!" Chrétien rubbed his hands. "Dolç is very nice. And smart."

"And Dolç is already in your domus," Ramón-roger said, "if her journey went as planned. The Crux Lunata pursued Dolç here, but I believe she traveled safely on to Toulouse. I added to the mercenaries who brought her this far."

"*Ai*, no!" Yusuf jumped up, nearly toppling his desk. "At Lérida they said that Dolç and her children had gone to Barcelona. My father will be distressed not to find her there."

"Peace, Yusuf." Pedro tapped his hand. "Tomorrow's courier will likely get to Barcelona before Tomás does. Write a message for him."

Yusuf nodded and settled back to his work, while Durán churned in distress over Pedro's interrupted command to marry Dolç, who was not far away in Barcelona.

"*Ai, cor dolç.*" Chrétien smiled, but he wasn't laughing at Durán in the same way the count did. He was just plain happy. "My mother will be overcome with joy. We get sweet, beautiful children with no effort from either of us. And with Dolç in charge of the household, we won't have to worry about managing the servants any more. What could be better for the peace of the domus?"

Ramón-roger had returned to his conversation with Pedro. "My niece Ermengarde is fifty if she's a day. And rich as a queen."

"My wife María is a queen," Pedro said. "And she didn't turn out to be as rich as she claimed."

"Ermengarde got half the Aude valley from her grandfather and two castles from her dead husband. And she's a miser, so she hasn't lost one shiny morabatin of what she inherited. Claims she doesn't need a man around anymore than the abbess of a women's monastery wants an abbot." Ramón-roger was head-to-head with Pedro, back to their planning and plotting. "She'd make a perfect bride for Senhór Chrétien, don't you think?"

"Have mercy!" Chrétien cried out, but no one in the room responded to his beggary.

·

Later, alone together, Durán's hand drifted from shoulder blade to the mound of Chrétien's buttocks, which were as perfect as any man's could be.

"Rashid is an extremely handsome man, don't you think?"

Chrétien flipped over under his hand. "No. He's a freak with a pointy chin and limited personal grace. He's sits his horse stiff as a sword scabbard. He can't handle a quarterstaff even as well as you. Though he's a decent enough fellow."

Durán didn't say more. He stroked the indenture at Chrétien's hip where muscle mass meets bone.

"What are you thinking, *cor dolç?*" Chrétien whispered.

"That if we ride out tomorrow with Thierry and a few of the others, you and I can be home in time for the late harvest. That your mother will be busy preparing koupepia and almond pastries. I'm thinking how delicious it will be if Numa makes us eat too much and then lets us take a nap afterward."

"You aren't thinking about food." Chrétien made that sweet movement which meant he loved Durán. "You heretics are such unrepentant liars."

"We merely see the world in a different way." Durán kissed Chrétien's teasing mouth. "It's how God made us."

■

Sebastián at Le Seu de Urgell
September 10

"Here's a clean shirt." Taresa tossed it to Sebastián, but he wasn't ready to catch it. The shirt fell to the floor inside their tiny room. "No, I didn't wash it myself, but I did find the best among the laundry women."

Sebastián was oiling his leather cuirass, rubbing hard. Since the beating it took over summer on the frontier, no amount of oil ever seemed enough.

"My pleasure," she said, though he had said thank you. Then she repeated it in a string of other tongues. "*De nada. Ès benvingut. De rien.* 'You're welcome, Serena Taresa. You're such a good wife. Life is so much easier with you here.'" She picked up the shirt, folded it, and laid it with his gear. "Can we start again? We once liked each other."

Before he could decide what to say, Taresa said, "I'll begin. First, I respect and admire you. I am grateful to you deep in my heart that Matheus is dead."

Sebastián rubbed harder at a worn spot on the cuirass. "Matheus died because of what he did to my mother. And what he tried to do to Valerós. It had nothing to do with you."

"Yet I'm happy about it. And I consider you a noble and honorable knight for that act. And for being the greatest Catalan hero in the battle."

She touched him, stroking that scar where he'd been made a bonfraire. The top of her robe wasn't tied tightly and slipped to reveal her collarbone and the first curve of her breasts. At least here in Urgell, she didn't dress as a boy.

"*Ai*, Senhór Sebastián. Can you not forgive Pedro for commanding you to marry me?" She sounded playful, but she crossed her arms, standing over him where he'd begun to stitch up the tear in that blue Beaurain surcoat. "Are you holding me away so you can beg a bishop for an annulment?"

"What? After what they did to Isabella and Durán, I'd never beg a bishop for a crust of bread if I was starving."

"Truly? You don't intend to end this marriage because it's never been consummated? Because you can't forgive me?"

She took away the surcoat and settled in his lap, the way she had in the laundry-women's camp. She spoke into his hair, one hand at the nape of his neck. "Is it because I threw you out for calling me a laundry girl?"

"You could have told me who you were."

"We argued this before. I hid to escape Matheus." She tugged at the ties of his shirt, running a hand down his chest, brushing her thumb over his nipple. "Can you not forgive me for marrying Felip when Pedro commanded that? I had no more choice than you and I have now."

"You seemed to enjoy it."

"Felip was a sweet boy. My playmate from childhood. We might have been happy. And I like his grandmother. Constanza of Xirgú will be so sad that he's gone to heaven. Though perhaps she expected it, sending another man off on crusade."

"This wasn't a crusade, only an enterprise of—"

She kissed him, stopping each attempt he made to speak by pressing her tongue into his mouth, coaxing him down onto the narrow bed. When he again tried to speak, she said, "Think about one thing at a time when you're making love."

"Where did you learn that?"

"From the baggage-train women. I learned more there than any new bride in Christendom ever learns from her aunties and sisters."

She knelt over him, the way she had once in a twilight hour, moments before they were interrupted by a call to arms. Without waiting for him, she untied her robe, cast it aside, and then untied and cast her skirt away. She grasped both his wrists, forcing him to cup her breasts.

Which were soft. A sharp V had been burned on her chest, where her shirt was open to the sunshine. The rest was ivory white. And soft as velvet.

"This is how to begin again." Taresa climbed off him, and tried to help him undress, which served to slow down how fast he could peel off leggings and his shirt.

"You have more hair everywhere," she said, her fingers in the mat on his chest.

"What next?" His voice croaked, though he was months and leagues past worrying about it breaking. They stood pressed against each other, her breasts mashed into his last rib, his face in her hair.

"You pick me up and ravish me," Taresa said. "The first time is always a ravishing. That's what the laundry-women all say."

Except it wasn't. It was long and slow, and took considerable time to find where elbows went, and required stopping for a moment when it all seemed too incredible to move.

And she didn't really know how any better than he did.

"Didn't you ask your father for advice?" Taresa whispered in his ear, tickling, when they lay side by side for a moment, catching their breath. "Father Anselm says Tomás of Morella knows more than any man about making love to a woman. What advice did he give you?"

What had Tomás last said? *"Why should any brave woman need your forgiveness?"*

"To show respect." Sebastián had her in his arms again. Her shoulders so soft, her back like silk, except for the hard ridge of her spine, which he traced, counting the boney bumps. "Will you forgive me for calling you a laundry girl?"

"That I shall not do. I'll hold it in my heart as a caution."

"What warning?"

"That you are an arrogant and selfish boy."

He should have known better, but Sebastián began a long, exhaustive iteration of all he'd done, everything he'd seen, that should command any woman's respect. That declared he was a man. A hero in Aragón. Words that seemed to have stunned Taresa into silence.

Except then she said, "See? Arrogant."

"I'm not calling you Serena, ma dòmna. It's not a good name for you. Only Taresa. *Furiós* Taresa."

◼

Isabella at Castell-de-Valerós
September 29, Feast of Saint Michael the Archangel

Isabella had come home to Valerós a decade earlier, when Pèire rescued her from the Montcavas in Toulouse. In the same way she did that day, Isabella stopped where the road turned to reveal the valley and villages.

Tomás slipped from his horse and came up beside her, his arm curving around her, familiar again, after weeks of living side by side through every day and night. She leaned against him, wondering if it would ever be enough to fill the abyss they'd lived through since last Michaelmas.

"We left in a hurry last time." Tomás murmured in her hair, pulling her even closer for a moment.

"*Òc.*" Isabella and Tomás had galloped out that day in pursuit of Sebastián's kidnappers, in a swirl of lies, deceits, and misunderstandings. "I've been homesick ever since for each tree and vine."

"*Ai, kalila.*"

They decided to walk and so waved Father Anselm and the others onward. The bordoniers, soldier-farmers who each carried a purse of silver from Pedro, said goodbye and separated, riding to their villages to find their families. Leading their horses, Isabella and Tomás walked through the first village in the lower valley, past the little barrel-vaulted church, which had been newly plastered and whitewashed. The road wound through the village, and they stopped a dozen times to greet people she recognized. She promised to sit with the women the next day, when they'd be spinning in the sun, and tell all the stories of her adventure.

"Where is everyone?" she asked Évrard, the ancient Catalan who tended the olive oil press outside of the village.

"People hid in the hills when that new seigneur came and began to hunt heretics. That seigneur lied, saying our Sebastián had died."

"But Pedro sent Marshal Guillem home. Surely our people are all safe now."

"Òc. But we have been too busy in the fields with harvest to fix our houses. That's what winter is for. For now, it's fine, living under the stars in the summer."

"Fix houses?"

"When the false seigneur came, his knights searched houses, looking for heretics' gold and their idols. Some people were burned out of their houses."

A longer legacy of Matheus's evil to repair.

In his slow way, Évrard continued on, naming the families who had fled and who'd be happy to see Valerós men returning now to finish the harvest and put things to right again.

"The way God wants it," he concluded.

On their way again, Isabella and Tomás mounted and rode slowly up the trail toward the castle. She felt her old job, steward of Valerós, settle over her like a comfortable cloak. Those apple trees needed better pruning next spring. And the peach trees in the lower valley, Pèire's pride, needed limbs propped and the orchard grass scythed. That almond grove looked fine, but along the way, they'd seen only one pair of pigs browsing in the shade of the orchards. The first chore was to discover which villagers had lost animals under Matheus's usurpation, and to use the silver from Pedro to restore animals to people.

Half the vineyards needed a lot of attention next spring.

Pedro might have sent enough knights with Marshal Guillem to retake the castle, but too many men had been off with the Aragón army's expedition when they were needed here at home to restore order in the fields and villages.

"Time enough," Tomás said, as if he heard her thoughts. "We have the winter to work. And the bordoniers are overjoyed to be here and not riding through dust in La Mancha."

The path veered sharply up into the hills, where the local peaks were trapped in low clouds, though the ragged limestone pinnacles on the opposite side of the valley glowed in afternoon sunshine. The many-curved steep path was slick with mud in places, from the previous day's rain. They dismounted and walked again where the deep forest gave way abruptly to brush land.

Brush land far more beautiful than the matorral Isabella had been used to since late spring.

Where the stony path became precipitous, with sheer drops to one side, they passed two crags, the limestone as familiar to Isabella as the lines and scars on her own hand. A solitary pine, adrift far from the forest, grew in a crack in a limestone outcrop.

A small grove of olive trees, sheltered from the wind in a narrow valley, huddled alongside a stream.

The trail zigzagged up the cliff, requiring tedious and careful hiking. The sun broke through the low overhead clouds, or boiled them away. Tomás and Isabella rounded another limestone outcropping, and there the castle perched, as if it grew out of living rock, standing where it had been built before the saints first carried the story of Jesus to Rome.

.

In the months since he arrived home, Marshal Guillem hadn't yet gotten to restoring farmers' cottages, but he had rid the castle and the surrounding hillsides of both Crux Lunata knights and bandits preying on people who'd fled for the hills. He'd set the castle right again and restocked supplies for resisting siege.

And Felicia, Isabella's sister, was pregnant. And happily serving house-knights and family in the dining hall at night and in the main courtyard at breakfast and after *migdiada*. The surprise there was Jacques and Thierry, who'd arrived two days before, sent by Chrétien, who had gone home to Toulouse with Durán ahead of Pedro and the army.

"Chrétien thought you'd worry," Jacques said, "when you didn't find Senhóra Dolç in Barcelona. But everyone is at Fontcours for the winter. I delivered Dolç there for you."

"And Quelo?" Tomás asked. Perhaps only Isabella heard that note of longing in his voice.

"Is being spoiled by his sisters and Numa and Fortuno. It's noisy at Fontcours these days."

After the first delirium of their homecoming welcome, and after drinking wine and eating Valerós sheep's cheese and late-harvest peaches in the courtyard, Tomás and Isabella slipped away, walking down the trail to where that spring cascaded from the limestone rock face and bubbled in a large pool before seeping down the steep slope toward the valley. At the place people called Heart Springs, where the village priest said blessings every midsummer, they stripped to bathe, to wash away a year's road-weary dust.

Isabella nestled in his arms. "Are you disappointed to be here when your sons—our sons—are in Toulouse or with Pedro?"

"No. Òc. A little." He wrapped his arm around her. "A great deal. But we shall see them all next summer. And I'm content at this moment to see you home. And happy."

Stone pines loomed over them, as familiar as the faces of family and knights around the courtyard table in the castle.

Overhead, a booted eagle drifted in the afternoon updrafts, though perhaps not the same eagle she'd watched from the parapets years before.

After they'd shrieked about how cold the water was, Tomás gripped her and then they counted to three and submerged together in the pool, emerging like half-drowned river otters, laughing.

Sun glistened off the water drops on Tomás's skin, in his hair.

He touched that dip at her throat and then slowly outlined all her old wounds with his finger. "*Eu vos amor!*" he shouted. "It's no longer a secret anywhere on God's own earth."

"No." Isabella traced that scar across his lips, knowing it tickled, and caused him to shiver and scatter water drops everywhere. "Only you, *amador*. Only you."

Tomás embraced her and pulled her into the water again.

Bathing in that stream proved an icy blast after the hot baths of Zaragoza and Barcelona. But the water at Castell-de-Valerós, pure as tears, tasted sweeter.

The water tasted like home.

END BOOK 4 ▪ ACCIDENTAL HERETICS

Heretics' Glossary

The non-English phrases in *Accidental Heretics* stories are for fun and color, not linguistic purity. The characters in these stories speak or read several languages.

A

Abu: An honorific name as the parent of a child ("father of…").

adouçar enfant Jhezu: Sweet baby Jesus.

Ai Dèu: O God.

alcade: A local judge.

Almogavars: Frontiersman foot soldiers in Christian Iberia.

Almohad caliphate: A Moroccan Berber Muslim movement in the twelfth century that came to rule North Africa and Islamic Iberia until Al-Nasir's defeat at Las Navas de Tolosa.

arming cap: The cotton or linen cap worn under a helmet.

aventail: A chainmail curtain to cover the neck and shoulders.

àvi, àvia: Grandfather, grandmother.

Ayyubid: A Muslim sultanate in the twelfth and thirteenth centuries, centered in Egypt, founded by the Kurdish general Saladin.

Azgaz: Turk bowmen who served as mercenaries for the Almohad forces in Al-Andalus.

B

baquelar: Villainous rogue.

barraganía: A form of concubinage in medieval Iberian as a contract between men and women who would not or could not marry.

barcelonese: Coinage under the Count of Barcelona.

batini: An unbeliever.

benvingut: Welcome.

Berbers: An ethnic group in North Africa. The invaders of Iberia in the eighth century were mainly Berbers. The Almoravid invaders who established a new dynasty in Al-Andalus in the eleventh century were also Berbers from Morocco.

bon amic: Good friend, or boyfriend.

bon día: Good day.

bon nuoit, bona nuèch: Good night.

bon vèspre: Good evening.

bonfraires: Members of a warrior brotherhood, La Confraria de la Crotz.

booty: Treasure; during the crusades, the primary way crusaders financed their armies or paid their mercenaries. Rather than "looting," these cultures thought of booty as legitimate plunder.

bordonier: A freeholder who arms and fights, freely, for a baron.

bruixa; bruja: Witch.

C

calla: Shut up!

cançó d'amor: Love song.

cançó d'guerra: Crusader song.

Candlemas: Feast of the Purification, February 2.

Castellano: The romance language spoken in the Castile regions of Iberia.

Catalan: In the Middle Ages, a language, not a political entity.

cavaller: A knight.

Cistercian Order: The White Monks, a reformist Benedictine order, who stressed manual labor and a return to the Rule of St Benedict.

cor dolç: Sweetheart; an endearment.

convivencia: "The Coexistence," describing the period of relative peaceful coexistence among Muslims, Jews, and Christians in Iberia under Muslim rule.

crux lunata: Lunate cross, featuring lunar crescents at each terminus; a pagan symbol; war tokenism imported to Europe by returning crusaders, adding the Islamic crescent in heraldic and other symbols.

cuirass: A rigid armor covering the torso. At this period, it was still made of leather.

D–F

Dar al-Islam: "The House of Peace."

Desperta, Ferro: Awake, steel! Historically, the battle cry of the Almogavars in a later century. In this story, it's taught by Valerós fighters from the Pyrenees.

Deus vult; Dieu le veut: God wills it! (A crusader battle cry.)

Dios ayuda a Santiago: God help St-James! (Castilian knights' battle cry.)

djinni: A supernatural creature in Arabian mythology.

domus: The larger economic household of a titled landholder.

don: A courtesy title for a gentleman from the landed classes.

donzel: A young gentleman, in training for knighthood.

eu vos amor: I love you.

fada: Fairy.

fadrin: A lad, a term of endearment.

francimand, francimandalha: Frenchman.

Franks, *franj*: At the time of this story, a reference used by Muslims and others for western European people.

G–I

gambeson: A padded jacket worn under armor or alone as a defensive covering.

goodmen, goodwomen: A reference to the people whom the Catholic Church called heretics; now commonly called Cathars.

hauberk: A chainmail shirt.

hereticated: Having decided to adopt a heresy.

hola: Hello.

Hospitallers of Jerusalem: A Christian military order, founded in Jerusalem to care for sick pilgrims.

Ibn: A patronymic name ("son of...").

J–L

Jhezu adouçar: Sweet Jesus.

Jhezu del tron: Jesus in heaven.

jongleurs: Medieval minstrels, who sang troubadours' songs.

jubba: An ankle-length robe.

khanjar: A Saracen short-sword.

kalila: Sweetheart, an endearment; Tomás learned the word from his Kurdish mother.

kazaghand: Mail coat favored by Muslim warriors in Iberia and north Africa.

Knights of the Order of Calatrava: A Cistercian-based military order; the first official order in Castile, founded in the twelfth century.

Knights Templar: A monastic crusader military order, the most elite of the crusader armies.

koupepia: Stuffed grape leaves, a traditional Cypriot dish.

lenga romana: The common tongue of the Languedoc in the Middle Ages, now called Old Occitan.

M

ma dòmna: My lady; an honorific for married, landed women.

Mare de Dèu: Mother of God.

membrillo: Quince jelly.

mestitz: A person of mixed heritage.

mainada: Little girl.

Michaelmas: The feast of Saint Michael the Archangel, September 29.

migdiada: Midday rest.

mon amics: My friends.

mon fraire: My brother.

Monsenyor: An honorific, such as for a king or a bishop.

Moors: People from northern Africa who settled on the Iberian peninsula under Muslim leadership. Colloquially at this time, a person of mixed heritage with a dark complexion.

morabatin: Gold coins in Aragón. A horse cost about 100 morabatins.

Mozarab: Iberian Christians living under Muslim rule in Al-Andalus. This is a modern term. In medieval times, they would have been designated *dhimmi* and required to pay a tax.

mutawwama: A chicken-and-cheese wrap, spiced with coriander.

N–Q

Nizari: At the time of the Crusader states, a legendary assassin cult.

Normans: Descendants of the Viking Northmen who settled Normandy, and later invaded Britain and conquered the Muslims on Sicily in the eleventh century.

òc: Yes.

Order of Santiago: A militia order founded in the twelfth century, with seats in both León and Castile.

paratge: A concept in Troubadour culture of kinship and justice, more than honor: natural balance, harmony, "what is right."

Parcite nobis: Spare us. Beseeching God, in Latin, in the plural imperative; a usage cited in the Cathar Lyon Ritual.

per l'amor de Dèu: For the love of God.

punxor: Prick.

puta, putana: Prostitute.

R–S

rafraf: A long tail on a turban.

renrén: Fool.

Saracen: Colloquial term used in medieval Europe for Muslims.

sarawil: Trousers.

scrofula: Tuberculosis of the neck; colloquially, part of an insult.

seigneur: A man of rank who holds land and rules a household.

senhór, senhóra, senhóreta: Titles of respect.

Sodalitas, fidelitas, virtus: Latin motto of the bonfraires: fraternity, fidelity, virtue.

surcoat: A long coat worn over other clothes or armor.

T – Z

taifa: An independent principality in Muslim Al-Andalus.

ultramontanos: Knights and foot soldiers from east of the Pyrenees who joined the united army in Andalusia for forty days, in expectation of total remission of their sins.

viscount, vizconde: A European noble rank, above a baron, below a marquis.

Visigoths: Germanic nomads who maintained a kingdom in Iberia from the fifth to the eighth centuries.

vivètz: Live!

vizier: A high-ranking political advisor, appointed by the caliph in the case of this story.

Walidi: Father.

Place Names

Valerós, Fontcours, Montcava, St-Féliu, St-Joachim, and Monasterio de St-Pere de Selva exist within the Accidental Heretics world, but nowhere else.

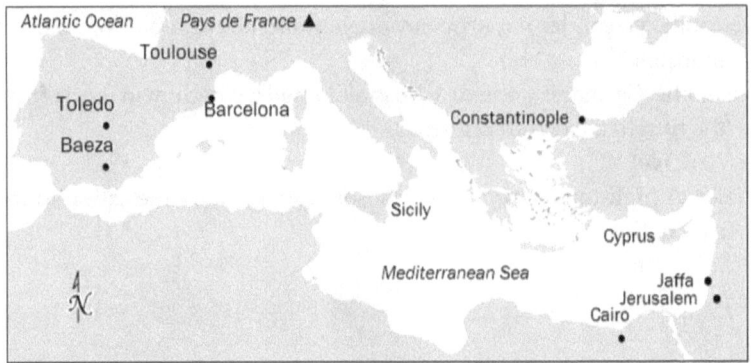

A – B

Al-Andalus (in country; Andalusia in Christendom): The land of the caliphates on the Iberian Peninsula.

Al-Arcos: A citadel in what is now Ciudad Real province. The site of a major loss by Alfonso VII to the Almohad caliphate in 1195.

Almería: A port and fortress city on the southeastern coast of the Iberian Peninsula.

Aquitaine: A duchy in what is now southwest France that was a key portion of the Angevine empire under Henry II and Eleanor of Aquitaine.

Aragón: In the mid-thirteenth century, a union of the Kingdom of Aragón and the County of Barcelona established the dynastic Crown of Aragón, with tributaries across the Languedoc at the time of this story.

Baeza: A cliffside city in the province of Jaén in Al-Andalus, at the edge of the mountains separating La Mancha from Granada.

Barcelona: A territory on the Mediterranean, now approximately the political entity of Catalunya, for which Pedro II held the title Count of Barcelona.

Benavente: One of the frontier castles taken by Alfonso on the way to Andalusia in summer 1212.

Béziers: A town in the Languedoc that was the scene of the first burning of heretics when the French-speaking army invaded to suppress what is now called the Cathar heresy.

C – D

Cahors: A town on the river Lot in southwestern France, north of Tououse.

Cairo: The seat of the Ayyubid dynasty that Saladin founded, with the third oldest university in the world.

Calatrava la Vieja: The citadel that guarded the road between Cordova and Toledo. Conquered by Castile in 1147, it was guarded by the Cistercian Knights of the Order of Calatrava. It was again conquered by the Almohads in 1195, returning to Castile in 1212.

Castile: At the time of this story, the Kingdom of Castile was one of the medieval Christian kingdoms in Iberia, centered around Toledo.

Constantinople: Capital of the Eastern Roman Empire, sacked in the Fourth Crusade in 1204, becoming the seat of Norman rulers for the next fifty years.

Córdoba: A southern city and province in Al-Andalus, considered one of the most culturally advanced and populous cities during the tenth and eleventh centuries.

Cuenca: A city in central Spain. At times living under Muslim rule, Cuenca came under Christian Castile in 1177.

Cyprus: An island in the Mediterranean, south of Turkey and north of Cairo. During the Third Crusade, its Muslim rulers were conquered by Richard Lionheart who sold it to the Knights Templar, who in turn sold it to Guy de Lusignan.

D – G

Despeñaperros: A gorge between steep mountains in the northern part of Jaén province.

Espanya: Catalan and Romance language word for Hispania, as it had been called by the Romans.

Famagusta: A city on Cyprus; formerly Tomás's home.

Ferral (Castro Ferral): A castle on the Sierra Morena frontier, defended and conquered multiple times between Christian and Muslim armies in the twelfth and thirteenth centuries.

Foix: A medieval county in what is now the Ariège department in south-western France, in the Midi-Pyrenees region. Ruled from the eleventh to the fifth centuries by the House of Foix, who owed allegiance to the Counts of Toulouse and Counts of Barcelona.

Girona: An ancient city in the northeast corner of Catalunya; part of the countship of Barcelona at the time of this story.

H – J

Holy Roman Empire: The successor in central Europe to Charlemagne's empire. During the high Middle Ages, this included parts of Germany, Burgundy, Italy, and Bohemia.

Iberia: The old Roman name for the peninsula now called Spain.

Jaén: A city and province in south-central Spain, geographically strategic between Castile and Al-Andalus.

Jerusalem: Captured by the crusaders in 1099, recaptured by Saladin in 1187, traded back and forth for several decades until finally captured by the Mamluks and lost forever by the crusaders.

L – P

La Mancha: An arid, high plateau between Toledo and Cuenca.

La Seu d'Urgell: A town in the Catalan Pyrenees in Spain.

Las Navas de Tolosa: A valley in the Sierra Morena where the united Christian armies confronted the army of the Almohad caliphate in what is considered a key turning point in what is called the Reconquista in European history.

La Solana: A town in what is now Ciudad Real province.

León: One of three medieval Christian kingdoms in Iberia.

Lérida: Now Lleida in western Catalunya, this city was the traditional royal residence of the kings of Aragón.

Malagón: A citadel on the frontier, in what is now Ciudad Real, subject in medieval times to repeated conquest and reconquest between Muslim and Christian forces.

Minerve: A town in the Languedoc that sheltered refugees from the massacre of Béziers and was subsequently defeated by Simon de Montfort and its own heretics burned by the conquerors.

Montpelhièr: A walled city in the Languedoc, near the Mediterranean, with the second oldest university in Europe.

Morella: A town near Valencia, taken from the Moors by El Cid, lost again later before finally becoming part of Aragón in the Reconquista.

Morocco: At the time of this story, a region in northern Africa, including Marrakesh, that was part of the Almohad caliphate.

Narbonne: A rich Mediterranean port in the Languedoc that was the seat of an archbishop and home to a sizable Jewish community.

Navarre: A medieval Christian kingdom, principally Basque-based and including land on both sides of the western Pyrenees.

Naxos: A Greek island in the Aegean Sea, alternately under Byzantine and Venetian rule.

Outremer: The Crusader States, the land overseas.

Pays de France: The historic personal domain of the king of France; most of this area became the province Ile de France.

Piedrabuena: One of the frontier castles taken by Alfonso, in what is now Ciudad Real province.

Provence: A county on the Mediterranean, ruled by the counts of Barcelona; governed by Pedro's brother Alfonso at this time.

R – Z

Roussillon: A region in the southeastern Pyrenees and foothills.

Serra del Montsec: A range in the Catalan Pyrenees.

Sierra Morena: A mountain range running east to west across the southern part of Iberia.

Seville: The capital in Al-Andalus for a series of caliphates from the eighth through the thirteenth centuries.

St-Sernin: A Romanesque basilica in Toulouse.

Toledo: A city in central Iberia, taken from the Moors by Christian forces in 1085, and then serving as the capital of the Kingdom of Castile.

Toulouse: A county in the Languedoc, whose count owed allegiance to the king of France at the time of this story. The city, on a major trade route between the Mediterranean and central France, was a bishop's seat.

Tunis: A city in North Africa that served as the seat of the caliphate after the conquest of the Almohads in the twelfth century.

Úbeda: A town in Jaén province. Conquered and held briefly by Christian forces in 1212.

Urgell: A county in Catalan-speaking lands between Lérida and the high Pyrenees. Pedro d'Aragón and the count of Foix defended the rights of the countess of Urgell to inherit.

Valencia: A region and ancient Roman port city on the Mediterranean peninsula. Seized from the Moors by El Cid in the eleventh century, then retaken a hundred years later and still held by the Moors in Pedro's time.

Valdepeñas: A town in what is now Ciudad Real.

Zara: Now Zadar in Croatia, this Dalmatian city on the Adriatic Sea was a stopping place for crusaders waiting for transports from the Venetian doge in 1204.

Zaragoza: A city in Aragón on the Ebro River. Originally founded by Caesar Augustus to settle veterans of the Cantabrian wars, it was subsequently conquered by Visigoths and Muslim invaders. It was taken by the Aragón king Alfonso I from the Muslims in 1118 and made the capital of the Kingdom of Aragón.

About the Author

E.A. STEWART is an American writer whose *Accidental Heretics* series explores intrigues in France and Spain in the early thirteenth century. Annie Stewart worked for many years as a technical writer and project manager in Pacific Northwest software companies.

Ms. Stewart lives and writes in Seattle.

To learn more about these series, visit:
www.eastewartauthor.com

ACCIDENTAL HERETICS SERIES
Book 1: *Bone-mend and Salt*
Book 2: *Trebuchets in the Garden*
Book 3: *Crux Lunata*
Book 4: *Song of Valerós*
The Mad Woman of La Catalane: A Novella
The Blue Door… and More Accidental Heretics Tales

LEGENDS OF VALERÓS SERIES
The adventures continue in these standalone stories
featuring characters from the Valerós world.
Wheel and Serpent: 1
Traitor: 2
Hero: 3

Acknowledgments

Thanks to Elizabeth Bjorkman, Jacyn Stewart, Susan Urban, Martin Fossum, and Laurie Cropp. And thanks to Waverly Fitzgerald for Mondays and Thursdays at Liberty on Fifteenth Avenue East.

Author's Notes: Las Navas de Tolosa

The battle of Las Navas de Tolosa is often cited as the first notable win for Christian forces in what came to be called the Reconquista, having more effect than the frontier raids and trading of territories tin the preceding five hundred years. The battle remains strong in the mythos for participating Iberian kingdoms that came to be united under the king of Castile.

Only fragments of eyewitness accounts exist of the battle. We know that Alfonso of Castile and Pedro of Aragón planned for years to prepare for it, and that León, Navarre, and Portugal contributed a limited number of knights, who arrived late in the campaign. We know that a significant number of "ultramontanos" — crusaders from the other side of the Pyrenees — went home after completing the forty days of campaigning to which they had committed.

We also have sufficient mathematical capabilities to determine that the letters and records written close to the time of the battle exaggerate the number of men present for the battle. One analysis I found estimates that men would have stood shoulder to shoulder, unable to move, if that many bodies were in the *navas*.

As readers know who've followed the earlier *Accidental Heretics* stories, I have a specific view, believing that thirteenth century chroniclers discarded or altered the record of Pedro's actions in the last two years of his life, because he decided to support the Occitan seigneurs after Simon de Montfort seized Toulouse. Pedro appears in earlier records as a more-than-competent administrator and military commander — that is, up until he changed how he supported the Church's efforts to stop heresy in the south.

374

I've taken advantage of gaps in the written record to imagine actions that differ from what was recorded ten, thirty, and fifty years later, when the unified Crown of Castile needed good legends that included the León and Navarre latecomers. *Song of Valerós* is a work of imagination, focusing on how individuals might have lived through the events, in a world where a complex mix of ethnic, cultural, and religious peoples coexisted in ways not known elsewhere in Europe.

For readers who want to learn more about the battle and surrounding history, beyond what can be gleaned from Wikipedia, here are a few good online references. These are in Spanish, but translate well in any online translator tool:

> Hispania Historia blog post
> http://bit.ly/2bzX10I

> Grandes Batallas web site
> for a detailed discussion of the battle array
> http://bit.ly/2bcSjRp

> Arturo Pérez-Reverte, "The Burden of the Three Kings"
> http://bit.ly/2aVzIJ1

From Jugum Press

HISTORICAL AND CONTEMPORARY FICTION

Nzinga, African Warrior Queen by Moses L. Howard

Nzinga is a brilliant leader during a time of violent upheaval. This fictional biography brings to life the 17th century flourishing African kingdom, now lost, where early explorers' maps of West Africa call out: "Here reigned the celebrated Queen Nzinga!"

Nine Volt Heart by Annie Pearson

He said, "I love you." She said, "You don't even know the real me." He said, "Great song lyrics. Key of G? Can we try close harmony?" Jason and Susi meet by accident in Seattle. Secrets, songs, and stalkers quickly entwine their lives in unpredictable ways.

This Charming Man by Ajax Bell

A chance encounter with an intriguing older man inspires Steven Frazier with visions of a more rewarding life. A vibrant snapshot of Seattle in the early 1990s, this story captures the drama of coming into one's own as an adult.

A Summer in Peach Creek by Michele Malo

Teenaged Faith travels to Peach Creek, West Virginia for a visit with relatives in 1932. When a scandalous murder occurs, Faith discovers the corrupt underbelly of Logan County. As summer progresses and peaches grow, Faith finds her own moral center.

PERSONAL VOICES IN HISTORY SERIES

Journey into Gold Country: Memories of a Forty-Niner

by Ralph Buckingham; foreword by Charles Barker

The California Gold Rush, remembered sixty years later by a New England younger son who went to seek his fortune.

We Were Walimu Once and Young, edited by Brooks E. Goddard

True stories from the Teachers for East Africa and Teacher Education for East Africa experience in the 1960s.

Find print and ebook editions:

www.jugumpress.net

www.ingramcontent.com/pod-product-compliance
Lightning Source LLC
Chambersburg PA
CBHW021129260626
47169CB00005B/1521